SOLITUDE,

Population 1

A NOVEL BY

FRED LANDERMAN

i

ACKNOWLEDGMENTS

In writing this story I received help and inspiration from a variety of sources including the biggest supporter of my work, my wife Susan. My brothers (all seven of them) were an inspiration also, as was a very special friend Tom Orlando.

Editng assistance was from a very intuitive young lady named Kate Jackson, who didn't always like the content but helped me say what I wanted in the best way possible. Also, Dr. Paul Landerman for his valued criticism deserves to be recognized.

The one person who helped create the character of Jake Kozan was Mr. Kozan himself. Yes there is a real person who inspired this tale. I met him while working in Ridgecrest, California and we had many conversations about several subjects. My thanks to him for just being a good friend when I needed one.

I would also credit the many law enforcement officers I've met and talked with during the years for helping me understand how they think.

CHAPTER ONE

He looked through the binoculars, slowly scanning the terrain of the hillside across from him, searching inch by inch for any tell-tale sign that his enemy may be there. A fly buzzed aimlessly around his head. From the corner of his eye he saw an ant making its way back to an anthill. The quiet of the afternoon seemed to enfold him like a soft blanket. He knew he needed sleep, and the warmth of the sun on his back was relaxing, but to sleep now would be suicidal. He knew his enemy was very sharp and willing to kill. He would be lucky to get out of the desert alive.

"Damn", he muttered softly to himself. "You really got yourself into a mess this time, Jake Kozan."

Jake shifted his eyes down to the ground and then back to the scope again. It was an old trick he had used many times when hunting deer. He had used the same techniques when his mission took him into enemy territory while in the service. He'd had sniper training, but preferred being the spotter instead of the shooter. Sometimes a person can stare at something and not recognize it until they look away and then look back. There wasn't much cover on the opposite hillside, mostly creosote bush and sage with a couple clumps of Joshua trees. He wanted desperately to stand and stretch his tired, aching muscles. He had been lying in the same place since late morning when the first shot had almost hit him in the chest. It was only by chance that the shooter had missed him. There was a hole in the side of his shirt and another in his sleeve under his arm to attest to how close the bullet had come. He had taken two quick steps after the shot and then thrown himself sideways to the ground next to a large slab of rock. Whoever it was had shot two more times, both just barely missing him.

By carefully inching himself around, he had concealed himself behind a small clump of Joshua trees. They weren't a lot of cover, but better than none. He could only hope that the slab of rock he was partially beneath would conceal him from anyone coming from behind. He hadn't had time to look underneath the rock to see if there were any other tenants, like scorpions or

1

snakes. He hoped there was nobody home. He knew that the loose rock and gravel on the slope above would warn him of any unwanted visitors.

Jake had played this deadly game before in worse conditions than these and knew that if he allowed the enemy any glimpse of his position he could die. His still being here was a testament to his patience. He glanced at his watch and noted the time. He would allow himself a small sip of water an hour from now. The canteen he carried was only half full, so it was best to conserve what he had. He pushed a little more dirt from under his body, careful not to raise any dust that might be seen, giving away his position. He had been clearing rocks and small stones from underneath himself since getting there and placing them as a barrier against additional gunfire. He knew they were a pitiful excuse for a barricade, but it helped pass the time.

Jake rested his head on his arm and closed his eyes. The sun in the desert can damage the eyes if they're not protected, and he'd lost his glasses when he had run from the gunfire. His eyes were more likely to be damaged than others because of their color. They were a very light blue, almost gray. Someone had said he may be an albino if it weren't for his dark hair. He knew if he went to sleep his enemy could sneak up on him and it would be over. He fought back the urge to call out and tell his attackers that they were cowardly bastards, for shooting an unarmed man in the back.

He knew his enemies couldn't let him live to testify about what they'd done. He kept thinking 'they' because he wasn't sure if 'they' were both still alive. He knew for sure that one was as evidenced by the shots earlier. If he was very lucky one had killed the other and there was only one to escape from.

He picked another stone from beneath his body and placed it with the others. If he could hold out until dark, he might be able to walk out of there, unless they had infra-red scopes which wasn't likely. He checked his rifle again out of habit and wiped some of the accumulated dust off of the scope. He had five rounds in the rifle and nine more in his pockets, along with two extra magazines for the 9MM he carried. Up close he could make it a war, but at long distance he was at a disadvantage.

The shot startled him and brought him back to reality, along with the shower of sand that drifted down over him. Jake thought they had shot high just to remind him that they were still out there. He knew he wouldn't be going anywhere for at least a couple more hours if then. He glanced at his watch again and decided he could treat himself to a small swig of water. He knew he had to stay hydrated or he couldn't survive. His body was leaner than most men due to being in the desert so much. At just over six feet and weighing two hundred ten he knew he should have at least two quarts of water per day.

He thought of another time when he had been forced to lie still for over twelve hours before he could leave. That time when he left, he went just far enough and left enough of a trail for the enemy to follow. The results were exactly as he had planned: three confirmed kills in less than ten minutes. Tonight, he told himself, would be a similar situation and he would become the hunter instead of the hunted.

The thought of the impending night sent a chill down his spine. He knew that his opponents were not new to this game. If he were smarter, instead of being so vengeful, he should just walk away and leave them there in the desert.

It had all started when his friend TJ had asked him to go with him to guide a party interested in doing some gold prospecting. TJ made somewhat of a living by conducting guided tours of the desert. He had a small ad in one of the LA papers and it brought in quite a few tours each year. Most people didn't like going out into the desert during the summer months, so this tour was somewhat unusual. They planned to be gone for two or three days at the most, coming back on Sunday.

Jake thought that TJ even looked like what a "desert guide" should look like, taller than Jake by an inch and thin with a slight potbelly. His hair was white and on the rare occasion that he took off his sunglasses you could see dark brown eyes. For some reason known only to himself, TJ was always smiling.

TJ had scheduled the tour with a young couple in their mid-thirties. He said they had come from Los Angeles to "explore" a certain area in the Panamint Range, based on some information they had researched in various libraries. They acted as if they were married, but Jake had a suspicion that they weren't related to each other in any fashion. As a recent widower Jake knew that married couples were more familiar with each other than these two. TJ introduced them as Dean and Karen Davis.

She was tall and leggy, almost like a model. If he had to guess, he would have said 6'1" and 140 to 150 pounds. Her hair was light brown, not quite blonde, with some blonde highlights in it and she wore it short. She had blue eyes, but they were too blue so he thought they might be contacts. He noticed the small worry lines that were starting to show around the eyes. She was a beautiful woman, but the small scar along her left eyebrow and the slight bump on an otherwise perfect nose told him the story of some roughness in her past.

Dean was big, almost 6'3" and at least 240 pounds. He had dark almost black hair cut very short in military fashion. Jake had no idea what color his eyes were. They were constantly hidden behind dark glasses. From his manner and his walk, Jake would have guessed him to be an ex-Marine or Navy Seal.

TJ had suggested they meet at a restaurant in Inyokern and have dinner the night before they were to leave. The place was quiet and the four of them were seated in the back part of the dining room, perhaps TJ's idea so they could all talk more freely. Jake had the feeling that this was more of an interview than just casual conversation.

He tried several times to steer the dialogue toward the Davis' background and each time he was given an evasive answer. Most of the night, it was he who was answering questions about himself and his background. He answered their questions in general, but when they got too inquisitive, then he too would change the subject. Most of their questions had to do with his knowledge of the region. Normally, he would have loved to have an audience to impress with his extensive knowledge, but he felt these two were on a hunt for specific information about something other than what they had said and he wasn't about to give them anything even by accident.

It was early Thursday morning when they left Ridgecrest. The sky was showing gray and pink as they motored along in TJ's old Dodge Powerwagon. It was one machine that was sinfully ugly with dented fenders and faded paint, but for endurance in the desert nothing came close to being its equal. Every part had been removed and re-built with care, until the entire truck was like new except the body. TJ had a trailer made from another Dodge truck rigged behind. It too was a nondescript grayish green. Jake guessed that TJ had gotten them both from a salvage yard somewhere. Jake had also seen four more Dodge trucks covered with tarps parked in back of TJ's big barn. From the looks of the trailer, he didn't pay top dollar. The one thing TJ did pay top dollar for was supplies. He didn't skimp on food, water, or anything else that mattered when you were a hundred miles from everywhere.

There was a slight chill to the morning air as they motored along at the roaring speed of 55 miles per hour, but Jake welcomed the chill, knowing that the day could turn into an oven by noon. He wore a short sleeve shirt and welcomed the sun on his skin while TJ always wore the same long-sleeved shirt buttoned at the collar and the cuffs. Jake thought about the differences between them and smiled. TJ was fair-skinned and burned easily in the desert sun, while Jake had darker skin and welcomed the sun. The Davises sat in the back seat watching the nothingness of the desert roll by. TJ was his usual self with non-stop chatter from the time he got behind the wheel, talking about rock formations, how China Lake got its name, and gold.

"Your ordinary everyday citizen doesn't give a damn about gold, and doesn't even think about it unless somebody else brings the subject up. Then it seems as if there's a switch that gets turned on, and then they can't wait to find some, get some, buy some, whatever it takes until that switch turns itself off. With some folks that's a short time, and with others that switch don't ever turn off. I've seen ordinarily common sense folks go

[5]

absolutely crazy over the thought of finding gold and they just don't know how to let it go.

Old Stan Hobbs would be a good example. He was a good worker, could do most anything with his hands, carpentry, plumbing, whatever, but he just couldn't give up that itch to go looking for gold. It seems like every time some fool starts in talking about a "strike" somewhere, Old Stan would pack up and go. He's made some good finds here and there and worked them long enough to "prove up" and then he'd sell out and come back to Ridgecrest and sit for a while. He didn't care for the gold so much as the finding it. The sad fact of the matter is that most folks don't have a clue where to look, or even what to look for. I saw one fellow standing on a vein of Galena nearly a foot wide and didn't know it. Most of the time these so-called prospectors wouldn't know if they were four feet from a million dollars or a million feet from four dollars."

TJ was going on and on about different topics. It was probably the effect of too much of Margaret's coffee and too little sleep as they had both been up late going over every item and checking each piece of equipment. Jake chuckled to himself when he thought about how meticulous TJ was when packing for an outing. Sometimes it seemed as if they were going on a three month safari instead of a couple of days hike. Everything was stowed in its own place and properly secured according to a diagram TJ made up for each trip. He even packed extra tires and rims although he had a tire repair kit in the trailer.

"You never know what you'll need out there until you need it. It's better to have it and not use it, than need it and not have it," he would say. "You probably think I'm being too much of a Boy Scout, but I've helped haul quite a few people out of this desert, and not all of them were alive. I don't feel like ending up as breakfast for some buzzard or coyote."

The sun was just peeking over the hills as they passed through Trona. Karen made a comment about the Searle's Lake Yacht Club sign above the local tavern.

"It's just a bit of local humor," said TJ. "The lake is dry most of the time except for a few places. Just underneath the surface of

[6]

that water you see out there is a layer of calcium carbonate, the stuff they use in Rolaids and Tums. They use it for other things too, but I'm not sure exactly what"

As they passed the refinery where the ore was processed, Mrs. Davis commented about the smell.

"That smell is horrible. How can anyone live here?"

"Well, I guess they just get used to it. Either that or drive back and forth from Ridgecrest every day. Some of them do that, but housing in Trona is so cheap that a lot of the workers just live here."

TJ stopped at the gas station and turned off the engine. "I'll be right back, I need to get a couple packs of cigarettes and use the facility."

The Davises just nodded and sat there fanning themselves with folded up maps. Jake knew better about the cigarettes. TJ might smoke one or two cigarettes in a day, and there were two packs already in the Powerwagon. Jake had figured out a long time ago that TJ always left an envelope with directions where he was going with Mike Thorpe, the gas station owner who also happened to be a reserve deputy sheriff.

Jake tried to start some conversation with Dean and Karen, but neither of them seemed to be in a talkative mood. She just sat there looking off into the distance like there was no one around, alone in herself and her thoughts. Dean grunted a response or two to Jake's questions, but wasn't interested in talking.

As he waited, Jake thought about the day ahead and wondered what it was the Davises were looking for in particular. He and TJ had prospected the area they were going to and hadn't really found anything worthwhile, except some galena, a combination of lead and silver ore. If there were any signs of gold, they hadn't seen them, though they had found a few "possible" traces of gold here and there.

TJ got back into the Powerwagon and fired it up. They crossed the railroad tracks and headed north out of Trona. A Navy jet roared overhead as they cruised over the hill and down into the Panamint Valley.

"Looks like someone wanted to do some early practice on the range," TJ commented. He went on to explain the locations of the different gunnery ranges that the Navy had set up.

As they neared the turnoff toward the old ghost town of Ballarat, the western side of the mountains were still in shadows. The road was now gravel and TJ slowed down to about 15 miles per hour. Jake knew from past experience not to comment on the slow speed, having heard TJ's tirade about the road being made for driving not racing.

It was alright by Jake, because at that speed they didn't stir up a lot of dust and he could watch the different animal tracks alongside the road. Occasionally he would see a coyote's tracks, or even a burro. Sometimes in the early morning they would come upon a rattler moving across the road. He looked up and saw Sentinel Peak in the mountains to the northeast, one of his favorite guides. To the west he could see Olancha Peak and Mt. Whitney rising above the others, the sun just touching the tops of them.

They passed Ballarat and headed north and east on an even narrower gravel road. It hadn't been used much and definitely not recently. In the desert the rain is very seldom and tracks of any kind usually stay until the wind wipes them out. There were no tracks at all in the two ruts Jake was watching.

"Can't we go a little faster?" Karen asked. Jake sensed the tenseness in TJ's tone when he answered.

"Yes ma'am, we certainly could, but this old Dodge is just like me. Old. I've had her for quite a long time and I don't figure on being broke down out here in the middle of nowhere just 'cause somebody is itchy to get someplace. There ain't any Triple A out here to call, that is if we could call. In case you hadn't noticed, them fancy cell phones you got don't have any signal out here. So, if you don't mind ma'am, we'll just keep to this pace and I can for sure guarantee we'll get where we're going. And that means we'll be able to leave when we want." He nodded his head for emphasis and turned back to his driving.

They seemed to crawl along for quite some time until there was a turnoff toward the mountain. Jake noticed that the Davises seemed to be a lot more attentive. He saw them put their heads together and some message was relayed, though he couldn't hear above the engine noise.

The old Powerwagon slowed almost to a walk when TJ shifted to a lower gear.

"We get around this bend and I'll have to stop and lock the hubs so we can go four-wheel. That's the only way we'll make it up this trail."

After they locked in the hubs, TJ and Jake paused to stretch their legs and have a half cup of coffee. Jake didn't drink much coffee and the jolt of the caffeine seemed to make him edgy. TJ's wife Margaret made some damn good coffee, if you like it on the strong side. She called it hundred mile coffee because if you drank one cup black it would keep you awake for a hundred miles. Jake always had to put sugar in it to take the edge off.

Dean and Karen were now wide awake and examining the mountainside thoroughly. They each had gotten out a pair of binoculars and were scanning each section as if it were under a microscope. Jake wasn't quite sure what they were looking for and wasn't about to ask.

TJ on the other hand, wasn't so bashful. "If you can tell me what it is you're looking for, maybe I can help you find it."

"Not yet," Dean replied. "When we see it, we'll know whether this is the right canyon."

"Last night, looking at the maps you were sure this was the right one," TJ said. "Now you don't seem too sure. Is there a particular landmark or something?"

"We have a description of a certain rock formation with a petroglyph on it. That's all you need to know"

TJ stared at him in disbelief. "Maybe you don't know it, but this here is earthquake country. That rock formation may not even be here any longer. It might be scattered all over the place. And even if you did find the rock formation, the petroglyph might be gone. Some of the local punks have been known to spray paint over the petroglyphs. Others just dig under them thinking there might be gold and then they sink down until they're barely

[9]

visible or just fall over. I'd say your chances are one in a thousand of finding what you're looking for."

Jake watched Dean's face as TJ was talking. It was getting tighter with each sentence, as if TJ himself had destroyed the rock formation and the petroglyph. It was obvious that Dean wasn't happy with the thought that they might not find what they wanted.

They climbed into the Dodge and started up the mountain. The trail they were following ran alongside what would be a creek if it ever rained. Sometimes they were in the middle of the dry creek bed, mostly to the side of it. They moved slowly, sometimes an inch at a time because of the rocks in the trail.

Jake watched the two scanning the hillsides as they climbed, curious as to what was so important that they were looking for. From the expression on Dean's face when TJ had told him about the possibility of the landmarks not being there, whatever it was had to be valuable.

After an hour had passed, TJ pulled the Dodge onto a small flat area in a canyon southwest of Sentinel Peak. Jake remembered the place as one where they had camped before when they had been prospecting.

"If it's alright with you two, we'll make camp here," TJ said. "Then you two can do some wandering around and see if this is the right area."

Dean and Karen were eager to leave the campsite, but TJ warned them about taking along enough water and other equipment. "Keep an eye out for rattlers," he said. "They don't always warn you before they strike."

"I've got what I need to take care of snakes, I borrowed them from a friend," Dean replied. He pulled a pistol and holster from a backpack and showed it to Jake. He pulled out a box of cartridges and looked at the pistol, then at Jake. "You know how to load this?" Dean asked. He watched as Jake loaded the magazine and slipped it into the pistol. Jake watched as Dean checked the action and slid the gun back into the holster and then strapped it on. He could tell this was something Dean had done many times before, so why the pretense?

[10]

"In fact, I even borrowed one for Karen," he continued. "Will you help her with it?"

Karen watched as Jake loaded her weapon. It was an old Browning model, but it didn't appear worn. Jake noticed that hers was in a shoulder holster and she had definitely had practice on putting it on.

They walked away from the camp toward the east following the creek bed, but paused briefly to look back at TJ and the camp.

Jake made himself busy helping TJ set up the camp. When they had packed the night before, each item had been placed in an order so that when they unpacked it was an item they would need as they made camp. The tent went together quickly, and soon they had most of the camp laid out. TJ set up the camp stove and hooked up the propane tank. Jake knew that lunch wouldn't be too far off. He also knew that if he wanted something palatable it was up to him to do the cooking. TJ was really good at camping, but his culinary abilities were almost non-existent.

"You figured out what it is they're looking for?" Jake asked.

"Not yet, but I don't think it has anything to do with gold. If they were serious about some treasure or old mine, they would have done some studying of some maps or something."

"This area wasn't exactly well traveled by any of the wagon trains I've read about," Jake commented. "I wonder if there is some kind of family history that they have, or maybe they just got hold of some information out of the library like they said. Either way, we could be hundreds of miles from any real treasure."

"Yeah, but I already tried to tell them that and they didn't seem to care. I think I'll just keep my mouth shut from now on and try not to be too nosey, " TJ said.

Jake went back to work on the stew he was creating for the evening meal, just content to be out in the mountains again. Lunch would be Bratwurst sausages over the fire and boiled potatoes and sauerkraut. He wasn't sure if the Davises would eat sauerkraut, but if not that just left more for him and TJ. He enjoyed his outings with TJ, often content to just ride along and see the scenery.

[11]

Since his early days growing up in the foothills of California, he had always been wandering, most of the time just going somewhere to see what was there. He never thought of himself as an explorer of any kind, just footloose. His family had laughingly called him "Smoke" because one minute he'd be there and then he would just disappear. He had left home shortly after turning seventeen, traveling all over the western half of the states. He didn't have any particular destination in mind when he took off, just wanting to see what was "out there". His travels had taught him a lot about the country, but it had also taught him about being self-sufficient.

He'd travel to someplace "exotic" sounding on the map like Battle Mountain, Nevada or Cutbank, Montana and stay for a few days working at whatever odd job was available. Most of the time he would just walk around the town taking in the sights and sounds, never really wanting to be a part of the scene just an observer. Often he would just sit and watch the people at whatever they were doing. Occasionally he would be rousted for vagrancy by the local police, and have to spend a night in jail but it wasn't all that bad. A time or two he had hung around intentionally just so they would toss him in the can. Being young helped, most of the cops had a younger brother or a nephew his age and didn't mind if you spent the night in one of their cells as long as they weren't busy. Often they would find something for him to eat. Most of them just wanted him to move on out of their town which he would do as soon as he was released.

Jake chuckled to himself when he thought about those days. A whole lot of time spent just wandering, but not wasted time he thought. An education of sorts, those days, learning how to do different things, like the way to properly prune roses he had learned at a nursery in Oregon. Or when he'd learned how to set up bricks for the brick-layers when he had a short stint as a hod-carrier. He had done quite a few different jobs from washing dishes in a cafe to hoeing weeds in a peach orchard. He wouldn't forget the times on the road, the black burning asphalt under his feet in Arizona, the coolness of the breeze coming up

[12]

the canyons in the Sierra Nevada, or the dryness of crossing the salt flats after being dropped off at Tooele, Utah.

He remembered the back-breaking labor in El Centro, working for an old man building a duplex. The old man was in his seventies but definitely not lacking for energy. Jake couldn't keep up with "Old Arnold" no matter what. He would get up at 4:00 a.m. to work until it got too hot, then take a "siesta" until evening and then go back to work until he couldn't see. He had learned how to use a shovel and pick, digging the foundation footings, the trenches for the sewer lines, the trenches for the leach lines, and even the hole for the septic tank, because Arnold didn't want to spend the money to rent a backhoe. He had helped put together the plumbing, learning to solder the copper pipe properly so there were no "icicles" hanging from the joints. He had also helped put together the drain lines, using cast iron pipe because Arnold didn't like using that "new-fangled" plastic pipe. He said it was made from petroleum and someday we'd run out of oil to make the plastic. Arnold showed him how to put the pipe together and pack the joints with oakum and then tap the lead in around the joint before heating it up to seal it. He also learned the importance of making sure the drain line had the right slope.

Forming the foundation was interesting, something he hadn't done before and he like the feel of the hammer in his hand. It felt like what he was doing was important, something he could take pride in, maybe look back later and say "I did that".

He'd stayed with that old man five weeks, longer than he'd stayed anywhere. He especially enjoyed framing the building because it gave him a chance to use his math skills, something Arnold wasn't too good at. Arnold even commented on how it would be the first time he hadn't "wasted twenty trees" on a building because of his bad math. When he left, the duplex was framed and roofed with the siding on and Jake knew a satisfaction he'd never known.

"Hey!" TJ said. "You dreaming again?"

"Just thinking about when I left home," Jake answered. "It seemed like those days would go on forever, but they didn't."

"They never do, Jake. It's always something or somebody wants to try to take away the good times. You know, like the damn draft board or whatever. I barely made it home in time to keep from being a "draft-dodger" myself. Don't think I wasn't tempted to take off to Canada like a couple of others I knew. I learned a lot out there just bumming around, and it didn't hurt me any to go hungry now and then."

"TJ, you know that Margaret is just like my wife Sue was. You haven't been hungry in over thirty years, and she never let anyone else go away hungry either."

The thought of Sue brought Jake back to reality and his grief at her death.

CHAPTER TWO

Weldon Purcell woke up at three in the morning. His shoulder was hurting again. The arthritis that bothered his joints was starting to come back. His wife was still snoring as he lay there rubbing his shoulder gently. He knew what the problem was. It happened every time they turned on the swamp cooler. He had argued with her before about the effects that the cooler had on his arthritis. He wanted to put in air conditioning, but as usual she talked him out of it. If they were to buy a new house, they could have it built with the central air installed and with better insulation in the walls. He had tried to tell her that putting in air-conditioning and adding insulation in the attic and walls would be much cheaper than buying a new house. As usual his arguments were totally ignored, and so he didn't much bother with saying anything.

The house they lived in now was built in the forties and didn't have any insulation in the walls. It wasn't much of an inconvenience except in the summertime when the temperature could climb to over one hundred. Then it was almost unbearable even with the swamp cooler.

They had bought the house just after he had been hired by the sheriff's department. It was a big step at the time and he remembered his nervousness at the thought of a 30 year mortgage. He was just barely out of the Marine Corps less than a year and had thought the house payment was too much to handle. Now it was less than the payment on the Harley every month. He had thought about refinancing, but the interest rates were way higher than when he had bought the house, so lately any overtime he got went to making extra payments on the Harley. There were only four years to go and the house would be paid off. The Harley would be paid off in less than two.

He rubbed his shoulder again and slipped out of bed. Maybe the Tylenol would help this time. It didn't usually do much more than take the edge off the pain, but lately he had been doubling up on the dosage and that seemed to work. He should talk to his doctor about the constant pain, but wasn't too happy about dealing with a rheumatologist. The last person Dr. Winslow had recommended was a quack, he thought. He had gone to the rheumatologist for almost two years, before he figured out that he was being used as a guinea pig for a "study" the doctor was doing. He remembered how defensive the doctor got when he had asked to see the file. He had become more than curious when the doctor kept changing his medication every three months. He also remembered the doctor yelling at him that he couldn't have 'those files' when he took the whole bunch out the door with him.

Maybe he could talk her into putting in a window air conditioner, just for the bedroom. He walked to the kitchen and poured himself a small glass of milk. The other deputies would laugh if they knew he drank milk, but it was the only thing that he could take with the Tylenol and not have an upset stomach. That and he still liked the taste of cold milk.

As he sat at the table, Purcell thought about the job and the hours he'd been putting in lately. Homicide division wasn't exactly swamped with business in a county of only eighteen thousand people, but then it wasn't lacking for customers either. It seemed there was always somebody who had to prove their point by shooting or stabbing or clubbing someone else. They usually had six or seven homicides a year, along with a dozen or so suspicious deaths. And when someone died, it became Purcell's responsibility to figure out who did it and why.

Usually it didn't take long to figure the who or the why, due to the abundance of witnesses. But every now and then they would get a case that they couldn't get a handle on. He worked harder on those cases than the run-of-the-mill murders. Lately they seemed to take more out of him, and he had recently started thinking about retirement. Ten years and four months to go until he was sixty-two and eligible for Social Security, if it was still there.

He sat at the table and waited for the Tylenol to start taking effect. If he sat up for thirty minutes and then went back to bed it would be better for his stomach. He thought about the upcoming weekend and wondered if he should take the Harley out. More than likely the wife would have ten excuses why she didn't want to go, and he'd end up staying home and doing some projects around the house.

He sat for a few more minutes and then decided to go back to bed. He wanted a couple more hours sleep before he had to get up.

. . . . . .

Hernando Partida was always on the look-out for new clientele. He worked his way up in the Los Lobos gang in East LA, but then his mother had moved to San Bernardino. Being the "new boy" in the neighborhood had almost killed him, until he had told them of his affiliation with Los Lobos. They seemed to take it easy on him when they "jumped" him into the gang, knowing that he had been through the ceremony before. After that he was accepted into the gang and given assignments. He had started as a messenger, delivering whatever note or package they told him to wherever they wanted. It was easy work and it kept him from being beaten.

As time passed, they assigned him to a corner not far from his home. He was given a small amount of grass to sell and when he sold out he could go home. The first few weeks were hardest, Hernando would wait until late into the night before he quit. As long as he took the money and the remaining grass back to the gang he was alright. His mother was always yelling at him to come straight home from school and quit hanging out with those hoodlums. After the first few weeks Hernando could easily spot both the regular customers and the narcs. The weekends were the best, because of the anglo teens coming over from the valley looking to score. He always made it a point to charge them twice the going rate. He kept the difference in one of his side pockets just in case El Jefe caught him at it. Slowly he was building up quite a pile of money. He knew if his mom caught him at it or found the money there'd be hell to pay, but for now everything was cool.

He'd been working the corner for nearly four months when he first saw the new narc cruising the avenue. They were easy to spot. Most of the time they would try to dress up like the gang-bangers they were trying to catch, but the clothes were too new and too K-Mart to fool anyone except some stupid anglos. This guy was different, he didn't even bother to try to dress like a gang member. He wore a pullover shirt and Levi's that were well faded. His car was new and sounded like there was plenty of power under the hood. The man himself had plenty of muscle and he looked as if he wouldn't take any crap.

Hernando was nervous when the new narc pulled up at the corner.

"Come here, kid."

"No savvy English, mister." Hernando replied.

"Don't bother with that bullshit, kid. I want some good grass and I don't want to pay for it. You savvy that, kid?"

"I don't have samples, mister. You want grass you gotta pay like everybody else."

"You're not getting the message, kid. I want some free grass. If I don't get it, then I'll have the local narcs shake you down three, four times a day 'til I get what I want. Got it?"

Hernando stared at him for a second. His first instinct was to run like hell and hope he could outrun the man. But something seemed to keep him frozen to the spot.

"I can't give you any free grass. If I do they'll beat me up or maybe kill me and then I won't be here anymore. You'll have to pay me."

Hernando would have continued the conversation, but a patrol car turned onto the avenue a few blocks away and he took the opportunity to back away from the car. He saw the man look into the mirror just before he pulled away from the curb.

Hernando made it a point to tell El Jefe every word of the conversation he'd had with the narc. If it happened again or if the man had the locals start coming down on him, Hernando would not have to explain it again.

. . . .

The evening slowly slipped into darkness, allowing Jake to move and stretch without fear of being shot. He went into a low crawling position and started carefully down the slope toward the bottom of the ravine, being especially cautious not to make any excess noise. His plan was to follow the ravine to the northeast for a few hundred yards and then to head east and then south. He had in mind a particular abandoned mine that was about two miles southeast of his present position. If "Dean and Karen" were looking for him tomorrow, he planned to be in that mine hiding.

He wondered what they had done with TJ's body, more than likely, nothing. They didn't seem to be the kind to worry about niceties like burial, or even covering up. The attack flooded back into his memory.

Dean and Karen had been walking back toward the camp when they opened fire. TJ was nearer to them, and caught the first of the bullets. Jake was just turning toward them when the ambush started, and was missed completely. Dean emptied his pistol toward Jake and then stood there while Karen fired two more rounds at TJ and then emptied her pistol at Jake, who had grabbed his rifle and was running a zigzag pattern downhill as fast as he could.

He still couldn't believe he hadn't been hit by any of the shots aimed his way. He felt cowardly in having run while his best friend was being gunned down. He let the shame wash over him and in his mind he knew he would have to make them pay for their deed. It was the only way he could rid himself of the guilt he felt.

It was almost midnight when the moon started shining over the mountains to the east. Jake was nearly to the spot he wanted, so the moon would be helpful. He had been in the desert many times at night, and knew that landmarks seen by day seldom could be seen at night. He remembered a road from the southeast that led almost directly to the mine. He plodded along, sure that he would be able to see the tracks. He was feeling tired because of the lack of water and almost didn't hear the rattler in front of him, and when he did it sounded muffled as if it were far away. As tired as he was, he wasn't sure if it was a rattler or just snakeweed. In the dark, the two sounded the same. Snakeweed, when matured and dried had a seed pod that when shaken sounded like a rattler. He stopped, holding very still until he located the snake. It was coiled at the base of a small creosote bush to the left. He reached out with the rifle barrel and pushed gently against the side of the snake. It didn't strike at the rifle barrel, but moved slightly away. He nudged it again, and it moved farther away. Jake repeated this process a couple more times until he was sure the snake wouldn't be a problem. As he walked away he remembered a time when he and TJ had encountered a similar situation. Jake had wanted to kill the rattler, but TJ had asked him not to, saying that the snake was just defending himself and would leave if allowed to.

As he plodded along, Jake tried to figure out why they had been attacked. He couldn't think of anyone in his past that would want him dead, at least no one that was still alive. He wasn't too sure about TJ's past though. He didn't know about the years before he had become friends with him, but since he had known TJ there wasn't anything they had done or anything Jake knew about that could qualify for the kind of attack that he had witnessed.

He had met TJ when he and Sue had been looking at investing in some property in and around Ridgecrest. Jake had been at China Lake Naval Weapons Station for a class on desert warfare while in the service, and had spent his spare time wandering around out in the desert. For some reason the desert held a certain fascination for Jake. He couldn't explain it, but in spite of the harshness, he felt more at peace there than any other place he'd been. Maybe it was the quiet, or maybe it was that the desert had its own rules, and if you didn't obey the rules you could end up dead.

TJ wasn't a realtor, but seemed to know more about Ridgecrest than anyone else they had met. They had intended to buy a property that they could build a house on. Instead, they ended up buying a 40 acre parcel next to TJ and Margaret that they would lease to them for growing pistachio trees.

Pistachio farming was a long-term proposition, not having any income for about 6 to 8 years. As TJ had explained to them, if he bought the 40 acres that Jake and Sue were looking at, he couldn't afford to buy the trees for another 4 or 5 years. He and Margaret wanted to supplement their retirement income with the income from the harvest every year. He felt that 80 acres was enough for one man to handle by himself, except the harvest, which he would hire day laborers for. Jake had finally agreed to a lease that was more than enough to pay the annual taxes and provide them with a small income. TJ accompanied them to the realtor's office and was totally surprised when Jake asked if it were okay to write a personal check for the full amount. The money had come from a bachelor uncle of Sue's who, not having kids of his own, left his estate to Sue, her brothers, and a sister.

He felt the tears starting, and sadness at not having known more about his friend's past. He had never been one to open up about past experiences, and past indiscretions, but TJ was a good listener, and what was even more valuable was the fact that he knew how to keep his mouth shut.

Jake had always found comfort in TJ's ability to listen, knowing that when he did answer Jake's questions it would be something Jake should pay attention to. It seemed as if TJ had seen and done almost anything there was worth doing. TJ had been there for him when Sue was killed in an auto accident. TJ didn't say a whole lot of meaningless words, just sat there, listening as Jake poured his heart out.

He and Margaret had helped set him up in a small two bedroom house in Ridgecrest after the funeral. He couldn't bear the thought of living in Sacramento surrounded by Sue's friends and her family. He definitely didn't want to be part of their "pity party" as one cousin of his had called it. Everyone sitting around saying what a tragedy, what a terrible thing and the whole time thinking how glad they were it wasn't them. TJ called it survivor's guilt. Said he'd seen it in the military. Jake had also seen versions of it, a guy in a foxhole laughing insanely because his buddy was the one with part of his head missing.

[21]

Margaret had done most of the work, even before the funeral, helping Jake choose what clothes Sue should be buried in, cleaning out the other house and getting it ready for sale. Jake didn't want to go back there, afraid of the memories, and even more afraid of having to face his in-laws, as if a drugged-up truck driver crossing over the line was somehow his fault. He was disgusted with himself for having accepted an out-of-court settlement after seeing the truck driver's family in court, but he didn't like the thought of going over all the details in court.

The other driver's family had "dressed down" in everyday clothes trying to look like a family from "The Grapes of Wrath". He knew it was a ploy to knock down the settlement amount, but he didn't care after the coroner had told him that Sue was four weeks pregnant. He already knew from the investigator that his attorney had hired what amount of insurance the trucking company carried and so he had settled for just under the maximum amount.

Jake found the mine as the sun started to send its first rays above the ridges to the east. He stepped cautiously into the mineshaft, aware that others may have discovered its location. He pulled the small penlight from his pocket and turned it on. Its tiny bulb wasn't much help, but it did allow him to make out where things were. He went slowly toward the back of the mine, trying to recall the layout and looking for a shaft that might go off to either side and offer him some protection. He found a narrow entrance a few minutes later, but was disappointed when it appeared to be blocked by fallen rocks. He shone the little light toward the ceiling trying to find out if there was a danger of additional falling rocks. He checked carefully and couldn't see where there was any disturbed rock at all.

He checked the rock blocking the entrance and it didn't match any of the surrounding rock walls. Somebody had sealed this off intentionally, but it had been long ago.

He knew the little pen light wouldn't last long, so he sat down and turned it off. He closed his eyes and counted to a hundred, then slowly opened them and stared into the darkness. He could see light coming from the front of the mine, but when he looked the other direction he couldn't see anything. His weariness was more than he could cope with, and he put his head on his crossed arms. Just as he started to nod off, he jumped like he'd been shot. "Tracks," he thought to himself. "They'll be able to see my tracks."

He scrambled out of the mine and feverishly went to work with a handful of brush. He erased all the tracks back to where he had found the road. Then, he tracked down the road until he found a small game trail and followed it for a short distance. He was almost at a dead run when he came back to the mine. He repeated the brushing as he walked back into the mine. This time he went even farther into the mine, and after some additional checking lay down behind some rocks. He put his 9mm in the jacket he had rolled up for a pillow, and even though he could feel the gun it wasn't long before he was asleep.

It seemed as if he had just closed his eyes when he awoke. A quick glance at his watch told him he had been asleep for nearly three hours.

He shook his head and tried to recall his dreams, but there were none. Usually he could recall in detail what he had dreamt about and sometimes be startled by the dream becoming reality sometime later. He'd been told that this precognitive power he claimed was bogus, that he only thought he had this ability. Jake knew better, he'd already experienced it too many times.

Jake checked his canteen, barely one-third full. If he didn't get some water soon, they wouldn't have to shoot him, he'd dehydrate to nothing. That wasn't too scary, but between now and then, with the possibility of bouts of insanity, was something he didn't like to think about. His kidneys and back hurt from lying on the rock floor and also from the lack of water. His head throbbed and when he moved it hurt all the way down his spine.

He knew he had come to this mine for a reason, but at the moment he was too exhausted to recall what it was. He remembered that he and TJ had been here together a little over a year ago. He remembered they had looked in the main shaft at all the different possible ore-bearing strata, but hadn't looked at the small shaft that was now blocked. Then it came to him.

"There's a beehive in there," he recalled TJ saying. "Either that, or there's some water."

"How do you know?" Jake asked.

"Only two reasons bees would come in here, beehive or water."

"Couldn't it be because they want out of the sun?"

"No Jake, they use the sun as part of their guidance system."

Jake got up and sat on the box. He needed water and he needed more rest, but of the two he need water more. He drank two good swallows of the water in the canteen, pausing between them to let the water rest in his mouth. He gently shook the canteen estimating that there was one swallow left. If there was a beehive in the second shaft, he wasn't sure what he'd do. He really didn't want to think about that possibility.

It took Jake about an hour to remove enough of the rocks to be able to squeeze into the second shaft. It wasn't a man-made shaft. Apparently the miners had followed the original formation in to this area, and then when the ore vein went straight ahead, they followed it. Jake wondered if they had explored this natural cave and what they had found. He turned on the little pen light and looked ahead. He had two more batteries in his pocket, so the light should last for about seven or eight hours, but any time after that and he'd need more than a penlight.

The walls of the cave sloped slightly to the left, which made walking difficult. He had to constantly support himself against the side. There was almost no floor to walk on, being part sand and part fallen rock. He followed the cave back about forty feet where it started to descend. A touch of his hand to his face verified a feeling of dampness. Water glistened from the left wall. He was just about to start forward again when a bee buzzed past his head.

He continued crawling along, following the bee. His head throbbed from the lack of water, and he hoped that he wasn't just imagining the moisture he felt. The walls of the cave were sloping more and more to the left, he was almost at a forty-five degree angle. When he had gone nearly three hundred feet in, he stopped to rest. The light was dimming and he'd have to change the battery soon. He turned the light out and leaned against the rock to rest.

Eyes closed, Jake lay against the rock in the darkness. He thought about the attack, and again felt the self-loathing for not standing by his best friend. He couldn't get his own act of cowardice out his mind. All of his training in the military had been exactly the opposite of what he'd done. His memory was there, waiting for something to happen, to show him what a coward he'd been. All logic was pushed aside as he went through different scenarios as to what he "should have" or "could have" done. Logic would tell him that had he stayed, he'd be lying alongside TJ right now. The killers would be headed home and he and TJ would be so much buzzard-bait.

Jake opened his eyes. He must not let them get away with this act of violence. He changed the battery to the penlight and turned it on. He started forward again, but had gone only a few feet when he smelled a foul odor. A few minutes later he saw the cause of the stench. A young coyote had chosen this place to die, the apparent cause of death a snake bite. By careful maneuvering, Jake was able to get around the coyote without getting any of the rotting corpse on himself. He almost threw up it smelled so bad, but a few steps later the odor was all but gone. There was a slight breeze blowing against his face that had to be coming from somewhere.

The shaft widened out and he was able to stand almost straight up except for the wall on the right. It too soon widened and he felt the slope of his descent now decreasing. He looked ahead and there was light showing. Not the yellow glare of a lantern or flashlight, but a pale, almost bluish tint, like just before sunrise. He was so intent on seeing the light that he nearly missed the water hole.

The cave had widened to nearly ten feet at this point, and Jake was keeping to the left wall. If he hadn't put his hand on the trickle of water that ran down the rock, he wouldn't have stopped at all. The water ran under some rocks he was standing on and pooled slightly against the far wall before disappearing.

Jake was very cautious as he sipped the water. The water had an odd taste, but it didn't seem to be too alkaline, in fact it was slightly sweet. He and TJ had had several talks about finding waterholes in the desert. He was fairly sure that if the bees could drink the water, he could too. He slowly drank a small amount and then rinsed and filled the two canteens.

He wanted to get back to the main cave and get out, but for some reason he held back not wanting to leave. Maybe he could do some exploring, see what or where the faint blue light came from. Just as he was about to go, his stomach revolted, and he was spewing vomit back toward the darkness. It's poisoned, he thought to himself. He sat down and hung his head between his knees, wanting the throbbing in his head to go away.

It was like he could still smell the dead coyote, but that couldn't be right - the coyote was nearly forty feet away. Then it hit him, and he began pulling up rocks from the floor. When he saw the stain he knelt and smelled it. The water coming down the rock face was also going past the coyote and washing the rotten corpse, sending tainted water into the pool where it disappeared. The urge to vomit hit him again and this time he didn't bother to try to contain himself.

Jake emptied both canteens on the floor of the cave and went back to the wall where the water trickled down. By carefully cupping one hand and holding the canteen with the other, he was able to get part of the water, but it was slow work. After a couple minutes, he swirled around what water he had captured and then dumped it out on the floor. He repeated the process with second canteen. When he had enough for a couple swallows, he took a small sip. He let the water roll around his mouth and then spit it out. He then drank two small swallows and went back to collecting more. H e drank and collected water until both he and the canteens were full. He found an almost level spot that he could rest on and stretched out. Without meaning to, he fell asleep.

CHAPTER THREE

Jake awoke in a panic, unsure of his surroundings. His light was out, and he hurriedly fumbled to replace the battery. When he finally had it changed, he checked his watch. It showed ten after seven, but that didn't help being in a cave. Jake wasn't sure how long he'd slept after filling the canteens. He wanted to go explore the far reaches of the cave, but he kept telling himself that he had to get out and get to the sheriff's office and report what had happened.

When Jake finally made it to the mine shaft, he could barely see any light. He stopped just before stepping out into the open and scanned the area with the rifle scope. Several sweeps back and forth showed nothing. He started out and then stopped, putting down the rifle and scope and pulling out his binoculars. They were the light gathering kind and worked great in dim light.

He scanned the area twice before he realized what he was seeing. The tracks went across the road from north to south, and he followed with the binoculars to where they might have gone. He saw a glimpse of one of the enemy and threw himself backwards just before the shot. He ran to where the cave entrance was and scrambled into the cave. He turned around and stuck the rifle barrel over the rocks and waited.

After waiting for several minutes as nothing happened, Jake decided to taunt them.

"Come and get me, coward!" he yelled at the entrance. "Are you scared of the dark?"

When no reply came, he stuck his head out of the cave entrance far enough to see. There were two men there and they were just turning to leave.

"Hope you like the dark, Jake" the man yelled as he ran away.

Jake was just about to lean out and try a shot when it came to him, explosives. They were going to collapse the mine on him and leave him to starve to death. He wanted desperately to climb out and run out of the mine. Instead, he crawled further into the cave and prayed that the shock from the explosion didn't break loose any overhead rocks and bring them tumbling down on him.

When it did come, the explosion was louder than he thought it would be. The rock flew in all directions, even careening through the narrow entrance to the cave. The dust was terrible, but because of the breeze coming from the cave it seemed to stop at the cave's entrance. A few rocks fell from the roof of the cave, but none were close to Jake. He climbed out of the cave, made his way toward the mine entrance through the dust and the rocks. The opening had been completely closed off.

. . . .

Desmond Edmonds reached out toward the other side of the bed to wake his wife in the early dawn. He could see the first rays of light starting to shine on the wall of the bedroom and knew he should be getting up soon. He was always the first to get out of bed and today wouldn't be any different. His hand touched the emptiness of her side of the bed and he was startled. Then just as quickly the tears started to flow. She was gone two years now and he still wasn't used to it. She had been part of him and his life for so long it was hard to understand why she wasn't here. The will to get out of bed left him and he lay back wishing the whole thing was just a bad dream.

His mind replayed in vivid detail the crash and the minutes after. How he had tried to stop the flow of blood and couldn't. He had watched in anger as the life force had left her body, unable to do anything except look into her eyes and see them change to that nothingness that one sees in corpses.

He wanted to yell, scream, blame somebody, but there was no-one. The other motorist that had swerved into their lane was dead, killed by the steering wheel pushing through his chest. He thought about how he could get revenge on the family, but the other man had been divorced a year earlier and had little or no resources. Not even insurance on his car.

He swung his feet out of bed and sat with his head in his hands. He thought of all the things the kids had said about how she would want him to carry on and continue living. What a load of bullshit, he thought to himself. They didn't even know her well enough to know that she wanted more than anything to live a full life. They didn't know the number of times that she had kept dinner late so they could discuss the cases he was working on. Or of the many discussions they'd had on the quality of life, and if she were ever injured or sick enough to require being kept alive by a "machine" that she wanted him to pull the switch. Together they had written everything down in a "living will" with specific instructions. He wanted to take those documents out of the vault and push them under their noses.

If it weren't for being a coward, he would have committed suicide soon after she died. But the kids had kept him busy with so many things he hadn't had time to mourn properly. His youngest was especially tough on him, coming up with one thing after another to keep him occupied. She was his favorite child, but she could be a real pain in the ass, constantly checking on him. She joked about it, saying she wanted to know if she could spend the insurance money on a new Corvette.

He made his way to the kitchen and started the coffee pot. He glanced at the clock. Three hours before he had to be at the office. Mrs. Partida would be here at 8:00 a. m. She came every Monday, Wednesday, and Friday. Every week when he paid her she complained that he paid her too much, that there was so little to do. He thought about her comment and chuckled thinking he too would have another day at the office with not a lot to do. Since his wife's death, he had been doing little things, filing, handling small cases that weren't much more than filling out one form or another. He hadn't had a real case since her death, and right now he wasn't sure he could handle one.

Maybe he should look into what was happening at the courthouse, and see if he could get one or two small cases, although he wasn't sure if he really wanted one. San Bernardino was getting to be as bad as Los Angeles, and it seemed there were more drug cases than any other. He couldn't bring himself to defend a drug-pusher, no matter what. Besides, he only went

[29]

to the office to have somewhere to go, other than the mall with the rest of the geezers.

The worst thing he felt was that somehow he wasn't needed. Before, they had shared their days, him telling her about the current case he was working on. She would often ask questions that inside he considered silly, but didn't dare say anything because she was genuinely interested. She in turn would give him the play-by-play of what happened at home, especially when the kids were younger and actively involved in school, sports, and other things. Now there was nothing.

Maybe Julie could help him find something that he could handle, like maybe a messy little divorce. They were always fun, with the listening to who did what to whom, who said what, and who owed who how much.

. . . .

Jake sat on a rock and put his head in his hands. He tried to think what to do next. There was a possibility that only a couple of rocks stood between him and freedom. It could also have brought down half the mountainside. He got up and went to the back part of the mine and gathered what wood he could find. He tore some boxes into small pieces and bound them into a bundle with some old rags. He also gathered a couple of old tools that were laying about. He made several trips to get all these treasures into the cave and then several more to get them to the water hole. His penlight was faded when he shut it off. The only good thing he could think of was the coyote. It was buried under a pile of rocks that had come down during the explosion. The smell was still there, but the coyote wasn't.

Jake lay on the ledge where he had rested before and was almost asleep when he heard a faint noise. It came from the unexplored area of the cave. He quickly got up and moved away from the water hole. A few moments later a shadow appeared heading toward the water. In the darkness, he could barely make out the form and heard more than saw the animal. From what he could guess, it was a fox. It was too small to be a coyote and too

[30]

large to be a rabbit. He watched as it drank water and then slipped back into the darkness.

After the fox had gone, he shined his light to where it had appeared. He was disappointed when he saw the opening there was too small for a man to fit in. While sitting there he began chipping away at the wall where the water ran down using an old piece of rusted steel that might have been a drill bit. He soon had a small bowl cut into the side of the rock which made it a lot simpler to get to the water.

Jake checked his watch. Eleven forty-five. Why was it so important to know the time? It was in the back of his mind, but he couldn't remember why. He lay down against the rock and watched as the fire slowly died out.

. . . .

Margaret hadn't slept well. She never did when TJ was gone. She was used to having him around and didn't like it when he was gone. He was always doing something in the yard or in the shop. Just knowing that he was around was comforting to her. They didn't have to talk much even though it was in TJ's nature to talk a lot when others were around. When it was just the two of them it was as if they didn't need to do anything other than be together.

They had met in her hometown in Missouri when she was just seventeen. He was so handsome in his uniform that she just couldn't take her eyes off him. She knew she was considered plain and not good-looking by her folks. She'd heard their whispers at night when they thought she was asleep. They never knew how she'd cried herself to sleep afterward.

It was purely by chance that TJ had asked her out on a date. TJ and his buddy were visiting his buddy's folks over in Quincy, Illinois and had happened to stop at the Maid-Rite in New London where she was working. TJ's buddy was a quick-witted smooth talker and when he noticed that there was going to be a dance the next night he asked the waitress if she would go with him, him being a stranger in town and not knowing anyone. Margaret watched TJ roll his eyes in disbelief and just smiled.

[31]

The waitress, Ann, didn't know what to say, but before anyone else said anything TJ said, "Well, I guess you and I will have to go along and keep these two kids out of trouble." She'd never been out before and wasn't sure how to act. Momma told her to just keep her mouth shut and smile and listen to him talk.

The first date was just like Momma had said. He had talked and talked, and she had listened. Occasionally he would ask her a question that she would answer, but mostly she listened. It was late in the evening when he finally took her home. He asked her for a second date, and she said yes. They didn't do much on their second date except talk. Again TJ talked and Margaret listened.

He was being transferred overseas in a week, and he asked if he could write to her. He never said what he would be doing and she never asked. After he left, she felt this strange feeling like part of her was missing. The daily letters to TJ and from TJ helped pass the time. Even then he didn't say where he was and there were no legible postmarks on any of the letters. For two years they corresponded with each other. Two weeks to the day after he returned, they were married. After they completed their vows, she could almost hear an audible sigh of relief from her mother.

They honeymooned in San Diego, California and made several trips around Southern California. It was on one of those trips that they saw the Mojave Desert and Death Valley. TJ was totally in awe of the different areas in Death Valley and mostly China Lake. TJ looked into job opportunities in Ridgecrest and found an opening with the Navy in their contracting division. He spent a good portion of their first year of marriage away from her at one school or another.

Now she felt pulled apart whenever he was gone. He'd now been gone nearly three days, but was supposed to be back this afternoon. If he didn't return, she knew where to go to find out where he was.

. . . .

When he awoke, Jake checked his watch again. Five fifteen in the morning. He and TJ were supposed to have returned to Ridgecrest yesterday. Then it came to him, the letter that TJ always dropped off with the reserve deputy. Deputy Thorpe would open that this morning and call Margaret to be sure they hadn't gone home and forgotten to check with him on the way back to town. When they hadn't shown up, Margaret would start the authorities looking for them. Jake felt better about the situation than he had felt in days. At least someone would be doing something positive.

Jake's search of the remainder of the cave was less than joyful. He returned to the water hole and looked at the faint light that came from above. The walls were too far apart at this spot to try and climb up, but a little farther along they came closer together. By bracing his back against one wall and his feet against the other, he was able to climb part of the way to the top. He could only climb to a certain point before the walls narrowed and he was forced to climb back down.

He rested for a while, trying to think what to do next. He wanted out of the cave desperately. At last he decided that he would go back to the mine entrance and try to dig his way out. He could come back to the waterhole when he needed water and rest. At least it was a plan.

Jake made it to the mine entrance after some struggle. He still had some cord in his vest, so he rigged a guide from the cave entrance to the mine entrance. He used up what was left of the penlight to verify the mine entrance. As soon as he started moving the rock and rubble that had come down because of the blast, he wished he had more light. By carefully checking the distance one foot in front of the other he could stack the rocks out of the way against the south wall of the mine. He soon developed a simple routine, ten steps to the rock pile, dump the rock, ten steps back. He tried not to think about anything but moving the rock.

He was reminded how much he appreciated his eyesight every time he stepped against a rock and hurt his ankle, or dropped the rock only to have it bounce down the pile and hit his foot. He didn't know if was getting any better at moving rocks, but he was getting really good at swearing. His fingers dug out the rocks one by one, some large and some small. It's just a game, he told himself. Keep working and you'll keep winning, he told himself. He developed a chant to go along with the pace of his labor. "Take a seat, and you're dead meat. If you quit now, you're coyote chow." He knew it sounded stupid, but he didn't care, he wanted out so he could track down 'Dean and Karen'.

Jake kept at it for four hours. When he stopped to rest, he could feel the pain in his back and shoulders. He knew he shouldn't stop, it would be hard to get started again. He fumbled with the wrist watch, trying to see what time it was. Margaret would be looking for them by now. He lay down on the rock pile and tried to get comfortable. No use. He laid there and closed his eyes, just wanting to rest.

He awoke with a start, feeling the shake of the ground like an earthquake. He hadn't meant to fall asleep, it just happened. The shaking stopped just as he came fully awake. The fear of being trapped started at him again. An earthquake could loosen the rock above enough to bring everything down on top of him. He started moving the rocks again, pick up a rock, ten steps to the pile, drop the rock, ten steps back. He was on the fourth trip when he felt the rumble again. This time he knew it wasn't an earthquake. Somebody was trying to dig him out. He moved back by the cave entrance and waited.

After nearly three hours, Jake saw the first shaft of light at the top of pile of rock. He wanted to yell to them, but caution told him to wait until he found out who "they" were.

CHAPTER FOUR

Jake couldn't believe what he was hearing from the deputy. After all the trouble he'd been through, it was just too hard to believe. He cleared his throat twice before asking the question.

"Am I under arrest?" he asked.

"We have reason to believe that you were instrumental in the death of Thomas James Wagner, also known as TJ, and therefore we are holding you for questioning. Do you want an attorney present?"

"I don't even know any attorneys," Jake replied.

"Even though you're not under arrest at this time Mr. Kozan, I wouldn't advise answering any questions until you've talked to an attorney."

The other deputy walked over by Jake. He looked Jake over, as if he were something rotten.

"What happened, Kozan? Did somebody piss you off? Something happen you didn't like? Sooner or later, you're gonna talk. Crazies like you always want to talk about what you did and why you did it. And I know you did it."

Jake wanted to scream at him. His thoughts were all twisted in his head, how could they think he would kill TJ? The only friend who understood him, who accepted him "as-is". He looked at the deputy and merely shook his head.

"You're wrong." Jake said quietly. He wanted to say more, but knew it would be a waste of time. How could anyone understand that he and TJ had been so close, almost as close as a man and wife. He had loved that old man for who he was, but even now in his mind he knew that he didn't know all that TJ had been and would probably never know. Margaret could tell him her part of the story, but it would be just part of the story.

Jake submitted quietly as they placed the handcuffs on him. He was glad it was the first deputy putting them on and not the other. The other had a mean nature about him, as if he enjoyed pushing people around. They read him his Miranda rights after they put him in the back of the Chevy Blazer that was their squad car. All the way to the station the mean one kept up a running dialogue about what was going to happen to Jake when the "Big boys" at the jail got hold of him. Jake did the best he could to ignore him, and succeeded in catching a nap during the ride to the Inyo County Sheriff's in Independence before they arrived.

The interrogation room was a light tan almost beige color and recently painted. He was introduced to the detectives for the sheriff's department, Sgt. David Larson and Sgt. Weldon Purcell. Larson appeared to be in his late thirties or early forties. Larson was shorter and heavyset, while Purcell was tall and very thin and at least ten tears older. Larson reminded Jake of a bulldog because of the jowls that were just beginning and the bagginess under the eyes. Purcell looked like a bald eagle when he turned sideways. His thinning hair was plastered down over the top to help hide his ever-increasing baldness. His eyes were like an eagle too. They seemed to look right through you. Jake didn't hold out much hope for them releasing him. These types had had too many chances to hone their skills and seemed like they had already made up their minds about Jake.

Larson started the game, "You want to tell us your side of it?"

Jake started to answer, but then thought better of it. He just sat there and waited for them to get going. After all, if he didn't say anything, they couldn't use it against him.

"You really should talk to us, Kozan," Larson continued. "If we don't hear your version of the events, then we can't help you."

"Gentlemen, I would like you to bring me a telephone book so I can call an attorney."

"Now Jake, you don't need to do that. We just need you to answer a few questions and then you can go."

Jake sat silent, watching Purcell in the corner of the room. He had figured out quickly who was to play good cop and who was bad cop.

"Am I under arrest?" Jake asked again.

"No Jake, not at this time. But if you leave now it's not going to look good for you later," Larson replied.

The detectives soon had Jake placed in a neat 2-man holding cell. The other person was an older man, somewhat small in stature and apparently the quiet type as neither of them offered any conversation. That would be fine with Jake as he didn't want to know the life history of every con in Southern California. Jake lay back on the bunk and thought how comfortable it felt compared to the rocks he'd been sleeping on. He didn't feel sleepy at the time, so he lay there replaying the events of TJ's shooting in his mind. He knew that at some point in time the details would be important, if not to anyone else at least to him when he was released.

"In case you were wondering, they are holding me for embezzlement," the old man offered. "They say I took over three million dollars."

"Well, did you?" Jake asked.

"No," the old man replied. "But I wish I had. The people I was working for wouldn't have had me arrested if they thought I had any connection to the missing money. They're not the kind that goes to the law to solve their problems. "

"And what kind is that?"

The old man just looked at him and shrugged.

The rest of the evening went by without further conversation until lights out. After the guards had left the holding area, the old man asked Jake what he was being held for.

"They think I killed my best friend," Jake replied.

"Did you?" the old man asked.

Jake thought about answering, then decided against it.

The formal arrest came the next morning. Jake looked at each of the deputies and then down at the floor of the cell.

"Would either of you recommend a good attorney?" he asked.

Purcell chuckled and then stopped. "You mean you don't know?"

"Know what?"

"Someone retained Harold Richardson on your behalf yesterday. We don't know who it was, but they must have a lot of bucks, because Richardson doesn't come cheap. His standard retainer is half a million."

"You don't know who sent him?"

"No, but he's waiting for you in the interrogation room."

"Thanks, Purcell."

Harold Richardson was indeed a high-priced lawyer. Jake looked at him while Larson took the cuffs off. His suit was definitely high quality, and the rest matched the suit. Jake waited until the detectives had left the room, and then asked the one question he wanted an answer to.

"Mister Richardson, you can either tell me who sent you to represent me or you can return the retainer because you are fired."

Richardson stared at Jake for nearly a minute.

"Well Jake, I can't tell you that. I can tell you that the person retaining me believes in your innocence and wants you to have the best legal representation possible."

Jake walked over to the mirror and tapped on it with his knuckles.

"Purcell, please take me back to my cell. This man is not my attorney."

He heard Richardson snort as if in disbelief, and he turned. "You are not my attorney, and you will leave now. Go back to whoever it was and tell them it didn't work."

Purcell and a deputy came in and escorted Jake back to his cell. After he was locked inside, Purcell looked at Jake with a puzzled look.

"What was that all about?" he asked.

"Somebody wants to make sure that I don't get out of here. They hired the bigshot lawyer to make an impression on me, and it back-fired. The people that I know that care about me don't have that kind of money. And they would recommend an attorney they were familiar with, someone who had done something for them or their family in the past. Now will you recommend an attorney?"

"I'll talk to a couple of them. See if they're interested. That's the best I can do."

"That's more than most cops would do. Thanks again, Purcell."

The first attorney was David Williams. He was young and already starting to talk before he was even in the room. Jake waited patiently for him to wind down, and then when there was a short pause he intervened.

"Don't you want to know if I'm guilty?" he asked.

"It really doesn't matter to me," the young man replied. "What we need to do is strategize a defense and then work on playing any evidence the prosecution might have."

Jake listened patiently for another six or seven minutes while the attorney rambled on about defensive strategies, etc. He had almost tuned him completely out when he realized he was being stared at.

"I'm sorry, did you say something?" Jake asked innocently.

Williams gave him a disgusted look and said, "it's very important that you pay attention, Mr. Kozan. We have a lot of ground to cover and if you're not paying attention we'll be wasting time. Now, do you understand what an insanity plea entails?"

Jake smiled and thought for a minute. "Mr. Williams, I think that I would be better served having someone on my side that does give a damn whether I'm guilty or not. Thank you for time, and if you want you can send me a bill."

Jake was sleeping in his cell when the guard tapped on the door with his baton.

"Mr. Edmonds is here to see you."

"Who is Mr. Edmonds?" Jake asked, wiping his eyes to clear them.

"Mr. Edmonds is the lawyer that Purcell sent for you."

"What time is it?"

"Nearly four, be dinnertime soon."

Jake entered the interrogation room and waited for the guard to remove the cuffs. He looked at the guard and motioned to the cuffs.

"No sir," the guard stated. "Mr. Edmonds asked that you stay cuffed until he knows you better."

Jake laughed. "Mr. Edmonds is a smart man."

After the guard left, Jake waited for the lawyer to start talking. After a couple of minutes had passed, he realized that Mr. Edmonds was waiting for him to start talking.

"Have you been in a lot of murder trials?" he asked.

Edmonds took his time before answering. He seemed to be searching for just the right words. Jake would learn that this was just a tactic that Edmonds employed.

"If I take your case, this will be the fourth murder trial for me. Now, tell me why I should consider taking this case."

Jake looked at him, wondering what his answer should be. He thought for a minute and then replied, "because I didn't kill my best friend."

"Anything else, Mr. Kozan?"

"What else is there?" Jake demanded.

Again Edmonds paused. It was annoying to Jake to have to wait, but he smiled when he realized it was a tactic Edmonds was using to try to draw Jake out.

"Is something funny, Mr. Kozan?" he asked.

"No," Jake replied. "But I bet that delay tactic is very effective in interviews."

It was Edmonds' turn to smile, "I would imagine you to be highly skilled at poker Mr. Kozan. Most people think I'm just an old man trying to keep up."

The interview with Edmonds lasted for nearly an hour, mostly with "Mister" Edmonds asking questions and then listening carefully to the answers. When they were through Jake looked at Edmonds and saw the fatigue in the old man's eyes. He could tell that the process had been tiring for the old man.

"Mr. Edmonds, I think you should go home and get some rest."

"Perhaps," he replied. "I live in San Bernardino and I was asked by my daughter to take a look at your case. She has been acquainted with Deputy Purcell since their patrol areas are next to each other at the county line. I'm staying in the motel here in town. We'll continue tomorrow if I can get my daughter to drive me over here. Better yet, I'll get a taxi if they have one in this town. I don't drive any more since I had an accident about two years ago."

"I'm sorry to hear that. Was anyone hurt?"

The old man lowered his head and said softly "I lost my wife in that accident."

Jake didn't know what to say, feeling that any reply would be inappropriate.

CHAPTER FIVE

The trial was less than Jake expected, with the District Attorney presenting lots of circumstantial evidence and depositions from the "Davis" couple. The DA argued that though Jake had the right to face his accusers, their involvement with an undercover operation that was on-going would jeopardize their true identity.

Mr. Edmonds' closing argument was simple and un-wavering. "My client has been accused of murder of the one true friend that was his. He doesn't deny being in the desert where the murder took place. He hasn't attempted to run away from the accusations by two so-called eyewitnesses. He has asked that they present themselves in court to make their statements and thus be cross-examined so that the jury may see how flimsy this evidence seems. In every trial I have participated in, or been witness to, the accused has had the right to be faced by their accusers, except now. You as jurors have been asked to believe that the two people representing themselves as Mr. and Mrs. Davis are actually agents of the United States Government and that by having them appear in this court we will somehow diminish our 'National Security'. There is no forensic evidence that indicates guilt on Mr. Kozan's part. The weapon in his possession at the time of his arrest is definitely not the murder weapon.

It is clear to anyone examining the evidence that there is no motive. Mr. Kozan has no reason to kill Mr. TJ Wagner, but the District Attorney wants you to believe that Mr. Kozan just started shooting for no reason, a fit of insanity, or maybe it was heat stroke, or maybe for "no reason". The outcome of this trial is your responsibility. As jurors, you must decide whether or not the prosecution has presented evidence "beyond a reasonable doubt" that Mr. Kozan murdered TJ Wagner. But more than that, you should ask yourselves why.

Jake waited in his cell for the jury's decision. Mr. Edmonds came to visit him every day trying to keep his spirits up. Jake didn't feel like being "positive", in fact he felt like hitting something or someone.

Each day he waited, he could see the strength ebbing from Edmonds. It was something he didn't want to see, but he couldn't help himself. Each day while Edmonds was visiting, he forced himself to be up-beat and positive. He knew that any negative could cause the old man to crumble like a house of cards.

On the sixth day of deliberation, the jury came to an agreement of sorts. Because they didn't feel that the DA had proved murder, and because they felt strongly about the depositions from the "Davises", Jake was found guilty of a lesser included charge of second-degree manslaughter. Jake wanted to scream at the jury, but he held it in. He watched as Mr. Edmonds sat down in his chair.

"We'll appeal the verdict Jake", Edmonds whispered.

Jake could see that whatever strength Edmonds had left was quickly draining away.

"Go home Mr. Edmonds, be with your grandchildren. You did your best, and I can't find any fault with that."

"But we lost. We have to appeal right away."

"No, go home, please. We did everything we could to get them to see the truth. I don't understand how they could think I'm guilty of anything, but I'll be alright. I may need you in the future, may I call on you? You've been more than an attorney Mr. Edmonds, you've listened when I needed you to, you've been a friend."

CHAPTER SIX

Jake was sentenced to serve three to six years at a medium security prison outside of Susanville. When it was built, Susanville was designed to hold approximately three thousand prisoners, but now they had nearly six thousand there. They also processed prisoners that were 'low-risk', convicted of non-violent crimes. These were housed in temporary bungalows until they finished training for fire-fighting when they would be transferred to one of the work camps. Purcell had told him that Susanville wasn't as bad as some of the state prisons. It didn't help his mood any as climbed down off the bus. Located on the east side of the Sierra Nevada mountains it was in the high desert not unlike the area around Ridgecrest, but not quite as hot during the summer. He knew it could get extremely cold during the winter, having been through the area when he was younger.

Jake listened carefully as the guard went through his list of instructions to the prisoners. Apparently the guard had recited this list so many times he knew them all by heart. Jake stared straight ahead as another guard walked up and down the line. He seemed to be taking inventory, assessing which ones would make trouble and which ones wouldn't.

Jake had seen this tactic before in boot camp so he wasn't surprised when the guard suddenly stopped in front of him. He was almost nose to nose with Jake, but Jake knew better than to flinch or show fear. After a long minute, the guard moved on down the line.

After being strip-searched, cavity searched, and "disinfected", Jake was issued a uniform and assigned a number.....664317. He had been instructed to identify himself by his number and respond with a "yes sir" when his number was called. Jake had used the same "dehumanization" tactic with prisoners of war and understood what the desired effect was to be. He knew that sooner or later the guards would slip up and call him by his name. He also knew that he couldn't afford to get caught up in the prison mentality of being a member of a group. He'd heard a lot of stories about lone prisoners not doing well if they weren't affiliated with some group or gang. He also knew that he had to try to keep himself apart from the others.

He was taken to his cell and locked in. The guard told him that he was being isolated for his own protection until they had made an assessment of his potential for violence. Jake thought he should say something, but didn't. Having spent many hours with Mr. Edmonds, Jake had come to appreciate the value of silence. He had made up his mind to only speak when spoken to and then only to a guard. It would become his world then and they could only enter when and if he wanted.

The first few days were uneventful. He was allowed out of his cell to exercise or walk in an enclosed area of chain-link fencing that was twelve feet high. He also was visited by the prison "shrink" each day for three days. The psychiatrist (or psychologist, Jake didn't know which) would ask Jake questions about his family, his wife, his mother, his father, and other people. Jake made it a point to keep the answers to the questions to as few words as possible. He knew the shrink was trying to draw him out and engage him in a conversation where Jake would "reveal" some information regarding his past. Jake didn't allow him anything that could help or hurt. He used what he called the "Edmonds tactic" several times, not answering until the shrink had asked the question a second or sometimes third time.

At the end of a week Jake was assigned to a cell in the general population. His cellmate was an older white man who also seemed to have taken a "vow of silence". Jake felt lucky to have been assigned to this cell, although his curiosity wanted him to find out more about his cellmate. It was in the afternoon of the third day when the old man finally spoke.

"I'm Lawrence Miller, and I'm doing six years for arson. I currently have two and a half to go before I'm eligible for parole. I like it quiet and apparently you do too."

Jake waited for almost two minutes before he spoke, "I'm Jake Kozan. I just started a six year sentence for manslaughter, and I don't want to talk about anything. As long as you respect me and my space, I'll do the same for you."

The next few days were spent with a cautious optimism about the time he would have to spend. The greatest danger Jake could see came when they were out on the yard. Anything could happen there and usually did. It was the fourth day when a prisoner was shanked in the yard. Jake saw it coming but couldn't do anything. If he had warned the prisoner, he would become a target for the ones who wanted to kill the prisoner. When questioned by the guards later, Jake told them he'd had his back turned and didn't see who did the stabbing.

CHAPTER SEVEN

Three months passed before another stabbing took place. This time, the intended victim saw the shank and was able to protect himself. He still ended up with several stab wounds after it was over, but he was alive. Jake kept more and more to himself, trying hard to stay out of the way of the "gangs". There were four different gangs in the prison. The Hispanics were affiliated with the Latin Kings. The blacks were aligned with the Bloods. Some whites belonged to the Aryan Brotherhood, while others were known as the "Outlaws". Jake couldn't tell if it was the same as the Outlaw biker group. He knew each member of each gang by sight and made it a point to stay away from all of them. He had chosen a corner of the yard that afforded some safety in that he could sit with his back against the wall and see when someone would approach him. The next day after the stabbing he was sitting at his spot when a member of the Aryan Brotherhood came toward him.

"We think you need protection", the young skin-head said. He had an almost permanent sneer when he talked, which Jake didn't like.

"If you swear allegiance to us, we'll provide protection for you. But keep in mind that protection doesn't come free. We'll work out a fair payment for our services."

Jake just looked at him and didn't say a word. He knew that it was almost time to go back to the cell, so he turned and started to walk away.

The young skin-head grabbed his arm to spin him around. When he did, Jake spun with him and struck him on the chin with the heel of his hand. The sound of the jawbone cracking was almost like a small caliber gunshot. The skin-head fell to the ground holding his jaw and crying.

Jake walked back to his spot and sat down. His heart was pounding a mile a minute, but he sat as perfectly still as he could. He knew the other members of the Aryan Brotherhood had been watching, and he wondered how soon it would be before some form of revenge happened. He knew that the leader of the gang couldn't allow anyone to disrespect their power.

Jake was about to return to his cell when the guard stopped him.

"You better be careful," the guard said. "They are the nastiest bunch in here and they'll find a way to get back at you."

Jake looked at the young black guard and smiled. He wanted to say something but didn't want to break his rule of silence.

That evening in the mess hall Jake went to the furthest table like he usually did and sat down. He was surprised when Miller joined him as did two others he had seen on the yard. Both of them were loners like himself. There was no conversation, just a feeling that while they were seated together they could eat in peace. They were only there for a few minutes when another "Aryan brother" approached their table.

"The Reverend wants to talk to you....now"

Jake sat there for a full two minutes, knowing that the messenger would become impatient.

"Didn't you hear me? I said the Reverend wants to talk to you NOW!"

Jake slowly stood up from the table, noticing how quickly the messenger backed away from him. He stared at the young punk and then shook his head to indicate no.

"If you don't come with me he'll send some guys to bring you. And you won't like it when they get hold of you."

Jake was almost totally calm when he slapped the punk across the face. He thought the kid was going to start crying, but instead he was faced with a shiv. It was an almost automatic reaction when he slapped the knife away and then broke the kid's wrist. He didn't even bother to watch the kid as he left.

"You may not be the smartest man I've met, but you do have balls, " Miller said.

The other two at the table joined in with an amen, but they left as soon as they were finished with their food.

Two days later in the yard, Jake watched as some of the Aryan Brothers came toward him. He had already seen a couple of others take a position behind him. He stood up quickly and started toward them, his hand on the crude knife he had made the day before. He quickened his pace and closed the gap between him and the two facing him much faster than they had planned. As he came within range he kicked the one to his left in the knee sending him to the ground and then continuing his motion, he caught the other with a spinning round kick to the head. His motion had almost turned him completely around, so it was only a half of a turn to be facing his other attackers. The first one was way too eager and paid for it with a slash across the fore-arm. The other jumped back out of range and looked as if he was ready to run.

"On your face, on the ground," The guard yelled.

Jake dropped to the ground immediately. He didn't know what to do with the knife in his hand, so he held it out at arm's length away from his body.

The guard ripped the knife out of Jake's hand while standing on his wrist.

The trip to the interrogation room was brief, but painful. The handcuffs were applied too tight, and they used a nightstick through his arms to guide him where they wanted him to go. When they arrived at the room Jake was dumped on a steel chair that was bolted to the floor. They attached some shackles to his ankles and re-cuffed his wrists to the table. Although their actions were sharp and rough, Jake couldn't blame them. If he were in their position he'd do the same.

It was almost an hour before anyone came. Jake had almost fallen asleep on the table and he felt drowsy when the first guard started talking to him.

"Why did you attack those men?" the guard asked.

Jake didn't bother to answer. He knew they already questioned the others and they had probably had a story ready if things didn't go as planned. He thought about several different answers and rejected one after the other. It wouldn't do any good to answer to some guard who already had some idea that Jake was in the wrong.

"I asked you a question, and I want an answer."

Jake didn't even bother to look at the guard. He knew what would be coming, so he braced himself for the blow he knew the guard couldn't hold back. He didn't have long to wait and when it came he went with it and rolled his head. He thought to himself that the guard couldn't hit any harder than some of the girls he had known.

They continued the question and slap routine for almost another half hour. He couldn't tell if there was a signal from someone or not, but suddenly they quit and an old convict came in with a wet washcloth. He gently swabbed Jake's face and then left.

Jake wasn't completely surprised when the deputy warden entered the room. They had tried their usual routine and that hadn't worked so now it was time for a different routine.

"These guards tell me that you don't like to talk." The deputy warden said. He was in his early forties and appeared tougher than leather. His hair was thinning in the front and also turning gray. He kept it cut short and his face appeared freshly shaved.

Jake swallowed hard before talking. "I like to talk to intelligent people, Warden. I don't like to talk to your guards because they're too stupid and I don't want to waste my time. You tell them to leave, and maybe you and I can have a nice long conversation. If they don't leave, I don't talk. You also need to turn off the microphone, or better yet, bring in a transistor radio."

The deputy warden looked at him and then nodded. "Do what he said, and one of you bring my radio from my office."

It took several minutes for the whole thing to be set up. Jake waited patiently, and when the deputy warden placed the radio near the mirror he shook his head.

"Please put it on the table next to me."

The deputy warden smiled and did as requested.

The conversation was low and fast paced. The interference from the radio caused the deputy warden to ask Jake to repeat himself several times. When it was over, the deputy warden sat and looked at Jake as he were seeing a two-headed snake.

"Do you know how many people the Aryan Brothers control in this prison?"

[50]

"I can imagine it's quite a few, but I still don't want anything to do with them. What I want most of all is to be left alone to do my time and get out. If they keep coming at me, I'm going to kill the Reverend and as many as I can."

"You're not leaving much room for negotiation, Kozan."

"I'm not leaving any room for anything."

"You could end up dead if you keep bucking them."

"So could several of your guards if they keep backing the Aryan Brothers."

"There's no proof of that, Kozan. Don't make accusations you can't prove."

"I didn't start all this shit. You can stop it and I think you know who to talk to make it stop. Any more attacks on me and I'll start a war you'll never stop."

"I don't like people who threaten me, Kozan. You say any more and you'll spend the next two weeks in the hole, do you understand?"

"You can make it stop. If you don't, these deaths will be your responsibility."

The deputy warden stood up quickly. "I warned you, now you can spend some time in the hole."

The trip to the isolation unit was brief. He was stripped and searched thoroughly. His only consolation was that he passed gas as the guard was doing the cavity search.

He was shut in a four by eight foot cell with no windows. There was a bullet-proof glass panel that allowed some light in from the corridor. The bed was the same size as the one in his original cell, but there was no bedding, only the steel bunk. The toilet and sink were at the far end of the cell next to the bed. He had to sit on the bunk to get to the toilet, no room for pacing.

The evening meal was passed to him through an access panel in the door. The meal itself was small and cold. There was no beverage, and he was handed a plastic spoon to eat with. After he had eaten, the guard counted all the items eaten and inventoried the paper and the plastic spoon.

Jake looked up and noticed there were no lights or electrical outlets in the cell. Probably didn't want any prisoner to electrocute themselves. There was nothing else to do, so Jake lay on the bed and began going over in his mind all the details of the shooting of TJ.

He replayed the scene in his mind again and again. One thing he was sure of now, they hadn't meant to let him get away. He still couldn't figure out why they would kill TJ. He tried to remember the details of their conversation that night at The Sisters restaurant. The one thing that he did recall was that neither of the "Davises" had known what a petroglyph was until it was explained to them. Jake lay on the bunk running over the details again and again wanting desperately to find something to use. He wanted to track them down and have his revenge.

He was sleeping fitfully when the screaming woke him. It was a chilling scream, like someone was being tortured. He tried to guess the time, but could only figure it was after midnight sometime. The screaming continued for almost two minutes then ended as sharply as it started. He tried to return to sleep but couldn't. The time was creeping by so slowly it scared him. He had never really liked being in small, cramped, dark places and this time it was even worse. He had talked about it at length with a psychiatrist when he had a panic attack due to the claustrophobia, and together they had developed a technique to combat the fear. He began using the technique again, slowly crossing off the things in his mind that could bring about such a monumental fear. In less than an hour he was breathing normal, waiting patiently for the guard to make his rounds.

In the morning he began an exercise routine. It was one of the few things that the guards and the deputy warden couldn't keep from happening. After a few repetitions of each exercise, he sat and calmly began doing mental exercises with some math problems. He had always been good at math and clearly enjoyed being able to do the problems he was given. He could see somewhat by the light coming from the narrow window on the exterior wall. His sense of time was becoming slightly distorted, he had no idea what the time was when it was dark outside. During the daylight hours it was much better and he began to mark off the days that had elapsed.

He was almost done with the two week punishment when the guard announced that they had "found" a weapon in his cell. He knew better than to deny it. Any conversation with the guards would just be a waste of time. He went quietly when they took him to an interview room and cuffed him to the table. After almost an hour the deputy warden arrived.

"You screwed up again, Kozan," the warden said. "We found the shiv used to kill Darien Moss in your cell. Now you're going back to trial and then to Pelican Bay, you stupid shithead."

Jake smiled at the deputy warden and nodded, "At least I'll be rid of your dumb ass."

He knew the slap was coming and almost avoided it completely. He did get part of it on the lower jaw and it hurt but not seriously.

CHAPTER EIGHT

Desmond Edmonds was out when Jake called, but promptly called the prison and asked to speak to the warden. He was told that the warden was taking a couple of days of vacation and he could speak to the deputy warden. In just a few minutes, Des knew he didn't like this man. After listening for several minutes to the deputy go on and on about how violent Jake Kozan was, Des had a pretty good idea all was not as the deputy warden claimed. His hours of talking with Jake had gotten him much closer to who Jake really was than most other people could understand. He understood the motives behind the mask that Jake presented to the world. He remembered clearly the exact tone and facial expression that Jake had when Des had asked him about the things Jake had done in the war. But knowing and proving are two entirely different things the old man knew too well.

He called a judge at the courthouse that had been a business partner in the past, and after a not too lengthy conversation he had a temporary injunction against the transfer of one Jacob Aaron Kozan from Susanville State Correctional Center. He then called his youngest daughter, and with some rather strong language, convinced her that her driving him to Susanville would be one of the better things she will have done in her life. He packed some clothes and the files of the case, and they were soon on the road north.

Jake had been thinking about his situation and had a fleeting idea that was so crazy that it might be worth trying. He called to the guard outside his cell and told him he wanted to see the Reverend. It was almost four hours later before the guard rattled keys in his cell door and barked at him to stand back.

The Reverend slid into the cell and stood next to the door with his back against the wall.

"Take your time," Jake said. "It takes a while to get used to the darkness."

They both stood there in the darkness, neither saying a word, not wanting to be the first to speak.

"Dam, Reverend," Jake almost laughed. "I've never known you to be the shy and bashful type. I asked you here because I have a little situation that you might be able to help me with. I don't like the idea of being charged with a murder I didn't commit, and I think you have the resources to make this whole mess disappear."

"Is that what you called me here for? Then we don't have shit to talk about, cause you're going to Pelican Bay and I'll have this whole place to myself."

"Don't be too sure Reverend. The Warden took vacation so he can claim he wasn't aware of what was happening here. But, he does know that I have information that can bury him and the Deputy Warden and a few more of your employees. And, before they "convict" me of murder, there's still the problem of the trial and all the statements I can make about certain transactions that take place between you and the guards. And even if they do convict me, there's still Pelican Bay and a few rather curious reporters I used to drink with that might like to hear about some payoff at Susanville."

"You have four supposedly "tough" men in the hospital because you don't think things through like you should. It wasn't necessary for them to get hurt, but your stupidity caused it. You consider yourself a leader, a planner, a thinker, but you're just barely above the idiots you have working for you."

"If you can think past the end of your dick, I can make you safer, and richer than you could ever do by yourself. But first, you have to make this little murder thing go away."
Jake knew he was pushing the Reverend almost to the breaking point. He was hoping to make him angry enough to make a mistake. If that happened, he knew he could maneuver the Reverend into a position more favorable to Jake.

"What's the matter, Reverend? Don't like being called stupid? What really hurts is when you know it's true. I personally detest everything you stand for but I need you almost as much as you need me."

Jake almost didn't hear the slight shuffle of feet as the Reverend took a half step forward, but he did see the hand

[55]

holding the shiv, and caught it and turned it to bring the point around to the Reverend's neck.

"You're lucky I need you to help me or I'd kill you right now." Jake whispered. He slipped the shiv out of the Reverend's grasp and let it drop to the floor. "There are so many things I can teach you. Not just how to use these martial art skills, but other things as well. But I'll promise you this, if you ever attempt to harm me in any way, I will kill you without warning."

"Guard, Mr. Reverend and I are finished talking for now," Jake yelled. Under his breath he said to the Reverend, "Come back in two days and talk, or I start releasing information."

After they had left, Jake pushed the shiv down the drain in the floor and laid down on the bed. That evening instead of the regular cold food and nothing to drink, he was surprised with double helpings of warm food on a metal tray with real utensils and no less than four cartons of milk. Well, he thought to himself, maybe things are looking up, or the condemned ate a hearty meal, and then he chuckled.

The next morning after breakfast, Jake was doing some exercises when the guard tapped on the door with his night stick. "You got a visitor. Actually you got two visitors, an old man and a woman that looks like his daughter."

They went through the usual routine with the handcuffs and the leg chains and shuffled their way to the visitor's center. As it was a weekday, it was somewhat unusual for visitors to be granted access. Jake was curious, but held to his silence until they were in the room. He smiled, recognizing Mr. Edmonds immediately, but still didn't say anything until the guard had moved far enough away to not be able to eaves-drop on anything they said.

"I'm so glad to see you, Mr. Edmonds. I take it you got my call."

"Jake, what's going on?" Mr. Edmonds asked.

Jake began carefully out-lining what he had found out since being moved here to Susanville. Des started taking notes, but it was obvious he couldn't keep up. His daughter reached in her

[56]

purse and pulled out a small recorder. "By the way, Mr. Kozan, my name is Julie Larson and I'm Des's daughter. I'm a deputy sheriff for San Bernardino County, but I am also an attorney. To keep things simple, do I have your permission to act in your behalf on all legal matters?"

"Yes, of course." Jake answered quickly.

They talked until the recorder was full and then they decided to continue in the morning. Jake gave them the name of a bank and the account number, then quickly made out a power of attorney so they could access what funds they might need.

"Jake, I, we have money. This isn't necessary."

"Mr. Edmonds, I want you to be paid in full right up to today in case something "accidentally" happens to me in here. You understand my feelings about this and I really want you to not have to worry about money."

"Dad," Julie interjected, "Do as he says, it will help him feel better about himself. You know how upset you get when you owe someone money."

They parted, but not before Julie asked, "Why do they call you Rabbi?"

"What?" Jake almost exploded. "Who said that?"

"On the way in, I overheard one convict say 'Rabbi Jake has company' when we passed."

"I haven't a clue."

The next day their meeting was all about information Jake had learned during his stay. This time Julie had three recorders, but they only filled the one. Julie had found a court stenographer who could put everything down on paper for a fee, but Jake said no to the idea. When Julie questioned his decision, Jake explained about not knowing who all was related to whom, and therefor no one in this town could be trusted. Afterward, Julie was a little more understanding of Jake's decision, but still disgruntled.

"But aren't they required to take an oath not to divulge any information they learn during the course of their duties?"

"Yes, but so are the guards. The ones we're gathering information on."

"What do we do with all this information?"

"Absolutely nothing for now." Jake stated flatly. "If we start spreading this around, I'm a dead man. Now let's move on to new business."

At the term 'new business', he could see both of their heads pop up with a curious look on their faces.

"I want to buy some property." He quickly described the mine where he had been arrested, leaving out the part about it having a water supply. He asked them to find out what it would cost to buy the mine and a couple hundred acres there in the small valley. Knowing they would want to know why, he explained to them that when he got out of jail, he wanted someplace secluded.

"Whatever you say, Rabbi." Julie winked and then grinned at him.

The next day, the Reverend showed up outside his cell. Still being in solitary, Jake's door remained closed and locked. The guard stood off a respectful distance, being bribed to do so.

"I understand the Warden is supposed to be back tomorrow." The Reverend said.

"I see," said Jake. "Is that going to be good news for me or bad news?"

"Well Rabbi, to me it seems like good news for you. Now, I want you to outline how you're going to be of use to me. If I like what I hear, then certain evidence disappears and the guard who says it was you claims to be dyslexic and may have gotten the inmate numbers mixed up. Then you and I have a small "Peace Treaty" and you start doing whatever you think I'm going to need."

Because there was a solid door between them, Jake calmly started telling the Reverend about all the problems with his operation, and some of the ways that Jake could teach him how to improve things.

"Be very aware Reverend, I will not do anything illegal because I want out of here. I was put here based on some bogus charges and evidence supplied by a supposedly rogue CIA agent. I want out so I can track him down and make him pay for what he did. And what the hell is this "Rabbi" crap?"

"I read your file Jake. I could see a couple of things that showed me you didn't have a chance. One thing you should know is that two of the jurors were bought and paid for, and not cheap either. The judge was told what kind of verdict was expected and to steer his decisions in that direction. I can't believe I might actually be talking to an innocent man. As for the "Rabbi" I thought it sounded colorful. Most of these cons won't touch a man of God, but with the way you fight they're not sure what to do. Mine have all been instructed to keep hands off. "

They parted and Jake went back to his mental math exercises. He kept thinking of the water source in the cave. In his mind, he kept trying to calculate how much water could be "captured" in a twenty-four period. After a while he gave up and lay down on the cot to sleep.

A few days later Jake was returned to his regular cell. A quick check showed that most of his personal items had either been stolen, or gone through thoroughly. It didn't matter, they were just objects he thought to himself. He chuckled and then thought, I'm even beginning to think like a Rabbi.

At dinner time, when he went through the line he noticed he was being given the better food and a more generous serving of each item.

"Please, can I have a smaller portion?" He looked up to see a huge black man smiling at him. "God loves a generous giver, but we should also share with others, don't you think, Brother?"

"Sorry, Rabbi. I thought you might be hungry after spending time in the hole. It won't happen again."

"I appreciate your thoughtfulness, Brother." Jake responded and then moved on down the line.

Jake sought out and found a table with only two others sitting there, and sat at the far end. As soon as he was seated, he saw two of the Aryan Brothers move near to stand behind him at a respectable distance. He looked around the mess and saw the Reverend. He looked back to the two "guards" and then back to the Reverend and nodded. With a nod in return, the Reverend went back to his food. When Jake finished his meal, he got up and grabbed his tray to put it away. The young Brother near him reached out to take the tray and then just as quickly pulled his hand back. Jake looked at him and smiled, feeling the fear wash off the young man.

"Please ask the Reverend to meet me at the bleachers after breakfast, and bring his four best warriors. I'll take care of the tray myself, thank you."

CHAPTER NINE

Jake sat at the bleachers and watched as the Reverend approached with four bulky convicts in tow. His attitude was almost condescending, as if he had other things to do and other places to go. Jake had the feeling that the Reverend was trying to provoke him. Well, he thought, let's see how he does with nice.

"Thank you for finding the time to come along with your soldiers, Mr. Reverend. I'm sure you'll find the time is well spent when we are finished here today." He watched the Reverend's face while he was talking, and saw his expression go from disbelief to open curiosity.

One by one Jake had the four men tell him their names. The first started off by giving his inmate number, and then a snicker as he looked around at the others. Their laughter stopped when Jake quietly stepped closer to the man and asked in a whisper, "What is your first and last name, please?" The laughter had turned to fear and the big man nearly stuttered when he answered, "Ernst Buchold, sir."

The other three were prompt and courteous with their answers. Ernst seemed to be the only true Aryan out of the bunch, as the others were Jason Smith, Mike Sorenson, and Davis Collier. No matter, Jake thought to himself, you'll learn to believe in "White Supremacy" like the rest of the Aryan Brotherhood has never seen.

"Gentlemen, you are here to learn. Mr. Reverend has chosen you as the four best of his warriors, and as such you will act like the best at all times. You will learn all things necessary to be considered the best. How many of you can read and write?" With that Jake started asking questions about each of them, personal questions, probing to see what he had to work with. Of the group, three could read and write, Ernst couldn't which Jake found out later. "I want you to write a story for me about what you'd do if you were free." It was then that Ernst confessed that he couldn't write. Jake smiled and then addressed the group.

[61]

"If I'm to teach you, you must never lie to me. I am your Rabbi, someone who was considered vile and low by Hitler, but is actually a teacher, a mentor. If you lie then it makes all my teaching worthless, because the person I'm trying to teach doesn't exist. Now write me a story."

Sometime later the Reverend left, satisfied that Jake was doing what he'd promised. The few times that the guards got too close they were quite suddenly distracted by a scuffle that broke out nearby, choreographed by a couple of Aryan Brothers. Soon it was almost lunch and Jake gathered the notebooks and pencils, but not before each had had a chance to put his name in his book. Before they left, Jake advised them to walk together and stand up straight, proud of their position. "Whatever you do, stand proud and stand together."

Jake sat by himself at the end of a table during lunch, watching the rest of the inmates. He noticed a stir of conversation going on at the table where some of the Outlaws sat. Though he couldn't hear what they were saying, he could tell the discussion was rather intense. It couldn't be because of what he was doing with the Aryan Brothers, or could it? It was obvious that if they were discussing the Aryan's and the 'teaching' he was doing that there was a leak from inside. Wow, he thought to himself, the prison pipeline was faster than most news networks.

After lunch was over, he had his four pupils sit below him on the bleachers. He knew part of what he was going to say wouldn't sit well with any of the higher-ups in the organization, but he intended to make these four the "superior white race" that they talked so much about. "Today you will decide if you can believe in a principle founded on hatred and stupidity. Adolf Hitler was really pretty stupid about some things and extremely smart in other things, but he was a very charismatic person. In a time when the German economy was in turmoil, he gave the common people someone to blame for their troubles, the banks. And, because the banks were mostly controlled by the Jews, he gave the country someone they could see and hate. It was an easy sell; the Jews were different in a lot of ways from the Lutheran and Catholic Germans.

Hitler would have succeeded with his ideas if he hadn't tried to expand and conquer by invading Poland. Germany needed to improve their economy and the only way at that time was to start building up the war machine. But their war machine was useless without a war to fight and so began World War Two.

"White superiority" is not a new concept; it has been around since the beginning of time, probably when the Cro-Magnon man first met the Neanderthal. The idea of one race or tribe being superior to another is why we have wars, tribal conflicts, invasions, etc. But, to actually be superior to another race or class of people is extremely hard to define and impossible to achieve. You four will have the opportunity to prove, or disprove the theory of racial superiority. I don't know if you're up to it, but we will find out."

Jake could see the puzzled looks on their faces and worried that maybe he was losing their attention. From his shirt pocket he took a list of books. Most of them were easy reading, like Louis L'Amour or Mickey Spillane, which these guys could handle except for Ernst. For Ernst he produced a deck of flash cards with the alphabet on them.

"You three will each read one book on that list each day, and you will answer any question I ask about the book. If you can't answer correctly, it will prove to me that you haven't thoroughly read the book. You can go to the library after we have done our afternoon exercises, except Ernst who will stay with me all the rest of the day."

Jake led them through a series of simple exercises, repeating the series over and over until at the end of an hour the four of them were groaning and sweating. He dismissed the three to go to the library, but not before repeating his admonition of the morning, "Stand proud and stand together."

He and Ernst moved to the top of the bleachers so they could have a better view if anyone came at them. Two old cons moved their chess game far enough away to not be able to hear Jake or Ernst. The first couple of times Jake went through the alphabet cards in order, so Ernst wouldn't be confused. When Ernst began objecting to have to do 'this baby stuff' Jake just nodded and shuffled the deck. He would go through the deck, correcting Ernst when he needed, at a reasonably slow pace. After a couple of times, he increased the pace and when Ernst made a mistake he would flash the card six or eight times making Ernst say the letter each time and then he would finally move on. He kept shuffling and increasing the pace until Ernst did the entire deck mistake-free under thirty seconds.

"Good work today, Ernst. Tomorrow we practice writing the alphabet."

They left the bleachers together, just in time for the evening meal. Jake sat at his usual spot and this time he noticed that his cell mate wasn't there. He looked around and still didn't see him. Maybe the old man was eating late, he thought. It wasn't like Miller to be late for meal-time. He'd check when he got back to the cell and see if something was wrong.

When Jake entered the tier he could seen something was wrong. Guards were coming out of his cell with what appeared to be a body-bag. Oh my God, he thought, they've killed Miller. The guards rudely shoved him against the wall as they passed, instructing him to stay out of the cell. To make sure, they posted one guard at the entrance. The guard was obviously anticipating some kind of trouble from Kozan, as he already had his baton in one hand and the other had on a sap glove, an ordinary glove modified with pockets of lead shot sewn into the palm area. They could be very painful if used properly. Jake wasn't inclined to find out.

"Prisoner 664317 requests permission to sit in central area, sir"

"Permission granted prisoner. I'll notify the floor boss."

Jake sat in the central area and waited. Hopefully, the old man hadn't smuggled in any contraband material. If he had, they would probably try to pin it on Jake.

While he was sitting, he went over in his mind the few minutes before they had blown the entrance to the mine. There were several questions he had no answer to. Where had they gotten the explosive? They, the Davises, certainly hadn't had any with them, TJ had done a really good job of snooping in the

[64]

backpacks and had told Jake about the pistols. If there had been explosives, TJ would have surely told Jake. Another question was who was the other person outside the mine? It wasn't the woman that had yelled at him, and didn't look like Mr. Davis. Was there more than the two of them involved, and if so, who and why.

It was near mid-night when they let Jake return to his cell, and he was tired. They apparently hadn't found anything in the cell or they'd be interrogating him by now, but then maybe they were just waiting. Either way was fine by Jake, as tired as he was. He laid back on his bunk and was sound asleep in a matter of minutes.

. . . .

Ernst was still awake, mumbling the alphabet so only he could hear. He felt something in the way Jake talked to him. Almost as if he really cared about what Ernst thought and did. He smiled when he remembered Jake's words, "You did a good job today." He'd never had anyone say nice things to him before and it confused him. The Reverend had told them that Jake couldn't be trusted because he really was a Jew. He lay back still wondering what was right. He grew up in a home without any religious or moral grounds at all. His father was an alcoholic, either drunk or on his way to getting drunk. Plus he beat Ernst's mother when he thought she'd done something wrong, which was most of the time. He beat Ernst also, but not so much when Ernst got older and bigger.

He was seventeen when his mother killed his father. He had come home drunk and when he started to beat her, she hit him in the head with a cast-iron skillet. When he fell on the floor, she hit him three more times in the head to make sure he was out, and then grabbed a butcher knife and cut his throat. She then turned and told Ernst to take all his clothes and get out. He did just that, but not before taking what little money was left in the old man's wallet. He was eighteen when they arrested him for armed robbery of a liquor store. He would turn twenty-two this year.

[65]

CHAPTER TEN

Hernando Partida was hurt. He didn't want to go home and listen to his mom's questions. His ribs hurt like hell and he had a badly swollen eye and lower lip. He thought his right hand was broken, because he couldn't make a fist without it hurting in the bones in his hand. The strange narc wanting freebies had come back and this time he wasn't fooling around. He had simply held out his hand, and when Hernando started to argue, the man beat him. He not only took the drugs and money Hernando was holding for el Jefe, he took Hernando's personal stash of money. The man had taken over twelve hundred dollars of el Jefe's money and drugs along with another eight hundred of Hernando's. When he told the Jefe, he was beaten again by three of the gang. Now he didn't know what to do, and he wasn't sure where he could go. For the time being, he thought he'd find someplace to hang out, but first he needed some money. He hated not having money. It made him feel like the wet-backs who had just crossed the border.

It must have been destiny or fate that caused him to think of Mr. Edmonds. Hernando knew from his mother that the old man was out of town, up in Ridgecrest looking at some property for a client. He would wait until his mother went to sleep and then get the key to old Edmonds's house and see what was there worth taking.

He decided that maybe he should find another city to live in, like Palm Springs or Twenty-nine Palms. Maybe he'd try going straight for a while, he'd figured how much he'd made pushing drugs and it came up less than minimum wage for the hours he put in. He'd heard from a friend that had worked Palm Springs as a valet and had said sometimes the tips were really good. One woman had even slipped him a fifty and her room key. He didn't say any more about that, and Hernando didn't ask. The thought of having a straight job sounded almost too good, but maybe that's what he needed for a while. Then he would decide what he wanted to do.

He slipped in and out of his house without waking his mother, or so he thought. She just lay there, wondering what he was up to. She knew she didn't have very much control over him anymore. His father had left them years ago and hadn't returned. He had promised he would find a good job in Northern California, and would send for them. She had gotten two letters from him, one from Modesto with a little cash in it, and another from Sacramento with no cash. That had been over four years ago and she had never heard another word. She wrote letters to some cousins in Sacramento, but they hadn't seen or heard from him.

She lay back and let the tears come as they usually did when she thought about her husband. He was basically a good man, but sometimes when he had too much beer or tequila he would get very angry. She wasn't sure what or who he was angry at, just that she was the closest target for his wrath. He would slap her around a little then start crying and saying how sorry he was, that he was no good and that he didn't deserve her, but she shouldn't make him angry. She never did understand how she was to blame; she just knew it would be over by the next day. And then he would be a model husband, working at any job he could find and bringing her a small gift to express his sorrow at hurting 'his angel'.

She thought about Hernando and a thought ran through her mind that maybe he was starting to act like his father, only with drugs instead of liquor. On a hunch, she checked her purse to see if any money was missing. It was then she saw the keys to Mr. Edmonds's house were gone. Her heart sank, the many ideas running through her mind. She went back and forth with her thoughts for about twenty minutes, and then decided to call Mr. Edmonds. He had left her the number of the motel where he was staying, and her heart almost stopped when he answered his phone. Slowly, carefully, through several bouts of crying she told him what she thought was going on. She was almost relieved when he told her to relax; he would take care of it.

After hanging up with Rosa, Desmond quickly called his daughter Julie and explained the situation. She called and

[68]

dispatched a squad to his house just in time to catch Hernando leaving with several items. Mostly they were sentimental pieces made of silver that in a pawn shop might bring about one hundred or one-fifty. When Julie told Desmond of the arrest, he asked her to relay the orders to Hernando to keep his mouth shut, that he shouldn't talk until his lawyer got there.

"Dad, why are you going to represent this kid?" Julie asked.

"I don't know, just a hunch I have. That and he's Rosa's son."

"The arresting officer made it a point to call back-up immediately. The kid was beaten pretty badly."

"By the police?"

"No. The boy said someone else did it, but he wouldn't name names. The police know that he is affiliated with the local gang."

When Hernando shuffled into the courtroom, he looked around and saw his mother sitting a few rows back crying. He hung his head not wanting her to see his face. It was two days since he had suffered his beatings, and his body still hurt. His hand was swollen very badly, and he still couldn't take a deep breath without feeling a sharp pain in his side. He looked to the defendants table and couldn't believe it when he saw Mr. Edmonds was standing there. Now he was really confused.

He went to stand where the bailiff told him, next to Mr. Edmonds. He looked down at the table and saw a legal pad with a note in big letters. "Don't say anything." was on the note pad. As if to make his point, Mr. Edmonds tapped his finger on the note.

"We're going to plead guilty," Desmond said. "We'll try to get a lighter sentence because of your age, and hopefully we can get the judge to go along, OK?"

Hernando just nodded in agreement. He wasn't sure what was happening here, but he knew his mother always said Mr. Edmonds was a good man, maybe he really was. Right now, he wasn't ready to argue with him.

After pleading guilty, the judge was ready to sentence immediately. Desmond interrupted and asked to meet in chambers, alone. Hernando didn't have any idea what that meant, though he had watched some of the lawyer-type shows on TV.

In chambers, Desmond wasted no time.

"David, you and I go way back. This time I think this kid can be salvaged if given an opportunity. His mother is my house-keeper and I know I'm way out of line by asking this, but I want his sentence suspended. Give him probation, or community service, or anything you can think of without putting him in prison. If I have to, I'll swear under oath that I had asked him to gather that stuff from my house for safekeeping. I honestly believe, given a chance, he can be a good citizen instead of a criminal. And no matter what, don't speak of any of this to anyone."

Judge David Hartshorne was definitely not a liberal. He once fined a prominent citizen the full dollar amount for illegally parking in a handicapped space. When the offender made a comment under his breath, he was then sentenced to five days for contempt of court, and then another five when he protested.

He slammed his gavel down. "I hereby sentence you to the following; you will make full restitution to the victim. That means you will accompany the evidence officer to the evidence locker and sign for the things you had stolen. You will then take them to the victim's residence and personally give them to the victim with an apology. Then you will serve five hundred hours of community service to be used at the discretion of the victim. In other words, young man, you will do what he says. If he wants you to mow the lawn, then you mow the lawn. And finally, you will be placed on probation with the state services and report to them every two weeks. Before any of this happens, you will be taken to the hospital to have these wounds taken care of. Are these orders completely understood?"

"Yes sir," was all Hernando could think to say.

CHAPTER ELEVEN

Jake stared at Ernst, not believing what he was hearing. They had started their training, and Ernst's education, just a few days ago. Now here Ernst was reading from a book. It was a first grade level book, but it was a book. He looked up at Ernst and could see how proud the boy was. His look of accomplishment was too genuine not to be true.

"How did you do that? Did someone coach you?" Jake asked.

"Yes sir. I talked to my cell-mate and he didn't want to at first, said I was kidding him. I talked to him real nice and he said he'd help. He was kind of scared at first, but we did it. And he showed me a lot of words and how words are made out of the letters you showed me."

"That's really good, Ernst. You really are doing good."

Jake got the four of them together for their exercise session, and this time he really worked them hard. All of them were groaning by the time he quit. He laughed at them and called them a bunch of little girls. He kept at it until he knew they were mad, and then ordered them to do two more sets of each exercise. He himself was hurting when they quit. Only Ernst was still there ready to do some more, like a big engine that didn't quit until you turned it off. Jake just shook his head in wonder.

On the way to the mess hall, they were stopped by a couple of the Outlaws. Jake was hoping to avoid any trouble right now, these guys were just starting to act like a group and he didn't need anything to upset that.

He pushed quickly to the front, and confronted the bigger of the two.

"Something you wish to discuss?" Jake asked.

"Oh, listen to the little pussy, with the nice manners," he sneered. "Why aren't you girls over on the heavy weights like the big boys?" Everyone knew the weight-lifting area was Outlaw territory.

Jake thought quickly, and decided his best shot was take down this big man and be done with it. "It is so smelly there and

[71]

the weights are just so big I don't think I could lift them. Besides, you're always there and you are a pig, with bad breath."

The big man was like a lot of big men. He had been big when growing up, always using his size to his advantage, and not really learning how to fight. His attack was all wrong when it came, and couldn't have been better for Jake. With a quick leg sweep he put the man on the ground, and then grabbed his wrist and with one leg in the man's armpit and the other on his neck, he pulled back and twisted at the same time. Jake heard the distinctive "pop" as the arm was dislocated from the shoulder. Just as quickly, he then hit the man in his collar-bone using his fist like a hammer. He then jumped up and was ready for the second man, who stood there in shock. Apparently he had never seen the big man get whipped.

In an act of mercy, Jake had Ernst help the man to his feet. Then Ernst did something unusual in brushing off the man's clothes. Jake smiled and turned to the other Outlaw.
"Please help your friend to the infirmary; he has a broken collar-bone and a dislocated shoulder. He should have his shoulder re-set and then wrapped. He won't be doing any heavy work for a while."

When the two Outlaws had left, Jake turned to the others. "You can do the same kind of fighting if you listen and do as I say. Now, let's get something to eat. Stand proud and stand together." Jake could see they were tired, but they had enough left to straighten themselves up and march together to the mess hall.

After Jake had his meal, a guard stopped at his table and looked at the number on Jake's uniform. "You're the one I'm looking for. Warden wants to see you."

"May I finish my meal first, sir?" Jake asked.

The guard looked around as if to make sure he wasn't being watched. No use, in here everybody was watching, all the time. "Well, alright. But make it quick. The Warden doesn't like to be kept waiting."

Before they left the mess hall another guard joined them and he brought along the hand-cuffs and leg chains. It was standard

[72]

for any prisoner to be in chains when being escorted anywhere in the compound he wouldn't normally have access to. Jake knew this but for some reason he was wary of these two. He was hoping they didn't do a beat-down on him. Some of the white guards showed favoritism towards one of the white gangs or the other. This time he was lucky, they didn't do anything to him, even being polite to him when they un-cuffed him.

The Warden came right to the point. "I have a request to visit from someone who is neither your attorney nor a relative. I'm not sure if I should grant this request, because it is highly unusual."

"May I ask who it is, sir? Perhaps then I can give you some information on this person."

"The person making the request is Margaret Wagner. Now you understand why I'm not sure I should grant this visit. I'm not sure it would be proper, you having killed her husband."

Jake almost screamed at him, but he held it in. "I see, sir. It is unusual. However, if in some way it could help bring her some closure knowing I'm behind bars, then I certainly wouldn't mind, sir."

"Well, that may be what she needs. Visiting day is three days away, so I'll let you and her both know tomorrow. By the way, you have some letters here. What are you doing, buying land Jake?"

"Actually, I haven't bought any yet. I wanted Mr. Edmonds to look into that area and see if it was available and for how much. I might not be able to afford it after paying Mr. Edmonds. I didn't have much to start with."

"I see. Guard, take the prisoner back to his cell."

Jake was about to jump out of his skin, he was so happy. Good news, two times. A letter from Desmond meant he was making progress, and Margaret wanted to see him and talk. He had almost forgotten about the incident of this morning with the Outlaws. This time there were three and they didn't care that he was being escorted by the guards. One had a shiv and stabbed the lead guard who grabbed Jake to try to keep from falling. The second guard must have had some warning because he already had his baton out and was swinging away. Jake went down on his back and did a double leg kick to the groin of the nearest Outlaw. He connected really well because of the high-pitched scream coming from the man. Jake jumped to his feet just in time to block another stab at the second guard, who had his back turned. Jake then clasped his hands together and swung them like a baseball bat at the one with the shiv and connected at his nose. There was a loud crack and the second one was down. Jake turned to see the guard with the baton start to pull the shiv out of his partner's leg.

"Don't!" Jake yelled. "It may be in the artery. If you pull it out, he'll bleed to death before you can get help. Please take my leg irons off, sir."

The guard looked at Jake as if he wasn't sure he could be trusted. Then he shook his head no.

"Then give me your belt, I need to make a tourniquet above the wound. Hurry!"

"Officer down! Officer down!" the guard yelled into his radio, and almost immediately the siren went off.

"Get on the ground. Do not move. Get on the ground." The warning was repeated several times. Jake worked feverishly on getting the tourniquet in place and just had cinched it to where it should be when he was hit alongside the head. Everything went black.

When he opened his eyes, Jake was in the infirmary lying in bed. Standing next to him was the guard who had given Jake the belt.

"How's your partner?" Jake managed to squeak out. Damn, his mouth was dry.

"He's going to be alright, thanks to you. The Doctor said you were right, if I had pulled the shiv out, he would have bled to death. We owe you one, man."

"Yeah right," Jake responded with a grin. "Buy me a beer, and we'll call it even."

"The warden said to let you know, your visit is granted."

"Who hit me?" Jake asked. "Didn't they see what I was doing?"

"That was one our guys, and he hit you because he saw a prisoner bending over a guard, and thought you were attacking the guard."

"Yeah, OK. Tell him I owe him one. And from the way my head feels, he ain't gonna like the payback."

"Then you won't find out from me who it was."

Jake spent the rest of the evening trying to get comfortable in the bed. He wondered if there was some kind of psychology behind having the most uncomfortable beds in a hospital. Maybe it was supposed to make you want to leave sooner. Or maybe the bed-buyer was a total masochist, the more pain the bed inflicted, the more that freak liked it. Either way, there wasn't any position that was comfortable. The throbbing from the blow to the head didn't help his disposition either.

He finally got some sleep later that night, but only after giving in and asking the nurse for a pain pill. He didn't like using any form of narcotics, even those prescribed by doctors, but sometimes it was necessary.

When he woke again, Jake sat up in bed. His left hand was cuffed to the bed, same as when he went to bed. This time there was a note tucked into the cuffs. He opened it and saw these words, "I owe you my life, Guard Crenshaw." Jake just smiled and lay back in the bed. He slowly drifted back off to sleep thinking how nice it was to have friends.

CHAPTER TWELVE

Desmond sat drinking coffee in the dining room when Rosa and Hernando arrived. Rosa appeared very nervous, while Hernando looked calm yet curious. He looked at the clothes Hernando was wearing and shook his head. The boy was dressed in typical gang-banger fashion.

"You might want to go home and change clothes Hernando. We're going to be painting this house, and those clothes might get messed up. I would suggest work clothes."

"I ain't got any work clothes." Hernando was almost defiant in his tone.

Desmond smiled and then waited a full minute before replying. "Very well, you can't say I didn't warn you. And Hernando, I would very much appreciate being called Mr. Edmonds, or sir."

Before Hernando could say anything, Rosa grabbed him by the ear with the ear-ring in it and pulled him aside. What she said to him, Desmond had no idea, never having learned Spanish. Whatever it was, when Hernando returned he immediately apologized for his "attitude".

"Thank you Hernando. Do you know anything about house-painting? I know nearly nothing, but if we ask the right questions, maybe the man at the hardware store can help us figure it out."

So it began, the two of them trying to figure out what questions to ask, how much paint they would need and so forth. Together they browsed the internet, looking up the information they needed. They were almost done on the computer when Rosa interrupted them for lunch. They looked at each other and then at the clock and laughed. The morning was gone, and they hadn't even started on the house. But they did have a list of materials, and the measurements of the house.

After lunch, Desmond wasn't sure what to do. Because he no longer drove, he would have to have a driver. One problem, although Hernando could drive, he didn't have a license. And even if Rosa had a license, Desmond no longer had a car. His car was wrecked when his wife was killed, and he hadn't replaced it.

"Guess what. We need to get Hernando a license. Do either of you know where to get the license information?"

Rosa gave him the information he needed, and he and Hernando piled into a taxi and headed to the license bureau. Desmond stayed just long enough to grab all the pamphlets and booklets he thought they might need.

All afternoon the two of them sat there at Desmond's dining room table going over the books from the DMV. Desmond kept asking Hernando question after question until they were both tired. When Rosa came in and said it was time to go home Desmond asked if she could be there the next day, and she shook her head no.

"I have another house to clean tomorrow, Mr. Edmonds. I won't be back until after the week-end."

After they were gone he dialed Julie's number in hopes she would be home. No luck, he got the answering machine. He left a message for her to call as soon as she could. He went to the office looking for the day's paper. He had barely sat down when the phone rang. It was Julie and she sounded out of breath.

"What's wrong?" she asked quickly.

"Nothing," he replied. "I just wanted some help on picking out a car, maybe an SUV. You know a lot of the dealers and which are best to deal with."

"You scared me. You've never said 'call as soon as possible' before and I thought something was wrong. How is it working out with the gang-banger?"

"Hernando is doing fine. He's why I need to get a car. I have no way to get to the hardware store and back. And maybe I'd like to get out once in a while without having to wait for you or your sister. Anyway, I'm thinking of an SUV, like maybe a four-wheel drive wagon."

She laughed out loud and then said. "Oh my God, you're going through your second childhood!"

Before he could say anything, she gave him the names of three good dealers. Before hanging up, she laughed and said "Oh my God, a second childhood."

CHAPTER THIRTEEN

Jake was as nervous as a school-boy on his way to the principal's office. He wasn't sure what he should or shouldn't say. The Warden had arranged for him and Margaret to be in a separate room with only one guard. It was somewhat unusual, but given the circumstances of the past few days, not that far out of the norm.

When he got in the room Jake was hand-cuffed to the table. The guard told him he was not to attempt to pass any objects to the visitor, nor was he to accept any from the visitor. Any breach of the rules would cause immediate termination of the visit and the prisoner may be subject to solitary confinement.

Margaret was looking behind her toward the two guards that escorted her. She turned and looked at Jake and her tears began to flow. It took several minutes for her to regain her composure. She looked at the side of his head at the area where they had shaved his hair of before stitching the wound closed where he'd been hit with the baton.

"One of the guards decided to use my head for batting practice," Jake chuckled.

"Wait a minute," the guard intervened. "He didn't know what you were doing to the other guard."

Briefly, the guard explained the incident in the yard, and how Jake was now considered a hero by some of the guards.

"Do you consider him a hero?" Margaret asked pointedly.

"Yes ma'am, I certainly do." The guard stood up a little straighter. "It's nice to know of one inmate who isn't trying to kill me."

Jake just chuckled and said, "The day's not over yet, so who knows?"

The three of them laughed and then Jake and Margaret got down to their conversation.   The guard respectfully stepped back to a corner of the room. Before Jake could say anything to Margaret, she started.

"I know you didn't do it Jake. I have some pictures of the couple from the night you and TJ and them were at the Three

Sisters, but they're not very clear. A couple of agents I know in the FBI and a U.S. Marshall that was a friend of TJ's are all trying to track down the two of them. But first, we need to talk about your situation. Remember when you got all that settlement money and you asked me to take care of it for you? Well, I invested some here and some there on advice I got from that financial advisor that you said looked squirrely. He maybe looked squirrely but his advice was really good. You won't have to worry about money for a while after you get out. I gave all the accounts over to Mr. Edmonds because of that power-of-attorney you signed. I think he's a good man. He is definitely on your side. We're doing all we can to find the Davises, so you don't have to worry about it in here."

"Margaret, I think there are more than just the Davises. Before they blew the entrance to the mine, there was another man out there with them. I didn't get a good look, so I can't make an ID. I'm doing fine in here. I can still take care of myself. Can you be at my parole hearing? It would mean a lot if you were there and on my side of the table. If not, I'll understand."

"I'll be there Jake. Come hell or high water, I'll be there. TJ and I couldn't have children, and as such he treated you like the son he never had. There are some facts you need to know about TJ's will, but that can wait until after you're released. I feel so much better just having been able to see you, and tell you what I had to say. But I may not visit you again."

"What? Why not? Was the drive too much?"

She leaned forward and then her face got slightly red. "They did a cavity search," she whispered, embarrassed to have said it.

Jake was very quiet for a couple minutes, trying extremely hard not to start laughing. He hung down his head so Margaret couldn't see his face until he was in control again, and then he asked, "Is there anything you need, Margaret? If there is, contact Mr. Edmonds and tell him. He's a good friend."

"Well, we need to get someone to help harvest the pistachios. TJ always took care of that and knew who to call. I wouldn't have any idea."

"OK. Tell Mr. Edmonds to pay them out of my bank account until we get paid for the harvest. I do have enough to pay a crew don't I?"

"Oh my yes. You're in good shape."

Jake saw the guard looking at his watch and asked how much time was left. The guard responded with a shrug and said, "As long as you don't miss lunch, you can take your time."

"Then please sit down, I promise I won't try to escape. I know it can be uncomfortable having to stand the entire time."

The guard took one of the extra chairs and sat down, and Jake and Margaret went back to their conversation reminiscing about some of the things that Jake and TJ had gotten into together. They talked up until lunchtime and then they both said good-bye. Jake thanked the guard for his patience, and held his wrists out to be cuffed. The guard shook his head and almost apologetically put the cuffs on. They both knew that he'd get in trouble if he didn't follow procedure. Jake felt better now than he had in quite some time in spite of the bump on his head. Just knowing how Margaret felt was a large part of it, but knowing that she would be taken care of was also a factor.

Ernst was waiting for him when he got back to the cell. There was a bit of tension between him and the guard that may mean some past history. He thought for a second, and then said, "Thanks for your kindness toward Margaret, sir. She means a lot to me and it was very thoughtful of you to treat her like a lady."

"You're welcome, Jake. She is truly a lady. Reminds me of my grandma."

He uncuffed Jake and left, but not before looking Ernst over.

"What's the matter, Ernst? Usually you wait to see me on the yard. Did someone get hurt?"

"Just you, sir. We weren't sure you would be coming back. The Reverend sent me to make sure you hadn't forgotten your contract." Ernst said, not sure what was meant by the phrase. Jake could see the puzzled look on his face and knowing of his limited education decided to explain all of it later.

"Come on, Ernst. If we don't hurry, we'll miss lunch."

They made lunch in time, and sat at the table where Jake usually sat. Another inmate was at the other end and looked at Jake and started to smile. Jake turned to see him better and instantly recognized him and started to say something but the other prisoner shook his head no. As the man left, he whispered to Jake to meet him at the bleachers after lunch. Jake wasn't sure what the situation was, so he just nodded yes.

"Who was that?" Ernst asked.

"A bad man, Ernst. I knew him a long time ago and from what I know now, he's a very bad man. Don't start any trouble with him, and tell the others as well."

At the bleachers the new prisoner was waiting as were his four trainees. He turned and told the four to start their warm-up routine, that he had some old unfinished business to take care of. He then walked slowly to the other end of the bleachers and faced the man, his face tight. He almost whispered when he addressed the new inmate.

"How are you, Alex? How much time do you have left?"

"I'm good, Jake. I've got less than four months to go, but I'm in a situation that's not good. The Outlaws have a hold on me and in order to pay it off, they want me to take you out, or bust you up. Either way, they need to prove they're the big dogs here."

"Give me one now to prove you're trying to do your job. I'll take it, and then walk away, okay?"

"Yeah, but I'm not sure it'll work." He struck out just as he finished the last word, and lucky for Jake, he wasn't quite as fast as he used to be or was doing that on purpose so Jake would think he slowed down. Jake had rolled with the punch and then fallen to the ground, but was on his feet just as fast. He then backed away from Alex with his hands raised.

Jake walked back to his group and wiped what little blood there was onto the sleeve of his shirt and then smiled. He could see the doubt in their faces, as if their hero were found out to be mortal. Ernst seemed especially sad to learn that Jake didn't whip the man.

[82]

"Gentlemen, let's get to work. You're not working hard enough to build the strength you need. You just saw a man hit me, and you all think I should have whipped his ass. Maybe I could and maybe I couldn't. I knew him from a long time ago and he was a "real" bad-ass then, I'm not sure what he is now. I'm not sure I can whip him, and right now I don't want to find out. Remember there's a time and place for everything. Now let's get to work."

He left his group working with Sorenson in charge. He would have left the group to Collier but something about him didn't seem right. Jake would have to wait to find out more on Collier. He walked toward the heavy-weight area and approached slowly. He stopped a little distance away and watched for a minute before asking if he could use some of the smaller weights. He saw the big man he'd had the trouble with and looked at his shoulder wrapped in bandages.

"How's the shoulder doing? I'm truly sorry I had to do that. If I had let you get hold of me, you probably would have killed me."

The big man laughed and said, "I damn sure was going to try. I will say you're one tough son-of-a-bitch. I see you met our new employee, he might be a bit tougher than you."

"I thought I knew him from somewhere, but I don't know. Anyway, I came down here to see if the ladies and I can use the smaller weights like one, two, three, and five pounds. If we use the big weights it builds big bulky muscles, and it slows us down."

The big man nodded and sent one of his men to gather all the small weights and transport them to the "ladies by the bleachers". Jake accompanied him, smiling as he thought out the scheme that was brewing in his mind.

CHAPTER FOURTEEN

Desmond was working on his third cup of coffee when the doorbell rang. Hernando was standing there looking somewhat disgruntled.

"How come I have to work on a Saturday? I didn't think I was supposed to work on the week-ends. What's up with that?"

Desmond looked at him and shook his head. "I guess I was wrong about you after all." He then shut the door and started back to the dining room. He got two steps before the doorbell rang again. He turned back and opened the door.

"Come in and close the door."

He sat down at the table and Hernando followed suit. Neither of them said a word for nearly a minute.

"I don't understand, Mr. Edmonds. I didn't know I had to work on week-ends."

"You don't. And you're not here to work, you're here to study. The license is going to be yours, not mine. If you don't want to study, go home. Go back to pushing crap for el jefe and people like him. Stay in the ghetto, and stay stupid. Keep pushing that crap and soon you start using that crap and then one night you get a hot-shot and they find you with a needle sticking out of your arm. I must have been crazy to believe what your mother said about you being a good kid, just needing a chance. If you really want that chance, then it has to be completely done my way, everything. I'll be in the kitchen making more coffee."

It was several minutes later when Hernando stuck his head into the kitchen and asked, "May I have a cup of coffee, too?" "Oh, excuse me. Please?"

"Yes you may, now let's go in the dining room."

They studied the Rules of the Road book over and over. It was late morning when Julie showed up at his house. They all piled into her car and headed to one of the dealers she knew. Des knew pretty much what he wanted and had a good idea what to ask. The first salesman approached them and Julie brushed him aside saying who she was here to meet. A middle-aged man with slightly balding hair came up and greeted them.

"Julie, it's so good to see you again. My wife and I are ever so grateful you could help us with that problem. Now, just exactly what are you interested in?"

Des went down the list of what he wanted to have and so forth. The salesman, John, kept trying to steer Des toward a smaller version SUV that he happened to have on the lot. Des just sat back and used the silent stare routine he'd used when he first met Jake at the sheriff's office.

Hernando watched and just before the salesman started to say something, he jumped into the conversation. "Come on, Mr. Edmonds. The other guy had everything you wanted, but it was the tan color, and he was almost four thousand cheaper. Julie said this guy was a friend, but I'm not too sure. Maybe we should just go."

Des didn't even blink. He just looked at Hernando and nodded. "Perhaps you may be right. We have too much to do to keep wasting time, and operations are supposed to start next week."

Des reached in his pocket and withdrew a small calculator. He did some quick numbers and then wrote down a number that was exactly four thousand less than the number "John" had quoted. "Do we have a deal?" He showed the number.

John swallowed, and then said, "I'll have to run this by my boss. You start filling out the credit app while I talk to him."

Des sat there waiting for the salesman to return, Hernando kept looking toward where the Manager's office was and then back to Mr. Edmonds. He was just itching with anticipation of what was going to happen.

"Aren't you going to fill out that credit app thing?" he asked.

"We won't need a credit app, Hernando. Just sit and please be quiet. You did a very smart thing just now, I was only going to ask for two thousand less on the price. Now, keep calm and let's see how we did." He then reached in his pocket and started writing a check for the amount that he had showed the salesman. He had just finished when John returned.

[85]

"Is there a problem? I see you haven't filled out the application. I had to do some talking, but I got the manager to agree to your price. So now what's wrong?"

"Nothing," said Des. He turned over the check and looked at it and at the number he had given John before. "You'll see these are the same, so I'd appreciate it if you would have the vehicle cleaned, waxed, and delivered to the address on my card," at which, he handed John one of his business cards. "Is Wednesday all right with you?"

John just nodded, and sat there, which prompted Des to remind him that a receipt would be in order.

They all waited until they were in Julie's car before they said anything, and then it was "Yeah!! That was fun!"

Julie stayed around Des's house the rest of the afternoon until it was time for Hernando to head home. She volunteered to drive him, and Des thought perhaps it was because she was going to have a word or two with him.

"Did you give him the big talking to that you wanted?" Des asked when she returned.

First she grinned and then she laughed, "Yes, but not like you think. I asked him a lot of questions and we talked quite a bit about his mother, and even a little bit about his father. There are some real issues there, so I'd go light about the father if I were you."

"I thought as much. He seemed somewhat confused as to the father's whereabouts or if he's even alive. Other than that, I think he's a basically good kid. Oh, by the way, can you take him to the DMV for his test on Tuesday?"

"I think so, but I'd better check my schedule. I may have court."

"Thanks, Julie. I love you. I'll talk to you on Monday. I need to try to get hold of Jake tomorrow and let him know I spent some of his money. It's hard to get him to the phone on the weekends."

"Be sure to give him a kiss from me," she said and grinned."I think I could go for an ex-con like that."

[86]

"That wouldn't be such a bad thing," Des said seriously. At that Julie just shook her head and left. She remembered how disappointed her father had been when she had announced her engagement to her first husband. He hadn't said anything against the marriage. As she recalled, he hadn't said anything at all after the announcement until she had broken down that morning and told him of her husband's affairs and that she wanted a divorce. The only thing he said then was, "We'll be here for you, no matter what you need."

Des was worried. He hadn't heard from Jake and usually the news that he had sent Jake in the letters would cause someone to call as soon as they could. Then he remembered that Margaret visited him and maybe she had an idea what was going on in there. Before he could get the phone, it started ringing. He picked it up and it was Margaret.

"Wow, I was just thinking of calling you. What's going on?"

Margaret told him of the visit with Jake, but didn't mention the cavity search. She also didn't mention anything about the letters that Des had sent Jake. She told him of the need to find some people to harvest the pistachios soon. Des told her he wasn't sure who to get, but he'd work on it. Maybe the Growers Association could help him. He himself didn't know the first thing about how they were harvested, but that certainly wouldn't stop him from finding out. He asked Margaret if Jake had mentioned the letters he'd sent.

"No Mr. Edmonds. With all that happened to him that day I'm not sure if he remembers getting the letters. There was quite a bit happening from what I heard."

"Is he in trouble again?"

"I don't think so, but with him you can't always tell. He has that way of keeping so many things to himself, and then he just explodes. Or, at least he used to, not so much anymore."

Des got the information he needed from Margaret as to the location of the orchards, and asked that she look up last year's people's names and how much they were paid. They said their good-byes and Des went to his office and poured a two-finger nightcap. He hadn't had any liquor in quite a while, not since the funeral. Then he'd gotten completely and un-ashamedly smashed.

He finished his drink and made his way to the bedroom. He felt a slight draft coming from the living room, and so he turned to check the front door to make sure it was closed and locked. He made it halfway when he saw a man standing there with a knife. "So this is what little Hernando has going, a sugar daddy. Well, Sugar Daddy you better give it up and right now or I'll gut you right here."

Before Des could move he saw a flash of movement from behind the man and heard a loud crack like a baseball bat. Probably because it was a baseball bat made of shiny aluminum, and there was Hernando holding it. The man had slumped to the floor, out cold. Des was in shock. "What? Who? How," the questions were forming but he didn't seem to be able to speak.

Hernando looked at him and said, "I saw him about four blocks from here. I was coming back to see if I could get the book of rules so I could study tomorrow, because we're not working are we? Anyway, he's one of the gang I ran with and I didn't figure he'd be here to help you. Oh, and I borrowed the bat from your neighbors down the street."

A quick call to 911 and San Bernardino Police Department was on the scene, the man, Jesus Alvarado, being held on the floor by the bat-wielding Hernando was put in cuffs and charged with attempted murder.

"Thanks, I owe you Hernando."

"No Mr. Edmonds, I'm just protecting my chance to get out."

CHAPTER FIFTEEN

Jake sat in his cell, disappointed at the news from Des. All his hopes, his ideas, his dreams of having his own enclave out in the desert were gone. Or maybe not, Des had stated that there were exceptions to the rules. The EPA was in control of the entire bureau for the abandoned mines. But if it was determined that the mine owners had "proven up" the property, there still could be a chance. The whole mess gave him a headache. He didn't understand a lot of what Des had said, but he did tell Jake not to give up, he was still investigating the mine's legal status.

Life goes on, he thought. His students would be waiting, as well as all the other gang-bangers in this shit-hole called a prison. He made his way to the bleachers, not failing to notice one of the Outlaws leaving from behind them. It appeared as if Collier was just coming around from in back. He shook his head, some of these "cons" deserved to be here he thought. They all believe that the victim is just going to roll over and do what they say. So when one victim resists, it surprises them and being stupidly optimistic, they do something desperate and often violent. Collier was one of those who believed like that. His big score was supposed to be carrying a briefcase full of money, but was instead only carrying some legal briefs. Collier shot him for a grand total of seventy-three dollars that was in his wallet. His "big score" netted him almost five dollars per year for the time he'd serve.

It was in this same foul mood that he started them on their exercises with the weights. It was a new routine for them, and leave it to Collier to question why they were only using two and three pound weights. Rather than explain it to them, he had Collier put a single two pound weight in each of his hands.

"Now, we start shadow-boxing. Me without weights and you with weights. Let me know when you are getting tired."

It was less than three minutes when Collier called it quits.

He had each of them do the same exercise, one at a time. He saved Ernst for the last, knowing the lasting power he had. As he expected, Ernst did ten minutes and was still going when Jake told him to stop.

"As you watch your Outlaw friends over there with the big weights, you might be impressed with the amount of weight they can lift, and curl, etc. but that isn't what builds strength and stamina. They probably wouldn't last any longer than you, Collier."

Jake had been watching Collier the entire time he was talking, and could see the nervousness in his demeanor. At the term "Outlaw friends" Collier had almost jerked his head, but held himself in check.

"Now let's start with the new weights and pay close attention, because if you do these properly, they'll help build strength, speed, and stamina. If you don't do them right, they won't help you at all no matter how hard you work at it."

Jake pushed them hard for an hour, and then when they rested, he asked for the 'book reports' on the books they'd been told to read. All of them did well at describing the book's storyline, but none could answer when asked if they felt there was a moral issue or was it just a story.

Jake had hoped for better, so assigned them to each read the same book, "Tucker" by Louis L'Amour. It was a short book so it wouldn't take them long. They could have it read in a day and then pass it on. Maybe this time they would take a little bit more time and try to figure whether there's a moral or not.

"Have any of you signed up for the Firefighter classes?"

The question took them by surprise to say the least. They looked at each other in surprise and their mouths partly open. He saw a slight smirk on Collier's face and knew he was right on with his idea about him having a connection with the Outlaws.

"The Reverend said that was the Outlaw's gig and we shouldn't butt in," Sorenson explained. "They get paid extra when they are on the fire-line and we aren't invited to join the party. We asked about it, but Reverend said we aren't strong enough to take on the Outlaws."

"I think I'll talk to the Reverend and see if I can change his mind. There has to be more to it than that. The Aryan

Brotherhood has nearly the same amount of members as the Outlaws, so it has to be something else."

It was nearing lunchtime so Jake dismissed them and walked to the Education Office. The same eager young man who had helped him procure the notebooks and pencils for his group was behind the desk. He was a senior at Cal-State University at Chico, doing an internship semester at Susanville. He was more than helpful in looking up the past few years concerning the Firefighter class enrollment. Jake noticed that the same senior guard was in charge of who enrolled each time. Jake asked the intern if he could cross-reference the gang affiliation of each of the students, and could he keep the results to himself until Jake can back in a day or two. As usual, the student was on it before Jake had even left.

After lunch the Reverend was waiting at the bleachers. He nodded to the group, and motioned for them to go to the other end. He then sat down as if he were a king holding court.

"I understand you wanted to talk to me? There seems to be some things happening that I wasn't aware of. Please be seated Jake." His tone was very disdainful, as if it were something he'd rather not do.

"Well Reverend, I was wondering why you haven't signed up any of the AB's for the Firefighter class. It would seem like a great opportunity to bring in more cash to the AB's fund and I believe we could project a positive image to the media while doing it. If we could get a newsperson or two that I know to show your positive attitude toward the rehabilitation program here at Susanville, I think it will help promote your vision. When people turn on the five o'clock news and see blacks killing people and then opposite of that they see you or the best looking skin-head we can come up with doing a 'good deed' they'll start asking themselves why the Aryan's are always getting bad press."

"You should have been a salesman, Jake. After listening to you for one minute, I'm ready to go join the Hare Krishna and start passing out flowers at the fucking airport. What is this going to do other than what you said? I'll tell you. It's going to piss off the Outlaws and we could end up in a gang war. Also, the guard who enrolls people in the class has control over who gets in and who doesn't, because he's on the Outlaws payroll. You can't get past that little fact, can you?"

"If you'll let me, I'd like to try. I think he might be persuaded, if I approach him with a fair deal."

"Like the deal you made me?" the Reverend asked.

Jake smiled like a Cheshire cat and replied, "Yeah, just like the deal I made you."

"You really are a smooth son-of-a-bitch Jake. Just be careful you don't try to be too smooth, you might end up dead."

Jake's smile disappeared and he lowered his voice, "I told you never to threaten me again. I'll forgive you this slip, be sure it's the last."

"There's one other thing Jake, I understand that the Outlaws have a new bad-ass after you put Davis out of action."

"Who?" Jake was on his feet in one step and right in the Reverend's face. "Who did you say?"

"Davis, Dean Davis, the big man that you broke his collar-bone." He started to say more, and then he stopped. "What is it?"

"It's the name; Dean Davis was the name the bastard used that killed TJ, my partner. It has to be a coincidence, there's no way they're connected."

"What about the new hitter?"

"He was just transferred in from somewhere, and I haven't found out about him yet. I used to know him many years ago, but people change and I don't think there's any way he can remember me. We only met briefly, and it was such a long time ago."

Jake thought about the situation and decided it was time to move up the lessons. He showed the group a couple of basic martial arts moves, and had them do the movements over and over in slow motion. Because he wanted the time-table to go faster, he had them add the weights they'd used in shadow-boxing. After merely ten minutes, they were whining and complaining. All except Ernst, who was just like a machine. He did whatever Jake asked and didn't stop until Jake told him to.

[92]

Jake wasn't sure what kind of intelligence factor Ernst might have, but it would be nice to find out.

They stopped early because of their whining about the weights, but Sorenson said he wanted to stay by himself. Jake said no to the idea, telling them of the eyes that had been watching them all afternoon. If they were caught alone, they could get seriously hurt or killed. He asked Ernst to stay with him and dismissed the other three with the usual, "Stand proud and stand together."

He took Ernst with him to the Education Office and hoped the young intern was there with some information for him. He didn't see him and was about to leave when Tyler, the intern, came out of the bathroom. He looked at Ernst and Jake could tell he was somewhat intimidated. Ernst had that effect on people until he started talking, then they realized how harmless he could be.

"I have the information you asked for," he said, unsure what he could say in front of Ernst. Tyler didn't want to get in trouble and he didn't want Jake in trouble so he just stood there.

"Thank you and I have another favor to ask. Ernst has never been to school and so has never been tested for what his intelligence might be. He has just recently learned the alphabet and is working on words at a first and second grade level. What else he may have learned in his life, I don't know. Is there some way you can test him? If not, I'll understand Tyler, I don't want you to get in trouble, and you've been a lot of help so far. Would you see what you can do?"

Tyler's face lit up and he almost giggled. "Oh, wow! This is great. I can call my professor and run it by him. We can make him a test subject, uh what's his name?"

Ernst reached out with his hand and grasped Tyler's hand firmly. "My name is Ernst Buchold, and your name is Tyler. Do you have a last name, Tyler?"

Tyler stammered and started to pull away, but Ernst held his hand firmly. "Uh, my, my name, I mean, my last name is Walker." He flushed and looked down. "I'm sorry Ernst, it's just that you're so big, I was, well, I, I don't know what to say."

"It's okay, Tyler. Sometimes I scare people. I don't mean to. Can you help me learn to read? Jake's been trying to teach me but he's so busy all the time. He did teach me all the letters and all the numbers and even some of the words. Can you help me Tyler?" His voice was childlike and very calm, so Tyler couldn't help but smile.

"It will be my pleasure, Ernst."

Jake was in awe. It was the most he'd heard from Ernst at any one time, and he was truly impressed. Tyler reached under the counter and handed a package to Jake. It was a manila envelope with no writing on the outside. Jake had a sudden thought, and asked for another envelope like the one he had.

He handed the first envelope to Ernst. "See this gets back to me at my cell, okay Ernst?" He then took a marker off Tyler's desk and wrote the word "Guards" in block letters on the outside of the empty envelope. Tyler watched and smiled.

"Ernst, you can't tell anyone about what we're doing. Not even the Reverend, he doesn't understand sometimes. And please be sure nothing happens to our friend Tyler."

Jake then left and as he suspected he was being followed. He decided to make it a little harder for them and up the ante at the same time. He passed one of the yard guards close enough so the guard couldn't help but see the package. He then started back towards his cell, and could see they had a few men blocking the way. He switched his direction and headed toward the other side of the yard. Again they started closing in on him. He played the switch-back game a time or two more. He then bolted towards the cell block and when they almost had him he threw the package toward the yard guard, and went inside the block. He was on the second tier when Ernst came in from the other end smiling. He didn't have anything in his hands, but when he got to Jake's cell, it appeared from inside his shirt.

"Well done, Ernst, very well done."

Jake looked at the information and right away knew how the senior guard had been manipulating the system. When the volunteers entered the firefighter program, they didn't have to do any other duties during the week-long course. They were also paid the higher rate of pay while in class and when on the line fighting fires. Jake could see how a prisoner would be in no hurry to stop a fire, especially if it meant he'd be losing money by doing so. Also, most of the 'volunteers' had already been certified and didn't need to be certified again, but were re-enrolled by the senior guard. Jake knew there had to be an incentive for the guard to violate protocol, so how was it happening? The funds the prisoners earned went to their canteen fund, so no cash changed hands. There had to be some way the guard was getting his cut of the monies earned.

"Jake?" Ernst was still standing at the cell's door. Jake had completely forgotten about him being there.

"Ernst, I'm so sorry. I forgot you were here. I just feel so comfortable when you're around, I forget. Please accept my apology."

Ernst looked confused, so Jake explained in simple terms that you apologize when you do something wrong to someone else, and if you are sorry you did it, you tell them you're sorry.

"But you didn't do anything to me Jake. Why did you say you were sorry?"

"Because it was rude of me not to acknowledge you were there Ernst. I should have said something to you before I started reading this paper," Jake said. "Now, was there something else you needed?"

Ernst hesitated for a moment and then asked, "Jake is it true you're a Jew? That's what the Reverend said, and he said Jews can never be trusted. Is that true?"

Jake thought for a bit and then responded, "Jews are people like everyone else Ernst, some of them good and some bad. They're called Jews because they because they practice a different religion than Christians. Their religion is very old, from before the time Jesus was born. I don't know much about them, except they have been poorly treated for many years. No, Ernst, I'm not a Jew. I'm not sure exactly what I believe in. I know that there is a God, but don't know what to call him, because there are so many different religions. As for trusting a Jew, why should a Jew be treated any different from anyone else? If you have a friend and he helps you and doesn't do things to harm you, can you trust him? How much do you trust anyone Ernst?"

"I don't know. But I like Tyler; he says I have 'opportunities' ahead of me. I think he might be a queer, but I don't mind. He won't do anything to me."

"I suppose not," Jake laughed. As Ernst caught on, he started laughing too.

CHAPTER SIXTEEN

Desmond hung up the phone and leaned back in his chair. It creaked a little when he did, and he smiled as he remembered when they had picked it out at the furniture store. He hadn't wanted to spend as much as the chair would cost, but she kept at him until he gave in. He could still recall what she'd said, "This chair will outlast three of those others and you know it. You should always invest in quality." He never liked admitting when she was right, so he had kept quiet.

He turned and looked toward the dining room where Hernando was still studying for his driver's license exam. He could see the features all twisted up and could tell he must be having a hard time with some portion of the reading material. He shook his head and smiled at the boy's determination. He hoped he was getting through to him, but wasn't sure if any of it did any good. He remembered when he was seventeen and how stubborn he'd been, always arguing with his father, so sure he was right. He remembered the Mark Twain quote, "When I was young I thought my father to be the dumbest man I'd ever met. A few years later and it was surprising how much the old man had learned." Des chuckled and turned back to his project.

All morning Des had been looking on the Internet for a lead as to the ownership of the mine. Between the Internet and the phone, he'd made some progress. So far, he'd tracked it down to a corporation in the Sacramento area. Like any good attorney, he wanted to know most of the answers to his questions before he asked them. It was slow and tedious work, with lots of dead-ends. The current owner was a corporation named Bryson Homes. Des was hoping he would be able to negotiate a deal for the mine without breaking the bank. So many times a corporation sitting on a pile of money and experiencing solid cash flow would buy properties like these on a flyer. With a little more digging he would have the information he needed, and could negotiate better. He smiled at the correlation, he was digging for information on a mine so they could start digging for gold, or whatever Jake was so interested in.

By lunchtime he extracted some more useful tid-bits about the mine's ownership. The person who filed the original claim and did the necessary work to "patent" the mine and gain ownership was a man named Ellis Chambers. He had left the mine to his daughter Eleanor when he died. It had been deeded to the Bryson Homes Corporation a few years later without explanation. But Des had looked into the Bureau of Statistics for California and culled through the Marriages until he found the marriage of Eleanor Chambers to one Donald Bryson. They divorced just two years ago with a healthy settlement in favor of Mrs. Bryson and their one son. Des had a thought, but it would have to wait until after lunch. Whatever Rosa was cooking smelled wonderful. Des's mouth was watering by the time he got to the kitchen.

"What is that wonderful smell? Whatever it is, I want some."

"Well then you better wash your hands and call 'Nando to the table also. I'll have it ready when you get back. And what you're eating is called enchiladas de pollo, or chicken enchiladas. Try it with some of the salsa verde on it, but not too much."

It was the first time Des had heard Hernando called by any other name. 'Nando had kind of a ring to it, and was more pleasant sounding than Hernando.

At lunch they talked about how the studies were going, and Hernando just rolled his eyes. Des answered a couple of questions about what he was doing, and was surprised when Rosa volunteered to talk to some cousins in the Sacramento area about the Bryson Homes Corporation.

"What would your cousins know about Bryson, Rosa?"

"Mr. Edmonds, when you are Mexican you blend right into the walls, like you're invisible. People aren't very careful about what they say in front of us, and so we pick up information here and there. Too many times they say things they shouldn't. They don't think we know anything so they talk and talk without even thinking whether we could be listening. What's even worse is when they talk about us when we're right there in the room. I'll call from your office if it's okay. Long-distance calls cost money and I can't afford them."

[98]

She quickly finished her plate and after cleaning her dishes went to his office. He could hear her talking rapidly in Spanish to someone. Figuring it might be a while, Des turned back to Hernando.

"I heard your mother call you 'Nando. Would it be alright for me to call you that?"

"Of course Mr. Edmonds, if that's what you want. My middle name is Eduardo, and she used to call me Eddie, until he left." He lowered his head as if suddenly remembering something very hurtful.

"What would you like me to call you? Anything you like?"

"I liked being called Eddie, like I was part of something then, if you don't mind Mr. Edmonds."

"Of course, Eddie, and when we're alone like this, just call me Des. That's what my friends call me, and because you saved my life, I consider you a good friend."

The moment was interrupted when Rosa returned with a scowl on her face and chattering something in Spanish. She stopped abruptly when she almost ran into Des, and quickly began telling him about how stupid that girl was to carry on with a married man. She realized what she was saying and stopped.

"I'm sorry Mr. Edmonds, but that girl is so stupid sometimes. The company you wanted to know about is having money problems, big money problems. They had three crews working full-time and now they only have the two carpenters working part-time on repair work. Something about a bond that can't be freed up because they haven't sold any houses. And another bond company won't touch them because the bank that has the papers on those houses said something about misrepresenting assets value. I'm not sure what that means, but I thought you would. That stupid girl, she's messing around with a married man. She finished school and got her degree, but she says she doesn't want to be a lawyer now, so she won't take the bar exam. What a stupid one."

"Rosa, thank you so much for your help. I'm going to tell you and Eddie to go home and have a nice dinner. And when you come back Wednesday you'll have some extra in your paycheck. Eddie, you be here at 9:00 a.m. in the morning."

Rosa looked at him with curiosity every time he said Eddie, but she didn't say anything. Des imagined Eddie would get an earful on the way home.

Des went back to work and soon found the bank that was holding the papers on all of Bryson Homes' properties. It must be my lucky day, he thought. He knew personally one of the board members and maybe he could get a little more information. The part that Rosa had said about misrepresenting assets might be helpful later. His third call got him through.

"God-damn secretaries, never seem to get it right as to who I want to talk to and who I don't," Jackson yelled into the speakerphone. "What can I do for you, Des? It's been quite some time, ever since your wife…well, anyway. What can I help you with?"

"First, pick up the phone, you sound like you're in a damn tunnel. And then tell me what you can about Bryson Homes Corporation. Are you and that blonde still married?"

"I'm having the secretary pull up the files on Bryson Homes and yes Cindy is still my wife, but she's a red-head, at least for this week. You remember that old song, that woman she gets meaner and uglier every day, but I still got her boy, and that makes me the Winner. Well, one of these days I'd like to lose. She's banging the pool boy and anyone else she can, daring me to say anything about it. Christ, I wish I'd taken your advice back then and made her sign the pre-nup, but she talked me out of it right after giving me one helluva blow job. Hold on a minute."

The phone automatically went to the elevator music that Des despised so much. It was two minutes later when Jackson came back on the line.

"Des, you and I go way back, so believe me when I say I will make copies of this entire file and overnight it to your office. But there's a couple things that may seem incriminating to me so I'm going to black-line those items. It might take two days."

"Send it to my home please. Are you still drinking single-malt scotch? I'll send it to your office. Thanks buddy."

Des decided it might not be a bad idea to find out what he could about Ellis Chambers, and his estate. His work on the internet was paying off, but he couldn't get any line on what Chambers was taking out of the mine and where he was having it assayed. On a hunch, he went to the map directions from Ridgecrest to Chambers' home in Pomona. After printing out the directions and a small map, he started looking for assayers. There were three assayers along the route and two of them were in Ridgecrest. Jake had mentioned a man named Stan Hobbs during their many conversations, so Des thought he might be able to use his knowledge of the assayers to good advantage.

His phone call paid off, Stan knew both assayers and also knew Ellis Chambers. He didn't think much of Chambers' mine or his mining abilities. He did tell Des which assayer had done the assays for Chambers. Stan also told him not to divulge any information that he wanted kept secret, the assayer had a big mouth and liked to impress people with how much he knew. Des thanked him and hung up after assuring him that what he'd said wouldn't be repeated. Stan felt much better after Des mumbled some words about attorney client relations, etc.

After some consideration, Des thought it might be time to contact Mr. Donald Bryson of Bryson Homes, Inc. The phone rang three times before a man answered.

"Hello?"

"Oh, yes, is this Bryson Homes Incorporated?"

"Yes, of course. The receptionist has the day off. This is Donald Bryson, how may I help you today? Are you interested in one of our premier homes?"

"No, Mr. Bryson. I represent a client who may be interested in a property your corporation owns. That is if the selling price is reasonable. The property is the Ellis Chambers mine. He's somewhat of a recluse and would like to use the mine as a home. Although he's not poor, he's not exactly rich either. He asked me to look into it as a possibility and so I am. Had you thought about selling that property?"

"Not really, who am I talking to?"

"I'm sorry, my name is Desmond Edmonds and I'm an attorney from San Bernardino where my client lives."

"Well Mr. Edmonds, I hadn't thought about selling it until just now. Let me get back to you and maybe we'll discuss this further. Can I call you tomorrow?"

"Just a moment," Des partially covered the mouthpiece on the phone with his palm and then mumbled, "but we have to be in Tonopah tomorrow, and Wednesday's when we go to the one down by Shoshone."

He uncovered the mouthpiece, certain that Bryson had heard every word and said, "Maybe it's better if I get back to you. My client is somewhat of a character and often he says things and then later doesn't follow through. How about I get back to you in a few days, and if he's still interested we'll set up a time and place to meet. Thank you for your time Mr. Bryson. Will you be in on Thursday?"

"Yes," Bryson quickly responded.

"Good. We'll call on Thursday." Des could feel the hook being set as he hung up the phone.

He quickly dialed Jackson's number again, and got through on the first try.

"Jackson, Des here. If Bryson contacts the bank regarding the value of the assets declared for his bonds, can you stall him for a few days? I'd like time to go through the files you're sending me before I deal with him."

"Sure Des. No problem. You got some kind of deal going on? If you need finance, make sure you call me personally. I'll be insulted if you don't. Talk to you in a few days."

Des looked further into the Ellis Chambers estate and the will. He found that Chambers also had two sons and they had inherited some adjoining claims for a total of 320 acres next to the 160 included in the mine. He started looking for the two of them and found the oldest, Ellis Jr., living in the same house as his father. Apparently the house was to be sold and the proceeds divided among the three, but Jr. wanted the house and made them offers which they accepted. He was still making payments on a first and second mortgage and from his income statement on the loans not making much money. He had no clue where the second brother, Elvan could be. He contacted a locating service he used in divorce cases sometimes and gave them the information he had on Elvan Chambers. They were pretty good at tracking people down.

He called Ellis Chambers Jr. and a young girl answered the phone.

"Hello?"

"Hello, is your father there?"

"Hello?"

"May I talk to your father?"

Before he heard another "Hello?" a woman grabbed the phone.

"Can I help you?"

"Yes, I'm trying to contact Ellis Chambers Jr. Is he available?"

"No, he's sleeping and I'm not waking him up. Who are you and what do you want?"

"My name is Mr. Edmonds and I'm an attorney. I need to talk to Mr. Chambers about a property that he inherited." He didn't get to finish his statement because the phone went dead. He tried calling back several times, but no one answered. He then thought of a way he could make sure Jr. would talk to him. He quickly wrote out a check for two hundred dollars to be paid to the order of Ellis Chambers Jr. and included a note that the money was for the task of talking to Mr. Edmonds for one hour, after which he would sign the check. He then put it in an overnight envelope and called them for pickup.

The other young Mr. Chambers was more of a challenge. He had disappeared about two years ago after a few minor run-ins with the LAPD. As he knew of no way to find out if a person was in prison, he called Julie. After explaining the situation, Des asked if she could help. She said she would, but only if he promised to take her with him on his next trip to Susanville.

"But you don't need to; I've got Eddie to drive me, or will have when he passes the test tomorrow. You are still taking him, aren't you?"

"Who are you referring to? I thought his name was Hernando."

"Oh, yes. It is. His full name is Hernando Eduardo Partida, but his mother called him Eddie up until the time his father left, said it sounded more American. Also, I'm the only one allowed to call him that and only in private. Sort of a bonding thing, he calls me Des in private and Mr. Edmonds the rest of the time. He saved my life you know."

"Yeah I know, now I have things to do. See you in the morning, love you."

"Yeah, love you too."

Des sat back in his chair, "Yes dear, it has been a really good day. I feel useful again. I think you'd like Jake, and Hernando, or Eddie."

CHAPTER SEVENTEEN

Jake awoke in a sweat. The nightmare this time was a whirlpool, swirling and pulling him into the darkness. He tried to cry out, but he couldn't make any sounds. He thrashed about in the water like a drowning man and it just kept sucking him in. He awoke just before it covered his head.

"Something the matter, man?" his new cell-mate asked. The man was medium build and blacker than any man Jake had ever seen. He kept his head shaved as well as his face, and Jake could see lots of scars on both. He had only briefly glimpsed the man's torso, but there were scars there as well.

"Bad dream," Jake managed to squeak out. His throat was parched dry, and his body was hot. He rolled off his bunk and reached over and turned on the water. He managed to get a few handfuls into his mouth. He lay back down on his bunk not wanting to go to sleep again.

"My grandma said that sometimes dreams can be warnings, depends on what they are and all."

"Did your grandma say anything about dreams that you have that later come true?" Jake asked.

There was a long silence. Then a cautious reply, "It sounds like maybe you got the gift. She always say that folks can see what's comin' in they dreams got the gift."

"I'm not so sure that's true. Sometimes I see things happening and know when and where I saw it before, but other times it's like I know what's going to happen and can't do anything about it. By the way, they didn't tell me your name, or should I just call you 'Hey you'?"

"My name is Josiah Albert Robertson. The Josiah is from the Bible, 'cause my grandma is real religious. Albert was part of my father's name, or so my mama says. His last name was Robertson, which makes sense 'cause lots of white folks had their slaves take the family name kind of as part of they ownership an' such. The white Robertsons was part of the Klan and they took it serious. If they seen a black man even lookin' wrong at a white girl, they'd hang him."

[105]

Jake listened carefully and noticed how Josiah slipped in and out of the slang talk as if it were amusing to him. He kept the thought to himself.

"What should I call you? Any name you prefer over another?"

"Josiah, or Joe. Either will do."

"Okay, Joe it is. My name is Jake Kozan. I don't know what all the names were for or where they are from, except my middle name Aaron is my mother's father's name. Most people call me Jake; sometimes they call me other names."

Josiah laughed, and it was a deep laugh, honest and strong. "I heard them call you Rabbi. What is that about? Are you a rabbi?"

"No. It's something the head of the Aryan Brotherhood decided to call me. He thought it sounded more mystical and religious. He said most prisoners won't attack a man of God. I think he's full of shit." Jake almost felt the tension in Josiah at the mention of the Aryan Brotherhood. He decided to take a different course in talking with Joe.

"It seems odd to me, Josiah, that they would house you in the same cell as me who is supposedly a White Supremacist. Why do you think they did that? Is there a reason you know of why they would do that?"

The silence lasted for a while. When he did reply, Josiah's voice was level and calm as if he had rehearsed this part before. "I was told that if you did anything that could be called racist, or acted in a manner that was not correct, I am to file a claim of racism against you no matter how thin the charge. I was told that they would consider reducing the time I was to serve if I could come up with something against you."

"I appreciate your honesty. So when do you want to start filing charges? Should I just start right now calling you coon, or nigger, maybe jigaboo? Just think, if you're really good at writing, you could be out of here in a week, nigger."

"You're trying to bait me, Jake. I already know about your martial arts abilities and I may not be able to take you in a fight, but you'll know I was there."

[106]

"You're right Joe. You probably won't take me in a fight. I don't want to fight. I want out and whoever sent you would be better off just leaving me alone and let me do my time. There isn't much time left for me to do, so why don't they just leave me alone? And Joe? From now on quit the ghetto nigger act, your education shows whether you like it or not. What is it? A bachelor's degree and maybe working on your master's? And if your name really is Robertson, I know more about your family ancestry than you do. My wife's mother was a Robertson and very much into genealogy. So from now on, boy, stay out of my way."

"Joe, one other thing, it's very dangerous playing both sides. My advice is to choose which side you think is right and play for them. You might live longer that way."

Jake rolled over on his side and was asleep in a minute. He woke refreshed as if he'd not had the nightmare at all. Joe and he didn't talk to each other. Jake didn't even think Joe was really a prisoner, which left him wondering who was behind this whole mess.

Out on the yard the four men were already at their spot when Jake got there. They did a quick warm-up routine and started into the exercise program. Today they weren't complaining at all which seemed unusual. At the end of the first set Jake called a halt, and gathered them close.

"We need to move our martial arts along faster than we've been doing. Tomorrow, I want each of you to bring four more of the Brotherhood to start training. You each will train four men and then when they are trained they will each select four men. In this way we will be up to where we need to be if we're to take on the Outlaws." Jake said the last part specifically for Collier's benefit. He now knew that Collier was a plant by the Outlaws, from the files that Tyler had given him. He also knew that Collier was being enrolled in the Firefighter class each year and supposedly out on the line as well. As the senior guard was the only one who did the paperwork, nobody ever questioned it.

After explaining how each of them would have first a squad and then a platoon to be in charge of there was a different attitude in their training. Now they were doing all that Jake asked and then some. They pushed harder and harder all morning and were reluctant to stop when it was lunchtime. They left after his usual "Stand together and stand proud." He was about to leave towards the mess hall when a guard stopped him.

"Your friend from the Outlaws will be back on the yard tomorrow. Just thought you might want to know," the guard whispered.

Jake bent down as if to tie his shoe and said, "Thanks, how's Crenshaw?"

"Good," he said quietly, then much louder, "Now get!"

"Yes sir." And Jake was on his way to lunch. Now he had another problem to try and solve. Things were way too complicated and he just wanted out. Right now he'd like to be in the orchard picking up pistachios with the crew. Anything but this rodeo he was in now.

He sat at the same table he always did, but today no one else was there. He sensed something was going to happen, but had no idea what it could be. So much for his magic powerful dreams, he thought to himself. He looked around and saw the two bodyguards posted near his table. They were the same ones as usual. Nothing else was out of place that he could tell. Damn Kozan, you're acting like an old woman, he thought. Next he'd be turning over tarot cards or tossing chicken bones. He laughed at himself, but for some reason the creepy feeling wouldn't leave him. Maybe the dream last night was having an effect after all.

Back on the yard, the four men were already going through a set of martial arts moves, very slowly and smoothly. It looked almost like a ballet troupe at practice. Yes, that's it. I'll show them how fighting is like a dance. Just then he was interrupted by the voice of the Reverend.

"What do you mean you want sixteen more men out here doing this fairy dance shit?"

"Excuse me Reverend; I'll be just a moment." He went to the men and told them what the Reverend had said and asked what they thought of it. Sorenson replied that maybe the Reverend needed a first-hand demonstration.

[108]

When Jake proposed the idea to the Reverend he thought the Reverend would turn it down. But he knew the Reverend couldn't refuse for fear that the men would then consider him a pussy. After all, he was taller than Sorenson and slightly heavier, so he should have an advantage. Quickly, the Reverend took off his coat and stood there as if waiting. Sorenson circled warily and feinted a few jabs at his opponent, being cautious.

"C'mon pussy," the Reverend yelled. "Just like when you first joined us, scared shitless and nowhere to run." The jab from Sorenson caught him on the mouth and it stung. It also drew blood, something the Reverend wasn't used to and he attacked violently, swinging with both hands but not connecting. He looked and Sorenson was on his left side standing and then suddenly jabbing again. His first and second jabs were blocked but not the third. It connected hard. Reverend attacked again, but this time cautiously and was promptly thrown to the ground. Sorenson was on him immediately, his hand at the Reverend's throat, his other drawn back as if to strike.

"That's enough." Jake called. He helped the Reverend to his feet and Sorenson helped to brush the dirt off. "I hope our little demonstration was enough to show the value of our training, sir. And we do appreciate you joining in on our exercise. The men are glad to know that you're not afraid to mix it up if necessary, right men?"

"Yes sir!" they responded loudly. The Reverend looked at Sorenson skeptically, not sure it was the same person he'd known before. He wiped the blood from his mouth on his sleeve which prompted Ernst to give him his handkerchief.

"Use this sir, blood is hard to wash out. Please, sir."

"Yes, thank you. I see your training is coming along better than I thought. Very good, men. Jake, Can I talk to you?"

When they were alone, the Reverend turned on Jake. "You suckered me, you bastard. You knew I couldn't refuse without losing the men's respect. That was a raw play."

"Quit your damn crying, you dumb shit, I just did you a huge favor. Men will only follow a leader they respect or admire. Up until now, you had neither from them. If I had challenged you, it would be expected of me to win. As it is now, you stood in there with one of the men and although you got whipped, you didn't back down. Now they'll follow you no matter what because they know now that you won't back down. If they thought you were a coward, how long do you think you'd be in charge, let alone in one piece? Not long. You just got a whole bunch of good PR among your own men. Now shut up and leave me alone. Do I get the additional men in the morning or not?"

"Yes." Reverend's voice was nearly a whisper. "I don't know why I just didn't have you killed. You're a real pain in the ass."

Jake laughed out loud causing the men to look their way. "You already tried that."

After the Reverend left, the men worked like they were on drugs or something. They did set after set of exercises and then double sets of the martial arts. Jake looked over at the weight-lifting area and saw a couple of the Outlaws trying to imitate the moves the men were doing but to no avail. Before the men quit, they were all sweating profusely, even Ernst. They all left towards their cells, except Ernst, who waited for a few minutes then headed toward the Education Office. Jake headed back to his cell to clean up before dinner. When he got there he looked at his bunk and could tell someone had been searching for something. Or maybe not, maybe they were putting something in his bunk. He went carefully, slowly so he didn't miss anything. He found a shiv tucked into the corner of his mattress. From the type of metal, it looked like it came from the welding shop area. He wrapped it in tissue and tucked it in his shoe before heading to dinner.

This evening instead of sitting where he usually did, he went to the table where the big man, Davis was sitting. He sat down uninvited at the one empty chair and began to eat his dinner. Davis stared at him in disbelief.

"Have you gone totally suicidal Rabbi? What are you doing here?"

"I thought I'd be nice and check how your arm is healing. If you like, I could show you some exercises that will help speed up the healing. But you probably know all those already. How is it feeling?"

Davis looked at him for a long time before he replied. "You are either the craziest son-of-a-bitch I've ever met, or you've got a huge pair of balls. What the hell do you care about my arm? You're the bastard that caused this."

"Not true, my friend. If you will recall, you attacked me and I defended myself. But that doesn't matter now. I really don't like hurting people, and I really am sorry that it came to violence. I would like to talk to you about this person you are sending against me. It's my understanding that he is supposed to either kill me or put me out of commission. Is that true?"

"Yeah, that's it. He owes us and to pay off his debt, he's to take you out. Either way is fine by us."

"Just suppose I don't want to fight him? What happens then? How will you collect your debt? I don't suppose you've thought about him losing, have you? What happens if we fight and he loses?"

Davis thought for moment. "If he loses, he still owes the debt. He won't lose. I've seen him before and he's too good to lose. And you'll fight; we'll make sure of that."

"Yes, I see. It looks as if you've got it all figured. You are smarter than I thought. By the way, how much is his debt?"

Davis was drinking when Jake asked the last question and nearly sprayed liquid all over. "What?" he gasped.

"How much is the debt? I may want to buy him from you and put him to work for me."

"You ain't got that kind of money Rabbi, unless you have an extra fifty thousand dollars just hanging around. I know from your canteen fund you don't have hardly any money, and that lawyer ain't the big money kind. Deputy Warden told me your lawyer hadn't had a case in nearly five years until he got yours. Don't even think about bull-shitting me about what you've got or ain't got."

Jake said nothing at first, and then he smiled. "Well it was just an idea. I didn't realize it would be that much. I thought it would be less. Have a nice day Mr. Davis, and if you want those exercises, I'll be happy to show them to you. I know one that will help that twitch in your shoulder muscle. Have a good day." He got up and left quickly. At the tray return he dumped the tissue-wrapped shiv in the garbage.

When he returned to his cell he was told to wait outside. He sat down as instructed and waited. A half hour later they came out of his cell, and Jake saw they were pissed off.

"We were informed you had contraband in your cell. We were unable to find any restricted items. You may now return to your cell."

"Yes sir, thank you sir." Jake smiled, but inside he was ice-cold. What if they didn't find what they wanted and planted something else for a later shake-down? That would be very likely if they were trying to frame him for something.

He looked at Joe or Josiah standing against the wall near the toilet. His face was calm, but he was a lousy poker player. His eyes kept wandering back and forth around the room. Everywhere except the bunk. Jake started cleaning up and putting away his belongings, saving the bunk for last. He had decided since their first conversation not to speak or talk around Joe. He finished refolding his uniforms and underwear, and started making the bunk. He flipped the mattress over, and pretending to fluff what filling there was he patted the entire mattress down. They had placed it back in the same place, but this time it was made of hard plastic.

He waited until lights out and then with toilet tissue he wiped and then wrapped the shiv and went to the door. There was room under the door to slide the shiv out, but Jake gave it a hard shove and was satisfied when he heard the clatter as it hit the floor below. Now he could go to sleep, maybe.

In a few minutes the lights on his tier came on and shortly the cell door was opened. He did as instructed and placed his hands on the wall for the mandatory pat-down, which didn't seem necessary. He was wearing underwear and nothing else. The guards instructed him to wait outside the cell, and this time Joe got the same instructions. Jake just smiled at Joe and sat down. Might as well be comfortable during this performance he thought.

He put his arms on his knees and then his head on his arms. He nearly fell asleep before they finished tossing the room. This time they went through everything including Joe's belongings. Joe had a sour look on his face when he looked at Jake. Just for fun, Jake thought he'd throw a zinger toward Joe.

"What's the matter snitch? Didn't find what they were supposed to? Maybe if you knew what a real con thinks like, you wouldn't be so stupid."

"Oh shut up."

"Whatever you say, snitch." He laughed and started putting away his clothes. He finished long before Joe, and lay there watching. Whatever he'd been, he wasn't military, and not a convict. Jake couldn't help but wonder about all those scars.

Joe then said something curious, "I really do like the dark."

Jake was puzzled, there was almost a sound of familiarity to his remark, but he couldn't quite place it.

CHAPTER EIGHTEEN

Des was reading the newspaper and working on his second cup of coffee when heard the knock on the door. He was about to get up when he heard the keys and Rosa's voice.

"It's just me Mr. Edmonds, and Hernando. He wanted to come by early to study some more before the test. He wanted to ask Julie about the driving test. He hasn't driven a car very much so he wanted to try hers a little bit before."

Des glanced at Hernando behind Rosa and started to turn back to his paper and then stopped. He looked and was astonished. Hernando or Eddie had his hair cut and was wearing dark colored slacks and a medium blue long-sleeve shirt. It was buttoned at the cuffs and also at the collar. He had on brown shoes and a brown belt.

"Wow, you look sharp Hernando. May I make one suggestion?"

"Yes, sir, anything you want Mr. Edmonds."

"Unbutton the collar button, and you'll feel more comfortable, unless you were planning on wearing a tie. I'm not sure how to say this, but when you wear your collar like that people will associate you with the gang-bangers. If you dress well, people will treat you better no matter what your background. Also, you might want to think about the ear-ring, it doesn't quite fit with the rest of your attire."

"Do you have a tie I could borrow, please Mr. Edmonds?"

"Certainly, come with me." And he headed towards his bedroom, but Eddie stopped as if frozen to the spot. The bedroom was where Eddie had taken most of items he'd been caught with. "Come on," Des said. "There's nothing in there that will bite you." They both laughed and then went in.

When they returned, Rosa took one look and started crying. Des and Eddie were both confused, having no idea what brought that on. Des, being older and having seen things like this before suggested that Hernando help him make a fresh pot of coffee.

"What's that all about? Did I do something wrong?" Hernando asked.

"No, Eddie. She just saw her baby boy turn into a full-grown man and right now she's crying tears of joy. You'll see more of this stuff as you grow older."

"You're a smart man Mr. Edmonds, a smart man."

"Not really, Eddie. I've just seen a lot over the years. Have you thought about what you want to do when you get older? What do you want to be?"

Eddie was about to answer when Julie opened the door. "Wow, you really clean up good Hernando. And a tie just like the one I bought Dad two years ago. Wow."

"Thank you Miss Julie, would you like a cup of coffee? We just finished brewing it."

"Oh my, and manners too, you were right Dad, he really is a gentleman," and then she laughed as Hernando blushed. She tucked his arm in hers and said, "Coffee it shall be, my handsome prince." This time they both laughed.

Des sat down to his now cold cup of coffee. "Hey," he yelled at the kitchen, "Can an old man get a hot cup of coffee around here?" Rosa was quick to gather his cup and as she turned Des could see the beam of happiness on her face. When she came back she whispered, "Thank you so much Mr. Edmonds. He is very happy that you like the clothes he picked out, he was so worried."

"Rosa, if I give you a check, will you be able to cash it and see it gets to him so he can buy more clothes like those and maybe a nice jacket too? Do not tell him I gave you the money, it would hurt his pride. Tell him you're loaning it to him and he has to pay it back when he starts earning some money. When he is driving for me, I want him to dress well. It shows he cares about his personal appearance and has self-respect. It may not be right, but you are judged by how you look, dress, and talk. If he dresses in a manner befitting the job, he will feel more comfortable. There will be times when he will accompany me to meetings and act as my assistant, and in so doing will be able to meet some very important people. How he conducts himself in these situations will help him later on when he may be sent to do business on my behalf. If these important people understand that he is my associate and not just an employee, he will have a big advantage over others his age. He's a very good young man Rosa, and I owe him my life. He has lots of opportunities ahead of him, and I do want to see him succeed."

Julie and Hernando came back in the room just after Des finished talking. He winked at Rosa and she laughed.

"What's going on in here?" Hernando asked, puzzled.

Before Des could answer, Rosa rattled off a string of Spanish that apparently made Hernando stand up very straight, with a somber look on his face.

"Yes Mama," was all he said. And then Julie took his arm again and out the door they went. Julie was running down a list of do's and don'ts concerning her car, Hernando looking more confused as she talked.

Des went back to his coffee and Rosa back to cleaning, both of them waiting to hear if Hernando would pass his test. In the back of his mind Des said a small prayer on Eddie's behalf. Des wasn't sure what to say so he just asked God to please help him.

He was wondering what he should do next when the package from Jackson arrived. It made for lots of interesting reading, and even after only a few pages Des could see that Mr. Bryson was a con artist. Quite a few of the assets listed were also listed as assets in a couple of enterprises that were subsidiaries of Bryson Homes, Inc. The most interesting part of the file was the part concerning the mine. Des saw that Bryson had claimed an asset value of $750,000 for the mine based on certain assays provided by the same assayer Stan Hobbs had warned Des about. It was beyond belief based on what Jake had told him about the type of mineral there, and what he and TJ had learned by taking some samples the first time they visited the mine. If Des remembered correctly Jake put the value in the $15,000 to $20,000 range. Maybe it was time to visit the assayer and see if Jake's estimate matched the information the assayer had.

Des kept reading through the rest of the file and found another tid-bit that would serve him well. Not long ago, the EPA began requiring mine owners to post a "remediation bond" to continue operations. The EPA set the amount of the bond on their estimate of costs to remediate the mine and surrounding area in the event that the mine-owner didn't have the funds. Because Bryson had set the asset value so high, the EPA had set a high bond. The annual premium wasn't a killer, but it was expensive. Bryson was in double trouble because the bonding company that provided his bond for the mine had learned about the bonding company that provided the bond for his construction company, and they compared assets. As a result, the construction company bond was suspended and also his ability to draw funds from the bank. To say he was in a tight spot was a severe understatement. Des kept writing note after note, feeling he would need them later in the week. Des was just about finished with the mine file when the door burst open and Hernando was running around the room.

"I got it! I got my license! Mr. Edmonds, I got it! Look. It's got my picture on it and my birthday, but I really don't like that picture. I got it! Yeah, oh and thank you Mr. Edmonds and Julie, you too! Look Mama, I got my license!" Hernando was wound up like never before, Rosa just stood there not knowing what to do or say.

Julie came in, "he only missed one question on the written test. He scored a 97 on the driving test. You should be proud of him Dad."

"I am Julie. I am. Now he's got work to do." At that Eddie's face fell.

"I know, Mr. Edmonds, back to painting. I'll go home and change."

"Not today Hernando, today we've got some different homework to do. Rosa, can we get some lunch or should we order Chinese for a celebration?"

He got a resounding "Chinese" as a response. Rosa told him to let her call it in. Des didn't argue, he was too happy to argue with anyone. Rosa came back and told him it would be fifteen dollars and five for the delivery boy.

"Why so cheap?" he asked.

"The cook is a friend. He knows me from my home town in Mexico."

[117]

They had a lively lunch, talking about all different subjects. Hernando hadn't finished high school, and both Des and Julie jumped on him about needing to finish his education, telling him how important it is to have. Rosa agreed with them and even said how stupid she'd been to give up going to school. After lunch Julie left after giving her "handsome prince" a kiss on the cheek and a big hug. Des and Hernando went to the office to talk about what they would be doing in the next few weeks. Des had just started laying out the plan Jake had to buy the mine out in the desert, when Margaret called.

"Mr. Edmonds? I have the information you needed to know about the harvest workers. TJ always hired six workers to harvest the pistachios, four on the sheets, one on the shaker, and one on the tractor pulling the trailer with the sheets. TJ drove the truck and the forklift himself to save labor. It took two weeks start to finish, and he paid two dollars over minimum wage. That way he got better workers. I've also got the place he'd call to have the workers sent out for him to choose. He always picked the workers himself. If you want, I can mail it to you."

"Margaret, do you have a fax or access to a fax? If you do just fax it to me, I'd like to be there on Friday." He gave her the fax number and said good-bye.

Des went back to the files on Bryson and laid out the plan to Eddie. They decided to do the same as they'd done to the car salesman, but with a different twist. Instead of saying a number, Eddie would "fumble" some of the papers so that a 'note' page on a legal pad would be on top of a stack of papers that Eddie set on Bryson's desk. He was to leave it there and Des would look at it, after an appropriate time lapse, and quickly pick it up. Des wrote it out in large letters so it couldn't be misread, the phone number of a realtor, Shoshone, 9600 +/-, Tuesday. They practiced 'the school play' as Des liked to call it for a couple of times, until they were confident in their parts.

"Is this how they normally do business, Des?" Eddie asked. "Why don't we just make an offer of what we want to pay?"

"Normally I would do just that, Eddie. But we're dealing with a person who lies and cheats, so therefore we have to use a little

[118]

deception ourselves. You can look in the files, but they will only confirm what I'm telling you. He misrepresented his assets to gain an advantage, or so he thought. Now he's in a bind, and needs all the money he can get his hands on. He cheated on his wife and she divorced him, and in the process got a very nice alimony and child support settlement, based on his past year's income. This year isn't so good, but he still has to pay that amount. He could go to court to ask for a review, but he can't afford the legal fees right now. If we let him see there may be other properties we have in mind, he'll probably accept our offer."

"How much are you going to offer him?"

"We, Eddie, we, you're part of this group now, like it or not. I was going to start at fifteen thousand, but now I'll probably start at twelve thousand five hundred. I may end up as high as twenty thousand, if he knows about the water. We won't discuss the fact that there's water there unless asked directly. Then we'll say we were aware of it, but that it isn't enough to support mining operations, we still have to import water."

"Mining? Is that what we're going to be doing? I know it's a mine, but I didn't think about mining. Is there gold there?"

"From what Jake told me, there is a minimal amount of gold in the type of mineral they were mining previously. He said it isn't enough to make a living; he just wants the property as a place to live. He plans on building his house out there. He really loves it out in the desert, says he likes the solitude."

"Solitude? What's that mean Des?"

"It means being alone, Eddie, which is funny, because people just like to be around him. He has a quality of being able to listen to people. I really like him Eddie. I think you will too when you meet him."

"I know Julie likes him. She was talking about him while I was waiting to take my test. I think she's sweet on him."

"Well how about that." Des mused. "Now, Mr. Licensed Driver Hernando Eduardo Partida, it's time for you to escort your mother home. Oh, tomorrow you will need to go shopping with your mother and get some more clothes like those. We'll be taking a trip on Thursday and maybe staying overnight, so you'll

[119]

need a couple of changes of clothes, and a suitcase. And Eddie, please shave those three whiskers off your chin." At the last Des grinned at him and Eddie laughed.

"Yes sir, Mr. Edmonds, sir," he replied and then saluted. This time they both laughed.

A good day, Des thought, a good day indeed, and Julie sweet on Jake? I guess that wouldn't be the worst thing that could happen.

CHAPTER NINETEEN

Jake didn't wait when he saw Alex headed towards him. "Guard, that man is trying to kill me."

"What?" the guard asked. "What are you saying?"

Jake pointed at Alex and said, "That man is trying to kill me. The Outlaws want me dead, and he's supposed to do it."

The guard looked at Jake like he was something really bad. What Jake had just done went against the very essence of the convicts. He had just snitched on another con and in public. "He hasn't done anything to you. Now get away from me, you're supposed to be a bad-ass, fight your own fights." He started to walk away.

"You don't turn your back on me," Jake yelled. He then ran toward the guard and jumped at him with both feet together. He was hoping the guard was quick enough to counter the move and he was right. The guard side-stepped and drew his baton and swung towards Jake's head, but Jake caught it on the shoulder. It still hurt, but at least he was conscious. Jake said, "I quit," before the guard could swing again. By then there were two more guards and they proceeded to rough him up while putting the cuffs and ankle bracelets on. Jake was smiling, hoping assault on a guard was worth at least two weeks in the solitary. Maybe they'd be less hard on him because of his actions regarding guard Crenshaw.

As he was being taken away, he could see Sorenson taking charge. He was sure that Sorenson could handle the job, especially with Ernst helping him. Ernst didn't like Collier, and the feeling was mutual. Smith was the wild card. He didn't say much and only spoke when spoken to. From what Jake could tell Smith was maybe the most intelligent of the three, with Sorenson coming in second. Smith was arrested for assault, a second time offender. Both times were for attacking the same man. Smith's claim was that the man didn't pay up on a gambling debt, twice.

Jake felt like Br'er Rabbit while he sat through the prison's version of a trial. Inside he was saying to himself, "please don't throw me in that briar patch," while on the outside he was trying to act defiant and belligerent towards the guards. They ended up giving him two weeks in solitary, which was what he'd been hoping for. He almost started singing Zippedy-Doo-Da on his way to the cell.

After they had him in his cell, the guard told him to stand away from the door. Jake was cautious when the guard started into his cell preceded by a new mattress. Prisoners in solitary didn't normally get mattresses; they slept on the steel bunk. It was flat steel slab bolted to the wall, welded completely at all seams so none of it could be made into a weapon. The guard pulled the plastic wrapping off the mattress and tossed it on the bunk. "Mr. Crenshaw said to say thanks," the guard said. Jake noticed it was the same guard who had waited in the room when Margaret had visited.

"Tell the guard I supposedly attacked it wasn't personal, I just needed some time alone so I can think things through. People were coming at me from all sides, too fast. And that convict Alex, really is going to try to kill me. Would you see if you can get the Reverend down here to talk to me?" Jake asked.

"I'll try, but I don't promise anything. I can't afford to lose my job over you."

The guard left and Jake began to plan his strategy for getting Alex out of this place in one piece. That would be one piece of the puzzle; another would be how to wipe out the debt he owed without breaking the bank. He had a faint plan in the back of his mind, and he started thinking more and more how it might work to accomplish both things at the same time, if he could get the Reverend to help without double-crossing him. It could be done, but he would need to involve several different people. One thing was absolutely sure. He couldn't trust Collier and the whole plan would explode in their faces if Collier was told any part of it. One part of the plan was to weaken Alex, and he knew how to do it. Just as he thought of it, he also thought they might try doing the same thing to him.

"Guard," he called, "Can I talk to you?"

He called a second time and then a third before he remembered that they came by the cell every fifteen minutes. When he heard someone approaching, he called out again.

"Yes?" the guard answered. Jake was in luck, it was still the same guard.

"Are you married?" Jake asked.

"What?" the guard came back, puzzled as to why Jake would ask a question like that. "Yes I am, why do you want to know?"

"I was hoping you were. Is she a good cook?"

"Yeah, I think so," the guard was hesitant, still curious why Jake was asking these questions.

"That's great," Jake said sincerely. He then laid out the facts about Alex owing a debt to the Outlaws and to pay off he was supposed to cripple or kill Jake. Jake was worried that the Outlaws might not be patient enough to wait until he got out of solitary and might try to poison him in here. Jake said he'd be willing to pay his wife for the meals, at which the guard said no, and walked away.

Fifteen minutes later Jake apologized to the guard, saying he wasn't trying to bribe him, but just give him enough money to pay for the food. The guard just looked at him and walked away again. Jake didn't hear from him again until almost end of shift.

"If you can figure out a way to pay my wife while you're in here, I'll bring you the food before my shift each day. Days I'm off, you'll be on your own, maybe Crenshaw will bring them to you. If he says yes, we'll do it. Now how do figure to pay my wife from here?"

Jake told him about Des and gave him Des's phone number and a code word to use, so Des would know it came from Jake. Jake asked the guard his name.

"Sam, Sam Battiste," he replied.

"Well Sam Battiste, whatever happens, please don't get in trouble over me, and tell Crenshaw the same thing. I don't want you to lose your job."

Sam left and Jake went back to his plan. Each step must be perfect, and also have a contingency in case it didn't go quite 'perfect'. One by one he went down the list, even to the people he could use. Each person must know his assignment, and what the back-up plan was to be. Some parts would be started right away; others would take a little longer to develop. First was to get to the Reverend, and let him know about Collier being a snitch for the Outlaws. As to whether he could be used or not would depend on how the Reverend felt about the plan. In the meantime, there wasn't much to do except eat, sleep, and exercise. As it wasn't mealtime, and he wasn't sleepy, so he began to exercise. He knew from the brief encounter with Alex previously, he would need all the strength he had. He pushed himself to the point of exhaustion before dinner. He would take a chance on this meal, and hopefully Des would get the money to Sam's wife right away.

Jake ate sparingly, chewing slowly and cautiously, nearly paranoid now that his mind was fixed on the idea of poison. Stop this nonsense, he told himself, but that nagging suspicion was still there. His stomach began to rumble deep down and he thought to himself, this it I'm going to die. He then farted loudly, and couldn't help but start laughing out loud. You damn fool, he thought, your imagination is going to scare you to death if you don't stop acting like an idiot.

He began recalling all the times he'd seen Alex fight, and there were several. Most of them ended quickly, abruptly. Alex wasn't one to waste time or energy. There were a few that were quite long and one in particular that Alex nearly lost. Jake remembered that Alex had a tendency to adopt a boxer's stance most of the time and would revert to that after a flurry of activity. Also his footwork was negligible, as he relied on more boxing and karate skills than anything else. Very seldom was he prone to try kick-boxing or moves using the feet or legs. Jake thought if he could take Alex's legs out from under him he might win this fight. Still, he knew Alex, and there was no quit in the man. He would keep fighting even while flat on his back. The key would be to take out his legs, but there wasn't room to practice in the tiny cell he was in now. He had to figure a way to get somewhere that nobody could know what he was practicing, and that had room for him to practice. He continued to exercise until lights out, knowing the guard in the hall would be reporting everything he did. Jake just didn't know who the guard would report to; he left it at that until morning.

Jake slept peacefully until about five in the morning. He awoke then, refreshed, ready to go to work. He knew he had almost two hours before his morning meal, so he put together a list of his 'top ten' exercises to do. He had finished twenty repetitions of each one twice and was ready to start on a third set when he heard a rap on the cell door. He was hoping to see the Reverend through the small window, but it was Sam Battiste. He had a package in his hand and was unlocking the portal. When he got the portal open, he slipped the package in and said, "Enjoy," and relocked the portal.

"How did you do that so soon? I didn't think Des could get any funds transferred until maybe tomorrow. What happened?"

"A courier came to the house about two hours after I talked to your Mr. Edmonds. He asked for the wife by name, and had her count out the money and then sign for it. There were instructions on what to do if we didn't use all the funds, and a number to call here locally if we needed more money. We told Mr. Edmonds we only wanted a hundred dollars, but he sent us a thousand, my wife cried, she was so happy. She's seven months along with our first and she can't work, so money's been tight. She's a clerk at Safeway and with both our paychecks we do alright, but she's worried. Jake, we can't take that much money, it wouldn't be right, I wouldn't feel right."

"Then consider it a loan until she has the baby and is back to work. Then you can start paying me back. But she still gets paid for making my food, okay?"

Sam mumbled a thank you through the door, but Jake was too busy eating some home-made bread with real butter to hear. The breakfast burrito had real meat and eggs with peppers. Jake was going to get fat like this but he didn't care. Jake ate quickly so they could get rid of the evidence before anyone came around. When his breakfast meal came, Jake was glad he'd had the other. The only thing he ate or actually drank was the carton of juice, but only after inspecting it for pin-holes. He mentioned it to Sam about the juice and Sam said he'd make sure it was there in the morning, and he was sorry that lunch was going to be a cold sandwich. Jake waved it off saying how grateful he was to have someone like Sam and his wife to count on.

Jake went about his planning and did some more exercises to pass the time. Sam passed in the hall as regular as could be. They had decided to wait until after the noon meal to have that 'cold sandwich', that way they wouldn't be rushed. Jake tasted the sandwich, and was surprised. It was made on home-made bread with roast beef and a slice of cheddar cheese, and something Jake hadn't had since going to prison, mustard. He savored every bite.

Another part of the plan was going to start at the noon meal. Sam's duty was to report what the prisoners ate and how much. He was also to inventory each item in and out of the cell like before. This time Jake would 'eat' a little of each item and send the rest back, but actually the food he supposedly ate went down the toilet. In that way it would seem that they were getting to him if they were actually poisoning him, and if not, it would appear as if he were sick.

The noon meal came and went and the Reverend still hadn't made an appearance. Jake asked Sam about it and was told that yes, he had passed the word along to a Collier out by the bleachers. That explained why he hadn't seen the Reverend, he thought, and he asked Sam to talk to Ernst this time. He described him to Sam, and Sam said he knew Ernst from an incident involving a homosexual. Ernst had picked him up in both arms and shook him 'like a doll' and broke the man's back. Sam said he'd get the message to Ernst but he didn't like the idea.

"Just tell him that Jake thinks he's doing a good job, and keep up the good work, you'll see a whole different person."

Sam went on with his rounds and Jake returned to his exercises. He found that if he removed the mattress from the bunk and doubled it, he could use it like a heavy bag for his practice kicks. He propped it against the wall on the bunk and by standing on the bunk he had room enough to swing his leg full length. This way no one would see what type of exercises or movements he was doing. Now he didn't need a larger room and he didn't involve anyone else, the less people that knew what he was doing, the better. He remembered what his father had told him after one of his brothers had told everyone about a 'secret' that Jake had shared with him. "If you have a secret and keep it to yourself, it stays a secret. If you tell someone else, then it's no longer a secret."

Jake thought about the Reverend and wondered just how much he could tell him of the plan. He still wasn't sure there was any real trust between them, so he decided to only divulge the parts necessary to get the Reverend's help. He would need him to have someone 'doctor' Alex's food, as well as set up the fight and the bets. If he could get Sam to 'divulge' the information about Jake not eating well, that would help boost the odds in Alex's favor. Hopefully, it would go as high as three to one in favor of Alex. Jake needed to be the underdog here, just in case he lost. He heard Sam coming down the hall and was about to call out to him when he heard, "Prisoner, stand away from the door." He did as told and was against the far wall when the door opened. Another guard entered the cell first, baton in hand. Then Sam entered, and the look on his face was all business. Sam instructed Jake to "assume the position" and spread his legs, Jake complied, curious as to why the pat down. The new guard watched closely as Sam did a completely thorough frisking of Jake.

"Very well," the new guard stated. "Has the prisoner exhibited any violent or unusual behavior?"

"No sir. None at all," Sam responded.

"Your report shows the prisoner having only eaten part of his meal, any explanation for that, guard."

"No sir, he said he wasn't hungry, sir"

"I see. I will need a full report after each meal. I won't have some convict going on a hunger strike on my watch, do you understand?"

"Yes sir. I'll see to it that the prisoner eats each and every meal even if I have to feed him myself, sir."

At that last comment Jake almost snickered, but caught it in time. After the two of them of them left, Jake thought that maybe he wasn't so paranoid after all with his ideas about poison in the food. It might be to his advantage if they thought he was eating the meals. They would assume that the poison was working, if their plan was the same as what he had planned for Alex. The thought of actually being poisoned with their intent to kill him resurfaced. Maybe if it was noted that he threw up after one or two of the meals they might back off. He'd have to wait to see how it worked out.

Jake was frustrated. He needed the time alone to exercise and to plan, but he also wanted to be out there getting the plan moving. It was frustrating having to rely on others to do what he preferred to do in person. He didn't trust the Reverend at all, he trusted Ernst, but Ernst could easily be tricked into giving up information that needed to be kept secret, and he couldn't involve Sam. He didn't want to take the chance that Sam might get caught and then fired, or even worse, put in jail. Prisoners don't take kindly to former guards who are sent to prison. Their life expectancy was shorter than a side of beef among a pack of wolves.

It was an hour before lights out that he heard a tap on the door. Jake wasn't familiar with the guard on this shift, so he backed to the other end of the cell.

The "stand away from the door," was barely heard, but he responded with a "Yes sir," and watched as the cell door opened, it was the Reverend. He turned and said something to the guard, who in turn replied, "thirty minutes, no more."

"What's going on Jake? My men are out there training themselves, which means you're not doing what we agreed to. You want to explain that?"

"Be glad to," Jake said. "I needed the time alone to plan, and maybe do some exercising of my own. I have a plan that may take the Outlaws down quite a ways, if not completely out of the way."

Jake explained the parts of the plan that he needed the Reverend's help on. Making Alex sick and/or weak would help insure that Jake would win. An old trick was to add soap to his meals which would give him diarrhea and weaken him. Another was to add flu serum to his food. Given as a shot it would protect him, but taken internally it would make him sick. Another way was to add marijuana to his food, or getting him a couple free joints, causing him to overeat and be sluggish. Jake knew that Alex liked weed, so it wouldn't take much to get him to light up. Jake also explained to the Reverend about Alex being "paid" by the Outlaws to cripple Jake or kill him. If the Aryan Brotherhood could turn it to their advantage by staging it as a 'martial arts match' then there could be bets placed and the Outlaws would be forced to participate or lose status.

They discussed the pros and cons and then Jake gave his suspicion about Collier to the Reverend.

"I had my own suspicions about Collier," said the Reverend. "Smith has been keeping me informed about everything you and the others are doing. He's family in a way, because he's my ex-wife's cousin, and very loyal. He told me I should trust you, but didn't say why. I think he sees you as a hero in some way. He said what you were doing for Ernst was a good thing. He also said I should stay out of your way, but I'm not sure what he meant by that. If there's nothing else Jake, I'm going to take care of the problem with Collier."

"Wait," Jake stopped him. "We can use Collier if we play it right. Do not use any of the four to contact the cook; we can't have Collier tipping off the Outlaws. What we can do is feed him information about my 'condition'. Tell them I'm not looking all that good, but you're going to bet on me anyway, especially if the odds are good, like three to one or better. If we can sucker the Outlaws into betting a big amount, at three to one we'll clean them out."

The Reverend looked at Jake for a minute and then said, "Okay, we'll do it that way for now. But it still comes down to one thing, you have to win. Do you think you'll win?"

Jake answered honestly, "if I don't I'll probably end up a dead man." He then turned away as the Reverend tapped on the door and left. What he had just said was clearly the truth. If he lost, lots of people, the wrong people, would lose money. He would be crippled or killed and unable to defend himself, with no-one to help him.

CHAPTER TWENTY

Des had in mind exactly what he wanted to say when he called the assayer. He let the phone ring five times before he hung up. He could try later, he thought. After all, not everyone starts right at eight a.m.

He refilled his coffee cup and sat back down at the desk when the phone rang. He answered on the second ring.

"Hello?"

"Is this Mr. Edmonds?"

"Yes, who am I speaking with?"

"Mr. Edmonds, you sent me a check for $200 so I would talk to you, is this some kind of gimmick? Are you a debt collector, or something?"

"No, I'm an attorney. Is this Ellis Chambers, Jr.?"

"Yes, I uh, it is. Am I being sued or something?"

"Mr. Chambers, if you will be patient, maybe I can explain why I want to talk to you."

Des laid out the whole story about representing an eccentric client who wants to live out in the desert and liked the area that Ellis had inherited from his father. He also told Ellis to consider carefully what he thought about a price for the property, because his client wasn't super rich, and he was looking at other places.

Ellis had a cautious tone when he told Des, the property was appraised at $40 per acre or so Donald Bryson had said. Bryson had tried to get him to sell it two years back, but he didn't like Bryson and didn't trust him. He asked a realtor in the Ridgecrest area for an appraisal, but she didn't say what it should appraise at.

"Ellis, listen to me. I think the 160 acres you own may appraise as high as $80 an acre, but I don't want to get in a bidding war with anyone, especially Donald Bryson. If I can acquire the mine property itself from Bryson, I'd be willing to pay $100 per acre for yours, but you mustn't discuss this with anyone. If anyone finds out we're interested in your property, it may just start that bidding war I'm trying to avoid. What did your father tell you about the mine itself?"

"Not much, he said it had some gold in it, but not a lot. He didn't think it would pay him to keep it, so he showed it to some people that were interested, but they didn't like the idea. They said it was too far out and had no water and no power, and the gold wasn't enough. He showed it one other time to a man from back east, but he said the same thing as the others."

"Thanks Ellis, I'll get back to you. Better yet, you call me next week if you can. Do you know how I can get in touch with your brother Elvan?"

"He's dead, Mr. Edmonds. Why did you want to talk to him?"

"He owns, or owned the property on the other side of the mine property, and I was hoping he'd be willing to sell. I guess I'll have to contact his heirs."

"He doesn't have any heirs and he doesn't own it, I do. He sold it to me before he died because he owed me money. I have all the papers, but hadn't transferred the deed, because things are tight right now. Is that offer for my piece good for his?"

"Yes Ellis. Be sure to tell no one, not even your wife. With this much money you could pay off some of those debts and those calls would stop."

Des hung up and sipped his coffee. It was still warm enough to drink, so he gulped down the remainder of the cup. He was about to get up when the phone rang again. This time it was Jackson.

"Hey buddy, got the bottle of single-malt. Thanks a bunch, but that favor wasn't worth a $100 bottle of Scotch. Your boy Bryson was asking when some funds would be released on his letters of credit. My branch manager in Sacramento told him to be patient there were just some 'minor discrepancies' with the assets pledged on the bonds, that everything should be straightened out in a week or so. I bet his ass is so tight right now he could shit B-B's. How's your little scheme coming?"

"Real good, I have a couple more calls to make and then we'll ready to discuss price with Mr. Donald Bryson. Thanks Jackson, love to Cindy," Des couldn't help but throw that last little zinger in there. He hung up, but not before hearing a 'fuck you'.

Des dialed the assayer's office again, and got the same results. He looked at the clock and saw it wasn't quite nine a.m. Today was the day the dealership was supposed to deliver the SUV, and Des was anxious to see it. He had ordered it with larger tires and rims, and when they told him those wouldn't fit; he ordered a lift kit to raise up the body a couple inches. He didn't want a "Monster Truck", just the ability to go off-road, like to the mine.

Eddie tapped on the door, and stuck his head in. "I thought they were delivering the new car today. Hasn't it got here yet?"

"Not yet, I was expecting it any time now. We'll wait an hour and then if it isn't here we'll call the dealership and see what's going on. Want some coffee? I'm going to make a fresh pot."

"I'll make it. How do you want yours, Des?"

"One sugar, one cream, thanks. What are you doing here? I thought you and your mom were going clothes shopping today."

"We are, after lunch. She has to clean Mrs. Roberts's house this morning. She called last night and said Mama hadn't cleaned well enough and she has company coming this afternoon and if she doesn't come back and clean it again, not to come back at all. I think Mrs. Roberts is scamming her, but she says she can't afford to lose any cleaning jobs. I wanted to see the new car, and maybe go for a ride."

"We might if it ever gets here and if I ever get another cup of coffee," Des said shaking his empty cup at Eddie.

"Yes sir. Right away, sir," Eddie was laughing as he left.

Eddie had just returned with coffee when they both heard a horn outside and almost knocked each other over trying to get to the door. The SUV was parked there, shiny and new. It was thing of beauty, all deep metallic blue color and black trim, no chrome. The tires and rims were black and had been polished. Des bent over to look underneath, to make sure they had applied the undercoating he wanted. They must have worked around the clock to get everything Des had ordered.

Eddie just stood there and looked. He was supposed to drive this? It was huge. Far bigger than he thought it would be. He might even have a problem getting in and out. He was about to

[133]

ask about that when the delivery driver clicked the remote and the doors unlocked, and at the same time a step rail came down from underneath. The driver was explaining all the features to Des, but Des shook his head and motioned toward Eddie. The driver came over and began again with the demonstration of all the features.

Together they walked all around the vehicle and as the delivery person explained each feature Eddie would try them out. Eddie was confused by the fact that the seats had heaters in them, not understanding why a person would need heaters in Southern California.

"We won't always be in Southern California, Eddie. Up in Susanville where Jake is, it gets really cold, and then you'll be glad to have those heaters. Try the remote start, see how that works. And ask the man to show you how the winch works."

As an added precaution, and knowing they'd be doing some off-road driving, Des had ordered receivers for hitches on both the front and back bumpers. Both bumpers were the heavy duty type. The front one had a medium duty brush guard, while the back one had the swing arm type spare tire holder with two gas can holders. He had even ordered the gas cans painted to match the body of the SUV. There was a heavy duty luggage rack on top with a tool box along one side.

The delivery driver showed Eddie the winch, stowed in the back of the SUV with its own hold down straps. He showed him the remote for the winch, how it worked, and even suggested that Eddie buy a pair of gloves to stow with the winch.

"Why would I need gloves?" Eddie asked him.

"If you've never operated a winch, one thing you should be aware of. When you run out the cable, sometimes they get barbs on them and if you grab the cable with bare hands, it can hurt. I know, I made that mistake my first time I used one."

"Thanks," Eddie said. "I'd have probably figured that out when I grabbed the cable the first time," and laughed.

"All the guys in the shop were really proud to have worked on this beast. They especially liked the colors you chose. That medium blue deep metallic is sharp against the gloss black. What are you going to call it?"

"What do you mean, call it?" Des asked.

"A lot of our customers have names put on their rides, like My Ride or Street Cruiser or like one guy called his Sweetheart. I just thought you'd have a name for it."

"We hadn't really thought about anything like that. We'll have to come up with a name I guess. By the way, where are the water cans?"

The delivery man checked his list, and looked in the back. The holders were there, but no water cans. "I'll have to check Mr. Edmonds. I know we sent four cans to the paint shop, but I only see the two on the swing arm rack."

Des looked at the two cans on the swing arm. "Those are the water cans, see the light blue top, and the word water by the spout? It looks like we're missing the gas cans."

The delivery man made a quick call, and then came back. "The guy who's supposed to pick me up hasn't left the shop yet, so he's checking on the gas cans. If they're there, he'll bring them when he picks me up. I'll need you to sign the delivery receipt sir."

"Not yet, I need you to show my associate how to check the fluids in the motor and the other things like washer fluid. You can do that while you're waiting for your ride, and my gas cans. How much gas is in it?"

"It's full sir, both tanks. And I'd be happy to show him how to check those things."

Des headed back to the house, hoping his coffee wasn't completely cold. It was luke-warm, but still drinkable. He started to get into the file that Margaret had sent him. It contained all the financial records of one Jacob Aaron Kozan, and Des needed to review it completely to see where Jake stood financially. He knew how much Jake had in his bank account, which in itself was a tidy sum, but he had no idea how many other assets Jake had. Right now, after buying the beast in the driveway, and the other expenses he had incurred, Jake had just over a hundred thousand in the bank. Des hoped that wasn't all of it, he'd feel bad if Jake got out of prison and was broke.

The financial consultant that Margaret had chosen to manage Jake's money was really good at picking the right things to invest in, but he was terrible at anything resembling record-keeping. There were receipts and sales slips from several different accounts in one file and even some file folders with a name on the tab, but nothing inside. Des could feel a headache starting just by looking at that mess. He thought for a second and decided this would be a great learning experience for a young associate he employed. He then remembered that Eddie and Rosa were to go shopping this afternoon, which meant he'd have to do the filing himself. He could feel the beginnings of that headache again.

"Des?" Eddie interrupted his thoughts. "The delivery man needs a signature before he gives us the keys. They found the gas cans; they were still at the shop. You want me to sign?"

"No, I'll do it. Did you check everything out with the man about where the oil goes and washer fluid and stuff?"

"Yes sir, and he suggested I keep a log of every time I fill up and what the mileage is and if I add oil, and that. He said it'll help me keep track of when to get the oil changed and the tires rotated and so on. What do you think?"

"I think that's a good idea since you'll be in charge of the beast."

"The Beast?" Eddie questioned. "Is that what you're going to call it?"

"I guess that's as good a name as any. What do you think?"

"I like it, the Beast. It even sounds like a beast, when you start it up it has a, you know, like a snarl. Yeah, the Beast, I like that."

Eddie helped Des until lunch time when he had to leave to meet Rosa. She was going to help him pick out clothes, and get a suitcase. Des stopped for a snack from the refrigerator and then continued sorting the various papers. He was getting an idea that the financial consultant was very good at reading the market, because he had bought and sold at the right times in the stock market. Even his purchases of bonds were very good,

[136]

often earning as high as twelve to fifteen per cent. Des just wished he had a clue as to how to file records. He was about to quit for the day when the phone rang. It was Donald Bryson.

"Mr. Edmonds, I'm so glad I got you. I have to be out of the office tomorrow, some business with the bank that I need to get straightened out. I thought about a price like you asked, and I could let the mine go for say one hundred thousand. It has the potential to be a very lucrative situation if a person really applied himself to the mining, instead of treating it as a hobby like Chambers did."

"Well Mr. Bryson, I did think about the mining operation, and as I said before my client is somewhat eccentric. So to be fair I'm thinking of going out there again and getting some samples of the gold-bearing mineral and having it assayed. That way we can put a fair price on that portion of the property, but truthfully, I don't think my client even cares about mining. He said it would cost way too much to have to haul water enough to support a mining operation. He just wants the mine as part of his "geo-symbiotic" theory of how one should live both in and on the earth. That's his theory, not mine. Like I told you, he's eccentric. But he's my client, so I have to do as he asks. By the way, do you know of a couple of assayers in that area?" Des couldn't help that last question. He knew what the answer would be before Bryson started talking. He wrote down the name anyway, just because.

Des told Bryson he'd think about what he'd said and get back with him, maybe next week, or the following week. He tried to put as much disappointment in his voice as he could.

After he hung up, he called Stan Hobbs, hoping against hope that Stan might be home. It was on the fifth ring and Des was about to hang up when Stan answered.

"What can I do for you, Mr. Edmonds? I was just about to go to the store and stock up. I'm leaving on Saturday for two weeks to an area east of Goldfield, Nevada that a friend told me about."

"Stan, are you familiar with the Chambers mine, southwest of Sentinel Peak, west of Mormon Butte?"

"Yes sir, I've been there a couple times with Chambers himself, didn't think much of the prospect. Too much work, not enough pay. Why?"

"I need you to go there first thing in the morning and get some samples to go to all three assayers in your area, even your loudmouth friend. I need the reports turned around and back to me by close of business Friday, but do not say who the report is for. I don't want my name on any of the papers, only an affidavit from you stating that all samples were obtained from the same strata in the Chambers mine. I'll pay you whatever you want if you can get it done on time. Okay?"

"Yes sir, Mr. Edmonds. It'll be my pleasure. Is this for Jake?"

"Yes Stan, yes it is. Thanks."

"No charge then, Mr. Edmonds. Jake staked me to a grubstake a time or two when I was flat broke. I'd be glad to do this for him, he never did ask for his money back even when I hit that good strike up by Tonopah. If I head out early enough, I can be at that mine by sunup and back here in time to get the reports by Friday morning. I'll still have to pay the assayers Mr. Edmonds; can you send that to me?"

"I'll send six hundred to the Western Union office in Ridgecrest; it should be there when you get back in town. Oh, by the way, when you get in the mine, about forty paces back from the entrance on the right you'll see some rock piled up there. Behind it is the entrance to a natural cave, and an artesian spring. I want that entrance concealed so no one knows it's there, okay?"

"Water?" Stan was stunned. "Jake found water? I was in there twice with old man Chambers and he never said anything about water, always brought out what he thought he'd need for mining. Son-of-a-bitch! Jake found water. That secret is safe with me Mr. Edmonds, now I know why he wants that mine. Son-of-a-bitch! Shit, I better gas up now and get on my way. I'll get it done Mr. Edmonds; I'll call you in the morning and let you know. Bye."

Des couldn't remember the last time he'd seen, or rather heard, anyone get that fired up over such a small tidbit of information. Not having lived in the desert, Des wasn't aware how valuable a water source can be. Still curious as to why Stan was so excited, Des decided to look up what he could find about water sources in the area. It probably was a waste of time, but it was more interesting than filing all those receipts. Besides, the more he knew about the area, the better he'd be able to help Jake.

On a hunch, he called Margaret, and asked if TJ had made any maps or marked any maps with spots where there was water. Margaret said she wasn't sure, but she could check in the vault.

"A vault, Margaret, don't you mean a safe?"

"No sir. When he had the barn built, he had an under-floor section with grates, like they have at some of these oil-change places, so he could work on the car and the equipment without having to install a lift. On one side of that is a room with a bank vault door and frame that he got when he was bidding on salvage materials at the Navy base. I thought it was a waste of forty dollars, but he put it to use. Only me, TJ, and Jake know the combination to it. I'll look after I've had dinner and let you know."

"On second thought, we'll be there on Friday to hire the harvest crew, let's wait and do it then. Enjoy your dinner. We'll see you Friday morning."

CHAPTER TWENTY-ONE

Weldon Purcell still had some doubts about Jake Kozan. He'd seen killers before and in no way did Kozan fit any of the profiles he usually dealt with. He was totally out of character of all the types he'd seen. Kozan was truly sad about his supposed victim being dead. And all the evidence presented didn't match the testimony of the two "government agents". Edmonds had tried valiantly to introduce testimony of others that the two men were best of friends, but wasn't allowed "character" witnesses. The judge had really bent the rules of evidence in favor of the prosecution, and against the defense. Julie Larson had talked to him a couple of times and Weldon got the feeling that she was more than just curious about Kozan. She admitted to only having had two face to face meetings with him, but those had apparently started a spark. He hoped she wasn't wrong about Kozan, she was a good officer and a good woman. Her marriage to his partner had been a bad mistake, one he felt responsible for. He'd been the one who introduced them at a retirement party. Now he was out here at the crime scene looking for what might be some crucial evidence.

Purcell remembered the conversation Julie told him about between Jake and her father. Jake had sworn that he'd been shot at by a rifle, but no evidence or testimony about a rifle was mentioned at the trial. That had started his mind turning, not a big deal in itself, but added to the fact that Jake said the woman had a 9mm pistol when they both denied having weapons. The weapon found at the scene was an older Browning 9mm that was registered to a Lawrence Simms of Compton several years ago. It was believed to be at his residence when the Los Angeles Police questioned the daughter of Mr. Simms, who was very surprised to find it missing. Her statement included the fact that Mr. Simms had passed away three years previously, and nobody had bothered to check his gun cabinet to see if anything was missing. The other weapons were all safely locked away; the 9mm was the only one missing. As Mr. Simms' grandson had some gang affiliation, it was probable that he had stolen it and sold or traded it.

Purcell had located the place where Jake had 'dug in' by the Joshua trees. Because Jake had said that the bullet hit the dirt near him, Purcell had borrowed a metal detector from a friend. He set the reading as broad as possible, so as to pick up a signal of anything metallic. He began sweeping the area slowly and deliberately, listening intently for the tell-tale beep. Because he was hearing nothing, he tossed a small pen-knife on the ground and swept it with the wand. The very loud beep in his ear almost made him pull off the head-phones. He knew for sure the detector was working. He went back to sweeping moving slightly slower. After a few minutes he was rewarded with a low beep. He began carefully digging the area out and after a couple of shovels of dirt he swept again. He still got the low beep so he dug out some more, spreading the dirt like before and then sweeping again. He got another beep and took out two more shovels of dirt. As he spread it out he saw a familiar gleam, but it wasn't brass or copper. Purcell laughed, he'd found a small gold nugget, about half the size of the nail on his little finger.

He continued his sweep of the area and found two more, smaller nuggets. He was about to give up when he heard a very strong beep at the far end of his sweep. He went over the spot in two different directions so he could pin-point the item better. He hoped it wasn't an old nail or garbage like that. When he got it out of the dirt, it was a full metal jacket slug, definitely from a rifle. The copper jacketing hadn't started to discolor yet, so it couldn't have been there long. He thought about what Jake had told Edmonds and looked at the area in front of him. He picked a couple of likely places where a rifleman might set up.

He broke down the metal detector and put it away in the pack, then folded up his little shovel and put the cover on it. He then strapped it back in its place on his belt and started across to find the rifle shooter's location. Purcell knew the desert and knew that often tracks in the desert remain for quite a while. They usually stayed in place until the first good wind, and then they'd be erased. There wasn't much chance of finding tracks, but he might find other indications of a shooter's position.

Purcell found the spot. It was higher on the slope than he figured it would be. He had to reference the Joshua trees several times and when he finally located where the shooter had lain, it was a wonder Jake was alive. Purcell used his binoculars and could see exactly where Jake had been hiding. Apparently Jake got to the spot before the shooter had an idea where he was, and just didn't recognize Jake as a human form.

Now Purcell was really puzzled. To him it was rather obvious that Jake had been telling the truth, so why was he in jail? The judge was one of the most obvious reasons for the guilty verdict. He had done everything except tell them to vote the accused guilty, with his jury instructions. During the trial he had made it a point to interrupt Edmonds when he could so the jury couldn't follow what Edmonds was trying to prove. And the worst was his sustainment of the prosecution's objections, many of which had no basis in law.

Purcell packed his binoculars and headed back to his squad. Because the budget was tight, he had to do patrol duty like all the others. Even the sheriff had pulled a couple of shifts so some of the deputies could take their vacation time with their families. As he approached where the Powerwagon had been parked he noticed what looked like part of a shell casing. He pulled it out of the dirt where it appeared the Powerwagon had rolled over it when they moved it out. He was careful to handle it with a tissue, and as a precaution he dropped it and the tissue in an envelope. It was a 9mm casing, but he couldn't remember if it was the same brand as the others that had been recovered.

Purcell was about to leave when a thought came to him. He unpacked the metal detector, and by lining up where TJ had been standing and the spot where the other casings had been found, he had a probable area where any missed shots might have gone. The crime scene investigator, his partner David Larson, had done a fairly thorough job of gathering the evidence at the scene, but had only found six casings all matching up with the Browning. He had just found number seven, and a Browning

[142]

usually had a ten cartridge or thirteen cartridge magazine. He couldn't conceive of a person going into the desert with only a partly loaded weapon.

In his mind, more and more things just didn't add up. He kept walking until he got to the spot he'd had in mind and then he turned on the detector and started sweeping. His efforts were promptly rewarded when he found a slug buried about six inches in the dirt. He worked the entire area for two hours and came up with seven more slugs. The coroner had pulled four out of TJ, and with these eight that would be twelve. That made more sense to him, even though he was missing a slug.

He piled into the squad tired and sore. The heat helped his arthritis, but not all the digging and squatting. When he got to the highway instead of turning right and heading toward Bishop, he turned south. It was a twenty minute ride to the San Bernardino County Sheriff's sub-station in Trona and hopefully some hot coffee. What he really needed was a nap, but that wouldn't happen. The Sheriff was easy going on a lot of the rules, but not if you were sleeping on the job. His favorite quote was "We stay awake at night so others don't have to." That, and "If you want to sleep on the job, become a fireman."

The door to the substation was unlocked, meaning that someone was there. Purcell looked around and didn't see anyone, so he called out a "Hello."

"Be right with you," a voice answered. "I'll be out in a minute."

He looked around and saw the coffee machine, just finishing brewing. He searched among the cups on the counter and found a clean one. He added a spoon of sugar to it and poured it full. He was sitting at the one empty desk when a reserve deputy came from in back. His nameplate said 'Thorpe' which Purcell recognized from the trial.

"Good afternoon, Deputy Thorpe. I was just taking advantage of your hospitality by helping myself to your coffee. You're the guy who owns the gas station, right?"

"Yeah, that and a partnership in the convenience store with Mr. Patel. What are you doing down this way?"

[143]

"I'm looking into the TJ Wagner murder. There's a slight possibility that the guy convicted of murder didn't do it. There are some pieces to the puzzle that just don't fit. Maybe I'm wasting my time, but I'm doing some more looking. It just doesn't feel right, him supposedly going all crazy all of a sudden for no reason. Did you know Kozan?"

"Yeah, and I thought he was okay. Quiet, but friendly, he didn't talk much. But, I only met him twice before the murder. Most of the time, he'd stay with that Powerwagon of TJ's. He was talking to the couple the morning TJ dropped off his planned location and when he'd be back. I thought it was funny that the prosecution didn't ask for the videos of that morning. I've been holding them, just in case someone like you wanted to re-open the investigation. I knew TJ, and he could be a loud-mouth and a jerk at times, but not so much that anybody would want to kill him. Kick his ass maybe, kill him no. You want that video, or should I make a copy and keep mine?"

"I would really like a copy of that video Thorpe. What you've just told me makes me even more suspicious of the judge and the prosecutor. When can you get me that copy of the video?"

"We'll lock up here and go to the gas station; you can have that copy in five minutes."

Purcell followed Thorpe and in five minutes had two copies of the video and was headed north toward Lone Pine and a late dinner. He called to see if the wife was cooking, but got the answering machine instead. When he pulled into the driveway, the house was dark and her car was gone, so he backed out and headed to the diner.

At the diner he treated himself to a small steak even though the red meat wasn't good for his arthritis, and even had a glass of wine to go with it. The lady who owned the diner kept a fairly simple menu and a better wine list. He thought she had taken some classes on wines, and her selection was simple but good. Her prices were slightly higher because of the tourist trade, but the food was worth it. He was in a celebrating mood having found the other shell casing and the slugs, and especially the video that Thorpe had saved, so he had an Irish coffee with a half shot in it. He was just sipping it when the wife and her girl-friends came in.

"I saw your squad outside and thought I'd check up on you; see who you're fooling around with now. What did you have for dinner?"

"Steak, " he knew not to volunteer any more information than necessary or she'd start on one of her tirades about how she has to watch him every second just like a little kid. "You weren't home so I thought I'd try some real food." He knew he'd pay for that last remark later, but right now he didn't care. He was feeling too good to let her spoil his mood.

"Now," he said and stood up abruptly. "You ladies have a nice evening. I have some work to do at the office." And he left. He figured he'd sleep on one of the cots in the jail rather than listen to the crap he knew he'd hear if he went home. When he got to the office, he locked all the new evidence in his desk and was lying on a cot ten minutes later, falling asleep.

CHAPTER TWENTY-TWO

Des awoke refreshed, and for the first time in a long time he could reach over where she usually lay without getting sad. "You were right, Nancy. The kids will be alright and so will I. I'm actually feeling like I'm contributing, you know, needed. It feels good. Being around these young people has made me feel younger, more alive than I've felt in a long time. I hope I'm doing the right thing. I know it feels right, and I guess that's what counts."

He showered and dressed and had his second cup of coffee when Eddie showed up.

"It's going to take me forever to pay for all those clothes we bought yesterday Des. My Mom said she would loan me the money, but I have to pay her every payday. We got so much stuff, I don't know if I'll ever wear it all. We even got a suitcase like you suggested."

"Good, we're going to Ridgecrest this afternoon and staying in a motel tonight. Tomorrow we have to pick out some people to harvest the pistachios for Margaret. Did you get any work clothes?"

"Yes sir, we got four pairs of jeans and six work shirts, and also two weeks' worth of underwear and socks. I didn't get any work boots yet; I wasn't sure what kind to get. Oh, and I got a work coat, the kind with a liner for when it gets really cold."

"Sounds like you're all set. Now we need to map out the route to Ridgecrest and we'll be ready."

They heard the fax machine and looked at each other. Des saw the top part of the fax and it was from the assayer he'd spoken to, but the phone number showed it coming from Bryson's office.

"This is going to be fun," Des said out loud. Eddie looked confused, so Des explained the phone call he'd gotten yesterday and what Bryson's proposal was. He then quickly instructed Eddie what he wanted him to do when Bryson called.

"You think he's going to call you?" Eddie asked.

"I'm positive he'll call," Des said pointing at the assayers report. It was the same one that had been given to the bonding company and the bank. They discussed a few points while they waited, a new form of the 'old school play' as Des called it. The phone rang while they were talking.

"Mr. Bryson, how may I help you today?" Des sounded cheerful, happy.

"I just faxed down the assayers report on the Chambers mine, and thought I'd follow up with a call. If you study it, you'll see the report shows more potential than many of the local gold mines. It would justify the costs necessary to bring in water."

He was about to go on, when Eddie interrupted. "Mr. Edmonds, the Shoshone people are on the other line. Should I get a number so you can call them back?"

"No," Des said quickly. "Don't let them go. What was their last price?"

"Forty eight thousand," Eddie said, reading from his notes.

"Good, keep them on the line, I'll just be a minute," Des said, not bothering to cover the mouthpiece. "Mr. Bryson, to be honest, we're looking at another property in Shoshone that is a better value. It's only eighty acres compared to your one-sixty, but it also has a mine, but it's non-productive although that doesn't matter. It does have water, and that is a big plus. Do you know of any water on your property Donald?" He almost held his breath, hoping for the right answer.

Nearly a whisper, Bryson answered, "None that I know of."

Des was totally pleased, while Eddie was grinning from ear to ear. Quickly, Des said, "I'm not ruling out the possibility of buying your property Bryson. So to be fair, I'm going to Ridgecrest on another matter, so I'll go out there and maybe take a sample or two and get two more assays done. I'm not saying your guy is wrong but everyone can make a mistake now and then, especially if they were working late and maybe tired. When I get those other reports I'll be in touch, thanks Donald." He hung up and then started laughing.

They were about to head to the kitchen when the phone rang again. Des answered with a tentative "Hello".

[147]

It was Stan Hobbs. "I just dropped off the last of the three sets of samples to the assayers like you asked. The reports will cost you just under four hundred, being a rush job. I'll pick them up first thing in the morning and drop them off at Margaret's house. Right now I need some sleep, I left right after I talked to you and I've been up all night. Did you say I could pick up the money at Western Union?"

"I wasn't sure how much it would cost, so I wired a thousand to you. If you don't need it all, give the remainder back to Margaret, or to me. I'll be at Margret's tomorrow morning as well."

To kill the time, Des showed Eddie the files he'd started on for the different transactions the financial consultant had done. Together they were starting to get an idea that Jake had more money than he knew. Eddie kept asking Des questions and for the most part Des could answer, but some things were just unexplainable. There should be a master ledger somewhere that showed how much Jake had, and many of the stock purchases were in street name through a stock-broker that held the actual stock itself. Des was curious about that; he had never done stock purchases that way. He usually got the certificate for the shares purchased a week or so after he bought them. As they were going through the different receipts, Eddie pointed out one that showed the purchase of some bonds.

"Isn't this the same company that is holding the bond on Bryson?" he asked. Des looked and the name was the same. The face value on the bonds was fifty thousand. Des decided to call the broker to find out what he could on the bonds. The agent wouldn't give him any information until Des faxed the power of attorney Jake had signed. Then he reluctantly told Des that the bonds were still current and that because there were no instructions as to where the semi-annual payments should be sent, they were being held in a money-market fund that wasn't paying much right now. Des asked if it were possible to sell the bonds and have the proceeds sent to Jake's checking account along with the monies in the money-market fund. When the agent said yes Des gave him instructions as to where to transfer the funds. The next question the agent asked really shocked Des.

"Do you want the proceeds from just those bonds, or all the proceeds being held in the money-market fund?" the agent asked. "He has other bonds here."

"Can you send me a listing of all the bonds Mr. Kozan has with your firm, and also I'd like to see a copy of all the transactions, please. For right now, I believe we'll only liquidate those bonds I mentioned, and withdraw the total funds that are in the money-market account. Can you give me a total of what that might be?"

"Yes, the total of the MMA is one hundred thirty-one thousand six hundred forty-one and fifty-four cents, and we'll have to wait and see what those bonds sell for. I'd imagine you'll get close to face value on them. Anything else, sir?" the agent was being very professional.

"Not for now," Des said and then he sat down and shook his head. He looked at Eddie and said,"Remind me tomorrow to find out from Margaret who this financial genius is. I need someone like that handling my finances."

Des told Eddie to go home and pack enough clothes for a week, and include some work clothes. He asked Eddie if Rosa would be alright by herself. Eddie wasn't real positive with an answer, which indicated there was something going on. It took a few minutes, but Des finally got an answer.

"Jesus Alvarado's mother lives about six houses away from us, and as long as I'm there, they aren't doing anything yet, but I don't know what's going to happen if I leave her there alone for a week. I don't even want to think about going for three weeks."

Des thought about it and could see the problem. It's funny how our actions are guided sometimes by the needs of others, so we're never really free to do what we want. If he thought it out, he knew he'd find a solution sooner or later.

"Eddie, call home. Tell your mama to pack some nice clothes for a week too, she's going on vacation. Has she ever been on vacation?"

"I don't think so," Eddie stared at him like he'd gone totally crazy. "At least none I ever knew of."

"Call her; she's going on one now." Des laughed. "And then you take the Beast and go home and pack." Des decided that if he was going anywhere, he'd better pack too. First, he decided to give Margaret notice that they'd be there this evening.

"Hello, Margaret? Desmond here, we decided to drive up this afternoon, so we'll see you this evening. Would you like to join us for dinner? It might be late, though. I'm not sure how long it should take us."

Margaret laughed, "You are sure wound up, aren't you? To get here from where you are it shouldn't take more than an hour and a half to two hours depending on traffic."

"Yeah, I guess I am. We've gotten some good news this morning and things are starting to come together. Do you know a good restaurant? "

"There are a couple of chain restaurants in town that serve good food, but they're a bit pricey as far as I'm concerned. Why don't you just eat here at my house? I haven't had company in ages, and haven't cooked for anyone else either, so it will be my pleasure to have some people here for a change."

"We'll call you right after we check into the Carriage Inn; we're booked there through Sunday morning. I plan on heading back early Sunday morning to miss traffic."

"I hear that's a nice place to stay. Most of the visitors to the base prefer that place, at least the VIP's. Give me a call if you break down on the road."

"How am I going to do that Margaret? I don't have one of those cell phones; I just can't get myself to get one. My daughter has one, and uses hers all the time, so I guess I'm just old-fashioned that way. Maybe I'll get one before I leave town. I'll see you this evening."

After a stop at the bank to cash a check and then a cell phone store, they headed toward Ridgecrest, Hernando driving the Beast, Rosa reading the driving directions, and Des in the back reading the cell phone instructions. If he could figure this cell phone out, he might get caught up to the current century.

[150]

CHAPTER TWENTY-THREE

Jake was worried, he was placing more trust in the Reverend than he wanted to, but right now the Reverend was his only pipeline to the outside, except for Sam Battiste. He didn't want to jeopardize Sam's job by involving him any more than necessary. He did talk to Sam more and more, he was a likeable guy and Jake felt at ease in their conversations, but Jake couldn't talk about anything that Sam might be forced to report.   They did talk a lot about Sam's earlier days as a gang-banger, and how he'd finally decided that it wasn't the life he wanted. Sam was lucky enough to meet a social worker that helped him relocate to a new city and even get his GED and a job. Jake told him about Ernst and how he'd never learned to read or write until now, that Tyler said Ernst was like a great big sponge soaking up knowledge. Sam agreed that Ernst was a different person than the one he'd first met. He no longer had that defensive attitude, and his posture was now tall and proud. They both laughed at the fact that Ernst probably had no clue what 'White Supremacy' was really all about; he was just going along to belong to something.

Jake's exercise routine was being questioned by quite a few people on the outside, but all Sam would do is his "Aw Shucks" routine and tell them he didn't pay much attention to that stuff. He would tell them, and honestly, that Jake wasn't eating much of the meals the kitchen sent, like he just wasn't able to digest them, said they bothered his stomach. Jake told Sam how lucky he was to have a gourmet cook in the family.

Right now Jake's problem was how to get Des to send a large amount of money to his canteen fund, without anyone knowing where it came from. Another problem was did he have enough money to place the kind of bet he wanted to place, so that he could take a lot of money away from the Outlaws. If he could get three to one odds, he wanted to place at least eighteen thousand dollars on himself. The big man, Davis, had said that fifty thousand was the amount Alex owed; hopefully he was telling the truth. He had to approach Sam with it, and hope he didn't blow the whistle on the whole thing. As a guard, Sam was obligated to tell everything he knew about any illegal activity that might be planned. Many of the guards were 'on the take' in some way or other, but not Sam. In the past, Jake had found that the best way to deal with honest people is by being honest. Sam knew about the upcoming fight and so far hadn't said anything. Jake was going to tell him all the why's and when's of the plan and then hope that Sam would understand enough to stay silent.

"Sam, can I talk to you about something really important?" Jake asked through the door. The dinner portal was open, that way they could talk without having the door open or yelling at each other.

Sam came to the door and squatted by the portal. "What is it Jake? What kind of 'real important' is it?"

Jake explained slowly the entire story, beginning with the trip to the desert with the Davis couple and ending with what was happening now. He then told Sam of his plan to fight Alex and to bet on the outcome of the fight with enough money to force the Outlaws to cancel what was owed or pay Jake enough money so he could buy Alex's debt. He also told Sam of his not wanting to get Sam in trouble for not reporting what he knew.

"Can you understand the problem I have Sam? Alex may be a totally different person than the one I used to know, but he saved my life in combat and I'm obligated to try to repay that debt. I don't know of another way, so this plan is what I've come up with. I know I'll get punished for the fight, especially if it's reported that I'm the one who attacked Alex. They'll probably add charges of assault or something, but if I can get Alex out and away from the Outlaws it'll be worth it to me. But I need to get a message to Mr. Edmonds so he can figure out how to get the monies into my canteen fund. The decision to report this plan is yours Sam, either way I won't think any less of you. If you decide to help, I have an idea that might save your butt down the road, in case there's an investigation. Now, you better make rounds, or somebody may come looking for you."

[152]

Sam didn't answer, just stood up and walked away. Jake knew he'd just dumped a big pile on Sam's shoulders and was hoping Sam could understand why. Ironic, Jake thought to himself, a guard and a con, both plotting something illegal so they could help another con that might not even be worth it. Life can sure be a screwed up mess at times. He went back to his exercises; they were only thing that had some form of sensibility. Lunch would be coming soon and time for another acting job.

Lunch came and went, the only fun part was checking to see if it had been tampered with. It had, and not just the food on the tray. Jake squeezed the juice carton that came with the meal and saw a dribble of juice coming from a pinhole in the bottom corner of the carton. He opened the carton and dumped the juice in the toilet, along with food on the tray. There were two cookies that looked appetizing, but he knew better than to take a chance. They went down the toilet also. Sam picked up the tray and was very quiet, not his usual self. Jake could understand, he had a lot to think about; after all, a lot could go wrong. When Sam brought Jake's other lunch, he opened the portal and handed the bag to Jake, again saying nothing. Sam's wife had made him a beef tongue sandwich. Jake wasn't ordinarily fond of beef tongue, having only had it twice before and both times it hadn't tasted good. This time it was a totally different taste, spicy and yet rich with the beef flavor. She had put horseradish and mustard on her home-made bread and Jake thought he'd better re-think his ideas on beef tongue. She had included a piece of sharp Cheddar and a couple of sweet pickles. There was a small jar of what was iced tea, now room temperature tea. Jake savored every bit of the meal, knowing that if Sam decided to report what he knew, this would also stop. He finished and they had just gotten rid of the bag and jar when Sam's boss came down the hall. Both Jake and Sam just watched, not knowing what was coming next.

"I came to see if the prisoner is doing any better at eating what we've been serving him. Can you give me a report, Guard Battiste?"

Jake thought to himself, if there was ever a time for prayers, it would be now. But, instead of telling what he knew, Sam's report was absolutely beautiful.

"Sir, the prisoner has repeatedly complained of stomach problems since being sent here. He has tried to comply with your wishes, but I'm sorry to report that if he does, it just ends up in the toilet, if you know what I mean, sir. I've given him some of my lunches from time to time, and because my wife makes home-made bread it seems to stay down. Like you, I don't want to see a prisoner being forced to eat food that doesn't agree with him, so, if I can have your authorization, I will bring some food from home for him, sir."

"Bring food from home?" the senior guard looked at Sam as if seeing him for the first time. "Won't that be a hardship on you and your wife? Isn't she expecting? Your first I believe?"

"She doesn't mind sir. As far as cost goes, if the prisoner would agree, I would draw out enough money from his canteen fund to pay for his food sir. That way, no one can accuse us of impropriety sir."

"I see. Your plan has merit, Guard Battiste. It's refreshing to see a guard that actually believes convicts are human. I'll check your plan against regulations, and then get back to you. Prisoner, do you have anything to say?"

"No sir, Guard Battiste said what needed saying, sir."

"Very well, carry on." And then he left. Jake turned and looked at Sam. "How long have you been thinking about that idea?"

"Not long Jake. It just kind of came to me when I saw the senior guard coming down the hall. As to other, I want to talk to my wife. She's got a part in this, too. We'll talk about it in the morning."

Out in the yard Sorenson was leading the squads through their exercise routines. He had taken over like Jake wanted, and was now pushing the men at a strong pace. He believed what Jake had said about the Outlaws getting ready to take the Brotherhood out completely. What he wasn't sure of was the when, it could be any day. Because of this, the pace he was keeping on the training schedule was harsh; he'd had two quit already. He knew he wasn't any great public speaker, but he felt he had to do something to build up morale. He hadn't been told of any part of the "plan" by the Reverend, so he wasn't sure what he was going to say. It was Ernst that gave him the inspiration. When two of the men had gotten into a scuffle, before the guards were even aware of it, Ernst had stepped between them and told them to stop fighting and "stand together and stand proud". It gave Sorenson the opportunity he needed.

"Gather round and listen up," he commanded. Nearly all of them respected him by now, after all hadn't he taken down the Reverend? "We are working hard here and some of you have short tempers. We're the Aryan Brotherhood, all of us. That means we're brothers, every one of us. We walk together, eat together, and if necessary fight together. But we don't fight each other, because that's what they want. If you fight over some little comment, then you are not the supreme race. Then you're like them, a bunch of punks. We are better than that; we learn everyday because knowledge is power. We train hard every day so we have physical power to go along with the mental power. Even Brother Ernst, who couldn't read or write when he began, is now reading a book a week. Why? So he can become a better, smarter, and stronger person. We are all growing tougher and stronger each day. If we stand together and stand proud, we can defeat any enemy, anywhere. Right?"

Their response wasn't as loud or encouraging as he'd hoped, but they did respond. He took the two combatants aside and informed them that another incident would cause them to be removed from the training program and possibly the Brotherhood. They both were quick to understand the thought of not having any protection from a gang, so they assured Sorenson of their future co-operation. Sorenson knew his elevated status among the Brotherhood was temporary, and only because of his quick victory over the Reverend. He relished it while he was in charge; the authority wasn't something he was used to. He was more used to being a follower than a leader.

In Jake's old cell, Josiah Robertson was not sure what to do. He'd been sent to try to discredit Jake and make him out to be a trouble-making racist; he couldn't do that if Jake weren't here. He didn't want to go to solitary to accomplish his task; he wouldn't be able to do anything. All he could do now is wait, but the people who had sent him there didn't want to wait, they expected immediate results. The idea with the shiv had failed, and now he was stuck being a prisoner and hoping his cover wasn't blown. They had run a scan of all the names of the convicts at Susanville, but nothing had showed up from that. He was just hoping that nobody popped from his past that might remember him. There was one possibility that might have known him, but he'd been transferred out to one of the conservation camps. He wished he had another look at the file that had been put together as a cover for him; the whole thing had been so fast he'd barely had time to look at it. He lay back on the bunk, waiting for dinner; there wasn't much else to do.

CHAPTER TWENTY-FOUR

Dinner at Margaret's house was good, the food simple but fresh. She had put together a simple salad and made a vinaigrette dressing with orange juice and sesame oil and a bit of minced garlic. The main course was a beef loin with a pan sauce, and a type of au gratin potatoes that had four types of cheese in it, and also a warm "fried slaw" made from shredded Napa cabbage, carrots, and apples. During dinner Margaret and Rosa got to know each other better, and it didn't hurt that Rosa had continually complemented Margaret on the food. Hernando was being most polite in spite of the fact that he was tired from driving. It was the first time he'd driven on the freeway or on a highway and he was extremely uptight, at least until they got onto highway 95 headed north to Ridgecrest where the traffic was much lighter. From then on he drove like a pro all the way, even the parking at the Carriage Inn where Des thought the spaces were a bit small for the Beast. Hernando backed it into the space on the first try like he'd been doing it forever, and Des noticed the grin on his face.

Des could easily understand why Margaret and TJ had gotten along so well, from what Jake had told him about TJ, he loved to talk, Margaret being the perfect counterpart because she was a great listener. She answered Rosa's questions about how she'd prepared the dishes, and asked her about where she was born and so on. In no time she had Rosa telling everyone her life story, about where she was born and grew up. Rosa was the third daughter of a schoolteacher, one of seven children. She had grown up in Culiacan, on the mainland side of the Gulf of California. They enjoyed the area because of the abundance of seafood; they were only miles from the seashore. She was surprised how much beef was eaten in the United States; in Sinaloa Province they didn't eat much beef. What cattle that were raised there were usually shipped elsewhere for purchase. She surprised everyone when she told of how her grandmother was born in Northern California in a town called Marysville. Her great-grandparents had come north to work the fruit harvest, and

[157]

her grandmother was born late in August just before they were to head south again.

They were about to start on dessert when Des's new cell phone rang. He fumbled with it for a second, and then said hello. It was Julie, returning his call from earlier in the day. He had called to let her know his itinerary and his new phone number.

"Welcome to the modern world, what brought this about?" she asked.

"Actually it was Margaret's idea. She suggested it was time for me to start using some of the modern technology. So now I have a new cell phone. What's going on?"

"I got some information today from Purcell about Jake's case, and I thought you might like to see it if you're still planning on filing an appeal. Where are you now?"

"I'm at Margaret Wagner's house, just finishing dinner. She's at the end of Quasar Lane. No, really, that's what it's called, ask your dispatcher for directions. We'll be here having dessert, I hope. How long will you be?"

"I'm at Red Mountain right now, so it shouldn't be more than thirty or forty minutes."

Hernando asked Margaret what he was to do tomorrow, and how the pistachios were harvested. Her knowledge of pistachios was actually quite extensive, including their origin in Persia, now modern-day Turkey.

"Tomorrow we'll pick out a crew, and if we're lucky we'll have some of the same people that were here last year. I'm hoping I'll get to see Indio again. He looks like he's five hundred years old but don't let his age fool you, he's really got some strength. I just like being around him, he just makes me feel good, you know, like nothing bad could happen while he's next to you.

If he comes back, pick him first, it makes him feel important. His job will to be the gleaner, picking up the nuts that don't get on the tarps, and shaking the upper limbs with his long pole. It's stored out in the barn, he wanted us to keep it here, said he'd had it for many years. He told me he got it in the mountains south of here when he was a boy harvesting mesquite beans and the fruit pods from the Saguaro cactus before the vaqueros

[158]

came to that part of the country, but I have a feeling he was pulling my leg. There's also a couple that has come back for two years now, if they show up. They're good workers, and they have their own little trailer they stay in.

One thing Hernando, I want these people treated with respect. TJ said it was important that each of us feel worthwhile and are respected for our abilities. He also said that just because a person works as a fruit or nut harvester, it doesn't make them any less important than another. He wouldn't allow any drinking or drugs on the property, he'd had some personal problems with that before I met him, and if they wanted to drink, they could wait until after work. If they showed up hung-over, he paid them for two hours for the day and sent them on their way, not to come back. If you have a problem with anyone and think they should be fired, tell me and I'll have their check ready at the end of the day. Be sure you're right, but don't back down. In the morning, if the couple is back, I think their name is Medina; he can be the one to operate the shaker. He is very good with it, doesn't break limbs or bruise the bark. Des says you recently left a bad situation involving gangs, he didn't say any more than that. He also said you're already a man, ready to take on a man's duties. I trust his judgment and it's my hope you live up to his comments. It's a great thing to have people place their trust in you, and in turn be able to trust others. Oh my. I'm rattling on and on, let's get dessert."

The dessert was a green colored gelato, with nut pieces in it and a hint of citrus. It was served with biscotti that had pieces of dried fruit and nuts in it. Margaret had a satisfied smile on her face as she served coffee, Rosa couldn't seem to stop saying 'Thank you', Des could see Hernando's eyes struggling to stay open, so he suggested he have a cup of coffee.

Julie showed up as they were doing the dishes, obviously disappointed at having missed dinner. She was especially disheartened when she learned what it was. Beef tenderloin was one of her favorites. She cheered up when Margaret offered to make her a plate. She quickly radioed in for dinner break and was cleared. Between bites, she began telling Des about

[159]

Purcell's feelings about the case, how he thought Jake had been cheated on every part of the trial. Des was more than in agreement, he was still angry that he hadn't been allowed to introduce quite a few items of evidence. Julie continued with what Purcell had done, using the metal detector to find the casing and the slugs in both areas. She saved the best for last, reaching into her shoulder-bag and bringing out the video of the Davises and Jake at Thorpe's station.

They moved to the living room and turned on the video player, waiting a moment before inserting the disc. Hernando's head was nodding until it got to the part that showed Dean Davis's face. He jumped up out of his chair and nearly knocked Des over getting to the DVD player. He hit pause and looked at the face on the screen for a long minute, then he turned and looked at Des and calmly stated, "That's the son-of-a-bitch that beat me up and took my money and drugs."

Des was watching Margaret; her face was like chiseled stone. She stared at the picture as if burning it into her mind. She calmly asked Julie, "May I make a copy?"

"Of course," Julie replied. "Technically, it belongs to Dad; Purcell made this copy for him, so I guess it's up to him. Okay, Dad?"

"Margaret, if you're going to make a copy, why don't you take it to the people on the base to make a copy? They have the better equipment, don't they?"

She didn't answer. She was still staring at the screen, Hernando standing next to her doing the same. They both had their eyes fixed on the face of a killer, and a man who beat up children.

Julie broke the silence asking where she could wash her hands before she had to go back out on patrol. Margaret directed her to the bathroom, and came back to the living room. She turned to Des and quietly said, "We have to get Jake out of there, he'll know what to do. Maybe you should call Purcell and compare notes, get the appeal started. If Jake doesn't want to pay the cost Des, I will. I don't have much, but it's yours if you get him out. He was the closest thing to a son TJ ever had and he meant a lot to both of us, means a lot to me."

Julie had come in on the last part of Margaret's plea, she looked at Des and said, "We're going to file next week, or maybe I'll file next week. I believe Jake's innocent and I like him, so an appeal is going to be filed. I'm hoping my dad will join with me on this, but either way Margaret, we will appeal."

Des raised his hand, "Before you have me tried and sentenced for not caring about Jake, you'd best remember that he told me not to file an appeal. As his attorney, I'm bound by his wishes, so before either of you start anything, let me have time enough to talk to him. If he still says no appeal, then I'll resign as his attorney, and you're welcome to try to change his mind. That sound fair to you, Margaret?"

She didn't say anything, just nodded yes. Des could see the tears just starting at the corner of her eyes, so he asked Hernando to walk with her on the front porch, so she could catch some fresh air.

Des called Purcell at the number Julie had given him and ended up leaving a message. He was hoping to connect with him in the morning to swap notes. He called the number for the guard, Sam Battiste. His wife answered, Sam was out. He didn't like to keep on calling her Mrs. Battiste, so he asked her name. "Angelina," she replied. He asked her to leave a message for Sam to call him at the new cell number, as soon as he could. Then, he wasn't sure why, he asked how the pregnancy was coming along.

"I'm just starting the third trimester and all of this is new to me. One day I'm feeling fine and the next I feel like I've been run over by a truck. I really shouldn't complain, it's just so many new feelings and sensations, I don't know what to do or what to expect. I don't have any friends I can talk to here, Sam was transferred here from Sacramento where we had quite a few friends, but Susanville is pretty much a white town. There are other black guards, but they don't hang with Sam for some reason, so he's the only one I get to talk to any more. I guess I'm just lonely, but I can't afford long-distance calls to my Mom. She always knew how to cheer me up when I wasn't feeling good, oh Mr. Edmonds, I'm just running on. I'm sorry, I'll tell Sam you called."

"Angelina, wait. Are you expecting a boy or a girl?" Des could hear the loneliness in her voice and thought he could spare a few minutes for a lonely girl.

"Sam doesn't want to know until the baby is born. I'm thinking it's going to be a boy, but you never can tell. I just hope the baby's healthy."

"Me too," Des said, "but with a mom named Angelina, that baby already has a head start."

She laughed and asked, "Are you flirting with me, Mr. Edmonds?"

"Maybe a little, maybe just enough to get you to laugh Angelina. Feel better now?"

"Yes, yes I do, thank you. You're a charming man Mr. Edmonds. I'll make sure Sam talks to you tonight," and she hung up.

They headed back to the motel and Hernando was unusually quiet, as if there something on his mind more serious than his current employment. Rosa commented that Margaret had stated that there weren't any housecleaners in the Ridgecrest area, that it would be a really good opportunity if they were to move there. Des agreed but asked what she would do with her house. She said she was only renting it and would be glad to get away from that neighborhood.

Des thought about that and wondered if maybe he should move as well. His other daughter, Michele, lived just south of here in Apple Valley, and didn't like going into San Bernardino any more. She said the old neighborhood had changed, and not for the better. She had asked several times if Des would move up by them, so she could help take care of him. Every time she said that, he felt like throwing a cane at her, show her he wasn't a total, babbling, senile old man. Maybe he'd ask Margaret about it in the morning, it would help not having to drive back and forth all the time. That made him stop and think how he'd get around anywhere with Eddie up here helping Margaret with the harvest.

Another thought flashed through his mind, he'd forgotten to ask Margaret about the financial consultant. He'd try to remember to ask her in the morning.

Even though it was late, Des answered a knock on his door. It was the maid; she had been instructed to turn down Mr. Edmonds bed for him. Des wasn't sure what to think, and apparently the curious look on his face was enough for the maid to explain. She had been instructed by Miss Rosa to take special care of Mr. Edmonds, he is a very important man. Des just chuckled and tipped her a dollar and thanked her for the 'excellent' service, he'd be sure to mention it to "Miss Rosa" in the morning.

CHAPTER TWENTY-FIVE

The message read, "Report to Sheriff Lutz's office, As Soon As Possible." Purcell had a hunch it was about his snooping around a supposedly closed case. If it was, he could handle Lutz, he'd been on the department two years longer, and knew all the history of Sheriff Lutz. Lutz had done exactly the same thing that he was doing right now, looked into a case because it didn't 'feel right' when the man was found guilty. A simple assault case had netted the man seven years, without the possibility of parole, a rather harsh sentence for a couple of punches to the face. Lutz had found the connection between the existing Sheriff and the man who was assaulted, especially the several thousand dollars that he had contributed to the Sheriff's campaign fund. A bit too much for a county sheriff in a county of less than twenty thousand population it seemed, and the next election was proof of that. Sheriff Jensen had won by a wide margin, only to lose to Lutz four years later.

Purcell decided he'd rather talk to Mr. Edmonds than listen to the Sheriff, so he called the number Edmonds had left the night before. He heard a "Hello", and then it went dead. He dialed again and this time got an answer.

"Good morning Mr. Purcell, I'm sorry about that hang-up. I'm not used to these cell phones, this is my first. I understand you have some information to go over with me, but I must caution you, Mr. Kozan had told me not to file an appeal. Do you think we should still get together?"

"Let's start with you calling me Weldon or Purcell. I hear Mr. Purcell and I feel really old. I think what I've uncovered will convince Kozan to change his mind on an appeal. I'm not a lawyer, but from what I've read in the transcript of the trial, the whole case should have been dismissed. He wasn't allowed to face his accusers, only a deposition that couldn't be cross-examined by you. Do you want to try to get together today?"

"Not today Purcell, I'm busy all day today and I'm trying to get a message to Jake. He managed to get himself tossed into solitary so a certain person doesn't have an opportunity to stick a knife in him. It will probably be sometime next week before you and I get together. In the meantime, keep digging at the case and keep track of your time, I'm sure Jake would want you to be paid for the time you spend on his behalf. Can you give me a call Tuesday or Wednesday?"

"Sure thing, there's something about this case that's not right and I really don't like that judge, he's greasy. As for pay, unless I have to take money out of my pocket, there's no charge, let's say this one's for Julie."

Des hesitated for a moment, "What do you mean, this one's for Julie?"

"Well, I kind of feel responsible for that first mess of a marriage, I was the one who introduced them and I knew David was somewhat selfish and a partier. I thought at the time that maybe Julie could straighten him out, but I was wrong. Now she acts like she's sweet on this Kozan fellow, so I'm trying to find out as much about him as I can, including the truth about this murder. I think he's telling the truth and more and more evidence is supporting that, but I want to be sure. Say, can I tell the Sheriff that you suggested I check things out? If so, he won't be telling me to drop the case and leave it buried. He's really nervous around attorneys and the mention of your name might keep him off my back."

"Sure, call me next week."

Des tapped on Hernando's door expecting him to answer, but instead Rosa stuck her head out of her room.

"He left early so he could talk to Miss Margaret. He wanted to know more about the equipment and the harvest. The crew was supposed to show up early and he wanted to be there when they did. He said he'd be back later. Would you like to have some breakfast, Mr. Edmonds?"

"Sure, why not." Des smiled, he imagined this was new to Rosa, not having to get up and go to work. In a way, this was kind of a vacation for him too. On a hunch, he called Stan Hobbs.

"Are you up and around Stan? Edmonds here."

"I just finished my first cup of coffee. Are we still meeting at Margaret's later?"

"There's been a change of plans. I need you to play taxi for me, if you would. First, you need to pick up the assayer reports from all three assayers. Then come by the Carriage Inn and pick me up, I want to see the mine itself. So far I've only heard about it from Jake and you and I'd really like to see that place, if you have time before you leave this evening."

"No problem, Mr. Edmonds. I can post-pone leaving for a couple days in case you need something else done. I'll see you in about an hour and a half."

Des joined Rosa at the table and ordered a light breakfast. He told her of his plans for the day, and then asked what he could do for Rosa.

"I can't think of anything Mr. Edmonds. I thought I'd maybe walk around a little and see what there is here in Ridgecrest. They have a bus here and a taxi company, so if I get tired I can get back here alright. Besides, 'Nando will be back after he's through at Miss Margaret's and I want to know how he did on his first day. I still think of him as my boy, and I forget he's a man now."

"Well, I may not be back by dinner this evening. If not, go to the restaurant here and put dinner on the rooms. All you have to do is show them your keycard and then sign the bill. You'll be fine, I'm sure."

"You be careful out there in the desert Mr. Edmonds, you're not a young man anymore and it would be bad if you got hurt. We need you, 'Nando and me, and so does Miss Margaret and Miss Julie."

"You're too young to worry so much Rosa, how old are you anyway? You can't be more than thirty-four or thirty-five, so why do you worry so much?"

"I'm thirty-five Mr. Edmonds. I don't know why I worry, I just do. 'Nando was born when I was just eighteen. His father and I had to get married because I got pregnant; my father was very disappointed in me. We were working harvesting crops in El Centro, south of here when 'Nando decided to be born. We were

[166]

going to go back to Culiacan the following week, but he wouldn't wait. My father was a teacher in the schools in Culiacan and he wanted me to study and go to the university, he even had some money saved up to help me pay the tuition. When I had to get married, he was very disappointed and gave the money to my younger brother. We came north and my husband found work as a laborer, at least most of the time. I saw a paper in the laundry that said this lady wanted someone to clean her house, so I've been cleaning houses since then. Sometimes I wish I could get out of cleaning houses, I went to a restaurant to see about a job one time but they wouldn't pay me as much as I make cleaning houses. Maybe I'll look around here and see what there is."

Stan was just walking in the restaurant when Rosa finished speaking, so Des introduced them and headed for the door.

"The bill Mr. Edmonds, you didn't pay the bill, and your briefcase is here also. Maybe you are getting old and forgetful," she wagged her finger at him.

"Rosa, would you sign the bill, both of them actually, and put them on the room. I'll see you tonight, I hope."

Stan was a pretty good guide, talking about the different parts of the town and how most of the town was either in the Navy or supported by it. As they neared Trona, Des asked if he knew Thorpe and where his station was. Stan pulled into the station a few minutes later, and they went in to see Mike Thorpe. "Mr. Edmonds, I'm glad to meet you. We don't get much chance to rub elbows with high-price attorneys like you, it is an honor sir."

"I'm not sure it'll be that much of an honor when you find out we're planning to file an appeal. I know you're a reserve deputy for San Bernardino County, so I don't know what your feelings are about this case," Des said. He was watching Thorpe's expression as he talked, but he couldn't get a read on what the man might be thinking.

"I'm the one who gave Purcell the tape of TJ, Jake, and the Davis couple. I still don't understand why the prosecutor didn't investigate any further than he did. One of the things TJ said before he left that morning was that he had an uneasy feeling about the two. He wasn't sure, but thought he'd seen the guy somewhere in his past. That was the last thing he said to me, other than 'See you in a few days' but I think that was for their benefit, not mine."

Des thought for a minute and then said, "I need to have you write a deposition of exactly what you just told me about that morning, and anything else you might remember. It's very important and I'd hate to have something happen to you before we put you on the witness stand. Will you do that for me please?"

"I will be happy to. Jake's helped out the department a time or two when we had some lost tourists. He's a great tracker, like a friggin' bloodhound. Where are you headed now, I could have that done and in your hand in an hour if you don't mind waiting."

"Actually, the thought of stopping to see you just popped into my head as we approached Trona, we're headed to that mine where they tried to bury Jake alive. Stan knows the roads and he promised we'd be in and out the same day, that is if his Jeep holds up."

"It should hold up, unless he's changed mechanics. You still taking this old relic to McCain's Stan, or did you change to that new oil-lube place?"

Stan laughed, "Still at McCain's, he's always let me have credit until I can get the repairs paid off. You know I wouldn't change."

Des wandered outside while Stan and Thorpe discussed the route in and out of the mine area, his nose was greeted with an exceptionally sharp odor. He was grabbing his handkerchief when Stan came out. Stan took one look and said, "We better go while you still have sinuses." Their departure was hasty, but not before hearing Thorpe tell them to stop back on their way out and he'd have the deposition ready. The rest of the drive to the mine was spent trying to clear his poor sinuses of all the mucus.

Stan was a careful driver, picking his way slowly on the rough road. Des thought they were over-rating it by calling it a road; it should have been called a trace of vehicle tracks. He didn't really understand Jake's love of this desert; it was barren, desolate, nearly void of any life, but absolutely quiet. Only the noise of the engine and their conversation interrupted that almost total silence. They neared the area where the mine was located and Stan stopped the jeep. "From here on we walk, do you have some comfortable shoes?"

Des showed him the boots he'd pulled from his closet when packing. They were old worn and very comfortable. Des felt over-dressed with the rest of his clothes and promised himself to buy some jeans when he had the chance. Stan took off walking toward the mine and Des just stared. He was traveling at pace that marathoners would envy. He let him get a little farther before he yelled at him.

"Hey, if you want me to go along, you better slow down. From the maps I read, we are just about forty-five hundred feet above sea level, and I'm not a kid. Now slow down."

Stan had a sheepish grin on his face when Des caught up with him. "I'm sorry Mr. Edmonds, I get out here and I just want to go full tilt. When we get up this ridge we'll be about a half mile from the mine, it's almost all level meadow. So can we go now?"

When Des got to the top of the ridge, he began to see why Jake liked this place. There were a couple of trees at the upper end of the meadow, and it looked like a long-stemmed grass over the entire area along with an abundance of mesquite bushes, some of them rather large. They grew in a line that began at the trees and extended to a wash at the lower corner of the ridge. He got the thought that there may be water under the meadow, held there by the formation of the mountains and the ridge. He looked and looked at the terrain to see if he could figure where the property lines might be. He was about to ask Stan, when he came up and pointed to a small pile of stones to the south of them. "That's the southwest corner of the property; the northwest corner is up the mountain there. You can't see the other two corners from here, let's go to the mine."

Des looked at the entrance of the mine, nearly closed by the blast. Stan showed him where to step and handed him a light that he could wear like a ball-cap. They turned it on and went inside, looking at the walls as they went. Stan explained to Des the band of rock they were mining was on a slight slope toward the rear of the mine. He commented that Chambers hadn't worked very hard at it, or he would have been able to make more from it. The fact that Chambers wasted a lot of water didn't help either. Water is a precious commodity out here, Stan reminded him. With that they moved further back in the mine.

"Do you see it?" Stan asked.

"See what?" Des responded. "Is there a difference in the ore or something?"

"Look around and see if you can find it. If not, then I did a really good job. The entrance to the cave is near you."

"I'm sorry Stan; I can't see what you're talking about. Can you point to it, please?"

Stan pointed and Des couldn't tell where the mine wall stopped and the cave entrance started. "I took the time to carry some ore from farther back in the mine and piled it here so it would blend in with rest of the wall. Unless someone knows exactly where to look, they won't find the entrance. It's exactly forty-three steps from that big rock at the entrance. You should remember that, just in case."

They exited the mine and let their eyes adjust to the sunlight. Stan commented that there used to be a small seep at the upper end of the meadow, where the trees were. Des wanted to see it so they hiked on over to the trees, the grass around the base of the trees had been cropped right to the ground. "Probably sheep, "Stan said. "They come down off the mountain every now and then, usually in the spring. They like the fresh grass, and they usually have their lambs then."

Des looked at his watch and so did Stan. They both nodded in agreement and headed back to the jeep. It was better to start back while they had plenty of sunlight, that way they could see the road better. Des felt kind of sad at having to leave, it was so quiet and peaceful there in the meadow. He was definitely beginning to understand Jake's love affair with the desert. There might be miles of harsh terrain with nothing interesting in it, and then an oasis in the middle of nowhere. He knew he had to get this property for Jake, no matter what. He also knew that if it meant playing hardball with Bryson, then that's what would be too. When they got to the jeep, Stan did a complete walk-around, checking the tires and for any fluid leaks that might be showing. There were none so they climbed aboard and headed back to town. Des took the opportunity to study the assay reports from the three assayers, all of them nearly identical. The percentage of gold in the ore wasn't enough to warrant a full mining operation, more like a hobby than anything. But, in order to keep the mine, which Jake wanted, they would have to show some mining or the EPA would shut it down under the Mine Recovery Act. The samples also showed copper and silver, with a trace of lead. Des thought the refinery costs alone would prohibit anyone from making money, as Chambers had probably found out by shipping a few tons of ore to be refined. Apparently it would be about a break-even situation, if it maintained the percentages it had now. Des was now officially curious, what did Jake know that everyone else didn't?

They stopped at the station in Trona and got the deposition from Thorpe, and a promise that he'd be there to testify if they needed him. The sun had just gone down behind the mountain when they pulled into the parking lot of the Carriage Inn. Stan said good-night and drove off, headed for home. Des saw the Beast in the parking space, and headed up to his room. He barely got in the room when the phone started ringing. It was Hernando.

"We were hoping you'd get here soon, we were getting hungry. I was ready to eat an hour ago, but Mama said to wait. Are you hungry? Can we go eat?"

"Give me ten minutes Eddie; I'll meet you and your mother in the dining room downstairs. I need to knock off some of this dust and wash my face. I also want to try to get hold of Bryson tonight if I can. I'm going to make him an offer, and I hope he sense enough to take the money and run. See you in a few minutes."

The phone call to Bryson was short, but not sweet. Des made him an offer of twelve thousand. Bryson countered, saying it was worth three times that at a minimum. Des chuckled and said he'd go sixteen thousand and no more and that would include the fact that he, as an attorney and officer of the court would not report Bryson for the fraud of pledging assets to both bonding companies. He then said that Bryson had one hour to make up his mind and call him back at his cell number. Des got to the top of the stairs when the phone rang. Bryson had decided that Des had made a fair offer and he would sell for sixteen thousand. Des told him to be at Inyo County courthouse on Monday afternoon no later than three o'clock and they would exchange papers. Des would give him a cashier's check for sixteen thousand, and Bryson would deliver an unencumbered deed to the mine.

Des then called Ellis Chambers Jr. and told him to be in Ridgecrest as soon as he could with the deeds to both properties. He could only imagine how badly Chambers would want to tell someone of his good fortune. Des smiled to himself, thinking that dinner was going to be the right end to a day like this.

The phone rang just as he sat down with Rosa and Hernando. Not wanting to interrupt dinner, he decided to let it go and shut off the phone. He ordered his dinner and then asked Hernando how his day went.

CHAPTER TWENTY-SIX

Hernando had started the day early. He was very nervous, not sure if he could handle the responsibilities he'd been given. He'd listened carefully when Margaret had explained how the pistachios were harvested. He left the motel at 6:30 anxious to get started on the day, his breakfast a quick couple of eggs and hash browns. He'd checked the Beast very carefully before starting it up, looking at all four tires, and even opening the hood and checking the oil. It also was a responsibility of his and he was proud to be the driver. He thought about the low-riders of the neighborhood at home and doubted that they would be of any use out here.

He got to Margaret's house at 7:00 and didn't see anyone, so he sat in the Beast and waited. About ten minutes later, Margaret came out on the porch wearing a robe. She motioned for him to come in, so he piled out of the SUV and made his way toward the house. He almost made the porch before he was stopped by a huge dog snarling at him. He froze, not sure what was going to happen. Margaret stuck her head out the door and yelled, "Frio!" and the dog went straight to her. She motioned for Hernando to come in, but he was still frozen to the same spot.

"Walk slow and keep your hands down by your side, he won't bother you. He's big, but he's also a big baby. We got him from the couple who will be here this morning, I hope. Last night I told you their name was Medina, it's not. Their name is Mejia, his name is Frank and her name is Guadalupe or Lupe. Frio was the oddball of the litter and much different than the other pups. We decided to give him a place to live where he can run. His mother was a Rottweiler, but smaller than Frio by a third at least. Just be calm around him, and there shouldn't be a problem."

Hernando came into the house and sat at the kitchen table while Margaret got dressed. Frio kept rubbing against Hernando, nearly knocking him of the chair. He didn't stop until Hernando started scratching him behind the ears. He was doing that when Margaret returned.

"Well Hernando, you now have a friend. Would you like a cup of coffee?"

"Yes ma'am. Can you go over the way the nuts are harvested, so I can be sure we're doing it right? I want to do a good job, Mr. Edmonds has trusted me to do this and I don't want to let him down."

As they drank their coffee, Margaret explained once more the routine. The tractor pulls the trailer alongside the tree until the wheels on the trailer are even with the trunk of the tree. Then the tarps are pulled away from the trailer and spread so the ground under the tree is covered. The shaker grabs the primary limbs of the tree, one by one and shakes them until he's sure he has most of the nuts off the tree. The gleaner, Indio, taps the upper limbs with his pole to try and get any other nuts that might be hanging on. He follows right behind the shaker, and then they both move off while the tarps with the nuts are pulled into the trailer and the nuts go into the bins on the trailer. When the bins get full, they are rolled off the back end of the trailer and left on the ground until they are loaded onto the trucks. Hernando should warn everyone to be very careful not run into the iron posts sticking up between the trees. Next to them are the connections for the irrigation lines, and if they get broken there will be water all over the place. When there are enough bins to fill a truck, Margaret will call the trucking company and they'll haul the bins to the processor in Bakersfield. After the trailer finishes at a tree, Indio goes around and picks up any nuts that may have fallen off the tarps or through the gaps between the bins.

Hernando asked how the bins are loaded onto the trucks, and Margaret explained about the forklift attachment on the back of the tractor in the barn.

"Does it have a clutch?" Hernando asked. He was hoping it didn't, but Margaret said yes.

"Ma'am, I don't know how to drive anything with a clutch. I've never been around any cars like that, or any other things with a clutch."

[174]

"Well today you don't have to; you only have to decide on a crew. You have all week-end to learn to drive the tractor and the forklift, and maybe the shaker too, in case the Mejias don't show up."

The first few showed up early, which Hernando took as a good sign. He introduced himself and asked their names, as luck would have it the Mejias were the first two he met. As he was talking to two others, he saw a figure far back in the orchard heading towards them. Frank Mejia looked and said that it was Indio. In a few minutes he was in front of them, standing perfectly still as if waiting to be told what to do. Frank explained that Indio didn't speak any English, only Spanish. He wasn't sure how old Indio was, but that he had always been old, even when Frank was a boy in Mexico. He had seen Indio a couple of times when he was growing up, then not again until he came here to work. As Hernando looked at him, he noticed his attire was not like any he'd seen except in National Geographic when he read an article on East India. He had a blouse-like shirt made of loosely woven fabric and pants of the same material. He wore thong sandals that appeared to be hand-made.

"He knows his job Mr. Partida, you won't have to tell him what to do. He's a very hard worker, you can count on that."

"Mr. Mejia, please call me Hernando, it doesn't feel right being called "Mr. Partida". I don't feel like I've earned that respect yet."

"Thank you Hernando, your mother would be proud of you for showing respect to your elders. I hope I can keep that respect. From what I saw yesterday when we were signing up, you may need some help. A few of the workers seemed to be a bit rough, and not pleased at having to harvest nuts."

"Thanks Frank, we'll see if we can keep from hiring them unless we have to. When the others show up we'll see what we have to work with."

He didn't have long to wait, the remainder of the people showed up in three cars. As they piled out, Hernando saw one that had definite gang tattoos on his arms. There were two others that were hanging with him and dressed nearly the same.

Five others came to where Frank and Hernando were standing, the three gang-bangers hanging back from the rest. One of the five was asking Frank questions about what time they would start in the mornings, how long they had for lunch, general questions about working conditions and so on. When Frank told him he didn't know, the man looked shocked.

"I thought you were in charge here," the man said. "Don't tell me it's this kid here, couldn't Mrs. Wagner find anybody else?"

Frank looked at Hernando and winked and then stated, "Mr. Partida comes highly recommended by a friend of hers and after talking to him this morning, I respect his authority in spite of his age. Is his age a problem for you?"

"No, no," the man said hastily, although Hernando could see he wasn't sincere. "I just assumed it would be you in charge."

"I'm not sure I want to take orders from a punk-ass kid," one the bangers said, almost a challenge to Hernando. "Did you get permission from your mommy to be here?"

Hernando felt the anger in himself rising, but he fought down the urge to retaliate against this person. A month ago he wouldn't have hesitated a second, he'd already be on him. He remembered how Des would wait before answering a question, so he mentally counted to ten and then as calm as he could keep his voice, he answered.

"I appreciate your concern for my well-being, especially because I'm so young. I've never seen gang members that displayed concern for other people's feelings like you have. Now if I may talk to each of you, one at a time, please relax until it's your turn. Frank, would you like to start?" Hernando could the fire in the gang-bangers eyes; he'd just been put down in front of a bunch of people, and by a kid. It wouldn't be a problem for Hernando; he didn't plan on hiring him now.

He and Frank walked away from the group until he was sure they couldn't be heard. "Thanks for your support Frank, you already have the job. Miss Margaret told me that you really are gentle when you shake the trees, only using enough power to get the nuts down. She also told me to hire you, but it was to be my decision, so you're hired. What time in the morning did they start last year?"

Frank explained to Hernando how everything had been done last year, and said he didn't see any reason to change, unless Hernando could improve on something. They both decided that Frank would be in charge of the crew in the field and Hernando would be in charge over everything.

Hernando interviewed everyone one at a time, even the gang-banger. Hernando noticed that Indio was only fifteen feet from them and had his pole in his hand, a fact that Julio, the banger, also was aware of. Something about Indio made Julio very nervous; he barely heard the questions that Hernando was asking him. When Hernando was done, Julio jumped up to scurry back by his friends. Hernando motioned for Indio to join him, and motioned for him to sit next to him. The entire conversation was conducted in Spanish, which Hernando felt wasn't Indio's native language. The gist of what Indio said was, I come, I work, you pay, I go home, very basic and to the point.

After the interviews, Hernando went into the barn to calm his nerves. He nearly jumped out of skin when Indio spoke to him; he had thought he was alone.

"You have a lion's heart, and are far wiser than you are old. The one outside wants to fight you, but it will prove nothing. Just be good to those who work for you and they will respect you and work hard. The old man and his daughter who is with child are very poor; I think they will do a good job." He then turned and went outside.

Hernando had his list now; it would be Frank and Lupe Mejia, Indio, the old man and his daughter, and one of the young Mexicans who had come with the Mejias. He walked out into the sun, and motioned for them to gather around. He called off the names and thanked the others for their time, and assured them there would be a check for each of them for showing up, they could pick up the check at the employment office. He turned and headed back toward the barn when he heard running feet coming toward him. Before he could turn to see what was going on, he heard a thud as someone hit the ground. He looked and

[177]

saw Julio face-down in the dirt. Indio commented in Spanish, "he tripped over a stick", but Hernando didn't see any stick, just the pole that Indio held.

The rest of the day was spent ordering port-a potties; cleaning out water cans, and practicing driving the tractor. Frank took Hernando to a fairly wide open area and showed him how a clutch worked and then had him shift the tractor into the lowest gear possible.   Hernando was rough at first, but soon got the hang of putting in the clutch, shifting gears, and then easing out on the clutch. After two hours, Hernando was ready to try the forklift, so he thought. Because the forklift was at the back of the tractor, Hernando was having trouble remembering which way to turn and which lever to use to raise and lower the forks, etc.

After two hours, he was ready to give up when Frank intervened. Frank and Lupe had finished parking and jacking up their little trailer, so Lupe was helping the young man that had come with them that morning. He had a small tent that he planned on sleeping in at night. He would get his meals from Frank and Lupe, so he didn't have to cook. Frank asked Hernando why they didn't use the other forklift attachment that was in the barn. They went into the barn and there it was; a lift for the front of the tractor. Before Frank could ask any more, Hernando was headed to the house. Frio met him on the porch, growling a little until Hernando spoke to him. He asked Margaret about the forklift attachment, if it would be alright to use it, she said yes and then asked what the young Mexican was doing. When told he was putting up a tent, she said no. He headed back to share the good and bad news when Margaret called him back. She asked Hernando if he thought the boy could be trusted, and when Hernando said yes she told him to have the boy sleep in the shed just behind the barn. It would be safer there, with less chance of a snake or a scorpion crawling into his bed. She also told Hernando of the three cots stored in the far corner of the barn, saying he'd be more comfortable on a cot than on the ground.

It took them barely an hour to hook up the new attachment and remove the old one, even the Mexican boy helped. The boy,

Javier McManus was twenty-two and married, his wife was pregnant or she would have come as well. They already had one daughter, and this time he was hoping for a son. He knew more about mechanical things than either Frank or Hernando, he was working as an apprentice at an auto repair shop near Cabo San Lucas, but it didn't pay as much as he could make as a laborer here in 'el Norte'.

When Hernando asked about his last name, Javier explained that back in the past one of his ancestors came from Ireland to fight in one of the many revolutions as a mercenary and decided to stay. That also explained the reddish tint to his hair and the lighter tone to his skin, as well as the few freckles across his face. After some more practice, this time with the forks in front, Hernando felt he could handle loading the bins onto the truck. Frank had him practice with a couple old bins that were on the slab on the west side of the barn. He had a problem getting them stacked on top of each other at first but with more practice he was ready.

"And that was how my day went," Hernando told Des. "I think Miss Margaret was pleased, she was smiling when I left this evening."

"Good, because I have some good news too, Bryson agreed to sell at my price, and so did Ellis Jr. It looks like I'll have to stay for a few more days so I can finish up with them. How was your day Rosa?"

"I walked around town like I told you this morning, and I stopped at a laundry and looked at the place where people leave notes. There were several that wanted someone to clean their house, so I called them and found out I can make more here than I can at home. I think maybe I want to move here, but I would have to get a car or a van to carry cleaning things first.

I still have a few friends there in the neighborhood, but not like it used to be before the gangs took over. Now everyone is afraid to go out of their house at night. They don't sit on the porch and talk like we used to, they're scared they might get shot by a drive-by. Now I think about moving here, but I'm not sure

[179]

where I could live or how much a house would cost. What do you think I should do, Mr. Edmonds?"

Des thought for a minute,"Rosa, that decision has to be made by you. This town is somewhat better than your neighborhood, but from what Hernando said there are gang-members here also. You'll have to deal with them sooner or later, and on your terms. I'm glad you looked for some opportunities as a house-cleaner here; you can be employed right away. If it makes your decision any easier, I'm thinking of moving here too. I can still practice some law, and maybe talk my daughter into joining me. My other daughter doesn't like visiting me at the old house, says it reminds her of her mother and she doesn't like how the neighborhood has gone 'down-hill', so you may have your first client already Rosa. Now, I'm going to order a drink, would you like one Rosa? Not you young man, you'll have to wait a few years."

Des ordered a single-malt scotch and Rosa asked for a tequila reposada. When Des questioned what that was, she explained how they took the best of the tequila, re-distilled it and then aged it like whiskey for a few years. When the drinks arrived, she let Des have a small sip. He was surprised at how smooth it tasted, similar to a whiskey, but with its own distinct flavor, not the raw harsh taste tequila usually had.

"Here's to a very good day for all of us." Des remarked, and raised his glass in a toast.

CHAPTER TWENTY-SEVEN

It was late when Jake woke up, or rather early morning, according to the lack of noise. He'd had another dream, this time about being enclosed in a stairwell. When he tried to go forward, the stairs tilted down, and when he stepped back, they tilted back. It was like he was going nowhere; he couldn't stop himself no matter what. He was sweating, and he also felt chilled at the same time. He swung his legs down off the bunk, trying to calm the closed-in feeling he had in the small cell. He resisted the temptation to scream, it would only add to his current feeling of helplessness. He did the deep-breathing exercises he'd used before and slowly got the panic attack under control. He wanted out of the cell, but for more reasons than the claustrophobia that bothered him.

He had almost a full week left on his confinement in Ad-Seg as the guards termed it. Ad-Seg, or administrative segregation sounded much nicer and less punishing than solitary confinement. He laughed at the thought, the PC police coming down on the warden for not using the proper wording in sending a prisoner to "Ad-Seg". Oh my God, he thought, I'm losing my mind. He laughed out loud and didn't care if anyone heard; he was tired of this hole and had figured a way out.

Within minutes a guard was outside his door. He tapped on it with his baton, saying "Keep it quiet in there."

Jake knew the guard couldn't see him, so he stuck fingers to the back of his throat and vomited loudly. "The bastards are trying to poison me, with this food. I keep getting sick after I eat. I need to see the doctor. My stomach is really hurting."

"Be quiet while I check the reports from yesterday, nothing we can do tonight anyway unless you're bleeding. I'll be back in a little bit." He left muttering something, but Jake didn't catch what he said, nor did he care. Jake was just sorry he'd had to throw up some of Angelina's good cooking.

He didn't have too long to wait for the guard, so he thought he'd try a little power of persuasion with him. "What did you find out, is there something you can give me for my stomach, like Pepto-Bismol, or Tums, or Rolaids? I can't even drink the water; it smells of chlorine so much I can't stand it. Can I at least get some bottled water?" He was deliberately trying to sound desperate so the guard might concede to one of his requests.

"I'll see what I can do," the guard said and then walked off. All Jake could do now is hope for a visit to the infirmary in the morning, and maybe get some rest.

He was lying on the bunk when he heard a tap on the door. "Prisoner, stand away from the door."

"Yes sir," he replied trying to sound weak. The guard from before entered, as did the senior guard from the previous day. Jake was doubled up, holding onto his stomach with his arms when they entered, so he stood up slowly and went to assume the position against the far wall as was the procedure. The senior guard told him to lie back down on his bunk and put his arms by his side.

"I see the food finally caught up with you prisoner. Have you been vomiting?"

"Yes sir," Jake answered. "I'm afraid that someone may be trying to poison me sir." He went on to explain the situation between the Aryans and the Outlaws. He also explained that he had agreed to teach the Aryans some basic martial arts techniques and exercises in exchange for protection from some of the other gangs, and because of this the Outlaws had gotten another prisoner to attack him with the intent to either kill or cripple him. He also told him how he'd deliberately attacked the guard so he would be sent to Ad-Seg and thus protected from this other prisoner, but apparently they didn't want to wait and were possibly poisoning his food. The senior guard nodded in agreement, telling the night guard that he personally had noted this problem with the food in his reports.

"There's nothing we can do until the infirmary opens in the morning. I'll have the guard bring you a bottle of water, but we aren't allowed to dispense any medications, not even an aspirin. Is there anything else prisoner?"

[182]

"Just that I was surprised to see you here this late at night sir."

"I put a note in your file to be notified by the guard on duty in the event of any stomach problems you may experience. Your guard called me so I could see for myself. Now, try to get some sleep."

Jake was suspicious, but kept his thoughts to himself. The senior guard was either totally a whack-job, or possibly a homo, or maybe both. Either way it didn't hurt to have him playing 'angel of mercy' on Jake's behalf. After they left, he managed to get back to sleep, this time with no dream. When he awoke again he could hear the night guard in conversation with someone who sounded like Sam. Mostly it sounded like Sam was getting a report from the night guard about Jake throwing up and complaining of there being poison in the food. The senior guard had left orders to transport Jake to the infirmary as soon as it opened, which would be in an hour.

Sam thanked the night guard, waiting until he left before giving Jake breakfast from Angelina and then telling him of the conversation he had with Des. Des understood what Jake was trying to do, but didn't like the idea of the fight, said too much could go wrong. Des also told Sam to pass on to Jake that he would soon own a "four hundred and eighty acre sand-box", as Des put it. They were to get the deeds from Chambers Jr. this weekend and from Bryson next week. Des also told Sam that the money Jake wanted would be there in his canteen fund by mid-week, at least twenty thousand dollars from as many different sources as he could get.

They were so busy talking; they nearly didn't get rid of the evidence of Angelina's breakfast when the senior guard showed up. He was escorting one of the trustees that delivered the food, and had a scowl on his face. When the trustee reached for a food tray that had a small piece of tape on it, the senior guard stopped him. "Let me see that tray," he demanded. "Open it right here where Guard Battiste and I can both see it." The trustee complied, but they both could see he was nervous.

[183]

"Did you put anything in the food, or in the drink?" senior guard asked. The trustee shook his head no, but Sam didn't believe him.

"Assume the position prisoner, right now." Sam began a very brisk and thorough pat-down and came up with a small envelope with traces of a tan powder on it. While he was looking at the envelope, the senior guard squeezed the juice carton and watched as the juice came out of a pin-hole in the corner. He then took his pen and separated the fried sliced potatoes and noticed the smallest amount of tan powder on the edge of two of the slices. He and Sam both looked at the trustee and Sam demanded an explanation.

The trustee was fairly young; maybe even one of those who would be taking the Fire Fighter training class in a few weeks. If that were true, then he was definitely affiliated with the Outlaws. The senior guard, having had the benefit of the conversation with Jake in the small hours of the morning, decided to "park" him in one of the cells until they could transport him later to face charges, although neither Sam nor the senior guard were sure exactly what those charges would be. The senior guard radioed to have another trustee finish delivering the breakfast trays to the prisoner because this trustee was suddenly indisposed. The senior guard took the tray of food along with the juice carton and left, mumbling something about wanting a 'transfer out of this shit-hole'.

When he was gone, Sam said to Jake that when he transferred to the infirmary, he wouldn't be able to get any more of Angelina's food to him, and that he would have to give the money back to Mr. Edmonds. Jake asked if giving the money back would create a hardship, to which Sam answered yes.

"Sam, you've gone way beyond what you should have to help me, so I'm going to consider the remainder of the money a loan. When Angelina has the baby and gets back to work, you can work out a repayment schedule with Mr. Edmonds, okay?"

"Jake, that's more than fair. But, I can't be seen doing any more favors for you, you understand?"

[184]

"Yeah Sam, and I was thinking that you should write down everything you know about this whole fighting and gambling thing. Don't date the letter; just address it to the Director of Corrections in Sacramento. If anyone asks later why you did that, you can say you didn't know who to trust here. Then, a day or so before the fight, you mail that letter. That way you're covered and I'll feel better."

The other guards showed up and escorted Jake to the infirmary and some time out of the hole, maybe more than a day or two. When he got to the infirmary, the doctor was waiting for him and so was the senior guard.

"This is the prisoner I was talking about doctor, he was vomiting last night, and so far hasn't had anything to eat that I know of."

Before the doctor could start his exam Jake said, "Sir, Guard Battiste knew I was hungry, so he shared a little food with me. I don't want him to get in trouble for that, sir. I just thought it would be best if you knew."

"Very well, is it staying down?"

"So far, yes it is, thank you sir. What did you find out about the food, sir?"

"I took it to a lab in town to have it examined; they'll have results in a few days. Then I'll make a final report about this. In the meantime, I've asked the doctor to keep you in the infirmary isolation unit and only allow Officer Battiste and Officer Crenshaw to check on you. From what Battiste and Crenshaw have told me, you can be trusted to not cause trouble. Doctor, if any other guards come and try to interrogate the prisoner, notify me at once. I live in the Guards Dormitory just outside the main gate. Anything else prisoner?"

"No sir, you've covered it. And, thank you sir."

The doctor did a fairly thorough exam and when he was done he told Jake he didn't see any signs of poisoning. Jake repeated to the doctor what he'd told the senior guard about the upcoming trouble between the Aryan Brotherhood and the Outlaws. The doctor listened carefully to what Jake was saying, and then said he might have a way to keep anyone from trying to get to him for a few days. He drew a sample of Jake's blood and put it in a container and added a mailing label to the Center for Disease Control, Atlanta, Georgia. He laughed and explained to Jake.

"All these big, bad convicts think they're tough until faced with something they can't see like a germ or a disease. Then they will kill each other to get away from here. I'll clue Crenshaw and Battiste what we're doing so they can act out their part, full isolation suits, etc. Anyone on the outside looking in will see what we want them to see, the only problem is getting food to you without anyone catching on. I'll have to think on that for a while, but I'll come up with something. Ha, all the big, bad men."

Jake asked the doctor if it was normal to take multiple stool samples from a patient with an 'unknown' condition. When the doctor answered yes, Jake told him he may have a way to get the food into isolation without anyone catching on. As for the food, Officer Battiste's wife is an excellent cook, and she had sent him some food before. He didn't want Officer Battiste or his wife or Officer Crenshaw to get in trouble, so he may want to discuss this with the senior guard before doing anything. They both agreed the plan would work, but the doctor precautioned Jake that he might have to really provide a few stool samples in case they got a guard in here who was nosey.

Jake was given his hospital garb, and the doctor set up a saline drip IV and even added a bag of a mild sedative solution for appearances. One thing Jake found out, the beds in isolation were much better than the ones on the ward; nothing to do now but wait for the rest of his funds to get here.

CHAPTER TWENTY-EIGHT

Des had been on the phone all morning, talking to anyone he could get to in order to help put money in Jake's canteen fund. There was a one thousand dollar limit per person that they could deposit in his fund each month. The rules did not state that the number of donors was limited, so Des was grabbing all the people he could get, even Purcell and Thorpe. He had each of them write a little note stating how they thought he might be able to use it in the up-coming times. It was just cryptic enough to have the Warden puzzled, but not alarmed. He had gone down the list of Margaret's employees and would personally talk to them on Monday to enlist them as well. The two assayers didn't escape the net Des was casting either, nor did Stan Hobbs. He asked Margaret if there were a few friends on the base that might be talked into helping, her reply was puzzling to him not having served in the military. Her words were, of course they'll help, they like their paychecks. It was only after he thought about it for a while did he understand.

It was getting close to lunch when the desk called. There was a visitor for Mr. Edmonds waiting in the front lounge. He started to call Eddie's room then remembered that he and Rosa were looking for a house to rent. He straightened his clothes and grabbed his briefcase and his room key. He was leaving the room when the maid asked him if everything was okay and was the service to his liking. He told her he'd never had such fine service and he wanted to thank her for making him feel so special. He left her standing there chattering about how Miss Rosa would skin her if she didn't do a good job, etc. He made his way on down to the front desk and inquired where the person was that wanted to meet with him. The clerk pointed to a young man in not too decent of apparel and sneeringly stated that would be the 'person'. Des didn't like the clerk's attitude, but now was not the time to do anything about it.

"Mr. Chambers, I presume?"

"Yes Mr. Edmonds, I'm Ellis Chambers, uh Junior." The young man was rather tired looking, and not well dressed. Des knew he was holding down two full-time jobs, and he definitely looked it. He was much too young to have the wrinkles and worry lines he had on his face.

"Are you hungry Ellis, I'm starving. I skipped breakfast this morning and was about to get lunch when they told me you were here. Would you like to have lunch, it'll be my treat?"

Ellis looked as if he was about to fall over, as if no one had treated him nice in quite some time, so he just shook his head yes. They found a table farther away from the rest of the lunch crowd which wasn't big on a Saturday. There they could talk in private, without any interruptions other than the waitress. Ellis acted as if he wasn't sure what to order, until Des reminded him that he was buying lunch, anything you want. Ellis asked if a steak would be alright, he hadn't had one in quite some time. Des nodded and asked the waitress if they could order one of the steaks from the dinner menu. She went to check with the cook and came back with good news. Ellis ordered a T-bone and Des went for the six ounce Filet Mignon.

"Did you bring all the papers we need to transfer ownership of the properties? I hope so; I have the check already made out in your name. I was lucky enough to find a bank open this morning so I could get a cashier's check. I do have one favor to ask though." He went on to explain how he needed to send money to Jake's canteen fund and would he, Ellis, mind sending him a thousand dollars and a note thanking him for the business. He looked up to see a confused look on Ellis's face, so he asked what the problem was. Ellis asked if the thousand was supposed to come out of his cashier's check, a rather angry look on his face. Des laughed, and said Oh my God, no. I have another check here and a hundred for the charges to send the money, plus I still have to sign that check I sent you. Ellis looked relieved and then laughed.

They spent the rest of their lunch talking about Ellis and his wife both working, but never catching a break on anything. Their two kids were great, but always coming down with something that prompted a trip to the ER, and they didn't have insurance and because they worked, they didn't qualify for welfare. The paperwork part of transferring the deeds would be finished on Monday when he met with Bryson at the Inyo County Courthouse. He had Ellis sign in front of the desk clerk who acted as a witness and was also a notary. Ellis promised Des he'd have the money wired to Jake's fund by Monday afternoon. Ellis left smiling and walking a little taller; maybe things would start looking up for him now.

Des went back to his room, and started making out checks to the people on his list that had agreed to help. Margaret called and gave him the names of six more people from the base, and said she'd be by later to pick up checks and have dinner at the motel with him and Rosa. She also said she had a proposition for him and for Rosa concerning places to live. He was just hanging up when Eddie came to his room.

"Hey Des, me and mama may have found a house to rent that's not too expensive. She said it's actually cheaper than the one we rent now in San Bernardino. Mama is in her room making some phone calls to people that wanted someone to clean houses. If she can get enough clients lined up, we're definitely moving here. What about you, what have you been doing?"

"Nothing Eddie, I've been laying back doing nothing, waiting for my assistant to finally show up for work, but he doesn't work on Saturday I've been told. Actually I've been rounding up people to help me put money into Jake's fund, and I've nearly got what I need. With what I have here and the ones working for Margaret, we'll have more than twenty thousand dollars in his fund by Tuesday. Did you and Rosa stop for lunch?"

"Yes we did, but it wasn't much. Rosa wanted to try the taqueria on the south end of the main street, thinking it might be good, but it wasn't. The place wasn't clean, the service was slow, and the food was not really good, but they were still busy while we were there."

"Well, I have not seen the great town of Ridgecrest, so if I can talk my chauffer into driving me around, I'd like to do the grand tour. What do you say? I have a couple more checks to make out yet, and maybe we could even run over to Trona and drop Thorpe's check off to him. Give me a few minutes and go tell

Rosa where we're going, and that Margaret is joining us for dinner this evening, not to rent the house just yet. Got it?"

Eddie nodded and bounced out the door. Damn, I wish I had his energy Des thought. It's a shame that in your youth you're given abundant energy and very little wisdom, but in your older years you have less energy and lots more wisdom.

On a hunch, Des called Margaret and asked if it were possible to meet the financial consultant who had done such a wonderful job on Jake's behalf. Margaret chuckled and told him that the person he wanted to meet was actually the daughter of the financial consultant, but she was at school in Los Angeles attending USC. Margaret said she'd check to see if possibly she had come home for the week-end, and if so, would she be interested in having dinner with them. Des told her of his plan to tour Ridgecrest and then go to Trona to deliver a check to Mr. Thorpe, that he would return in time for dinner with them.

Eddie tried to be as informative as he could about Ridgecrest, but because he didn't know much, there wasn't much to tell. Des could see a different 'attitude' in the town, different from other towns in that here most of the residents were transients stationed at the Navy base for a term of duty and then transferred elsewhere. Because of that, the houses seemed to be kept in better order than in some neighborhoods and towns he'd observed. They traveled a few of the side streets, and saw several "For Sale" signs in the yards. Unlike Phoenix or Las Vegas, the landscaping in the yards here was austere bordering on non-existent; he imagined a lawn-mower repairman would starve to death here. Some attempts had been made to make the yards like those in the cities of the Midwest that have an abundant rain-fall and ample water supplies. More and more, he was beginning to realize what a gem of a property Jake had found.

He said so to Eddie, and with that both were reminded that they better get to Trona and back so they could get the checks out to the rest of the people. On the way, Eddie asked Des about what he thought of him going back to school. Always having been a strong supporter of education, Des told Eddie he thought it to be a great idea, but what about his mother. Wouldn't she need to have help; if she started a new business here. What about transportation for carrying the cleaning equipment and supplies, how did he plan to get that? Des had plenty more questions, but he held them to himself, he didn't want to scare Eddie out of the idea of going back to school. He suggested that Eddie write down what his goal is, and then a plan on how he could achieve that goal.

The stop at Thorpe's station was brief. Thorpe took the check and went to his partner's store and had the funds on their way in a matter of minutes. Des introduced Eddie to Thorpe as a business associate, and asked if there were anything they could they could do for him as a return favor. Thorpe laughed and said no, it's nice to know people who will go the extra mile just for a friend. On the way back Eddie commented on how he had Thorpe wrong. When he first saw him, he thought he would be a total hard-ass, but he turned out to be nice guy. Des said most people are like that until you get to know them.

At dinner, Des met the financial consultant that had invested Jake's money. Margaret introduced her as Jayantha Prabatma, a junior at USC studying banking and finance, but everyone just called her Jan. Her father was legally the person signing the papers, but Jan had been the person making the decisions, sometimes after much argument with her father. Jake had met them at after Jan had been handling his finances for more than a year. Margaret knew Jan's father from the accounting office on the base where he worked. She had asked if he knew someone capable of investing some money, and he volunteered.

He had a problem with the English language, so he asked Jan to translate for him and soon she was the one making the decisions. Although she was only eleven at the time, she was choosing stocks for reasons only she knew and they mostly were winners. Though she was young, her choices were solid and soon she was buying stocks using Jake's money and also some bonds. Des asked her about some of the other transactions, such as selling short, etc. and Jan just laughed. She said sometimes she'd get hunches about a stock and would do a short sale, selling stock she didn't own at a later date much lower than the current price. When the stock falls to the price she predicted, it's sold and she keeps the difference between the two, minus commissions of course.

"Sounds risky, "Des said. "Do you ever lose money on short selling?"

"Sometimes, yes I do. But I'm glad to know that I made Mr. Kozan money, he's nice. I hope he's happy with what I did, he always treated me like a grown-up, even at times when I acted like a child."

"What are you going to do when you finish school Jan? Do you have plans for the future?"

"I don't know if I want to go on in school or take a break for a while. My father wants me to help him in his accounting business, but I really don't like accounting. I really liked what I was doing for Mr. Kozan, it was kind of exciting. My father was very upset when Margaret asked for all the files back; he thinks Jake doesn't trust us anymore. I didn't know what to think."

"Jan, I may need your help in figuring out what all of the papers mean. When I got them, they were and still are a jumbled mess; I can't make sense of a lot of it. I'd be willing to pay you for your time, if you help us."

"I have to check my schedule for classes, if I don't get a heavy load of homework, I can help you on the week-ends."

Des was about to speak again when Margaret interrupted, "I understand Rosa is contemplating moving to Ridgecrest and starting a cleaning service, if that's true I have an idea that may be of help to her and me." She turned to Rosa and asked, "How would you like to live with me at my house? If you'd be willing to clean the house a couple times a week, you wouldn't have to pay rent. I'd sure feel better having you and Hernando live with me. Also you could use the old station wagon until you can afford to get a better car."

"As for you Des, Jake's house is empty and I think it would be better for you than trying to buy right away. It needs to be cleaned; I haven't been over there in over two months. Now, if I can have those checks you made out, I'll get them to the guys on base to send to Jake."

"You need to send money to Jake?" Jan asked. "My father and I can help."

Des quickly explained the limitation on the amount that may be sent to a prisoner by any one individual. She said she understood, and she would explain to her father that Jake wanted Des to be in control of all the monies, that he'd done nothing wrong. He then made out checks to Jan and her father. He also asked Margaret to explain to the Mejias what the situation was and would they help. She smiled and said of course they would, just make out the checks.

"That puts us over our goal," Des said. "Jake only wanted eighteen thousand and we will be sending him over twenty thousand. He has a specific use in mind, that I can't tell you about now because of the risk involved. Thank you all for your help." With that he raised his glass in a toast to the group, and everyone cheered and clapped.

Rosa and Eddie huddled with Margaret about the living arrangements there at her house, while Des questioned Jan more about her financial abilities. They were in the midst of their conversation when Stan Hobbs showed up at the table, he looked dirty and dusty.

"Mr. Edmonds, unless you need me this coming week, I'm headed out of town and would like to get that check wired to Jake."

"Sure Stan, I've got it right here in my briefcase. I thought you weren't in any big hurry. What's wrong?"

"I don't know, I've just got a hunch this might be a really good find, and I'd like to get there before a bunch of amateurs screw up the whole area."

"Okay, here's the check and I hope you hit it big, I really do. You deserve to have a good one for a change."

Des was very impressed with Jan's financial knowledge, but he found out that her father wouldn't let her watch cartoons when growing up, said they didn't teach anything. She watched the financial channel at first because of the ticker scrolling across the bottom of the screen, but the more she watched, the more she understood. She thought of it as a game at first, and started picking certain stocks and writing them down and 'pretend' buying them. As she got better at it, she showed her father and they invested small amounts each month in the stocks she picked. It wasn't long before they had a sizable sum of money to show for her 'game-playing'. When the opportunity to manage Jake's money came along, they jumped at the chance, and it went up from there. It was the commission from handling Jake's money that paid for her tuition at USC. She wasn't sure they could afford it now that Des was in charge.

Des assured her that she and/or her father would probably be re-instated to the consultant position after the records were straightened out and filed properly. He also told her of an idea that he had in the back of his mind regarding an old friend who was on the board of directors at a very large bank. Jan laughed and said that she still wasn't interested in being an accountant, even if it was at a very large bank. Des re-assured her that what he had in mind wasn't accounting.

Rosa and Margaret had come to an agreement on the living arrangements at her house, now they had to figure out how to get what belongings they had out of San Bernardino and up here. Des was facing the same problem at his house, and he had much more furniture and belongings than Rosa. He decided it would be better to review the situation in the morning after they all had some rest.

CHAPTER TWENTY-NINE

Jake woke to a nightmare, his arms were cuffed to the side of the bed, and he was staring into the face of his old friend Alex. A shiver of fear ran through him as he thought what might happen next, the thought wasn't good. He was about to speak when Alex put his finger to his lips indicating that Jake should be quiet, and then he winked at Jake. In a whisper, he told Jake how he'd gotten into the isolation unit, it seemed that Officer Crenshaw was an old friend and had smuggled him in.

"We don't have much time Jake, Crenshaw says you have a plan to get me out from under the Outlaws, so you better fill me in quick. I have to be out of here by 5:00 a.m. at the latest. The Aryans are betting small amounts on you, but nobody has bet any big money. What's your plan?"

Jake looked at him and then said quite bluntly, "How can I trust you Alex? I haven't seen you in how many years and the first thing you tell me is you're supposed to kill me? All I can tell you is that you and I are going to fight in a few days, but I want it to be out in the open where everyone can see it. Also, I want you to wait at least five days so I can get 'better' and out of the hospital. Fighting me when I'm sick is no kind of victory Alex, not even you could be that low. Deal?"

"Okay Jake, deal. You have my word on it, and the guys on my tier appreciated the weed. I don't do that shit any more. I'll see you in five days and I hope like hell you know what you're doing. By the way Jake, I've got a nine-year old son now and for his sake I really do hope you can do whatever you're planning. If it's what I think it is, don't expect any favors from me, I won't lay down for you or anybody else and you know that Jake."

He left quickly, guided out by Crenshaw. Jake lay back bewildered. He was trying to figure it out when Crenshaw returned, apologizing for the cuffs, he wasn't sure if Jake would wake up swinging or not. He also told Jake that Alex had been a fairly quiet prisoner at Oroville Correctional Center, where he had first met Alex. Crenshaw said that when he left Oroville, there weren't any major violations on Alex's record, just a few minor scuffles.

Jake was worried now more than ever before. Why did Alex want to see him personally, what would that accomplish other than to shoot down the idea that Jake was sick. If Alex were to spread the news that Jake's 'sickness' was a scam, the odds would drop to even and he couldn't finish his plan. He lay back on the bed and wondered if Alex was really worth this trouble now. Back when he'd known him, he'd have gladly laid his life on the line for him and did several times. It was like Alex to go into a bar and insult everyone in the place just to start a fight. If there was anything Alex was good at, it was fighting. Often, Jake had resorted to buying a round for the house to keep Alex from getting stomped to pieces. The Alex he knew then had been worth it, but that was then and this is now and both he and Alex had changed. It might be enough now that Alex had a son that he was serious about getting out of prison and going straight.

Jake remembered in detail the one time in the war that they had faced almost certain death, and Alex simply said I'm tired of getting shot at. He instructed Jake and the two others with him to lay down cover fire and he would attack the closest group of the enemy. Jake thought it was either the bravest or the dumbest thing he'd ever seen, but in a few short minutes Alex had killed the group in front of him and was working his way towards the others. The remaining enemy had run away in terror, afraid of this berserk attack method. It wasn't until days later that Alex told Jake that if he ever pulled some shit like that again, Jake should shoot him in the head. That was long ago and another time, Jake thought to himself.

He was laying there reminiscing when Sam brought breakfast, definitely not from the mess hall. Angelina was an amazing cook; everything smelled great and tasted better. He told Sam he couldn't understand why he wasn't fatter than he was with Angelina's cooking. Sam just laughed and told him when they were first married; he did gain a lot of weight so they agreed to eat smaller portions. Sam also told Jake that Alex had been to the old man, Mendez, and was giving three to one odds of the Outlaws money that he would beat the Rabbi to the ground. According to Alex, he had seen Jake in the isolation unit and he was recovering, but in five days he would beat Jake into the ground right here in the yard where everyone could see. Sam said Mendez was making the Outlaws put up the money now, not later when the fight starts. Jake asked who was Mendez, and what did he have to do with this.

"Jake, Mendez is the bag man for the Latin Kings. They control any and all gambling that goes on in the prison, including outside bets on football games, etc. They get a percentage of the total and in turn guarantee that the winner gets paid. Mendez may look like a harmless old man, but he's known to have killed over twenty people both here and in Mexico. More than once the victim was hacked to pieces with a machete. If he makes the Outlaws put the money up front, it's because he believes there may be a problem collecting 'after the fact'. He has only done that a couple other times, one man had the money and placed it with Mendez, the other one didn't. Be careful Jake, he's not some old fool, though he acts like one whenever the guards are around."

"Thanks for the heads-up Sam," Jake answered. "I'll very careful when I talk to him. What happened to the man who didn't have the money?"

"He's buried in the prison cemetery," Sam answered.

Jake needed to exercise so he asked Sam to close the curtains of the isolation unit. He would have to work hard for the next four days to make sure he was in shape, he knew Alex would be. He had seen Alex up close and he looked as fit as ever, maybe he couldn't take him. The doubt in his mind started to come back, nagging at him; reminding him of the many times he'd seen Alex take a punch that would knock most men out. Alex would look at them as if he had been slapped instead of hit, and then the barrage would come. He would overwhelm his opponent with so many punches, hard punches, that he had no choice but to go down or surrender. Jake thought about that and several other things as he exercised, even Alex's son. Alex having a son was the wild card in the deck, was it for real or something Alex made up to throw Jake off his game.

He stopped exercising long enough to tell Sam about it and asked him if he could find out. If he were to talk to Tyler, the young intern at the Education Office, he may be able to find out. Sam said he'd try tomorrow; the Education Office was closed on Sundays.

Jake exercised intermittently for the rest of the day, but his thoughts kept returning to the idea that Alex had a son. He thought about his own baby, unborn in Susan's womb, and his sorrow came back as fresh as if they had died yesterday. He sat on the bed, wondering if he had pissed off the gods, maybe he was doomed to live his life alone. The thought of a family overwhelmed him, the desire starting to build inside him. He and Susan had been very happy for the few years that they were together, and then it was wiped out in an instant by a careless driver. He never did learn whether the baby would have been a boy or girl, not that it mattered now. Now he was in prison, convicted of a crime he didn't commit, against the only man who seemed to understand him. Now he felt alone, cut off from friends, working for a group of 'skin-heads' whose ideology he despised. He wondered if his circumstances were all part of some 'cosmic plan' the gods had cooked up. He never had been a religious person, he had left that to Susan because she enjoyed the services and the sermons and seemed to return home every Sunday refreshed.

Maybe there was a particular God, he wasn't sure. Each religion from Christianity to Zen Buddhism seemed to think they were the only religion that had a 'lock' on what was going to happen after death, but so far Jake had never met anyone who had died and returned saying "it's this one." He didn't feel very religious right now; he felt more like smashing something or someone. Sam saw the look on his face when he brought dinner, and didn't say anything to Jake.

Jake had just finished dinner when the doctor came in with a telephone and handed Jake a note with a phone number on it.

[198]

Jake dialed, wondering what might be at the other end. He was pleasantly surprised when Des answered.

"Jake, are you alright? I called Sam's wife to see if she could get a note to you and she told me you were in an isolation unit in the infirmary, what's going on?"

Jake filled Des in briefly on the 'tampered' food and the senior guard placing him in isolation so they couldn't get to him. He then asked if Des had figured out a way to get the money into his account, and Des told him the good news.

"There should be twenty-two thousand dollars in your account by close of business on Wednesday. I can't be privy to any illegal activity, as an officer of the court I would have to report it immediately. On Monday we transfer deeds to the property, and my daughter and Margaret want to file an appeal immediately. When we last discussed this case, you instructed me not to pursue an appeal, if you won't allow me to do that Jake, then I will resign as your attorney. What's the answer?"

"When I said that, I was tired and angry and confused. Des, so many things have changed since then, I would be happy to have you file an appeal. Just don't spend too much of my money, that is if I have any left. I'd like to have something to live on when I do get out of this so-called correctional facility, okay?"

"For now, it will only cost you the filing fees; my daughter is going to be working this 'pro-bono' for the experience, plus I think she has a crush on you. Who would have thought?"

The last statement shocked Jake. Julie was a very good-looking woman; at least he thought she was. Maybe the gods weren't so cruel, if a woman like that thought he might be worthwhile. He told Des to keep up the good work and to check on him on Friday or Saturday to make sure Jake was still alive, and be sure to give Julie a hug.

"One more thing Jake, I may be moving into your house for a while. That way I won't have to pay for motels and such when we start your appeals process. I plan on moving to Ridgecrest in the near future, but need some time to find the right house. Would that be alright with you? And we may be coming up to Susanville this week-end to get your signature on the deeds and the appeals papers, if so I'll bring Julie with me. Bye for now."

Jake mumbled an answer to Des's question and hung up, very much happier in his mind now that there was good news. The thought that Julie might be interested in a wreck like him really lifted his spirit; after all it might turn into something. He hadn't talked to her all that much, most of the time it had been him and Des doing the talking. She had asked a few questions also, but nothing of a personal kind, and especially nothing that might indicate an interest in him. Now his curiosity was up and he began to wonder about her, was it maybe some prisoner groupie situation, she didn't seem the type. He knew she'd been married before by the different last names between her and Des, why had she divorced? These and other questions ran through his mind and he realized they were a distraction from the goal he currently had. There wasn't much use in thinking about things that might never come to be if he didn't win this fight.

With all these thoughts in mind, he went back to practicing his leg kicks with more determination than before. In his mind he began to visualize himself winning, seeing Alex fall to the ground. He practiced until late and went to bed completely exhausted, with a smile on his face. His last thoughts before he drifted off to sleep were that maybe he needed a haircut and a shave, and that he was now looking forward to Friday.

CHAPTER THIRTY

Mondays are for some people the hardest day, the beginning of week, back to the old grind. Des had felt like that until he'd met Jake, and then the days took on meaning, giving him a reason to get up in the morning, wanting to dive into the day's work. Maybe his daughter was right; maybe he was going through a second childhood. If he was, it couldn't have happened at a better time, he needed the new strength he seemed to have now. Today was going to be busy, for everyone not just him. Margaret had to go to work, Hernando had to get the harvest started, and Rosa had to call the moving companies to get quotes on moving her house-hold contents as well as a quote for moving Des's. Julie was going to be his chauffer to the courthouse and act as lead attorney on Jake's appeal. They weren't actually filing the appeal today, merely the notice of intent. After lunch with Purcell, they were to meet with Bryson and transfer papers for the final piece of property, and then they would file the deeds and head home. It was definitely going to be a busy day.

On a hunch, Des called his office to talk to one of his partners. He hadn't been in the office in weeks, merely calling in to see if there were any cases for him to handle. Each time he got the same answer, nothing at this time. If his hunch was right, they probably as tired of having to "carry" him as he was of being "carried" and he could sell his partnership fairly quickly to the partners themselves or to one of the junior partners. Before the receptionist could say there was nothing for him, he asked to speak to Landon, one of the three other senior partners.

"Hi Landon, Des here. I wanted to run the thought by you of having the firm buy me out of the partnership. I think it's time I retired, or maybe open an office with my daughter. Try to think of a mutually agreeable number, will you?"

"I'm glad you called Des. The partners and I were talking about this very thing last week, wondering if you'd be amenable to the idea of stepping down. As for Julie, you know we'd be glad to make her a junior partner just on your say-so, all she has to do

[201]

is call. How about I let the others know about this call and get back to you later this week, say Thursday?"

"Great Landon, I'll leave my numbers with the receptionist. Thursday it is."

He'd had room-service send up coffee about an hour ago, but he was out already. He was just about to call when there was a tap on the door. When he answered, there was the maid with another tray with a full coffee-pot and clean cups. She was chattering something in Spanish, obviously angry with someone. Des raised his hand and she stopped what she was saying only to continue in English. "I told them that fory-five minutes from the time they deliver the first pot they are to deliver the second pot and they say no he didn't call for a second pot we don't send him a second pot until he calls for a second pot. I told them that you are an important man too busy to be dealing with idiots like them just to do what I say but like idiots they want to argue all the time."

Des stopped her by raising his hand again, "Rosa was right, you are a jewel, a rare and precious gem, never before have I been taken care of like this. If I were just twenty years younger, I'd be asking you to marry me. How cruel life is that I meet you when I am so old." He could see her face begin to blush and knew he'd said the right things. He took a ten from his wallet and held it out to her, saying, "Take this small token of my appreciation for your outstanding service and the kindness you have shown me."

She giggled and almost dropped the tray and coffee-pot. She set them down and gently took the ten, then left muttering something in Spanish, waving the ten in the air like a trophy, passing Julie in the hall.

"What was that all about?" Julie asked. Briefly Des explained and Julie laughed. "That explains the comments she was making about someone only being as old as they feel. I thought maybe you were chasing her around the room or something."

Des snorted, almost choking on the coffee he'd just sipped. "Oh my God, I don't believe it. Her and me? Please Julie; give me a little credit here, will you?"

[202]

Des finished his cup of coffee while Julie went over the notice of intent, this was her first since passing the bar and she wanted it to be right. Des nodded his approval and so she put the form away. She did a quick touch-up to her lipstick while he was loading all the papers and the checkbook in his briefcase. He smiled as he recalled when the girls were in their teens and would spend hours at a time in front of a mirror applying and often re-applying their make-up so that it was just right. They would do all that just to go out with a boy to get a hamburger and a coke. Teen-age girls either didn't understand or didn't care that teen-age boys had no clue whether a girl was wearing make-up or not. Boys at that age were only interested in one thing and it didn't have a whole lot to do with lipstick and eye-shadow.

"Can we take the Beast?" Julie asked. "I've been wanting to drive that thing since you got it, and now seems like a good time. We can swap with Hernando on the way out of town."

"Sure, but we better get going. I want to see how he's doing on the first day on the job; he left out of here really early. I guess he didn't want to be late on his first day."

They parked in back of the barn where they could see the harvest crew working back up the row toward them. It was amazing to watch, Frank and Hernando had the whole operation working very smoothly and efficiently with a certain rhythm to it. After they left the tree, old Indio would scramble around picking up any wayward nuts off the ground, even pulling a few weeds here and there that were sprouting at the base of the tree. He may be old, but he definitely doesn't lack for energy Des thought.

They exchanged keys with Hernando and were soon on the road north to Independence, and the Inyo County courthouse. Julie took to driving the Beast as if born to it, testing its power by passing a few slower cars. She also tested the seat warmer and really liked that. She set the air-conditioner on maximum cool and in seconds they were both chilled to the bone. Des laughed and commented that maybe he wasn't the only one experiencing a second childhood. Julie ignored him and kept fiddling with the different accessories, one by one. Des finally broke the silence by asking what she thought of Jake's chances on appeal.

Julie pondered a moment and then replied, "I think he's got a good chance, if we can get him out of this little town to a venue that's larger. I've gone over the court transcripts several times, and I believe I can show bias on the judge's part, but I think what is most important is the fact that he was or I mean you weren't allowed to cross-examine the two Davises. That by itself should have been cause for a mistrial, but the judge blew right past your objection. I hope the Appellate Court isn't as closed-minded as the judge was, because if there has to be a re-trial, I would most definitely ask for a change of venue. Also with the additional evidence that Purcell has been able to find, I believe there's a better than fifty percent chance of a dismissal. What do you think?"

"Julie, I believe Jake is a very fine young man and if I didn't believe in his innocence I wouldn't be here in this car headed to file this Notice of Appeals. He's not like most men I've had the displeasure of defending from time to time, he's sincere in his beliefs and honest to a fault. I like him. In fact, I'd heard that you like him too, is that true?"

Her answer of, "I think he's interesting," didn't match up with the slight flush on her face, so Des couldn't help but ask directly, "You do like him, don't you?"

This time her answer was more direct, "Yes, I do like him. When we talked to him there in prison, I felt a certain feeling that he was a very trustworthy man, someone who wouldn't lie to me. I know he might not tell me the whole truth, but I have this feeling he would never lie. I think about him and I'm not sure what to think. I know he was married once, but I don't know any of the details, is she still alive, is she dead. How come he never said any of that when we were talking to him? Is he that private a person? I just don't know what to think."

Des calmly explained the circumstances of Jake having been married to Susan and also the facts regarding the accident that killed her, and how Jake was in a way still grieving for his loss. Because of this, he wouldn't open up to people for anything as personal as the loss of his wife, that he, Des, had experienced the same thing and was just now starting to realize a refreshment of sorts by being inundated with all these tasks that he was doing for Jake. He finished his explanation as they were approaching the city limit sign for Independence and fortunately they found a parking slot big enough to accommodate the Beast. As they were entering the courthouse they saw Purcell leaving and waved at him. He changed course and came over to them.

"Glad you're here. I was just heading to the Sheriff's Office to see Lutz, when I'm done there do you want to get lunch? It'll be about an hour, how about we meet at the restaurant down the street there at 11:30?"He pointed to a small restaurant two blocks down and across the street.

"Sure," Des said. "We won't be that long; we just have to file a Notice of Intent on Jake's case. We'll meet you in an hour."

The filing was quick and easy, Des posted the filing fee with the clerk. Julie then asked if it were possible to obtain a list of the jurors on Jake's case and the clerk went to a file cabinet and sorted though the files and the returned empty-handed.

"Is there a problem with releasing that information miss?" Julie asked.

"The judge has placed a hold on that file, meaning I can't release any information regarding that case. If I do, I could lose my job."

Julie then asked, "May I speak to the judge, please."

"He's not in today; he won't be back until Thursday. He and the Prosecuting attorney went fishing."

Des pulled Julie back and whispered, "What are you doing? I have those names in my file." She replied in a whisper, "I know, I saw them this morning. I want to see how much control the judge has in this Podunk town." Des just nodded.

Julie turned back to the clerk and very politely said, "Very well. Thank you for your assistance in this. I hope I can call you in the future, do you have a card?"

The clerk, obviously bewildered by the sudden display of politeness, fumbled around a bit and finally came up with a business card. She gave it up after explaining in detail how her cell phone had changed and scribbled the new number on the card. They decided to walk to the restaurant and maybe browse the shops along the way. In spite of the tourists, the shops were not doing all that well, mostly souvenirs to send home to kids and grand-kids. A few of the stores had closed, with the ominous 'Out of Business' signs in the windows. Des thought Main Street isn't doing as well as Wall Street is, and if things didn't turn around soon there won't be much of a Wall Street either. They made their way to the restaurant, a few minutes early, but then so was Purcell.

"Hello Weldon," Julie said holding out a hand. "You're looking good, the arthritis treating you alright today?"

"You know how it is Julie, one day's good and the next bad. I never know how I'm going to feel until I wake up." He motioned for them to sit and waved to the waitress.   "Honey, get these good folks something to drink, will you?"

They ordered drinks and looked over the menu, both pages of it. Julie looked at Weldon and asked what the best on the menu was.

Purcell smiled and said, "I usually order the special, it's always different each day, but it's almost always good. There have been one or two times I was surprised, but not usually, the one time was a poached fish in pureed carrot and turnip sauce. If you don't want to gamble on the special, try the Reuben sandwich, it's really good but the corned beef doesn't agree with my arthritis, so I only order that if I'm feeling really good, or really adventurous. That and the venison burger is good, but ask for it with the sauce on the side. The cook puts this sauce on the venison burger, but it's too hot for me. A little of it on the burger makes it taste great, but too much and you'll regret it."

They ordered and Julie asked Purcell for an up-date on what he'd found out about the evidence on Jake's case. He sipped his iced tea and looked around the restaurant to see who was there, obviously concerned about who might overhear. Something or someone must have alarmed him because he asked Julie to wait until after lunch, then they'd all take a walk by the park or just sit in their car. Des had ordered the daily special, which was stew, and he remarked how tender the beef was and how it tasted unlike any other beef stew he'd had before. Weldon waved the waitress over, and said, "Honey, tell Mr. Edmonds what the stew is made of today."

Without hesitation she recited,"Bear meat, carrots, potatoes, onions, garlic, parsnips, celery, broth, and spices. Is there a problem?"

"Not at all," Des answered. "I've never had bear meat before and was curious, that's all."

They finished lunch and made their way to the Beast and climbed in. Then Weldon began to tell them what he knew.

"When I went out there, I found everything just like Jake described it in his testimony and when I talked to him. I found a rifle slug near the exact spot where Jake had hidden, a newly fired slug full-metal jacket from a .308 rifle, the same kind snipers use. It's an extremely popular caliber with the military and the different agencies. I didn't find anything else at that spot, but I re-traced the supposed foot-steps of the Davises and swept the entire without a single blip from the metal detector. Going the opposite direction, based on Jake's testimony, I found several 9mm slugs all from the Browning found at the scene. Even though there were Jakes prints on the 9mm casings, I don't believe he did the shooting, it doesn't add up with the location of the other slugs I found. One thing is certain; I've never seen a murderer blow half a hillside to bury himself in a hole he couldn't get out of.

I also did some background work on the jurors and one in particular is suddenly spending more than usual. There are a couple others that seem to have more money than before, but they might have reasonable explanations. I'd need warrants to get the bank statements and deposits for these people, but that means going to the same judge that put Jake in prison and that would tip him off to the fact that we're re-opening the investigation. The prosecuting attorney has already hinted that I should leave things alone in this case, that the jury made the right decision.

Sheriff Lutz may have tipped him off, because he called me on the carpet about spending hours on a closed case. When I told him I was working on my own time, he backed off, but I'm worried he may be feeding info to the judge or the attorney. He made it to Sheriff by digging dirt on his former bosses, so I wouldn't put it past him to try to sabotage any evidence we come up with. Lutz has been known to bend a rule or two if it was to his advantage, I've seen that myself."

"Is it possible that the new slugs and other evidence might end up missing?" Julie asked. Purcell nodded and smiled.

"What if they weren't turned in to the Sheriff's Department, but to a well respected attorney who represents the accused? I just haven't gotten around to telling Lutz that I have this evidence or the video of the Davises at Thorpe's station in Trona. Which would you call that counselor, incompetence or malfeasance?"

Julie laughed and then commented, "Weldon, you are a fox, an old desert fox. Thank you so much for thinking of that. Just for the record, where is the evidence, other than the video?"

Purcell took a manila envelope from inside his coat pocket and handed it to Julie. She looked inside and grabbed a large notebook from her briefcase. She quickly wrote out a receipt for the contents and put down the origin and dates of discovery, and by whom. She then had Purcell sign as well as Des as a witness. It would be crucial to maintain a chain of evidence on these items if they ever went to court.

Des motioned to Julie to look toward the courthouse. A man with some large envelopes in his hand was pacing back and forth, checking his watch.

"I think my three o'clock appointment is early," Des said. "Weldon, would you do me a favor and accompany me while I do a little business with this man? You won't have to do anything, just stand there. I'll do the talking."

They disembarked the Beast and walked toward the man. When they were close enough, Des said, "Mr. Bryson?"

He turned and answered, "Yes, I'm Donald Bryson. Are you Mr. Edmonds?"

"Did you bring the necessary papers Mr. Bryson? I do hope I haven't made this trip for nothing."

"Well, there's one thing we need to talk about, can we talk alone?"

"Mr. Bryson, if it has to do with the price, then I must inform you that the deputy is here to arrest you should attempt to back out of our deal. Now, what is there to discuss?"

Bryson's demeanor crumbled in the face of possibly being arrested, "Nothing I guess," he mumbled and held out the papers.

"Good, if you'll follow me we can have everything transferred, notarized, and recorded and you can be on your way back to Sacramento," and with that Des went into the courthouse, with Bryson in tow. They came out thirty minutes later, with Des smiling and Bryson walking quickly towards his car.

Julie and Purcell had had the chance to discuss the case and Jake. Purcell had said to Julie that he thought Jake was innocent, and that he wasn't inclined to charge for his hours in investigating for them. When Julie protested, he explained how he had felt bad about her and David Larson, that he felt somewhat responsible for her pain. With that he had gone back to work so Lutz wouldn't have anything to berate him with.

When Des returned, Julie fired up the Beast and they headed south towards Ridgecrest. The first few minutes were quiet and then Julie asked why Jake wanted that particular piece of property way out in the middle of the desert.

"As far as I can tell, he wants to build a home there where he can have some privacy away from other people, or as he put it, solitude. I think he is one of those people that although they may be alone, they aren't lonely. He seemed to be at peace with himself, secure in the knowledge that he is capable of handling any situation that might arise. When he is alone, it's because he chooses to be, not because he hasn't any friends. In handling his affairs, I've seen several instances where he has helped others just because they needed help; no other reason and no worry about if he would be paid back. People just like him and there's no explanation for it, other than he makes you feel good when he's there.

Anyway, he was trapped in the mine and found water, clear drinkable water, enough to sustain his home with careful rationing. Water is a precious commodity in the desert, so finding a continuous source is kind of like hitting the lottery. There is also water in the little valley that he now owns most of, a small seep at the upper end of the valley that could be pooled and used for irrigation or other uses. From what I saw of the valley, there is water held there in the ground far longer than any of the areas outside the valley, meaning that there is possibly enough water underground to warrant drilling a well. How he might power that well, I don't know, but I do know the gold is one of the last things he's concerned about. We'll ask him some of these questions when we see him Saturday. Are you planning on going up there with me?"

"If I can get the time off, which shouldn't be a problem because I haven't taken a vacation day since before David and I split the sheets. Are we driving up Friday and coming back Sunday?"

"That's the plan if we can get someone to cover for Hernando, that's a long drive all by yourself, and I'd feel better knowing there's two of you to do the driving. Besides, he is my chauffer after all, and it's time he earned his pay. Speaking of pay, remind me to call the probation office when I get back so I can let them know Hernando has made full restitution to me."

"Why don't you call them right now with that cell phone you bought, or did you forget about the new toy already?"

Des looked at her and finally said, "You are way too much like your mother, a real pain in the ass sometimes. Now, how about you drive and I make phone calls while you be quiet, okay?"

She smiled and said, "I take that as a compliment, being compared to Mom like that, thanks."

Des called the probation office and talked to the officer in charge of Hernando's case, giving her all the information she needed, but before they finished talking, the PO reminded him to tell Hernando that he had an appointment on Friday and to not be late. With a little begging and pleading, Des was able to get the PO to change the time to late Thursday afternoon.

He then called Margaret's house hoping she might be home, but no luck. He didn't like calling her at work; the feds were funny about people conducting personal business over government

[210]

phone lines. He called back to the house and this time left a massage for her to call him about Hernando being off Friday. They were just pulling next to the barn when the phone rang, it was Margaret. Des told her to hang up the phone and come out by the barn.

"Hi Margaret, I need to know if you can get someone to fill in for Hernando on Friday so he can drive me to Susanville to visit Jake on Saturday. Do you know anyone that will do that for one day?"

"I know a couple of the enlisted men who might fill in for the day, I'll ask tomorrow. They really did a good day's work today; between him and Frank they're ahead of the first day last year. I was worried about the old man that Hernando hired, but he seems to be holding up his part of the work. He was struggling at first, but Frank showed him a few tricks on how to handle the sheets and he really did better. I think he'll be here until we're done. Is there something special you're seeing Jake about, or just a visit?"

"Actually, I need to have him sign several papers, including the appeals documents. And I wanted to make him aware of a few things that we found out about some jurors and the judge. Is there a message you want to send him?"

"Only that I'm praying for him Des, only that I'm praying for his release. Remember, if you or Julie need money for his appeal; let me know and I'll get it to you."

"That part is covered Margaret. I talked to Jake and have his authorization to proceed with the appeal and to use whatever funds I need, but thank you for the offer. We filed the Notice of Intent with the county clerk this morning, so we have that part covered. Julie is drafting the appeal itself and I'll be helping her when I can. Let me know about Hernando's replacement as soon as you can, please?"

"He's going to be driving you up there, even if I have to take a day off to work the sheets myself. He's really good with these workers, he checks on them all the time, making sure nobody is getting too tired or over-heated. I've noticed that during break he always makes sure everyone gets something to drink, apparently

Frank told him of a worker passing out from dehydration last year. He asked if it would be alright to bring in some Gatorade instead of just water, so I told him to pick it up and I'd pay him for it. He's got a good heart Des, he cares about people."

"I'm glad to hear that, I was worried he might turn out to be another punk trying to take advantage of the opportunity."

When the crew reached the end of the row, Hernando called for them to quit for the day, they were all tired, but they were smiling too. Julie said good-bye, noting that she had midnight shift and had to get some rest. Des rode with Hernando back to the motel, and let him know of the up-coming trip to Susanville. Hernando started to protest until he heard that Margaret was getting a fill-in for the day and that Frank would be in charge. When they got to the motel, Hernando headed to his room for a shower and Des to his to talk to Rosa about the movers. They agreed to meet downstairs for dinner in an hour.

Rosa had contacted four moving companies and described the household contents of her house and then Des's house. She asked for separate bids for each house, and had written down the quotes from each company. Her written English wasn't the best, but it was legible and very neat. They decided to go with the one company for both houses and Rosa would call to see if it could be done next week. Both household's contents were to be stored in the barn at Margaret's.

When they met for dinner, Hernando looked tired. Des asked how his first day went and he replied that at first they were a little slow, but they got into a rhythm as the day went on. He said he was tired, but it was a good tired, like he'd done something good.

Rosa told him of the plans to move both houses to the barn, but she said she needed to get some of her cleaning equipment like the two vacuums and the carpet shampooer from her house as soon as she could. Des suggested they take the station wagon from the barn and drive it to McCain's to have it tuned up and lubed, and then Rosa would have some wheels, instead of having to rely on the bus or someone else.

"Why don't you drive, Mr. Edmonds?" Hernando asked. "Didn't you ever get a license?"

[212]

"I have a license. I think it's still valid. I haven't driven since my wife died in an accident. I just don't want to drive anymore."

"What happened; were you the one driving? Is that why you don't drive?"

"No, I wasn't driving. I was supposed to be driving, but I was tired so my wife said she'd drive, and another driver crossed the line and hit us head-on. I escaped with mere bruises, but I held her as she died in my arms. I just haven't driven since. Now can we change the subject to something else?"

"I'm sorry Mr. Edmonds, I didn't know. Forgive me for bringing it up."

"Of course Eddie, you're a good friend and you have a right to know these things. Someday I might try driving again, but not right now. Besides, if I drove, what would I need a chauffeur for?"

Eddie smiled and said, "Yes sir, Mr. Edmonds, sir. I really liked working today, it made me feel good. By the way, if you plan on driving that old wagon far, you might want to think about getting some new tires, those looked pretty worn and they had age cracks on the sides. The rims looked rusty too."

They finished dinner and went to their separate rooms. Des had one message from Jan, the financial wizard. She said she was able to work Friday and Saturday on the filing of the accounts and would he please call her.

"Hello, Jan?"

"Yes sir. I called because I wanted to know how much I would be paid for setting up the files and filing the accounts. Does fifteen dollars per hour seem fair?" she asked.

"Yes, I think so, but the files are in San Bernardino right now, I'll see if I can get Rosa to bring them back on Thursday when she goes down there. Can we drop them off to you, and you get started by yourself on Friday? We have to be out of town on Friday and Saturday."

"That will be alright Mr. Edmonds. I'll start on them Friday morning."

After hanging up, Des thought to himself; Mondays aren't that bad after all. It all depends on how you look at it.

CHAPTER THIRTY-ONE

Smith watched as Collier had another meeting with one of the Outlaws. He felt nothing but disgust for the man, selling out his own people that way. He admired Jake for his attitude, but also because he was loyal to those he was working with. He knew Jake had some other agenda he was working on, but it didn't seem to interfere with the Brotherhood's plans so it wouldn't matter that much. Smith also liked the way that Jake had helped Ernst learn to read and write, that was awesome as far as he was concerned. He now regretted his actions while in school, always acting up and not doing any of the homework or the required reading. He had finally quit school while only a junior, to take up a job that paid very little and went nowhere. He watched how Ernst devoured book after book, moving up in levels as his ability improved, and in a way he envied him for his hunger to learn.

It was time for the morning exercises, and Sorenson was there to lead as usual. He had stepped up to the job and was doing a fine job teaching the newer members all the martial arts moves they had been taught. Smith would definitely back him up, as would Ernst when it came down to trouble, but not against the Reverend whom he considered family. He joined the exercise group and did the full routine, smiling as he felt the burn begin in his muscles. It was a good feeling, a feeling that his strength was improving daily along with his confidence. Smith knew about the deal between the Reverend and Jake, and admired Jake for his actually teaching them the correct ways to exercise and to practice their defensive moves, he knew Jake could have just gone through the motions and not too many people would be any the wiser. He thought back to Collier and knew if he were given an opportunity, he'd take Collier out. The very thought of that made smile and work even harder, which Sorenson noticed and said "Way to go Brother Smith, that's the spirit we like to see."

Ernst got into the spirit too, waving his arms like a cheerleader, challenging the men to work harder, telling them that "If we stand together, we stand tall." Smith liked that

[214]

remembering it from the first time he heard the Rabbi say it. He began clapping his hands in rhythm and chanting "Stand together, Stand tall," as the men exercised. Out of the corner of his eye he saw the sneer on Collier's face and thought to himself, your turn is coming traitor. Again, the very thought of Collier going down made him smile.

Jake was in the isolation unit also exercising. He had the curtains closed and was going hard at the leg exercises; he knew they would be what would help him win. His concentration was broken when he noticed Sam standing there smiling. He motioned him closer and listened as Sam told him that his canteen fund now had fourteen thousand dollars with possibly more coming in later today. It seemed that Des had found a way to get the money to him; hopefully it all would be there in time to place a bet. He asked Sam if there were any way to get Mendez here so he could place that bet, Sam replied no. The best he could do is let Mendez know that Jake wanted to bet on himself at three to one and had several thousand dollars in his fund. Mendez would figure his own way to verify the funds if he didn't know already. When it came to finances in prison, there weren't that many secrets. Sam agreed to contact Ernst and have him relay the message to Mendez, Sam even felt more comfortable around Ernst than he had before, said that Ernst seemed more peaceful and less menacing now. He also told Jake about how Ernst was reading at the rate of two books a day, like he was addicted to learning. Sam told Jake he'd created a reading monster.

Jake looked at Sam and commented, "When a person is denied something for a long time, they begin to crave just that one thing. Like if a man were poor most of his life and then one day the bank manager comes to him and escorts him to the bank and says, "here, take whatever you want, it's your turn now so anything you want just take it." That man would be scooping up bundles of hundred dollar bills as much as he could carry. The same thing happens when you're in the desert and short of water. You ration it carefully, hoarding what little there is until you finally run out. And if you're lucky and make it out of the desert

[215]

alive, you don't guzzle down gallons of water like you see in the movies, you sip slowly savoring the feel of it in your mouth barely drinking any at all the first day, but the second day you drink and drink as if you can't get enough. That's the way Ernst is right now with learning, he was deprived of it all his life and made to feel stupid. Now, he's started to learn and it feels good and so he can't get enough, he is catching up for years of not knowing. I'm glad for him, I think beneath that big tough exterior of his is a kind and gentle man who was never able to express himself except through violence."

Sam looked at Jake and smiled. "You know when you first got here; you didn't say anything for weeks. Now, we can't get you to shut up. You do beat all Jake, you do beat all."

Jake laughed at him, "You're right Sam, I must have gotten a case of vocal diarrhea all of a sudden. Now I have to get back to work, thanks for the news. Let me know if Ernst gets through to Mendez, please."

Down in the yard a different conversation was taking place. This one was between the Reverend and Smith, whom the Reverend had asked to keep tabs on Collier. Smith reported the meeting between Collier and the Outlaw member earlier this morning and asked if he had permission to take out Collier. The Reverend told him to be patient, that Mr. Collier had a few more useful days left. He also told Smith that it would be okay to let slip that the Brotherhood wasn't too sure that Jake could take Alex, which is why the bets were so small at this time. He also said that Jake was to be out of the infirmary as soon as they figured out what kind of 'bug' he had, maybe as soon as tomorrow. The doctor wasn't exactly sure what it was, so he'd had samples of Jake's blood sent to the Center for Disease Control in Atlanta, and was supposed to have an answer later today. The doctor's assistant was keeping the Reverend informed of any changes and any new information that came in. Smith figured afternoon practice session would be a good time to pass along the Reverend's conversation to the other three, because the Reverend wants them to understand what is happening.

In Jake's old cell, 'Joe Robertson' was about at the end of the line. His superiors had sent him here on short notice, to get anything he could to discredit Jake, but Jake disappears into Ad-Seg and is untouchable. Joe was 'new fish' and as such didn't have any affiliation with any of the gangs and didn't have the resources to keep procuring contraband such as the shivs that he'd planted in Jake's bunk previously. He was sitting there trying to come up with a plan when a huge man appeared at the cell door. He knew he was one of Jake's students, but couldn't remember his name.

"What do you want, boy?" Joe sneered, trying to put as much insult into the question as he could.

Ernst answered in his soft childlike voice, "It's not what I want, it's what I know that Jake likes. He prefers to be alone. He calls it solitude and because of that I'm here to ask politely if you would transfer to another cell, please. I would appreciate that very much, and I'm sure you would feel better living with one of your own kind."

"Is that right, cracker? You here to chase me away, whitey, what's the matter, you too stupid to answer, or didn't they teach you that yet, dummy?"

Ernst started toward him and then stopped. "Your words can no longer bother me, because I do know what they mean. You're trying to make me angry so I do something wrong and get in trouble. Not this time, you won't get to me this time; I've asked politely and would like an answer. I'm not sure you'll be safe if you stay in this cell." With that Ernst turned and left, walking slowly away down the tier. Inside he was fuming, but at the same time proud that he had held his anger under control.

When Ernst got to the Education Center he still had a scowl on his face prompting Tyler to ask what was wrong. Ernst recanted the conversation with 'Joe Robertson' and when he was done he looked at Tyler. Tyler told him that he had done the right thing and that he was really doing lots better than when they'd first met, and that he was very proud of him. Tyler also told Ernst that he had the information that Jake had asked for about Alex Chang, Ernst could take it with him when they were done with their session today.

Today's session was to be about Herman Melville's "Moby Dick", a favorite of Tyler's.

Back in the infirmary, Jake had just been caught exercising by the doctor's assistant. Jake was sweating profusely, so there was no point trying to deny it, instead he said he was trying to exercise to 'get back in shape' because somebody was going to try to kill him on Friday. He also commented on how out of shape he was because he was sweating so much after a couple of simple routines, hoping the assistant bought his act. Apparently so, because the assistant told him he shouldn't try so hard, just take it easy at first, and then he left. When Crenshaw came in Jake told him what had happened, but was assured that the assistant reported only to the Reverend. With that good news and Crenshaw guarding the door, Jake went back to a full-blown hard-out exercise routine, pushing as hard as he could. Friday was coming and he wanted to be ready for whatever Alex might throw at him. As he exercised, his thoughts were about Alex's son if there was one, he wondered what it would be like to be a father. He had always liked children, and they seemed to always like him, but how could he be sure he'd be a good father?

The only example he had was his own father, stern but always fair. His step-brothers had always picked on him, but his father would only allow so much of the kidding around. When they got too rough, he would put them in their place, hard. With Jake, he always seemed to take a more gentle approach, as if he knew this was his last child. His mother also protected him from his step-brothers, but in a different way. She would take Jake to another room and let him play by himself when they got too rough with him.

His mother was barely ten years older than his step-brothers, the result of being the second wife of his father. She was the quietest and most gentle woman Jake had known, not because she was his mother, but because of the way she was. His father would sometimes go into these rages, and with just a touch she could calm him. Whenever Jake was around his father, he felt this feeling that there was this massive amount of power built up in the man even though he wasn't that big in stature. He also felt very secure in his presence, knowing that his father, in spite of his occasional rages, would never strike him in anger. His brothers had challenged their father's strength and his authority, physically fighting with him. Jake remembered seeing each of them get punished severely by their father, but when the fight was over he always helped them up and put his arms around them. Jake thought it was his father's way of saying, "You're forgiven."

Jake thought to himself that with his father as a role model, he could probably be a very caring and giving father. But if he was to be a father, he would need a wife, which started him thinking about Julie again. He personally thought she was a beautiful woman, not the Hollywood glamour-glitz type beautiful that people made so many comments about, but the deep comes-from-within beauty that a grown woman possesses. As he remembered, she didn't wear much make-up and didn't need much. Her hair was kept simple and natural; the cut was medium length and also seemed natural, not needing much more than brushing to keep it arranged properly.

He caught himself, thinking like a school-boy, and he chuckled. Maybe he should see if he could get the guards to slip her a note like in fifth grade. What the hell was he thinking, after Friday he might not even be among the living. With that sobering thought, he went back to exercising hard, pushing more and more on the leg exercises, changing up only to practice his leg whips and leg kicks.

In the Warden's office, the Deputy Warden was explaining to the Warden about the up-coming "grudge match" between the two combatants. Because the two involved had been causing problems on the yard, the Deputy Warden felt it would be best to allow the two of them to have their fight and be done with it. It would also help ease some of the tension that the other guards had mentioned was building up between the two gangs.

Fighting in any form was forbidden according to the Corrections Code, but if it were considered an "athletic event" the

Warden couldn't be held liable for any injuries that might occur. The Warden was a political appointee to the post and as such was very much in favor of not being "liable" and so he grudgingly gave his consent to the idea. He reminded the Deputy to be sure to have extra guards to control the crowd of prisoners that would be there watching.

CHAPTER THIRTY-TWO

Friday means a lot of different things to different people. To some it means the end of the work week, time to start unwinding, clearing off the desk, or finishing those last-minute little tasks that seem to arise out of nowhere. To others it means planning for the two days of honey-do projects, or soccer practice with the kids and maybe pizza after, or going to visit relatives. To Des it meant the end of a very satisfying week. Monday he had closed on the properties that Jake wanted, and at a very reasonable price. Tuesday and Wednesday he had helped Julie put together a very plausible appeal for a re-trial and a change of venue. He and Rosa had been able to get the old station wagon to McCain's repair shop; Des had been impressed by the cleanliness of the waiting room and the entire area as well as the garage. It was squeaky clean throughout, so much so that Rosa was impressed also.

McCain himself was a friendly sort; he suggested that he turn the wagon over to an older mechanic working for him. When Des explained exactly what they wanted done, the mechanic, Jim, asked if they wanted all the fluids drained and refilled as well. His thoroughness was admirable, Des thought. Jim also stated that he was particularly fond of this station wagon because he had owned it before selling it to TJ.

Thursday had also been a very productive day for Des. His partners in the law firm had made him an offer that was actually more than Des had in mind. To ease his mind, he told them he would allow them to pay it in quarterly payments so they didn't encounter a cash flow problem. They thanked him for that consideration and told him the papers and his first payment would be there at the first of the following week. Rosa and Hernando had moved out of the motel and were living with Margaret. Des had also checked out of the motel and moved what little he had with him to Jake's house, which Rosa had thoroughly cleaned.

Friday started early for Hernando. He was up and had coffee before anyone else in the house except Frio, his constant companion as of late. For some reason, that dog just liked to follow him around even when he was working. Once he had alerted the crew to the fact there was a snake at the base of one of the trees they were approaching, barking and growling until Hernando came to see what the problem was. Thankfully Frio had the good instincts not to attack the snake, which although small still had a very lethal bite. Frank started to go get something to kill the snake with, but Indio stopped him. Indio emptied his big plastic bucket of the nuts in it and with his pole he guided the snake into the bucket now lying on its side. He carried the bucket and snake to the far edge of the orchard where the desert resumed, and then turned it loose to find another place to lay in the shade.

This morning, Hernando was checking the fluids in the Beast, along with the air pressure in the tires and even the gas and water in the Jersey cans. He dumped the water cans out and rinsed them and then refilled them with fresh water. He was just finishing when a small car pulled up by the barn and a young man stepped out. He spotted Hernando and came over.

"Hi, I'm looking for Frank Mejia or Hernando Partida. Margaret asked me to help with the harvest today. Can you show me where they are?"

"I'm Hernando Partida, what did Margaret tell you about the harvest? I see you're at least dressed for the work, what is your name by the way?"

"I'm sorry sir, my name is Donald Arroyo, but most people call me Donnie. I'm from New Mexico where my uncle has a pistachio orchard, so I do know what to do. When Margaret said she was looking for someone to fill in for the day, I volunteered. I told her she didn't have to pay me, it gives me a chance to pay her back for the times she's helped me and a couple of the others. Besides, I miss being outside and the physical work."

Frank had joined them while Donnie was talking, so Hernando introduced them and told Donnie if he had any questions to ask Frank.

Frank reminded Hernando that he better get moving, it would be a long drive and Mr. Edmonds would want to get started

[222]

early. With that, Hernando waved good-bye to Margaret and Rosa who were out on the porch drinking coffee and fired up the Beast. He pulled up in front of Jake/Des's house a few minutes later, in time to see Julie struggling to get a suitcase from her trunk.

"If the fair lady would allow me, I will be glad to move her suitcase to this fine carriage."

Julie laughed and answered, "Of course, my gallant knight, it would be very much appreciated. Fair lady just got done working another midnight shift and is very tired. She will probably sleep in the back seat for the first four or five hours, that is if the gallant knight can handle this Beast."

This time they both laughed. Des was just coming out of the door and asked what was so funny. Julie explained that she had just finished a mid-night shift and would be sleeping in the back seat for the first part of the trip. They finished loading the suitcases and were soon on the road. Hernando enjoyed driving the Beast, he had become familiar with the way it handled and was looking forward to the first time he got to take it off-road. He didn't plan on doing any "extreme" four-wheeling like he'd seen on TV, just being able to go where he wanted in the desert. Even though he was technically still in a city, he thought of living here instead of San Bernardino as living in the desert. The desert was twenty feet past the end of the orchard, as they had experienced earlier this week.

. . . .

Friday morning and Jake was up and off to breakfast, having been released by the doctor two days before. His first session with the rest of the Aryan Brotherhood was very limited, with him bending over much of the time, attempting to sell the idea that he wasn't in top shape. It apparently worked, because later that day he went to meet with Mendez with Ernst acting as his bodyguard. He had verified the total amount in his canteen fund and was now going to place his bet of twenty thousand at three-to-one odds.

He knew the Outlaws would have to scrape to put up sixty thousand which was exactly what he wanted. He wanted them to have little or no 'wiggle room' when he attempted to buy Alex's debt. He had verified that Alex really did have a son, named Jacob, courtesy of Tyler in the Education Office. He hoped no one ever found out that Tyler had the ability to 'research' the prison records.

Tyler had also given him a copy of Joe Robertson's file, which was very interesting. Whoever had put together that fairy-tale either forgot about or didn't know about the 'three-strike rule' because they had Joe serving seven years for a third violent crime when the sentence should have read 'life imprisonment'. Tyler also showed him another anomaly in that one prison in the Central Valley where 'Joe' had served a sentence wasn't built until three years later, so he had to have served time sitting in a field for three years. Jake thought it would the courteous thing to do by informing the Bloods of this fact, so he had a meeting in the yard with three representatives from the Bloods, Ernst again acting as his bodyguard. When they met, it was quick and to the point.

"You wanted this meeting Rabbi, what's it about?" the slender young black man with shades asked him. "You expecting us to bet on you or something?"

"Not that at all, my friend. I came because I found out some information about a person of your color that I think you should know," and with that he handed the man a copy of what Tyler had given him. "As you can see, there are several discrepancies in this fairy-tale someone put together. I know this man was sent to get information on me, to make me look bad, and to discredit me any way he can. Whoever else he is supposed to be investigating, I have no clue, but I did want to make sure you were aware of this."

"So Rabbi, just exactly what do you want us to do about this, take out the trash because he's one of 'our color'?"

"No, though I do appreciate the offer, I just don't want there to be any misunderstanding should something happen to him. It would be a shame to start a war over someone neither of us has

[224]

any use for. At this time, I'm just asking you to stay out of the way," and he got up to leave. The small black man stopped him by raising his hand and the two extra-large men he had with him started to reach toward him.

"Stop," the young man said and they lowered their hands. "I have one last question; do you think you'll win this fight?"

Jake smiled and then answered, "I just got out of the infirmary from them attempting to poison me, so I don't feel exactly one hundred percent right now. You bet on who you want."

Jake and Ernst approached Mendez at his customary place at the top of the bleachers near the basketball court. This was Blood territory in the yard, the basketball court and the bleachers, but Mendez went wherever he chose without regard to whose territory it was. Jake wasn't that fortunate, he was challenged by a couple of the Bloods, but then quickly passed through to see Mendez.

"I came to place my bet on this fight Mr. Mendez. I want to bet twenty thousand on myself, will that be alright?"

When Mendez finally looked up at him, Jake felt fear. He had never felt like this before and when he looked into those eyes he wasn't sure if he was looking at madness or genius, but he knew he was seeing evil itself.

"You are kind to show an old man such respect Rabbi. I heard that you really don't like fighting, but here you are risking your life for another who may be trying to kill you. I asked myself if I would be able to do such a thing and cannot find an answer. Is the debt of friendship that great that you find yourself forced to fight the man you are trying to help?

He has sworn to kill you, or at the very least to cripple you for life, and he is not the only one. There are at least two others that will try should Chang fail. Your motive for your bet is very clear young man; you want to put the Outlaws in a position where they can't refuse your offer if you win. I knew what the Outlaws planned before Chang got here, and have been watching to see what you will do. I also know about the past between you and Chang, how you both served together and saved each other's life on more than one occasion. You don't have to fight this fight

[225]

Rabbi, you could just walk away, petition for a transfer. For the amount you're willing to bet, you can buy a transfer, so why go through with this fight?"

Jake asked permission to sit and when granted, he sat close to Mendez. "Loyalty, Mr. Mendez. Sheer stupid loyalty is the reason. If you're aware of our past history, then you know that Alex would do the same thing for me if the roles were reversed. There are nearly forty Latinos less than a hundred feet away, right at the edge of Blood territory, who would attack immediately if you gave the signal. Would they do so because they owe you something, not likely. If a man's loyalty can be purchased, then he is no longer a man, but merely a commodity. Now, will you accept my bet?"

"Of course my young friend, I will gladly accept the bet, and personally I do hope you win. I know Chang will not roll-over or quit, so you will have some hard work to do and in that I wish you good luck. Come and talk to me after the fight and remember my warning about the others. One of them is close to you every day, but it's not your large friend there."

At the mess hall, Jake noticed the eyes on him but didn't care, he was here to eat. He was given a wide berth in line because Sorenson was leading him and Ernst was following. He grabbed a tray as usual and looked at the usual powdered re-constituted scrambled eggs but before he could say anything the slender young man from the Bloods was there behind the line suggesting he try the over easy eggs and some crisp bacon. He winked and then recommended some fresh orange juice and the wheat toast with some marmalade.

Jake was instructed to sit at his usual table and his breakfast would be served right away. He did and was greeted by Alex sitting across from him, also waiting to be served. They were both given a cup of coffee and Jake was pleasantly surprised to find it was real coffee, not the crap swept up from the roasting house floor and packaged for 'institutional' use. Shortly thereafter, they were both served with breakfast, a vision that most prisoners only dream about. A pile of golden brown hash-browned potatoes was on one side of the plate, while three over easy eggs occupied the other. On separate small plates were toast, light brown with butter, and four strips of crisp bacon. Each of them was served a large glass of orange juice.

"Was this your idea?" Alex asked. "Trying to get me off my game, Jake?"

"Not my idea," Jake responded. "Besides, I know better than to try to influence you Alex, not that I ever could. Why would I attempt a cheap trick like this?"

"I didn't think it was your idea, but I had to ask. A man changes over the years, and I thought you might too, but I see I was wrong."

Jake went on with his breakfast, savoring each bite. It was almost as good as Angelina's cooking, but not quite. Soon they were both sitting enjoying the last few bites, Jake noticed that there wasn't any marmalade on the table and looked up to see a huge black prisoner approaching their table with the jar of marmalade in hand, at least what you could see of it. The man had huge hands, dwarfing an ordinary jelly jar like the marmalade came in.

"Sorry Rabbi, Brother Qwaami told me about the marmalade, but I was trying to make sure your breakfast was just right and I forgot. I'm really sorry, sir. I hope everything was how you like it, sir."

"It was wonderful Brother. Please tell Brother Qwaami thanks very much for treating my opponent and I to this beautiful and tasty courtesy. You could easily be a chef on the outside, your food is so good," Jake said. He could see the man beaming with pride, so he added, "Let's just keep the marmalade between us. I don't think he has to know unless he knows already."

"I don't think he does, and thank you Rabbi. I'll be sure to pass along what you said about the breakfast. He said he wanted to repay you for the information about your former cell-mate, whatever that means. I'll get you two gentlemen some fresh coffee now."

Alex watched as the man walked away and then commented, "Always the kind and gentle person, Jake. Do they really think you're a Rabbi, if they do they've never seen you in a fight before. What all do they know about you Jake?"

"From what I got from old man Mendez, they know just about everything there is to know except maybe my mother's maiden name, but I'd bet they probably know that too. They've seen me fight on a couple of occasions, once against four young Aryans, and then again against your owner, Mr. Davis of the Outlaws. He wasn't much of a fighter though; he thought his size would carry him through, like most big men. I was in a bad mood that day, so I guess I went at him harder than I ordinarily would. I'm pretty sure they know as much about you as well, wouldn't you say?"

"Yeah, I suppose they do," Alex responded. "My whole life has been nothing but violence for as long as I can remember, at least until my son was born. I don't know why, but something inside of me said enough, I can't keep living like this. I was going to tell his mother she was on her own, but for some reason, when I saw her holding the boy I knew I wanted to stay. I had a helluva time convincing her to marry me; I even had to promise to go to church with her. Do you remember the bar where we always hung out in Coronado, the kind of plain looking girl that was always there shooting pool? That's my wife now, her name is Merrian like in Robin Hood and Maid Merrian. She has a full-time job now, working as a clerk in an office, from what she tells me in her letters. I quit doing drugs and quit drinking except for a beer or two when I would get home, which is how I got into prison.

I stopped by the bar on the way home to pick up a six-pack and some ass-hole who knew me back when called me out. Believe it or not Jake, I really tried to just walk away, but that ass-hole wouldn't let it go. I was headed toward the door when he hit me from behind with a beer bottle. He tried to cut me with what was left of the bottle, so I spun him and he tripped over one of the chairs and went down, but the bottle was in his hand and it sliced his carotid artery open. He bled out before the ambulance could get there, I even tried to do compression of the wound to try to stop or slow the bleeding, but his buddies thought I was trying to hurt him more so I couldn't get to him.

That was the worst night of my life Jake. My son was just three when I got sent away, it was alright though because it was only an hour drive for Merrian to come and visit at first. Then I got into a card game and lost some money to the cons running the game. I gave them some markers to try to get even, but I never did. They arranged for me to get transferred to Oroville and I've been doing shitty little enforcer jobs for them ever since to pay off the debt, but all I seem to pay off is the interest and that keeps adding up. This fight is supposed to wipe clean all my debt if I win."

They both looked up as the big cook brought them a refill on the coffee, the mess hall was emptying out so there were very few prisoners left. Jake noticed three Outlaw gang members and Ernst and two others from the Brotherhood. Alex must have noticed the same thing, but he just sat and asked, "Who is the man-mountain that shadows you like a puppy-dog?"

Jake explained the circumstances around Ernst, how he'd grown up and how Jake had taught him the alphabet and some of the first words. He also told Alex about Tyler working with him so he was now learning to read. He was amazed that Ernst had learned so much in so little time, he was now reading two books a day, carrying a dictionary with him whenever he was reading.

The time had come to quit this trip down memory lane, Jake thought. "What time are we doing this dance, Alex? I thought maybe one o'clock would be a good time, what do you think?"

"That's fine with me Jake. Do you want gloves or no gloves; I rounded up a couple pairs of soft leather gloves, if you want."

"Good, Alex. I expect you to bring your best. By the way, Mendez warned me about two others who will be trying to kill me if you don't win, I think I know who one is but I don't have a clue who the last one might be. Watch your back."

They left the mess hall and went their separate ways, Jake returning to his cell to rest. He had not slept well, the thousands of thoughts going round and round in his mind. Laying there on his bunk, he thought about what Alex had said about his son and he knew he was seeing a totally different man. He was really mixed up now, knowing that Alex had actually quit his former life-

[229]

style. He didn't want to have to hurt him, but it seemed the only solution to the problem. If he walked away from the fight like Mendez had suggested, Alex would still be in debt and forced to resort to other measures to get at Jake. If they both walked, then the Outlaws wouldn't allow Alex to leave prison alive and owing money.

. . . .

Friday was a morning Sam Battiste wasn't looking forward to, but it was finally here. He had gone over everything twice in his letter to Sacramento, finally dropping it in the mail on Wednesday morning. He had talked all of it over with Angelina several times, and each time they concluded that Jake's advice to 'get out in front of this' was the best. Angelina had helped Sam with the writing because she was better at it than Sam. She was also the one who suggested that Sam send the letter with a 'return receipt requested'. He had thought about calling in sick for the day, but again he felt he should be there on the yard.

He was met by the senior guard who had taken an interest in Jake, and was told to accompany him to a visitation room. Sam was wary of what he might want, but when they were alone the senior guard pulled off his boot and removed a small badge. Sam was suddenly worried that his letter had already arrived at Sacramento and had been opened. The senior guard put his fears to rest when he told Sam who he was.

"I'm David Morris of the FBI. I'm here undercover investigating gang activities and the gang's interaction with a certain segment of the guards that work here. We've been able to clear you, and I may need your help today with whatever may happen. Can I count on your support?"

"Yes sir, I'd be happy to help."

"Good, I've already talked to Crenshaw and he'll be with us. I wanted to have at least one guard on each side of the basketball court, but I haven't gotten anyone other than you two. The least likely attackers would be the Latin Kings, so we can each take one of the other sides. You'll be by the Bloods, and Crenshaw by the Outlaws. I'll take the side with Aryans. I have a snitch that told me there would be a try to kill Prisoner Kozan if Chang fails. When that happens, the best that we can do is retreat to the center where the combatants are, understood?"

"Yes sir, and if I may suggest something, I think we should trust one person from the Brotherhood to help us. Do you know the big man that follows Jake, er, Prisoner Kozan around?"

"Yes, I've seen him. Big bastard, isn't he?"

"Yes sir, and he's as loyal to Kozan as a puppy dog. If I talk to him, he'll be there to help you. Shall I contact him?"

"Only if you think he can be trusted Sam."

They headed to roll call and just made it in time. They were all advised of the up-coming "athletic event" that afternoon and to be very aware of any suspicious behavior. The Warden had made it a point to order additional guards on the yard in case the "event" turned into something else. Sam hoped he done the right thing by turning in that report, many of the guards mentioned in it were here in the room. They left roll call and Sam immediately headed toward the area where the Brotherhood hung out. He spotted Ernst right away and ordered him to come over. On the pretense of doing a search, he had Ernst assume the position on the fence next to the bleachers. A few of the Aryans were too curious and too close, so Sam ordered them to back off. Turning back to Ernst, he kept his voice low when he talked.

"Do you think the Rabbi is your friend, and if he is would you be willing to help him?"

Ernst was caught off guard by the question, so he paused a moment before answering, "Yes sir, he's probably the only friend I have in here. Why?"

Sam quickly explained about the possibility of someone trying to kill Jake if Alex lost the fight, and the plan the FBI agent had proposed. "I told him that we could count on you to help us help Jake, I didn't make a mistake did I?"

Ernst turned partially so he could see Sam's face and then replied, "I think I know who it is sir, and I plan on being right next to him to stop him if he tries. You're a friend of Jake's too, aren't

[231]

you sir? I can tell by the way he talks to you, not like the way he talks to the other guards"

Sam didn't reply, he was watching the others watching him. He ordered Ernst to take off his shoes in attempt to take their attention off him and Ernst; he'd already spent more time than he should have in questioning Ernst. Loudly he said, "From now on you better be quicker doing what I told you to do, you understand prisoner?" He then winked at Ernst and walked away.

It was Friday and almost the end of the week.

CHAPTER THIRTY-THREE

The fight was a magnificent display of two animals going at each other. Jake and Alex had each arrived a bit early to look over the court. The Bloods had very nicely swept the entire court completely clean; there wasn't even dust on the court. There were three guards at each side of the court in addition to Sam and Crenshaw, to keep the spectators back. The guards all had full-size Ebonite riot batons in their hands, out and ready to be used. Alex offered Jake his choice of the gloves, and was almost gentlemanly in his action. Jake looked them over and chose a pair that fit snugly on his hands.

He then took the belt from his denim pants and tossed it to the side. He'd had his jeans re-tailored to be snug at the waist but loose in the legs so as not to interfere with the leg-kicks he was hoping to deliver. He removed the Jan Bradys from his feet and tossed them towards the Aryans. He removed his shirt and heard a few mutters from the crowd. He knew they were looking at his body and he knew what he looked like. The past two weeks, with Angelina's cooking and the constant workouts had toned him to almost no body fat. He'd had his hair cut short a few days earlier and also shaved his face. A few of the faggots made some comments but were quickly shut up by the other spectators.

Jake looked over to Alex and thought he looked the same as the first time they'd met. His body had a bit of fat, but that wasn't new. The only thing new that Jake could see were a few more scars, picked up along the way courtesy of his former life style. He was as fit as ever, Jake thought. He'd hoped that maybe they had gotten to Alex with the food and the other tricks, but it certainly didn't appear as if they had.

A large guard came to the center of the court and announced what most everyone here already knew.

"This athletic event is a grudge match at the request of the two opponents. Because this is a grudge match, there will be no 'rounds'. Each contestant will continue fighting as long as they are able. If one is unable to continue, the other shall be declared

[233]

the winner. Any and all styles of fighting are allowed and there is no such thing as a "foul". Do the contestants understand the "rules" as stated?"

They both nodded, impatient to begin. They were about to start when the announcer stopped them. One at a time, he patted down each of them to make sure neither had a hidden weapon.

"Spectators! The guards on the towers are armed today with rifles and live ammunition. If you are told to lie down, do so immediately or you will be fired upon."

"Gentlemen, you may begin and good luck to both of you."

The guard had just finished when Alex charged at Jake, trying his usual barrage of punches. Jake hit him with two swift jabs and backed up a little. When Alex started forward, Jake's timing was just right and caught Alex on the thigh with a very hard leg-kick. It was to be the first of many as they got into the rhythm of the fight, Alex hitting Jake with a barrage of punches at the head and the shoulders, some of them harder than others. Jake backed up again and waited for Alex to follow which he did and paid for it with another hard leg-kick. That only worked one more time and Alex, although limping slightly, circled the opposite direction.

Jake caught a hard left to the side of his head and it rocked him. Jake had only fought Alex once before and that was in a gym with the big sixteen ounce gloves on. Neither had won that day, they just called it a draw. Today it was all on the line, and they both knew it. Alex sensed that Jake was hurt and rushed him hard, but instead of boxing with Alex, Jake stepped into the rush and tossed Alex to the ground. He landed hard on the concrete surface, but before Jake could close in, he was up and on his feet. When he moved, Jake could see him favoring the right leg and knew he'd picked the right strategy. He tried a few more times to get Alex in the right position but not successfully.

He decided to box with him for a while and let loose with several jabs and then a right to the body. Alex wasn't quite quick enough to stop the right and Jake knew it was a solid hit to the ribs. Alex countered by throwing Jake to the concrete, but his leg didn't let him move quick enough to take advantage of Jake being down. Jake came up from the court with a rush, but was greeted with another barrage of punches, this time much harder than before. Jake got caught with another punch that set him back; as he was retreating he saw Alex moving forward and kicked him hard on the thigh again, more out of instinct than anything else. Alex tried to control it, but he fell anyway and was slower getting up, not that it mattered, Jake was busy trying to clear his head.

They both looked at each other and then as if one, they both charged. This time Jake just covered up to protect his head as much as possible and pushed toward Alex's chest. He knew Alex didn't have the power in his short punches as he did full-length, so he kept pushing until his head was an inch from Alex. He was partly bent over so when he started to straighten up Alex assumed that Jake was trying to head-butt him and pulled back a bit. Jake caught him with both hands open in the form of holding a basketball and it snapped Alex's head back. Jake knew that Alex would retaliate with a barrage, so he stepped back and caught Alex on the thigh again. Alex went down and this time was too slow getting up, and caught a kick to the side of his head which he only partially blocked. Jake was tired or he would have tried to finish Alex right then. Instead he allowed Alex the time to get up before they started again.

There were a few boo's at his display of gallantry, but they turned into a muffled choking sound as the person who booed was quickly "escorted" away. Jake was busy watching Alex get up or he might have noticed Collier working his way to the front of the crowd. When Alex was up, they both came together again and Jake noticed Alex's jaw sagging. He feinted a jab at Alex and spun him into another solid right to the ribs. This time he heard the bones crack, but wasn't sure if it Alex's ribs or his right hand. He didn't have time to check it out as Alex was back with another flurry of punches. Jake thought that either Alex was losing strength or he was just getting used to being hit. Jake reached under Alex's arm and simply tossed him over his hip. He attacked as Alex was just hitting the concrete, piling on punch after punch. Alex was in the wrong position to defend himself and Jake finished him with a hard kick to the side of his head. Alex went down and out. Jake just stood there waiting for him to get up, but he wasn't getting up.

Jake struggled with his emotions as he stood watching, waiting for him to get up, almost praying that he would get up. He didn't like seeing Alex like this, defeated, beaten severely. He looked for any sign of movement and saw that Alex wasn't breathing. He knelt over him and started CPR, yelling that he needed a doctor. He didn't hear the order to hit the deck, nor did he hear anything else. He felt a sharp blow to the side of the head and the last thing he remembered was Sam standing over him as the lights went out.

When he awoke, he saw bright lights and he was lying in a bed, a comfortable bed. He started to move, but couldn't. His left wrist was cuffed to the rail on the bed and his right hand was wrapped in a cast. He tried to turn his head but it hurt too much, so he just lay there. The nurse must have heard him try to move because she called to the doctor. The doctor wasn't the prison doctor, and from what he could see, Jake knew this wasn't the infirmary.

"Where am I?" he tried to say, but it came out sounding much different. "Where is this, and where is Alex?"

"I'm glad to see you're finally awake, we weren't sure you would make it. Your friend is still in Intensive Care, two floors up. You won't be able to get to him to finish him off. You're in the hospital in Susanville, in case you don't remember."

Jake laid back, tears coming to his eyes. Alex in Intensive Care wasn't what Jake wanted to hear. And the doctor was right, it was Jake's fault, he could have walked away. It was his own stupid pride that made him think he could solve every problem, save the damsel in distress, do whatever needed doing. For the first time, Jake prayed. He wasn't sure who he should pray to, but he just wanted his friend to get better, and this time he knew he couldn't help. He let the tears come, screw all that macho crap.

If he hadn't been so full of himself, none of this would have happened and Alex would be alright. He could have just paid the protection money to the Aryans and it wouldn't have started all this shit, he would be sitting in his cell reading a book. I'm sorry, he thought, and then he said it out loud. "Alex, I'm sorry. It's all my fault, but I was too stubborn to roll over and play dead. I'm sorry I had to hurt you; it seemed like the only way. I was wrong, there was another way. I didn't see it until now. Please forgive me Alex."

He knew Alex couldn't hear him two floors away, but it made him feel a little better just saying it out loud. In his mind he asked Buddha, or Mohammed, or God, or whomever to please help Alex live. The nurse had heard his out-burst and came in with a syringe and administered a sedative through his IV line. He was out within seconds.

CHAPTER THIRTY-FOUR

Des and Julie checked into the desk at the High Country Inn while Hernando parked the Beast and began unloading the suitcases. It was late but the restaurant hadn't closed yet, so they put their bags in their rooms and hurried downstairs. They got in before the doors closed and ordered dinner. All three of them were tired, Hernando and Julie from driving, and Des from re-reading the transcript of Jake's first trial, so conversation at dinner was minimal.

On the way north they had discussed quite a few things including Hernando's lack of a high school diploma. He knew he wanted to go back to school, but wasn't sure what to do. He had quit attending at the beginning of his junior year, and thought he would be out of place with the other students. Julie had him thinking exactly the opposite by the time they reached the motel.

None of them had heard anything about the fight at the Correctional Center until they turned on the local station and were just catching the last part of the news report. The reporter was using terms like riot and lock-down and Julie tried to catch what had been reported. At the last part of the half-hour news the reporter came on again and Julie was able to get a better idea of what had happened.

"An "athletic event" sanctioned by the Warden got out of control when the favored opponent lost the fight. The near riot caused five prisoners and one guard to be sent to the hospital in Susanville. The Warden reported that one inmate was killed and several other prisoners are being treated at the prison infirmary. The names of the inmates involved are being withheld pending notification of their relatives and the prison remains on lock-down at this time, according to the Warden."

Julie picked up the phone to dial Des's room but he was already on the line. "Julie? Are you there?"

"Yeah, I'm here. The phone didn't ring. Did you see the news; does this have to do with Jake? Is this "athletic event" what he needed the money for, to bet on a fight?"

"I don't know, he wouldn't tell me what for, only that he needed it. I think he's involved in this, but I'm not sure how. The only person I know to call is Angelina; I'm hoping she might have some information. You call room service and have some coffee sent up to my room and I'll call Angelina. And you better let Eddie know."

"Who? Oh, you mean Hernando. I'll knock on his door."

Des was on the phone with Angelina when Julie and Eddie came in, just nodding and saying yes now and then. But he was scribbling notes as fast as he could, and then he stopped.

"Do you have a copy of that report Angelina?" and then, "Can I make a copy please?"

He nodded again and then asked, "What's the address? I'm sending Julie and Eddie over to pick up that report, but I think Julie should stay with you until we know more about Sam's condition. Eddie can bring the report back to me."

Given the address, the two of them were on their way. Eddie returned in about thirty minutes with the report. It was neatly typed, about four pages long and full of information. Des read it all in less than five minutes. It outlined a lot of the illegal activities that had been happening at the prison, and it named names. Des thought if anyone found out about Sam sending this report, his life wouldn't be worth a nickel. He wanted to help Sam, but more important, he needed to know about Jake. He tried calling the prison, but only got a busy signal. He called the local TV station and asked if the names of the prisoners that were sent to the hospital were known. He was informed that the inmates identities were being withheld for now, until any family could be notified by the authorities from the prison. Des lied and told them his name was Kozan, could they tell him if a Jacob or Jake Kozan was one of the ones in the hospital and was again informed that the information would only be released only after he had established his identity.

Des was getting completely frustrated and was about to give up when Eddie asked if he could try something. Des just nodded and listened as Eddie dialed.

"Hello, I'm supposed to deliver some flowers in the morning and I need to know what room Mr. Kozan is in, please? I was late getting to my deliveries yesterday and the boss almost fired me, I have to drop off the flowers and go. I can't afford to lose this job 'cause my girlfriend is pregnant and we need the money. Yes, I'll hold." He covered the mouthpiece and looked at Des, "Anyone else I should ask about?"

"Yes, Sam Battiste. He's the guard that was helping Jake."

When the hospital came back on the line it apparently wasn't what Eddie wanted to know. "Can you tell me if he's there, please? I can just drop the flowers at the front desk and they can take them to his room. Oh, and I have one other delivery there, is Sam Battiste on the second floor? He is? Room 216, yes I got it, thank you."

Eddie turned to Des and said, "I learned all about lying from an old grey-hair I work for. Sam's in the hospital, and Jake's there too, but she wouldn't tell me. If he wasn't there, they'd let you know right away. She said she had to check to see if she was allowed to tell me what room he's in, that's how I know he's there."

"Damn, Eddie. That's some good work, have you thought about becoming a detective? We have to call Julie and let her know about Sam and also about Jake; she'll know how to talk to Angelina so she doesn't go into hysterics."

Des called and talked to Julie, filling her in on the situation with Sam and then went on to tell her about Jake being involved in the fight. There had been enough specifics in Sam's report that Des now knew exactly why Jake had wanted the money. Julie told him that Angelina had already let her know all about Jake's involvement, and how Sam was involved.

"Do you think he was doing the right thing Dad? I so wanted to believe that he was honest and not like these others. Now I don't know what to think. I almost wish I'd never met him."

"Julie, I love very much, so I want you to stop and take a deep breath. Before you start jumping to any conclusions, you should try to see things from his point of view. We don't have all the answers as to what went on and we don't know why he made the decisions that he did. Now, you have to tell Angelina that Sam's in the hospital and if necessary take her to see him. I can send Eddie to pick you up, that is if he doesn't start whining about not getting paid overtime. Tell them whatever you have to at the hospital, just make sure that Angelina gets in to see Sam and make sure he's alright. Eddie's on his way."

"Des? You weren't serious about me being a cop, were you?"

"I said detective Eddie, there's a big difference between the two, now get going."

After Eddie left, Des slipped off his shoes and poured the last of the coffee in his cup, already exhausted from a long day, and facing a possibly long night. He thought it would be useless to try but he called the prison again. He was surprised when he got a ring tone and then on the third ring someone answered.

"Good evening," he said pleasantly. "I'm Attorney Desmond Edmonds and I'm trying to find out the status of my client, Mr. Jacob Kozan. Can you tell me if he is there in the prison, please" He was put on hold and the next person on the phone was the Warden himself.

"Mr. Edmonds, what can I help you with?"

"Warden, it's so nice to talk to you again, especially in light of what happened today. Can you tell me the status of my client, Mr. Jacob Kozan?"

"Your client was involved in an athletic event today and was badly injured. So much so that he is now in custody at the hospital in town. I suppose you want to be able to talk with your client, is that why you called?"

"Yes, it is. Would you be able to arrange that for me please?"

"I'll make the call, but I don't know if he's able to talk yet. He was nearly comatose when he was taken off the yard. Anything else I can help you with?"

"Yes, if you could also include my co-counsel, Ms. Julie Larson, in your authorization?"

"Fine, I'll include her as well, good-bye Mr. Edmonds."

Des hung up with the distinct feeling that the Warden did not like him. Too bad, he thought, he thought the Warden was a pleasant man when they had first met. He called Angelina's hoping to catch them before they left, but didn't. He finished the now cold coffee in his cup and thought about calling room service, then decided against it. He pulled off his shirt and loosened his belt, then flopped onto the bed. Nothing to do now but wait, he thought. He didn't hear Eddie knock on his door, he was already sound asleep.

He thought he heard ringing and couldn't understand why there would be ringing. He then heard a voice and partially woke up. Eddie was standing next to his bed talking on the phone.

"Wait a minute; I think he's awake now. Hold on."

"Des, are you awake? Julie's on the phone she got in to see Jake, but they've got him on some pain-killers and he probably won't be awake until morning. She's in Sam's room with Angelina right now. Are you awake?"

Des shook his head trying to clear the cobwebs, and then he sat up. He took the phone that Eddie was holding out.

"Julie, how's Sam?"

"He's doing alright. He is beaten and has been stabbed twice, but neither is a serious wound. He was also shot in the leg. He was protecting Jake and one of the Outlaw gang members got to him with a home-made knife, I think Sam called it a shiv. Angelina's much calmer now, but she doesn't want to leave. She won't listen to me; she keeps insisting that she's alright. Will you talk to her please?"

Des waited until Angelina got on the line, "Angelina, what are you doing endangering your baby like this? Sam's going to be alright tonight, so I want you to go home and rest. Either do that, or I'll call the hospital and have you admitted, do you understand? I'm sending Eddie over to pick you up and take you home. Both you and Julie need to get some rest so you'll look beautiful when you return to see Sam. Okay?"

He hung up and looked at Eddie. "What are you doing in my room? How did you get in?"

"I told the desk clerk that you were my uncle, and I was worried about you 'cause you didn't feel good before you went to bed and you weren't answering when I knocked on your door. He

[242]

let me in with his pass-key and made sure you were okay. Shall I go get Julie and Angelina now?"

"Yes, please. And then you get some sleep too, I know it's been a long day for you too."

This time he was out before Eddie fired up the Beast.

CHAPTER THIRTY-FIVE

Jake started to move and then stopped. His shoulders hurt when he tried to move them, along with several other parts of his body. He wanted to open his eyes, but was having trouble clearing his mind. He remembered, he was in the hospital in Susanville. He succeeded in opening one eye only to see the room spinning around. He heard a voice that sounded far off, a woman's voice. He wondered what a woman would be doing in prison, he laughed at the thought. He closed his eye and went back to sleep.

He woke again later, his mouth dry. He tried to talk, but no sound came out. This time he got both eyes open, but again the room was spinning. He moved his left hand and was brought up short by the cuffs. He closed his eyes and the spinning stopped, his head starting to clear. Oh yes, hospital, prison, cuffs, it was coming back to him in bits and pieces. He attempted to talk again, not sure if he was making sound or not. He felt someone close to his bed, and he started to panic, fear creeping into consciousness. Tears started to roll down his cheeks, he could feel their heat. Why am I crying, he thought, I won the fight didn't I? The vision of Alex lying on the concrete beaten and not breathing came to him and he screamed, "No!"

"No, what, Jake?" the woman's voice was back again. "What do you mean when you say no? Who are you saying no to?"

"God, Brahma, Buddha, pick one, it really doesn't matter. Who are you?"

Jake, it's me, Julie. Julie Larson, remember? How are feeling?"

"Okay except I'm real tired and it feels like I've been beat up. How did you get into prison, I didn't know they let women in prison, when did they start doing that?"

"You're not in prison, Jake. You're in the hospital. Can you open your eyes?"

"No. If I do that, the room starts spinning and I might fall off. Can I have some water, my mouth is very dry. And can you get some for Alex too?" With the mention of Alex's name, Jake started crying again and saying, "It's my fault, Alex. Please, be okay and wake up. Please God, let Alex wake up. He has a son and he needs to wake up. I know it's my fault, I told you that. I said I was sorry, didn't I?" He lay back sobbing. He heard the voice from really far off calling his name, but he was too tired to answer. Maybe he'd answer later; right now he wanted to sleep.

It was hours later when he awoke again. This time when he opened his eyes, the room was dark and it wasn't spinning, at least not yet. His mouth was dry again; come to think of it she never did bring him his water. He rubbed his face with his hand, why was that funny? Then he realized he no longer had cuffs on his wrist. He started to sit up, but when he tried he felt nauseous.

"Can't a guy get a drink of water here? All I want is a lousy drink of water, what do I have to do to get some water?"

"To start with, quiet down, you're yelling. Everybody else here is sleeping, so be quiet. I'll get you a drink of water." The voice was a woman, but not Julie. She moved quickly and helped him with his water. It was a nurse. He drank too quickly and promptly vomited up what he'd drank. Most of it was on the covers, but a little was on his chin and throat. She didn't turn on the lights, just pulled off the blanket and wiped his face with a washcloth.

"How about you just sip on some ice chips? They'll make you feel better and you won't throw up again. Would you like to sit up a little? I can adjust the bed."

Jake nodded and lay back. He felt the bandage on his head for the first time and thought; I didn't hit my head, why is it bandaged? He could see his right hand and the cast, why was there a cast on my hand, he wondered. His legs hurt, so he tried to stretch and realized his left leg had a cast too. Why am I so beat up, it was just a fight, I've never been beat up before. He then remembered the fight with Alex, and it all came back, shocking him into awareness. When the nurse came back with the ice, he asked her to tell him if Alex was still alive.

"If you mean Mr. Chang, your opponent, he's alive, but not by much. You nearly beat him to death. What on earth made you so mad that you had to beat him like that?"

"I wasn't mad at him, he's my friend. I had to help him; I, never mind you wouldn't understand if I told you. Is he still in Intensive Care, I need to know, I need to contact his wife, she should be here. Is the guard outside?"

"No, an attorney was here today and demanded they take off your cuffs. She stayed here all day, at least until an hour ago. She's in the waiting room now, sleeping. What do you need?"

"Can you please wake her up, tell her I'm awake and need to talk to her. It's urgent, please?"

Julie came in a few minutes later, wiping the sleep from her eyes. She turned on the room lights and the room started spinning again.

"Please turn out the lights, they make me dizzy."

"Fine with me, I probably look like crap anyway. What's so urgent Jake? The nurse said it was very urgent."

"You look beautiful to me, but you can hear all that later. Right now I need to get in touch with Alex's wife. I don't think she knows about what happened, and she should be here with Alex. She lives in Coronado or nearby, is there someone you can call and find out where she lives?"

"Yeah, it's called a telephone directory. Do you realize it is three a. m. Sunday morning? What do you want me to say to her, I represent the man who beat the crap out of your husband and he thinks you should be here?"

"You don't understand, Alex and I have been friends for years and I was trying to help him. I'll explain it all when there's more time, right now I need you to get in touch with Alex's wife, her first name is Merrian. Please try to find her."

"Help him; my God you nearly killed him. You bet thousands of dollars that you can beat the shit out of your 'best friend', putting him in a coma, and you were helping him?"

"I was wrong, I know that now, but then it seemed like the only answer. Please Julie? He's got a son and I know I screwed everything up, you, me, Alex, everything. I'm sorry. Please just find her and get her here to be with him, he needs her. I never knew a man could change so much, he loves her and little Jacob so much, he told me that the morning before the fight. He was

[246]

supposed to kill me or cripple me to get out of a debt he owed the Outlaws, but he really didn't want to. I know I made a big mistake, and now I want to try to fix it, but I don't know how. Please Julie, find her and get her here?"

She looked at him lying there, not sure what to believe. She wasn't even sure she could trust him anymore, the doubt was that great. She finally said, "I'll do it Jake, not for you, for Alex, now go to sleep."

He started to protest, but the nurse was already administering the sedative. He was asleep when Julie left the room.

"Come on sunshine, it's time to get up," the voice was back, but it didn't sound right, it wasn't a woman's voice. "That's right, come on Jake. You can hear me can't you? It's time to wake up."

"Who are you, are you the doctor?"

"Open your eyes and you can see who it is."

"Are the lights on? If they are will you turn them off, please? They make me dizzy."

He felt the lights go off and opened his eyelids a bit; his eyes were swollen almost shut. He saw the senior Guard standing there.

"Oh, it's you. Did you come to take me back to prison?"

"Eventually, but not today. Are you feeling any better, when they hauled you off the yard you were nearly dead. By the way, the doctor told me to give you a souvenir; he pulled it from under your scalp. He said you either had the thickest skull bones he'd ever seen, or you were one very lucky man." He handed Jake an object, but Jake couldn't tell what it was, he was a problem focusing on objects.

"What is it?" Jake asked. "I can't see anything really good yet."

"It's a bullet. One of the guards tried to kill you after the fight. He's in custody in the jail in town, facing a charge of attempted murder among others. There were other guards involved and he's talking a lot and naming names. We've rounded up all of them, except one who took off before he was implicated. I've already notified the Bureau and they'll track him down."

[247]

"What? Why would you notify the Bureau? Do you mean the FBI? Now, I'm getting confused, why would a senior guard be notifying the FBI?" His head did hurt; he thought Sam had hit him with a riot baton, but why?

"Just lie still and let me explain, I'm David Morris, an agent of the FBI. I was undercover investigating the gangs and some of the guards. Sam helped me, as did Crenshaw, oh yeah, also that big guy, Ernst. We knew about one of the convicts that was supposed to kill you, but we didn't know about the guard. The guard was spending way too much money, but he told everyone he won it at the casinos. Our investigation revealed that what he won was nowhere near enough to explain the spending he was doing. He was smuggling drugs into the prison for the Aryan Brotherhood, your friend the Reverend. The Reverend was the one who paid him to kill you."

"Collier was the one we knew about, he had a deal with the Outlaws to give them information, but they turned it around on him and threatened to tell the Brotherhood about his activities if he didn't kill you. When Chang went down the last time and everyone knew it was over, he tried to attack you with a shiv. You had just dropped down to give CPR to Chang when he thought he could get you, but he didn't make it. Your friend Ernst hit him in the back of the neck with his fist; he went down on his own shiv, in the heart.

When I saw the gangs start toward you and Chang, I hit the panic button and the alarm went off. The guard on the tower thought he had a shot, but it hit Sam in the leg first. Sam was lucky, the bullet passed next to the thigh-bone and the femoral artery without damaging either one. He and Crenshaw took the first couple of Outlaws on to protect you and Chang, that's when he got stabbed. Crenshaw was cut up some, but not anything serious. He told me to tell you that you two are even now, whatever that meant."

"I checked on Chang before I came in here, and it appears that he's going to be okay. The swelling on his brain has gone down, and it doesn't appear that his liver is too badly damaged and should be back to normal function in a day or two. At first the doctor thought he'd have to remove his liver because he was pissing blood, but not now. He's starting to show signs that he's out of the coma, so they're watching him closely. I'm hoping he makes it and I think he will, he's one hell-of-a fighter. I think it was sheer willpower that was keeping him standing."

"Your lady attorney left about two hours ago, she was dead on her feet tired. She did say to let you know that she did get in touch with Chang's wife and your employee is going to pick her and the boy up at Reno Airport in about an hour. She also had some other words for you, but I'll let her tell you for herself, basically it was you're a bastard."

"One last thing before I go, Mendez said he would appreciate it if you stopped by and had a conversation with him. Be careful with him, he's one crazy old man. I wouldn't trust him, if it were me."

Jake was trying hard to take in all the information that the agent was telling him, but some of it didn't make sense. "What do you mean; my employee went to pick up Alex's wife? Do you mean Mr. Edmonds?"

"No Jake, I mean your employee, a Hernando Partida, his job is chauffeur. You're the only convict I ever met that had a chauffeur."

"It still doesn't make sense, but I'm sure Des will tell me about it. What time is it? And what day is it? I'm not tracking real well right now; I keep going in and out. Is there still a guard outside? I feel like a helpless baby here, and they might try to get me in here."

"Relax Jake; I'm your guard for the next six hours. I've already got some additional guards from other prisons to come up here to this prison, ones that I've personally vetted. It's four o'clock on Sunday afternoon. Would you like some ice or water?"

"Yes, I would. Thank you Agent, uh, Morris. Why the interest in me? I thought at first it was maybe you were gay, or something, but I still haven't figured it out. Sam thought maybe you'd screwed up at the last prison you were working at. Your file said you were single, so we weren't sure about you. Is Sam in trouble?"

"No, Sam's covered. He and Crenshaw are the only two that know I'm undercover, other than you, of course. My wife will get a kick out of that gay part, especially after five kids. The Reverend is in Ad-Seg and being guarded by three of my men, by the way. Your attorney told me about a deposition you made when you first met with her. It could be valuable to our investigation, would you consider letting me have it?"

"I'll have to think on that, Agent Morris. I need to figure out where I stand before I do anything else. All I'm concerned with for now is making sure Alex is going to get better, and getting his wife here. You did say my employee, uh, Partida, was picking her up at the airport?"

"Yes, I did. That was really nice of you to pay her air-fare, her and the boy."

Jake just smiled and closed his eyes.

CHAPTER THIRTY-SIX

Des had been on the phone so much he felt like it was permanently attached to his ear. Purcell had called with some really great news; one of the jurors suspected of taking a bribe had confessed that he had done just that. Purcell convinced the man to dictate his confession with two other deputies as witnesses, and was currently having it transcribed so he could have it signed. Des was trying to arrange with Eddie how they could get back to Ridgecrest, Eddie was supposed to be back to work in the morning and Des wanted to attach the confession to the appeal. He could then submit it right away and ask for an expedited appeal and/or possibly a pardon.

Eddie had suggested that he and Des catch a plane to Las Vegas and then one of the little commuter airlines to Inyokern. Then he left to pick up Alex's wife and son.

Des called Margaret and told her of the situation and asked if she could pick up him and Eddie in the morning. She said that she could and that Frank could handle the crew even if they were one person short. She also said that she had some good news of her own, but would rather discuss it when they were at her house. Des spent an hour getting arrangements made for the flights and ended up paying more than he wanted to for the tickets, but they would arrive late that night instead of in the morning. He called Margaret and made her aware of the changes. He and Eddie would have to check out of the motel and leave for Reno in about two hours to make that schedule. He thought of calling Julie in her room and then changed his mind; she had only gotten back to her room two hours ago and was probably sleeping. He decided to give her another hour at least.

He had another call, this time from Jan. She reported to him that the files were now done and in order. She also apologized for the mess they were in, she didn't do the filing for Jake's accounts, her father was supposed to and hadn't. Because of that, she didn't feel she should charge them for something that was a part of her commission, which she had already been paid.

Curious, Des asked, "Do have an idea of how much Jake's total assets are? I wouldn't want to be caught writing bad checks."

Jan laughed and answered, "Not to worry Mr. Edmonds, unless you write a check for more than two million dollars. I don't know what you've written out of his checking account, so if you need money, I can sell a couple of stocks. There is one thing, I wasn't able to balance the bonds account with statement that was in the mail Friday. Did you sell some bonds?"

Des quickly explained to her the sale of the bonds that Bryson was involved with, not wanting to see the bond value go down.

"See, Mr. Edmonds, you're never too old to learn something. That was very smart, it saved him money. I have school this week, or I would start working on Jake's portfolio again. Will I see you next week-end?"

"Yes Jan and thank you for your efforts."

He barely hung up when it rang again. It was Eddie.

"Mr. Edmonds, I have Mrs. Chang and Jacob in the Beast with me, should I take her to the hospital or check into the motel first?"

"Check in here first Eddie and then you can take her to the hospital. When you get done there, come back here, we have to leave for the airport in about two hours."

Des called the hospital and was put through to Sam's room, Angelina answered the phone.

Des quickly explained to Angelina about Merrian Chang and asked if she would mind driving them back to the motel if they needed. She said yes, she'd be happy to help.

"Angelina, are you feeling okay, are you getting enough rest? I don't want you to get too tired; it won't do you or the baby any good if you do. I can make other arrangements if you are getting tired. I just thought that with you knowing all the particulars of what this fight was all about would help her understand."

"You're a kind man Mr. Edmonds, I'll be alright and I'll do my best to help her. I thought it was very nice of you to pay for her airfare and motel that way. The only thing I'm worried about right now is where Sam might be in trouble some way. They might try bringing charges of some kind against him, I don't know."

"Angelina, don't worry about that. Is Sam awake?"

"Yes, hold on."

When Sam got on the phone Des said, "If they bring charges against you for anything, call me immediately, and don't answer any questions until I tell you to. As of this moment you're my client, understood?"

"Yes sir, but I can't afford a lawyer. We don't have the money Mr. Edmonds. We couldn't afford to have this baby if I didn't have health insurance."

"If Angelina promises to fix me a dinner, then the account will be paid in full. I do have one regret though; I still haven't met either you or Angelina face to face. Someday soon we'll change that. Talk to you later."

Des was packing when Eddie got back to the motel. "All delivered as requested Des, want me to pack?"

"You might want to, or you could just leave those clothes and buy new ones. It's your money; spend it how you want, Mr. Moneybags."

Eddie looked at him for a moment, a confused look on his face and then, "Oh, I get it, sometimes I don't understand you, but you were making a joke. I'll be back in a couple minutes."

Des rang Julie's room, but she didn't answer. He waited five minutes then dialed again, this time she answered on the fourth ring.

"Julie, Dad. We have to leave for the Reno airport in about forty minutes. Eddie and I are going back to Ridgecrest. Purcell called with some really good news. I'll explain on the way to the airport, now get up and get dressed."

Eddie had the suitcases packed and loaded into the Beast when Julie got to Des's room. He looked at her and said, "You look tired, you want me to drive to the airport so you can have a nap on the way?"

Julie smiled at him, "First the gallant knight tells the lady that she looks like crap, and then he tries to be nice. I think he needs to re-read the gallant knight manual. I'll be fine Eddie, thanks for the offer. Did Merrian get here? Is she at the hospital?"

"Yes, and yes. I left her with Angelina. Des called and Angelina said she'd talk to Merrian and try to explain everything. She also said she would drive her back to the motel when she needed. Des is probably waiting for us; he went down to check us out."

On the way to the airport Des went over what he'd learned from Purcell, and also told her about Margaret's cryptic message regarding more good news. Before he could say much else, she said, "You might want to think about getting that juror out of town to a safe place, he may be in danger if stays in his home. I don't know for sure of that, just a feeling I have. I called in before I went to sleep and got my vacation extended for three more days. Anything that needs doing up here should be done by then. After the appeal is filed, I may resign from Jake's case. Maybe I'm too close to it, or maybe my personal feelings are getting in the way, but I'm not sure if I can believe him anymore."

Des sat there in silence, his thoughts racing. He finally said, "Please listen Julie, I'm your father and I love dearly, but if you resign now you will end up regretting it. Jake never told you he was even interested in you, that was all your own infatuation. You let your imagination build so much that when you find out he's human and makes mistakes you can't bear it. Don't be guilty of pre-judging him, that's for small-minded people, not for you. Besides, I kind of liked the idea of having a millionaire in the family, but then a million dollars just isn't what it used to be. Jan told me earlier that he's worth over two million, but she hadn't included the bonds account. To look at him and the way he dresses, you'd think he sleeps in a homeless shelter,"

"How can you judge the way he dresses, all you've seen him in is prison clothes," she fired back. Then she started to grin, "You always knew what to say to get to me. You don't play fair, Mr. Edmonds."

"I can't afford to play fair when it comes to you and your sister; I love you both too much."

[254]

Julie left them at the airport and on the way back to Susanville she thought about what Des had said. Perhaps she had jumped to conclusions regarding Jake, especially the part about building something in her mind that maybe wasn't there. Jake hadn't said anything about being interested in her until just last night, or rather this morning. What was it he'd said about screwing everything up, including her and him? Maybe there was something there after all. Maybe she was just hoping, but there could be a chance they could get together.

She was tired and thought about going back to bed, but decided to check on Merrian and Angelina at the hospital. Merrian was here because her husband had fought Jake and lost, so Julie wasn't sure what kind of reception she would get. She found Merrian and Angelina sitting in the waiting area down the hall from Alex's room. Angelina started to get up, but Julie told her sit back down.

"Are you feeling okay?" she asked. "Des said you sounded tired on the phone, he was worried about you."

Angelina smiled and said, "I'm okay, just tired and it doesn't matter if I stand or sit, it's still uncomfortable. I was explaining to Merrian what Sam had told me about why Alex and Jake had to fight. She wasn't aware of the debt that Alex owed the Outlaws, but she did think that Alex was in some kind of trouble because his letters were very short and unlike the ones she got from him before. I tried to explain what Sam had said that if Alex didn't fight, the Outlaws probably would have killed him just to set an example."

"I'm beginning to understand now, Jake and Alex have been friends since long before I met Alex so I couldn't believe they would fight over something trivial," Merrian said. "Jake was always the one keeping Alex out of fights any way he could. I couldn't imagine him changing that way."

"I'm just glad you got here," Julie said. "When Jake woke up it was one of the first things he was worried about, getting you here and how Alex was. Have you heard any more on Alex's condition? I'm going down to Jake's room and he's going to ask."

"He regained consciousness briefly and went right back to sleep. The doctor is no longer worried about his liver, but there was some internal hemorrhaging so he's still got blood in his urine. He has a broken jaw, a fractured thigh bone, and several broken ribs along with lots of bruises. How can men be so brutal to each other?" Merrian shook her head and said, "I don't think I can ever understand that."

"Me either Merrian, me either," Julie said. "If you need me or are getting tired, I'll be down at Jake's room." She left the two of them and headed to Jake's room. She got to Jake's room just as the senior guard was about to leave, he introduced her to the guard on duty.

"He's sleeping at the moment Ms. Larson, but I think if you talk to him he'll probably wake up. He's been waking up for a few minutes here and there all afternoon, trying to learn if Mrs. Chang got here. I'm sure he wants to know."

She entered the room and Jake spoke. "Is that you Morris?" he questioned, his eyes still shut.

"No Jake, it's me, Julie. Merrian Chang and the boy, Jacob, got here about two hours ago. Angelina has been filling her on all the details. She wasn't aware of Alex's gambling debt, nor any of the things he was doing for the Outlaws. She also hasn't been told about the betting you did. She's going to find out sooner or later, but I'm not sure I am the one who can explain it to her. Wasn't there any other way to solve the problem, without beating him half to death?"

"I don't know Julie. I've been trying to think of all the different things I might have done instead of fighting, but I still haven't found one that would work. I thought about it before and wasn't sure then either. I tried to avoid the fight by getting put into solitary or "Ad-Seg" as they call it, but that only gave me more time to think. I could have stayed in Ad-Seg until Alex was up for parole, but I didn't think the Outlaws would just let him walk out of prison owing them fifty thousand dollars. They would have killed him just to prove to others that trying to skip out on a debt to them would get them killed."

[256]

"Fifty thousand dollars?" Julie asked. "How could he owe them fifty thousand dollars?"

"He got into a rigged game that the Outlaws were running. He kept writing markers, trying to win back what he'd lost, but like I said, it was a rigged game. By the time he realized what he was into, he was down fifty thousand. After that, they kept adding on interest, piling on more to his debt, forcing him to do what they wanted. He was beating other prisoners just to satisfy the 'vig', or interest.

When the Outlaws saw what I was doing, teaching the Aryan Brotherhood some martial arts skills, they perceived that as a threat to them and got Alex transferred to Susanville. I found out his problem when I talked to Davis, the leader of the Outlaw gang here, and asked if I could buy Alex's debt. When he told me the amount, I wasn't sure how much money I had and so I didn't try. If I had known I had enough money to hire a chauffeur, I would have asked Des to get me the money for that debt. By the way, do I have a limo too?"

Julie laughed and answered, "No, but almost like a limo." She went on to describe the Beast, outlining all the features it had. "Des decided to buy it so that he didn't have to keep spending money on airfare and taxis. The chauffer, Hernando, was Des's idea also. Hernando, or Eddie as we've come to call him, flew back with Des tonight to Ridgecrest to work on getting the pistachios harvested for Margaret. He's just a kid who was in trouble, so Des decided to try to help him turn his life around. Margaret says the crew admires and respects him, even old Indio. I like him too; he's trying hard to do the right things.

He was hoping he'd get a chance to meet you, but we kept him so busy driving people around he didn't get here while you were awake. We found out how much money you have just this afternoon from Jayantha, she said roughly two million dollars, but she hasn't included the bonds accounts. Had we known earlier, then maybe this whole mess wouldn't have happened. I'm beginning to understand a lot more about why you thought you had to fight, but why did you have to be so brutal?"

"Julie, Alex Chang is one of the fiercest fighters I have ever known. He knew what my plan was before the fight, but he came at me anyway with nearly every bit of energy he had. I wasn't sure I could defeat him until I saw him go down that last time, and I'm not really sure that he gave it his all. Maybe in his mind, he was hoping I'd win. After all, it was his doing that got the odds so high after talking to me in the infirmary. The Outlaws wanted to make sure he could beat me so they poisoned my food, trying to give Alex the edge. Sam and the senior guard caught the trustee that delivered my food with the poison and put me in the infirmary where I'd be safer. Alex came to see me in the infirmary, that's when he told me about his wife and son. His words to me then were, "I hope you know what you're doing." Do you know if his condition has changed?"

"He's showing signs of consciousness like he's out of the coma and his condition is improving. I'm glad you made me get Merrian and Jacob here, she's up there now with Alex."

"No, she's not."

Julie turned to see Merrian and Angelina standing in the doorway. "How long have you been there?" she asked.

"Long enough," Merrian said. "How are you feeling Jake, the doctor said you took somewhat of a beating yourself."

"I'm still alive Merrian, no thanks to that to that chili-eating Chinaman. He's one man I never want to fight again, ever. He really loves you, you know. He told me that the morning of the fight when we had breakfast together. He also told me that you made him start going to church. I would have never believed anyone could change as much as he did. I know he didn't really want to fight me, but they left him no choice. I'm glad he's doing better, do you need anything? If you do, please tell Julie and she can get it for you. She's my attorney and also has my checkbook so she can get what's needed."

Angelina laughed in the background and said, "Julie you have to teach me how you did that, I would love to know."

Jake opened his eyes and asked, "Who's that?"

"I'm your favorite chef according to what Sam tells me, he said you never left any of my cooking on the plate, not even the pickled tongue."

"Angelina," Jake said. "Now I understand why Sam is such a happy man, you're beautiful as well as a good cook. It's nice to finally meet you. I feel like I've known you forever, just from your food. Shouldn't you be sitting down?"

"Standing up or sitting down, either way I feel uncomfortable. I probably should go home and lay down, but I want to check on Sam before I go."

"Please tell Sam I said thank you," Jake said. "He saved my life."

"Before we go, I have some papers for you to sign Jake, but your hand is in a cast. Will you try to sign these so I can overnight them to Des?"

"Am I in trouble Julie? You sound worried about something."

"I'll tell you tomorrow Jake. Right now you need to sign these and then I can get these ladies home and I can get some sleep."

Jake signed them, or rather scribbled his name, and had Merrian and Angelina witness his signature. He had hoped to talk to Julie some more, but not with the other ladies present. His hope was that he could re-kindle any spark that may have been there, but now it would have to wait. He waited until they left and then tried to get comfortable, but to no avail, so he lay quietly hoping sleep would come.

CHAPTER THIRTY-SEVEN

Des heard the alarm and didn't want to wake up. Margaret had dropped him off at the house a little after 1:00 a.m. and gone home. He hit the snooze button, knowing it would go off again in ten minutes. He also knew he should be getting up and dressed, but after his marathon of phone calls and the flight on the little commuter plane, he was exhausted. He lay back with his eyes closed and tried to go back to sleep. When the alarm went off again he shut it off and swung his legs over the side of the bed, fighting the temptation of lying back down and sleeping for another couple of hours. He rubbed his hands over his face and realized that he hadn't shaved in two days. A shower and a shave would definitely make him feel better.

An hour later, while drinking his second cup, the phone rang. Margaret was on the phone.

"Good morning Des, can you come over this morning? The information I told you about is here and you should see it. It explains a few things that even I never understood about TJ until now."

"I would Margaret, but I'm waiting for the package from Julie if it comes today. She may not have gotten it in on time for an overnight delivery. I also need to talk to Purcell, plus I don't have any car or driver. Can you pick me up around noon?"

"I have to go in to work this morning, how about I meet you after work, around three or a little after?"

"Okay, how's Eddie this morning, tired I'll bet."

"Oh Des, I wish I had the energy that boy has. He was up early and checking on everything before I got up. He's really taking his responsibilities very seriously; I hope he doesn't forget how to have fun. He's so serious for being so young."

"I know what you mean Margaret, but I think he'll be alright. See you around three."

He tried calling Purcell, but got no answer. He then called the Sheriff's Office and was informed that the Deputy was in today, but he was currently in a meeting with Sheriff Lutz, so he asked the receptionist to leave a note to have Purcell call him. He went back to editing the appeal so he could insert the juror's deposition when he got it. When the phone rang he answered hoping it was Purcell, but it was Rosa.

"Mr. Edmonds, I need some help. When I was talking to the woman whose house I clean on Friday, she said I need to get a license from the city and insurance too. I got the papers from the city, but I don't know some of the words they use and I don't want to sign something I don't understand. And I don't know why I need insurance, can you help me?"

"Sure Rosa. Come by and I'll look over those papers and see about getting insurance. I'll be here all day." He was about to hang up when a thought hit him. "Rosa, are you able to come by around lunch time? I don't have any way to get out and get lunch, and haven't had time to stock up on groceries."

"Sure Mr. Edmonds, but how about I go shopping for you and get the groceries. Then I can cook those enchiladas you like."

"That would be great, see you when you get here."

He was just starting on the appeal when the doorbell rang and then the phone rang. He picked up the phone and said, "Hello, hang on," and then went to the door. It was the overnight delivery man, but the package wasn't from Julie. It was a check from his partners. He signed for the delivery of the check and went back to the phone. It was Purcell.

"Hello Purcell, what's going on this morning?"

"Quite a bit, I just got done with a meeting with Sheriff Lutz. He's had a couple conversations with the district attorney, and they're trying to get information from him on Jake's case. The two other deputies I had act as witnesses to the juror's deposition haven't told him anything. For now I told him I was still following leads, but he's still nervous. The DA and the judge have both been pressing him every day, wanting to know why I'm looking around. So far, I've told him that I'm just working for you and that I felt Jake didn't get a fair trial. There is some good news though, I got the deposition transcribed and the signatures notarized, so that's done. I'm bringing a copy down this evening, if you're home that is. How about six o'clock?"

"That sounds good. There is one other thing; Julie seemed to think that if we could we should get that juror to a safe place somewhere for a while. She said she had a feeling this wasn't done yet, what do you think?"

"If you can afford it, I can put him in a motel in Bakersfield for a week. Would that be alright?"

"Fine, let me know how much and I'll get you the money this evening. Anything else?"

"No, I'll see you at six."

Des went back to the appeal, working until Rosa showed up an hour later with a bunch of groceries. He helped her unload the bags from the old wagon into the house. When they were all unpacked and put away she started on the enchiladas, but not before handing him the receipt from the store.

Des looked at the receipt and laughed, "Well, I'm going broke, but I am going to eat good. Thank you Rosa, I'll write you a check." As he was making out the check, she brought him the application for the city business license, and the information about the insurance requirements. He looked them over and quickly had the application filled out and had her sign in the appropriate places. He then called a couple of local insurance agents and got quotes for business liability insurance and also a fifty thousand dollar bond. He told Rosa what the cost of the insurance was, and also suggested that she consider getting the bond.

"Not right now Mr. Edmonds, when I take this check to the check-cashing place, I'll just have enough money to pay for the insurance. How often do I have to pay this insurance, it seems very expensive to have for my business."

Des answered," You only have to pay once a year for the insurance, but why are you going to the check-cashing place? Don't you have a checking account?"

"My husband had one when 'Nando was very little, but they said he wrote too many checks and wouldn't let him have an account anymore. I just go to the check-cashing place and they cash the checks and give me the money orders that I need to

[262]

pay the bills. I don't think I could do a checking account, do you?"

"Of course you can, and we'll do that right after we have some of those enchiladas, it's easy to learn. And I'll help you get one opened today if you'll drive me to the bank, okay?"

"Sure Mr. Edmonds, let's have some lunch."

After lunch, Des had Rosa make coffee. He was still tired from the night before. He talked to Rosa about the checking accounts and how they worked. He explained the difference between business expenses and personal expenses and told her it was important to keep track of both of them. Rosa was eager to learn, but she hesitated when it came to the bookkeeping part of the conversation. She said it wasn't the math, but knowing what kind of expense goes where. Des had a thought, and suggested that she talk to Jan about keeping her business books in order. She would have to pay Jan a small amount each month, but would be assured that everything was in order. When it came time to file her tax returns, Jan would take care of that too.

Rosa told Des that tax returns were easy; she used to go to a man in the old neighborhood that would charge her a hundred dollars to fill out the tax form.

"What do you mean, the tax form, Rosa? If you have a business, there are several forms to fill out in addition to your personal tax return."

"He told me not to worry about that. He said that the one form was all I needed. He asked how much I made, I told him and he showed me how much I was supposed to pay and where to sign. That's what I did every year."

Des shook his head in amazement and finished his coffee. "Let's get to the bank; we can open both accounts today. Do you know what Margaret's address is?"

"No, I don't. I haven't had any mail coming since I moved. I closed the account with gas and electric company, and told the city I was moving so they don't charge me for the water. Did I do something wrong?"

"No Rosa, but you should fill out a change of address card at the post office anyway, okay?"

At the bank, Des deposited his check to his account and then he and Rosa waited for the new accounts representative to get off the phone. From what Des heard, the conversation wasn't about business. The young man was chatting with a friend about the previous weekend, recapping their exploits. After a few minutes, Des was tired of waiting and walked over to the Bank Manager's desk. He introduced himself and then told the manager that he would like to use his phone. He dialed up Jackson, and after a brief explanation of the circumstances, he handed the phone to the manager.

The manager hung up after several 'yes sirs' and went to the new accounts desk and grabbed all the forms necessary and returned. He was furious, but very civil to Des and Rosa as he filled out the forms for both accounts. Des offered to deposit the minimum amount necessary to open the business account, but the man graciously said it wouldn't be necessary. He escorted them over to the new accounts desk where the young man was still chatting on the phone, oblivious to his surroundings until the manager grabbed his phone and said "You're fired," and hung up the phone. He then apologized to Des and Rosa and assured them that kind of behavior wouldn't happen again. They left, and Des was smiling, he never could stand rude and incompetent people.

"Who did you call Mr. Edmonds?"

"A friend of mine who happens to own part of this bank. He and I went to school together. I thought he should know what one of his employees was doing, instead of his job. If I had someone working for me that wasn't doing his best, I'd want to know. Now, let's go and see the insurance agent."

The meeting with the insurance agent was short, but productive. Des was able to get Rosa on a quarterly payment for the insurance and set up another meeting in a month to discuss the bond. He also asked the agent to put together a proposal for life insurance for Rosa in the amount of one hundred thousand. He also asked the agent for a meeting later in the week to discuss his business insurance. When they left, the agent was definitely smiling.

[264]

Their next stop was the city hall to submit the application for a business license. The clerk didn't want to issue the license without an insurance policy number. Des handed her the agent's card, and suggested she call and verify that Rosa had just purchased a policy. She did and when she finished her call, she apologized and told them that lately people were trying to avoid costs by not buying insurance, or giving phony policy numbers. Des thanked her for the help and asked for an application for himself. When asked what type of business, Des told her attorney. She smiled and said, "You'll get plenty of business here, there's only two other attorneys in town and they're partners. It's expensive to go to them, and it takes time to go out of town to someone else. When do you plan on opening your office? I know a couple of people who would love to talk to you."

"I won't be open for a while; I have to find an office first. Do you know a competent realtor?"

She went to her desk and got two business cards. She gave them to Des and told him to call them both and explain what he wanted, and then they could come back with some listings. He thanked her and they left. Rosa's Cleaning Service was now officially in business.

Des glanced at his watch and asked Rosa if she could give him a ride to Margaret's.

"Of course, Mr. Edmonds. I was going there next after taking you home."

"I need to stop by the house first and grab my briefcase and some other papers, and then we'll go to Margaret's. Eddie can give me a ride back home when I'm done."

They got to Margaret's just past three, but Margaret hadn't gotten home yet. Des watched as Eddie and the crew worked the harvest, amazed at how coordinated their motions were. He was still on the porch, watching when Margaret arrived. She invited him in and went to get some papers from her bedroom. Rosa had made coffee, so he poured himself a cup. When Margaret returned, she had a packet of papers and an old diary. She handed him the diary first and asked him to read the pages she had book-marked. She sat and waited while Des read.

He read carefully following the handwritten text as it explained who TJ really was. When he was just past his sixteenth birthday, TJ was on guard duty, which was not uncommon when two clans are feuding like the Suttons and the McLeans had been for nearly a hundred years. From his post in the loft of the barn he could see the group of McLeans approaching the house. They weren't being sneaky about it, they had a white cloth attached to a stick as a symbol of truce.

The Sutton family came out to talk as they had done in the past, but what TJ saw was a young man, probably one of the McLeans, sneaking toward the back of the house and he had a couple of 'Molotov cocktails' in his hand. TJ waited until the young man lit the wicks and then shot him. If he hadn't, the Suttons wouldn't have had a house and who knows what else was planned. As it was, he disrupted whatever plans they had because the Suttons ran back into the house and opened fire on the McLeans that were still there.

To the Suttons he was a hero, but to the McLeans he was a coward who shot an unarmed man. TJ didn't like the fact that he'd had to kill someone, so he left the next day without telling anyone where he was going. He traveled north to Chicago and changed his last name to Wagner and had some phony papers made up. He then enlisted in the service and started his life over.

When he was done reading, Des looked at Margaret and asked, "How many other people know about this?"

"I don't know, maybe just those involved", she said. "What should I do about this?"

"Right now, you don't need to do anything that I can see for right now. I will have to study this some and then I can suggest what you should do, okay?"

"You'll want to read these papers, the will is in there and some other things. I'm not sure that they won't change your mind after you read them."

Des looked at the papers and decided to read the will first. When he finished, he looked at Margaret and asked, "Do you want to contest this will?"

"No, TJ and I talked about it before he wrote his will, and I didn't have a problem with it then and I don't now."

"But looking at this and knowing that Jake was convicted of TJ's murder, it may be a problem for him in his appeal. Has anybody else seen this Margaret?"

"I doubt it Des, it was in the vault and only me and Jake had the combination. Besides, I don't think there's many people that even know about the vault."

"Then as of right now, I'm your attorney and no one needs to know about this until Jake gets out. Can we put it back in the vault until then?"

"Yes, but shouldn't the next of kin be notified, now that we know who they are?"

"According to his diary, he left so they couldn't find him. I don't think he would want them included in his estate, do you?"

"No, I guess not. When I found those other papers, I was so worried that someone might figure it out and come here and cause trouble."

"It's possible they already have, what did you find out about the 'Davis' couple? Have any of your government friends found out anything?"

"No, not yet, but they're still looking into it. Why?"

"Can you ask them to check on a murder in Kentucky thirty-five years ago involving the names Sutton and McLean. Don't give them any first names; they might get too involved in this case, understood?"

"Yes I do, and thank you."

They were finishing the last of the coffee when Eddie came in. He was tired and dirty, but still curious.

"What are you doing here Des? Did I forget an appointment with the probation office, or something?"

"No, I'm here helping Margaret with some legal questions she had. Can you drive me back to my house after you clean up, please? I have a date with Purcell later to discuss some evidence he'd found."

"Sure Des, I'll be back in a few minutes."

[267]

On the way back to town Eddie mentioned having to go to the check cashing place and Des laughed.

"What's so funny?" Eddie asked.

"Ask your mother and she'll explain it all to you when you get home. We went through this same speech earlier today."

Eddie dropped Des off at his house and went on to cash his check. Des went back to work on the appeal, waiting for Purcell. When he arrived, they opted for one of the steak houses and headed there. After placing their order Purcell handed the package containing the deposition to Des. He read through it quickly and then put it back. He put the package in his briefcase, and asked Purcell about the juror.

"Do you think he'll be a credible witness? If we get an appeal and have to present him as a witness, do you think he'll survive a tough cross-examination?"

"I don't know Des, it took some pressure to get him to give up his confession as to accepting a bribe. Also, he kept referring to the man who talked to him as "one of those government types", but he had no name and a really vague description. I wish he was a little more solid, but if they find out we've got him, they might try to get to him and he could possible recant all his testimony saying he was coerced into it. I've got a good lead on the other juror involved, but I'm having trouble getting information on him. Like I told you before, if I go to the judge it'll tip our hand about the investigation. For right now, Lutz is going along with me in keeping quiet because he knows how much crap I can unload on him in the next election. How can we get the warrants to look into this other juror?"

"I thought about that, we may be able to prove that Jake's civil rights were violated by the one juror who accepted a bribe, opening the door to a federal investigation. I was going to make some discreet phone calls to a few friends and see if they can help us. What do you have so far on the second juror? Do you know how much he was paid?"

"I think it was twenty-five thousand, if they paid him the same as the first juror. What I think happened is that they paid the money to a relative who's holding it for a while. I've got a list of possible relatives that you can have. I understand Julie's still in Susanville, what's going on, she getting to know Jake a little better?"

Des thought for a moment and then explained about the big fight and why Jake and Alex had fought. He also told Purcell of Julie's first reaction, and how she almost quit the case.

"When I left her at the airport, she still wasn't sure what to do, so I asked her to give him some time to explain himself and why he thought he had to do what he did. She's like her mother, jumping to conclusions before hearing the whole story. I'm hoping she gives him a chance, she won't find anyone as decent as he is. There must be something going on or I'd have gotten a call telling me she was on her way home, so far I haven't heard a thing."

Purcell nodded and said, "This is one time that no news is good news, right?"

"I hope, she needs to be happy for a change. Did you find a place to put the juror for a week or two?"

"Yes I did, and it's not going to cost as much as we thought. I have a friend who works for the Bakersfield Police Department who will make some room at his place. His son just got out of the Army and would love to have a simple baby-sitting job. Between the two of them, they'll keep your juror safe. I'll get you the address before I leave your house."

"I'd rather not know. That way if I'm asked for his location I don't have to lie."

After dinner, Purcell drove Des back to his house and then gave him all the information he had on Juror#2 as they now called him. He left and headed north for home, hopefully the wife will be asleep by the time he gets there. He had come to ignore her more and more lately, her constant nagging about his hours being one of the reasons. When they did go somewhere together, she always wanted to invite her friends along. They would chat for hours about the TV shows and who was doing what in town, and for the pleasure of hearing all that garbage, he'd be rewarded with the opportunity to pick up the tab. He'd thought about divorce, but every once in a while when they were alone together, she would actually be civil.

CHAPTER THIRTY-EIGHT

Julie was sitting in the chair when Jake woke up again. He'd been awake several times during the night, many times not by his own choosing. The nurse had awakened him several times during the night, first for his blood pressure and then again to give him a pill. Those that thought the hospital was a place to get some rest were crazy. Jake thought he'd have gotten better sleep in a rail yard roundhouse. He looked over at Julie and smiled.

"How long have you been here?"

"Not long, maybe ten or fifteen minutes. How are you feeling this morning?" she asked.

"Not bad this morning, I could definitely sleep for another hour or two, but it's not likely in here. They must try to wait until you get to sleep before they take vital signs or whatever they call it. I think they're just pissed off at having to work mid-nights."

"Jake, I want to apologize for being mad at you earlier; my dad said I should talk to you and try to understand why you fought. He was right, I was angry because I thought there might be something between us even though you've never said anything like that. Des also said that I had built you up in my mind without getting to know you, and when you did make a mistake, I was angry because the image I had of you was destroyed. I was wrong in thinking there might be something between us, forgive me."

"I'm so happy you said that Julie. I was hoping there would still be a chance to talk to you about you and me. I've had a lot of time to think, and sometimes those thoughts were about you. Like you, there wasn't anything said that would indicate there was something between us, but I was really hoping there could be. I see you and I want so much to be able to just talk with you and learn more about you. I saw certain things that you did and it made me admire you for doing them, like the way you're always checking on Des to make sure he's okay. Maybe I did a little daydreaming about "us" when there wasn't really an "us". Will you give me a chance to see you when I get out?"

[271]

"Of course," she said. She was about to say more, but the nurse's aide brought in his breakfast interrupting the conversation. "I'm going up to check on Alex while you eat breakfast, he may be awake this morning".

Alex was definitely awake when she entered his room. He and Merrian were laughing, then crying and then laughing again. Little Jacob was sitting in the chair wondering what it was all about. She was about to ask when Merrian said, "He's trying very hard to tell me something, but with his jaw wired shut I can't understand a word he's saying. He said 'I dub you', but I think he meant 'I love you', I can't really tell."

Julie reached into her briefcase and got a steno book. "Here," she said, "this might help. Have him write it down for you."

Alex tugged on Merrian's sleeve and gestured toward Julie and then shrugged as if to say 'Who is that?'

"I'm sorry, I should have introduced you. Alex, this is Julie Larson. She's the one who told me you were in the hospital and then paid for the plane tickets to get me and Jacob up here. She's Jake's lawyer and set us up in the motel."

Alex seemed satisfied with that information for the moment, and started writing a note to Merrian, so Julie excused herself and said, "I'm going back down to see Jake, anything you want me to tell him?"

Alex nodded yes and then scribbled a note. "You are one stubborn SOB. I will NOT fight you again."

Julie read it and laughed, "I think he said the exact same thing yesterday. He'll be glad to know you're feeling better. If you need anything, let Merrian know and I'll see if we can get it for you."

She met the senior guard outside Jake's room. After exchanging pleasantries they both went in to see Jake. The senior guard didn't waste any time in asking Jake about the package of information he had. Jake looked at Julie and asked, "Are you the one who told him about the deposition? If you did, doesn't that violate attorney-client privilege?"

"Not if I didn't divulge the contents of the deposition, which I haven't. Now, I want to know why a senior guard is so interested in that deposition. Perhaps you should let me know what's going on Jake."

Jake looked Morris and asked, "May I?"

"You might as well," he said. "She's going to find out sooner or later."

Jake introduced FBI Agent David Morris and explained that Agent Morris was working undercover at Susanville gathering information on the connections between certain guards and gang members of the four gangs. He also let Julie know what danger there was in someone else finding out he was FBI.

"If either the guards or the gangs find out, he'll be dead before the next shift change. This is not the kind of place where we'll be taking the kids on vacation. Now, Agent Morris, what's in it for me? If I go back inside, and someone has found out that I "may have" passed on information to you or anyone else, I'll be dead. I suggest that you start figuring out how both Alex Chang and myself are going to be protected. I also want all the markers that the Outlaws are holding on Chang in my hand, before you and I talk any more deals. Consider it an act of good faith Agent Morris, maybe you can put the squeeze on one of the Outlaws to give up those markers or whoever is holding them. I know it doesn't sound fair, but that's what I'm proposing in front of my attorney, so we don't have any misunderstanding later."

"I have to hand it to you Jake, I knew you were tough, but I didn't figure you were that smart. I'm going to have to run this by my boss, but it's going to be a tough sell. I'm asking him for a lot based on information that may or may not be useful to us. We may already have a lot of what you're thinking of giving us. Anything else you have to offer?"

Julie interrupted, "Yes, but Jake hasn't been told this yet, Deputy Purcell has a juror tucked away that has also given a deposition regarding jury tampering, and he's got a lead on the second juror involved. We know the judge was also involved, but we haven't been able to get warrants for the juror or the judge without letting the judge know what we're up to. Would that help, Agent Morris?"

"It might help Jake a lot, but doesn't help my investigation at all. I wish you could give me something that I can use to prove that the deposition is worth moving you and Chang to another prison, maybe closer to Ridgecrest. Anything you can tell me?"

Jake looked at him and said, "Yes, leave the room. Come back in ten minutes, after I talk to my attorney." After he'd gone, Jake turned to Julie and asked, "Why is Purcell looking into my case, did you ask him to?"

"No Jake, I didn't. He told me about his investigation after he'd been to the murder site and had found some additional evidence. He told me that he thought you were innocent based on the testimony you'd given and the evidence being exactly what you'd said. He and I have been acquaintances for a long time. He introduced me to my first husband and felt responsible because he knew David was the type that cheated. When he thought that I was interested in you, he started looking into your background and your case because he didn't want me to be hurt again. Now what are you going to do about this situation?"

"I think I'll give him some information that he can easily prove is correct, and then we play "Let's Make a Deal", okay counselor?"

"Okay, what do you want me to do? I have to drive back to Ridgecrest tomorrow so I can be at work the day after."

"Just go back to work for now, when he comes up with a solid proposal that includes Alex as well as me, and then I'll get it to you. Now, how is Alex doing? Is he able to talk? How about Merrian, is she doing okay?"

"Hold on. Alex is awake and talking as much as he can with his jaw wired shut, but Merrian is worried that she may have lost her job. She didn't have any sick leave or vacation coming, so they probably fired her. She wasn't making much anyway as a file clerk, so it's going to be rough on her."

"No it's not, she's working for me starting yesterday, pick a reasonable wage for her and get her some health insurance, including the boy. If we can negotiate this transfer, she can move to near us in Ridgecrest. That way she can ride along when you come to visit me. There's certainly something we can put her to work doing, isn't there?"

"I'll have to check on that Jake; right now you don't have a business, just a chauffeur and the Beast to ride around in. Have you thought about what you want to do? Are going to try mining the old Chambers mine? And one other thing, how do you know I'm going to come visit you in prison?"

"Well, maybe I was kind of hoping that you would. Will you?"

"We better tell Agent Morris what he wants to know before he decides to leave. He might say to hell with the whole deal if you don't hurry up."

She called in Agent Morris and recorded Jake's statement on the two small recorders she had purchased before, giving one to the Agent to have transcribed. She reminded him that the 'deal' had an expiration date, so he had better get things moving quickly. He agreed that it should be done quickly and left, but not before getting another guard to stand watch. After he left, Julie moved closer to the bed and asked Jake, "Do you think there could be an 'us' Jake?"

"I sincerely hope so Julie. I would like that very much. Being alone doesn't always mean that a person is lonely, just that they haven't found the right person to be with. Since I met you I've begun to realize that I'm lonely when you're not around. When you're gone I feel like part of me is missing, do you understand?"

She was about to answer when a nurse came in, starting toward Jake, but she had a large paper bag in her hand and was about to reach inside when Julie yelled. "Stop!" She had dug into her purse and grabbed her backup pistol and was pointing it at the nurse. The nurse dropped the bag and raised both hands over her head; Jake was looking at her but not understanding.

"What's wrong Julie?" he asked.

"Her uniform is wrong; it looks like it came from a costume rental shop." She turned to the nurse and asked, "What's your name, and who sent you?"

The nurse was clearly shaken, almost to the point of tears,"Please don't shoot me, I didn't do anything wrong, I was just supposed to deliver the money. Mr. Mendez said to give the money to Mr. Jake Kozan and tell him thank you for a great fight. Please don't shoot."

"What's your name and how much money is there?"

"Mmm, my name is Hortencia Balderrama and Mr. Mendez said there's fifty-nine thousand in the bag. He said he didn't charge you as much as usual because you are such a great fighter and one of the 'good guys'. Can I please go now; I don't want to get in trouble."

"Wait," Jake said. "Why didn't Mendez wait until I was back in prison so he could pay me himself?"

"He didn't think you'd be coming back and he didn't want someone called 'Reverend' trying to claim the money was his."

"Thank you Hortencia, and tell Mendez I said thank you. You may go now."

When she left, Julie picked up the bag and looked inside. There was money in it all right, bundles of bills held together with rubber bands. She thought about it and then said to Jake, "You know that this money is probably drug money or worse."

He looked at her seriously for a moment and then said, "I don't care, and it's all going to Alex and Merrian to give them a start that neither of them has ever had. I don't want it, I was going to use it to buy Alex's markers from the Outlaws, but if Agent Morris comes through, I won't need it at all. If you still think it's immoral or wrong for them to have it, then take it out and burn it, okay?"

Julie sat there, taken back by his sudden seriousness. She started to speak a couple of times, but whatever she was going to say must not have sounded just right. Finally she said, "I think you're right, I didn't look at it that way, I'm sorry."

"Don't be, "he said. "I wrestled with the same thoughts earlier until I thought about Agent Morris. I hope he can do what we're asking."

She smiled and asked, "Anything I can do when I get back to Ridgecrest?"

"Yes, tell the chauffeur that he's going to be demoted to laborer for a while. I need someone to start clearing all the rock and debris away from the front of the mine, and I also want him to dig a small pond at edge of the property closest to the seep Des told me about. I want the animals to have a place to get water when they want without being disturbed by us when we're there. Can that pretty thing of mine travel in the desert, or should we have him use TJ's old Powerwagon?"

"For work out there, the Powerwagon would be best, I'll check with Margaret. Anything else, Mr. Kozan, sir?"

He laughed and said, "Yes, can you see about getting me a phone in here? I'd really like to be able to talk to people myself instead of relaying messages all the time. That way I feel less like a boss and more like a part of something. Plus then I can call you and talk about us some more."

She smiled and answered, "Now I'm definitely getting you a phone, Mr. Kozan, sir."

She picked up her purse and her briefcase along with the bag of money and departed, but not before stopping by Alex's room and leaving two thousand with Merrian for 'expenses'.

CHAPTER THIRTY-NINE

Eddie leaned on the shovel for a moment, catching his breath. It was almost siesta time, and he'd brought some of Mama's fine tortillas to make fajitas. He didn't mind that they'd be cold; in this heat it was better that way. He had about fifteen feet to go to finish this row and then he'd stop for lunch and a siesta. He'd do a couple more rows after siesta if it didn't get too windy. When the wind blew it was miserable to try to work, the sand and clay dust flew around too much. He was glad to be working, even if it was with a shovel. After all, he was getting five percent of the profits from the operation.

He thought about Jayantha and hoped she'd be coming home this weekend, he wanted to study some more with her. The GED test was going to be in less than three weeks and he should be studying more than he had been. He'd brought two of his books with him, so maybe instead of napping, he'd study some more. Probably the English instead of the Civics book, he had a difficult time understanding Civics. He could save the Civics text for studying with Jayantha, if she came home. He really liked her, not just for helping him, but because she was so easy to talk to. He didn't call her Jan like the rest because he thought her name had an almost musical sound to it. He'd better get back to work, he thought, or he wouldn't make much money this week.

The operation he was working on all started when he came home on a Saturday after digging out part of the pond for the burros to get water. His clothes were covered with the white dust from the clay that he had to dig through. Margaret looked at it and said it looked like that stuff they used at salon she knew. There they used the clay to make a cleansing 'mask' on the ladies' faces, peeling it off after it dried. Jayantha was there and commented that it did look like that, but that the clay they made it from was only found in China and in some places in Georgia. Margaret had asked her if she knew anyone who could check it out for them. The following weekend, when she returned from

[278]

school, she told them the good news. After a few phone calls to Julie and two to Jake, the three of them were part owners of the Jayantha Corporation, a subsidiary of JAKE, Incorporated; along with Jake who provided the finances and Julie who provided the legal counsel.

They had researched the selling prices for the same product on the Internet and decided on a selling price per pound, with discounts for bulk sales to salons and beauty supply houses. The orders started coming in faster than expected, so they hired Merrian to handle the office and the girl, Dayna Goodnight, who had helped them with the harvest, was packaging and shipping out the orders. Eddie hired Javier McManus to help Dayna on the weekends getting the big bulk orders ready to ship.

Dayna still hadn't told anyone who the father of her baby was; even though she was due to deliver in a couple weeks. The young seaman, Donnie Arroyo had been coming around to talk to Dayna on his days off. Rosa had met him a couple times and told Eddie that she thought he was a very nice young man. Rosa had rented part of the warehouse for her cleaning business and also paid Merrian to answer the phone during the day.

Jake had also hired Javier McManus to help Eddie clear the rocks and dirt from the mine entrance and begin leveling the area where the house was going to be, when Eddie wasn't excavating clay. He was working today in the back of the mine clearing out an area where some rocks had fallen during the blast. Des had told Eddie exactly where the cave started, and to try to widen the entrance to the cave when he couldn't work outside.

The two of them stayed in a little shack they had put up over a weekend with some help from Stan Hobbs and an old prospector that they called Prospector, because he never gave an honest answer when asked his name. One week he would answer to George Washington and the next week he'd be Joe Montana, never the same answer in two weeks. Stan had thought the old man was wanted for something somewhere, which kind of made sense Eddie thought.

Per Jayantha's instruction, Eddie had dug several test holes to determine how deep the layer of clay was. In some places it was just less than four feet and in others it was closer to six feet deep. She said she wanted to have an idea how much "product" they could excavate in the next few years. She also told Eddie that it helped to determine the total value of Jake's property, based on current selling prices for the clay. When Eddie questioned why the clay was so expensive compared to other types of clay, Jayantha told him about the different qualities of the different clays.

The white clay they were mining had a non-metallic base, unlike red clay which had iron in it, or grey clay that had aluminum oxide in it, both of them metals that weren't good for the skin. The white clay also had a slightly abrasive quality that helped to scrub the skin and remove dead skin cells. Either way, as long as it was popular with women, it would be valuable, but there were other uses for it as well. She told him that based on current prices; the clay that was in the meadow was worth several million dollars. It was nice to know that he was now worth five percent of several million dollars. He thought about how he at one time had wanted to be just like 'el Jefe' and shook his head. "Boy was I stupid," he thought.

He finished the row he was working on in time to watch Javier coming out of the mine with another wheelbarrow of rock. They separated the gold-bearing ore and piled it to one side to be processed later and dumped the other rock down the side of the ridge to help fill in where they planned on having a road. The rock and gravel that was excavated in leveling the area where the house would go was also dumped there. They had been instructed not to extract any more ore than they had to in widening the entrance to the cave, for some reason Jake didn't want it dug into at this time.

Jake had told them how to excavate the clay and given them an area fifty feet by fifty feet to work until all the clay was extracted from there, and then he would give them another square to work. Eddie had cleared the brush and weeds off the top and then piled the sand off to the side as he dug a row three feet wide to where the clay started. Then he would excavate the clay, getting as much pure clay as he could, loading it into plastic sand-bags that Jake had purchased. They were smaller and easier to lift than the big ones and he made sure the back of the Powerwagon was full as well as the trailer at the end of the week.

He would fill the wheelbarrow he was using and then run it up to where they had an area that was used for filling the bags. On Friday they loaded the sand-bags with clay and then wheeled them down to the Powerwagon and the trailer. When they were loaded, the two of them went back to town and stayed there during the weekend.

Each time Eddie finished a row, he filled that with whatever sand and gravel was available until it was even with the original. Then he was instructed to rake it somewhat level and spread some grass seeds over the area. Then he would start the generator and turn on the little pump and pump water from the pond through a hose to water the seeds he'd just planted along with those he'd done before.

Some of the grass was already starting to come up in spots, but Eddie didn't think it would last long when the animals found it. That didn't matter, he'd been told. What mattered was getting the plants to put down roots and help build up the soil so later they could plant a garden in that spot. Then they would build an animal-proof fence with netting over the top. They definitely wanted to keep out the ravens; a flock of them could ruin a garden in one day.

They were about to stop for siesta when they saw Prospector coming down from high on the mountain and they waved to him. He was leading his mule and the donkey was tied behind, he usually rode the mule. When he got close enough, they could see why he wasn't, his mule had been shot. The wound was a bullet-hole through the back leg that was still bleeding from both sides. The mule had bucked Prospector off and had gone on down the hill, he was three hours just getting everything put back together on the donkey and then rounding up the mule.

He told them that he had seen the person that had shot at him. He described the man and Eddie asked him to wait a minute. When he returned from the shack he had a picture of "Dean Davis" and showed it to Prospector. When he saw it, Prospector just nodded and said that's him. Eddie told Javier that they were going to start loading sand-bags right now and as soon as they had both vehicles full they were going back to town, even if it was the middle of the night.

Prospector asked if he could stay by the pond while the mule healed up and Eddie said yes, but don't let anyone know who is working this mine or who owns it. Prospector said not to worry; and then pulled an old pistol out from under the pack on the donkey. It looked like a museum piece it was so old. It actually looked like the ones Eddie had seen in the westerns on TV.

Eddie and Javier began loading bags as fast as they could, while Prospector tended to the wounds on the mule. When he finished that, he started putting together some beans and tortillas for dinner. Eddie told him to add the tortillas that he had in the cooler, and add the fajita meat to the beans. After they had filled the back of the Powerwagon and started on the trailer, Prospector called them and told them dinner was ready. They ate and then went back to work filling bags; even Prospector filled a few to help out.

It was late when they were finally loaded, but that didn't matter to Eddie. He had to warn everyone that the Davises were back, he thought. He gave Prospector the keys to the cabin and some instructions on how to start the generator and asked him to water the grass. He and Javier went rolling down the mountain, maybe a little faster than he normally did, but not endangering himself or the old Dodge. They pulled into the barn at 4:30 a.m. greeted loudly by Frio; he was making sure that Margaret knew he was doing his job.

He headed towards the house while Javier went to his cot in the shed. Eddie knew it was earlier than Margaret usually got up, but he was sure she'd want to know about this. She was putting on a robe as she came down the hall. He headed toward the kitchen and started to make coffee, but she gently pushed him out of the way.

"Who got hurt?" she asked. "What happened? Something must have happened for you to be coming in here in the middle of the night, what is it?"

He started to explain, but he was so tired, he just sat there. Finally he said, "No-one got hurt other than Prospector's mule. Davis shot him. I showed Prospector the picture of Davis that you printed for me and he was positive that it was him. I came to town so we could warn everyone; I don't know what he's planning on doing. We should call Des, and Julie and Jake, maybe that deputy that was investigating too. What was his name?"

"Calm down, you're talking ninety words a minute, have cup of coffee and then we can decide who we need to call. Did you bring Javier in with you; I hope you didn't leave him there. When did Prospector say he had been shot at?"

"He said he had just broke camp down and was starting to get the donkey packed when Davis shot, so it was early morning, maybe six or seven o'clock."

"Okay, we know he's in the area now. I'll call and see if I can get Purcell, though it might be too early. You have some more coffee while I get dressed, I'll be back in a bit."

Even though Eddie was tired, he didn't feel like sleeping. He wanted to be there if something happened. He poured himself another cup and sat back down, worried about Prospector; thinking what might happen if the Davises showed up at the mine.

Margaret came back to the kitchen and sat down. She looked at the clock and said, "It's early, but I know that Des would want know about Davis being back in the area. I'll call him right after I call Deputy Purcell."

Margaret called and the dispatcher answered the phone. When Margaret told her who she was trying get in touch with, the dispatcher informed her that Deputy Purcell wasn't working today, please try again tomorrow. Margaret asked if she could get his home phone or cell phone and was told no. She then

[283]

asked the dispatcher to contact the deputy and relay a message regarding the murder case he'd been working on, it was very urgent. When the dispatcher hesitated, Margaret stated that if she hadn't heard from Purcell in thirty minutes, she'd be calling Sheriff Lutz and she already had the phone number for him and then she hung up.

Eddie looked at her and said, "I didn't know you had the Sheriff's phone number."

"I don't," she said. "But she doesn't know that. Let's hope it worked." She phoned Des and his daughter Michele answered. Margaret asked her to wake Des up, it was important news. Des answered about three minutes later. When she told him of the situation, he asked if anyone had been hurt. Only the mule, she told him.

"What do you think he wants Des? He's already killed TJ and the CIA has terminated him, so what is it that he could gain by even being here?"

"I don't know Margaret, maybe he feels that Jake is a threat to him, although I don't see how he could be. I'm going to call him and Julie and let them know what's going on. It will be better if he knows now about Davis."

She hung up and told Eddie what Des had said. She started fixing some breakfast and made another pot of coffee. Rosa came in and began helping Margaret. Eddie thought Javier might still be awake, so he went to the shed, but he was sound asleep. Frio joined him on his walk back to the house, the rabbit fur around his mouth indicating he'd run down another one. Eddie thought, for a big dog, Frio was very fast. They both went back in the house and sat down to breakfast.

Des asked Michele to fix some coffee. He was glad that she had finally decided to move in with him after the divorce; it was nice to have her and the kids in the house. He'd moved out of Jake's house to one of his own when they had announced their marriage. That had all happened so fast it was like a whirlwind. Des had filed the appeal the same day that Agent Morris had announced that instead of being moved to another prison, both Jake and Alex were being paroled based on "their cooperation"

[284]

in an on-going investigation. Julie had driven the Beast up to Susanville to pick up Jake and drive him home.

Their route just happened to take them through Reno, so they thought it would be an opportunity they shouldn't pass up. Alex and Merrian had opted to go back to Coronado for a week, so they could pack up what belongings they had and move to Ridgecrest. The only person who got moved was Sam Battiste, when he was promoted to Special Liaison to the Governor in charge of reporting conditions of the various prisons throughout the state. He and Angelina were both moved to Sacramento right after their son was born.

Des called the hotel where Jake and Julie were staying, only to be informed that Mr. and Mrs. Kozan had left specific instructions not to be disturbed. The desk clerk was not going to put the call through no matter what Des said, so he told the clerk to have either of them call as soon as possible.

Margaret picked up the phone on the second ring, it was Purcell. He sounded like he'd just woke up.

"What's the big emergency Margaret, did somebody get shot?"

"Davis is back in the area, I thought you might want to know and I apologize for calling so early, but he shot at Prospector and hit the mule. I think he's gone over the edge and is looking to take Jake and maybe some others with him."

"Oh shit," was all Purcell could to say at the moment. After a long pause he asked, "Where was Prospector when he was shot at, and did anybody else see Davis?"

"Just a minute, I'll let Eddie tell you. He knows more about it than I do."

Purcell started to ask who is Eddie, but Margaret had already passed the phone.

"Mr. Purcell, this is Hernando Partida. I work for Jake out at the mine. Me and Javier were working out there yesterday when Prospector came in and his mule had been shot in the back leg. He said he was north of the mine, almost due west of Sentinel Peak when it happened. It was right after he broke camp and was packing the pack on the donkey. He was walking the whole

[285]

distance, so it probably was about three and a half miles north of the mine, nearly the same elevation though. Are you going to try to find him Mr. Purcell?"

"The first thing I'm going to do is inform Sheriff Lutz as to what you've told me and then he can decide what man-power he wants to put into this. The last few county meetings have been nothing but budget and where we can cut. He may say it's just a hoax and tell us to forget about the whole thing, but that doesn't mean that I agree with him Hernando. If you can, without getting in trouble, get some self protection to carry with you. Do you understand what I'm saying?"

"Yes sir, I do, but I just got off probation and if they catch me with the kind of 'protection' you're talking about, I could end up in jail. What else should we be doing?"

"Make sure everyone is aware that Davis is back in the area. Then let them know what I said regarding 'self protection'. When I say everyone Hernando, I mean anyone and everyone even remotely related to Jake's case and especially Margaret. Is there anyone that can be there with Margaret all the time?"

"Yes sir, I think instead of going back out to the mine, I'll stay right here and Javier will be here too. Thanks Mr. Purcell, and by the way, I left Prospector up at the mine. He has keys to the shack and wanted to stay while his mule healed. Can you check on him for me please? I know he's a crazy old man, but I like him anyway."

"Either I will or I'll have someone do it for you. I'll check back later with you, and if your mother has to go clean a house, make sure there's someone with her as well." He'd been talking so long that now his breakfast was cold. Margaret looked and told him not to worry and fed his food to Frio, then started on another breakfast. He wasn't quite as tired as he thought because he finished his meal and asked for seconds. He told Margaret what Purcell had said about 'personal protection' and wanted to know if she had anything like what he was talking about. She just laughed and told him to finish his food; the 'protection' was something TJ had plenty of, enough for her, him, Rosa, and even

Javier. She said she didn't think Frio would need any, because he didn't know how to reload.

When they got to the barn, she told him to wait while she went down to open the vault. When it was open, he came down and looked inside. There were several rifles, some shotguns, and a variety of handguns, as well as plenty of ammunition on the shelves. Eddie couldn't believe one person could have so many weapons, so he asked how TJ had gotten so many.

She said that over the years, working here on the Naval Station, sailors sometimes ran into a need for extra money. When they couldn't wait until payday, TJ would loan them money, but he always wanted something to hold for collateral. In some cases the sailor wouldn't be able to pay the loan and so he would forfeit his collateral, usually a gun or something equal in value. TJ had never sold any of them in case the sailor would come back months later to try to redeem his property. He didn't cheat them, they knew what they were getting into and TJ's interest rate was lower than the payday loan companies in town and he offered more money per item than the pawn shops.

Together they decided that the best weapons for the house would be shotguns and pistols, while Eddie and Javier would have the semi-automatic M-16's and each would carry a 9MM pistol. She told Eddie that TJ liked that combination, and nearly always carried it when he went into the desert.

She called Des and told him what Purcell had said and asked if he could stop by later, then he could pick out what he felt most comfortable with. She reminded him that with Michele and the kids in the house it would be better to have it than not.

CHAPTER FORTY

Jake sat up and swung his legs over the side of the bed, trying not to move too much and wake up Julie. He looked back over his shoulder and saw her wide awake and staring at him, "I was trying not to wake you," he said. "I guess it didn't work."

"Nope, it didn't. Where are you going?"

"Where I usually go first thing in the morning, and then I was going to make us some coffee. This place has terrible room service. And last night, the maid didn't turn down the bed for us. I don't know why I stay here."

"It's probably because you own this run-down old place, Mister Kozan. I happen to like the room service, especially the masseur. That was a wonderful rub-down; remind me to leave him a tip when we check out."

"Sorry Mrs. Kozan, but the staff is instructed to not accept gratuities, all services here at Plaza Kozan are complimentary."

"Fine, but hurry up in the bathroom, I have to go too. I'll make the coffee, your coffee is like Margaret's, you can stand a spoon straight up in it. Be sure to hang up your towel when you're done with it."

They had been back in town for three days now and hadn't seen or heard anything more about Davis. Eddie had driven back out to the mine with Stan Hobbs in his old Jeep, not wanting to tip off Davis as to who they were. Neither of them had been seen by Davis before, other than when he'd beaten up Eddie and took his money and drugs. Eddie didn't think Davis would recognize him now, he had changed that much. When they got to the mine, Prospector was getting ready to leave. He'd been staying in the shack, eating what provisions there were, but he left them a small pouch with some nuggets in it.

He told them that while there he had scouted around the area and hadn't seen any tracks or sign of any kind. He hadn't gone too far away from the mine, just a half mile in each direction, not wanting to be away from his pack and the mule. When he was at the top the hill above the mine he had looked with an old telescope he had and thought he spotted someone off to the

[288]

north, but they were too far away to recognize. He pulled Eddie aside and told him of another meadow that had the same type of clay in it, not too far away to the northwest. He had drawn out the directions on a piece of paper from the shack so Eddie could refer to them.

When he mentioned going to town to cash in some of the other gold that he'd found, Stan volunteered to take him into town and drive him back out. The old man thought that would be okay and they helped him stow his pack in the shack and then tethered the donkey and the mule on long ropes so they could graze what grass and weeds were there and still get to the pond.

On the way to town, Stan asked the old man which assayer he used. When he answered, Stan asked how much he was being paid for the gold, the old man told him and Stan nearly ran off the road. He told the old man what gold was currently selling for per ounce and Prospector wanted to turn around and get his "six-shooter" so he could kill the assayer. Stan and Eddie both talked him out of that idea and suggested that Prospector re-pay the man by selling him a mine. They worked out the details on the way to town. Stan said he had just the thing they needed to convince the assayer to part with a lot of money.

Stan stopped at his house and came out with a couple of tennis-ball sized pieces of quartz, what they called "jewelry rock." They all had very prominent veins of gold in them, so much so that Prospector wanted to know where they came from. Stan told him they came from a mine near Grass Valley in Northern California and that they'd been sent by one of the "Lucky Seven" who owned the mine, as a gift to Stan.

When Eddie asked what "jewelry rock" was, they explained that it was like a jewel in a pile of rock. When someone sees the pile with the jewel on it, they assume that there are more "jewels" in the pile. So when a con artist wants to sell a mine to someone, he shows them some of the samples which are all "jewelry rock." The buyer sees the gold in them and thinks he can make millions from the mine when there isn't any gold there at all.

This "jewelry rock" was just to help Prospector get back some of the money that the assayer had cheated him out of over the past couple of years. Eddie asked how he could help and was told to just be quiet. He listened intently as they discussed what they were going to do, and he knew just how he could help sell the "mine".

They stopped at another assayer's office and sold nearly all of the nuggets and dust that Prospector had collected. They kept back a little to sell to the greedy assayer. They got to his office just after lunch time and Prospector was greeted warmly. He pulled out the pouch that he kept his gold in and told the assayer that this was all he'd been able to gather since he was here last. He told him that his mule had been shot by some guy trying to protect what he'd found and so he had to stay with the mule until it was completely healed up.

After he weighed the gold, the assayer told the old man that he'd like to help him, but gold prices are down because of the economy. When he offered a price that was barely a third of what the other assayer had told them what gold was selling for, Prospector almost took the gold back. Instead, he shook his head and said, "If that's the best you can do, I guess I'll just have to make do somehow." He then showed the assayer the "jewelry rock" and asked if the man was interested in buying a mine.

"What do you mean, buying a mine?" the assayer asked. "Do you own the property that this came from?"

"No, I don't. At least I haven't filed on it yet, Maybe I'll do that when I get back that way, but I don't know how I can make it pay, I don't have enough money to buy food and get what I need to work that kind of mine and make it pay. Probably wouldn't pay anyway, gold being low right now."

Before the assayer could say anything, Eddie interrupted. "Does this mean we're not going back there Uncle? I liked it there; it was lots cooler and not so dry like the desert. Besides, I can help you, I'm strong enough now."

The assayer grabbed the samples out of the old man's hand and said, "Wait a minute, I want to look at these closer." He went to the table where he worked and looked at the rock under the big magnifying glass he had there. He came back and said, "how about we go partners on this mine, say eighty per cent for me and twenty per cent for you? I'll be the one doing the mining, all you have to do is sit back and I'll send you a check every month. What do you think?"

"Well, before I give up any information on where this mine is, I think maybe I should see some money up front, okay? Now keep in mind that these quartz veins are running all through that hillside, some of them are two and three feet wide. You think it over for a minute, me and the boy will be outside, we need to talk this over too."

When they got outside the old man turned to Eddie and said, "You're sure quick to catch on to things. What do you think he'll do?"

"He'll probably want to offer you a thousand dollars, but I don't think you should take it. I think you should hold out until he offers you at least five thousand. If he starts to quit on you, I think I can help. I'll remind you of that other fellow that was willing to pay you ten thousand for the whole thing, not a partnership, okay?"

Stan chuckled and said, "If you decide to quit working for Jake, let me know. You and me could make lots of money "finding" gold mines."

They went back inside and waited while the assayer looked at the samples some more. He finally said, "I may be able to come up with fifteen hundred, how's that sound?"
Prospector looked down at his boots and then finally said, "I was kind of hoping for more than that. For that piece of property, I would say seven thousand is a fair price, but if you don't have that kind of money, I'll understand."

The assayer coughed and answered, "I don't have that much money, will you take three thousand and we'll split it seventy five and twenty-five. What do you think?"

Before Prospector could answer Eddie tugged on his coat sleeve and said quietly, "that man in Lone Pine said he would go ten thousand cash, but he wanted it all, no partnership, remember?"

[291]

Prospector started to say something, but the assayer cut him off, "I'll meet you half way. I'll give you five thousand cash and I get ninety percent, is that a deal?"

"Now that sounds like a deal to me. Me and the boy can sit back and collect our ten percent and still have plenty of money. You get the cash and I'll draw up the directions, is there some kind of paperwork we need to sign or is my say-so good enough for you?"

"We've doing business for a couple of years now and didn't need any paperwork, I don't think we should start getting any lawyers involved now, do you?"

"No sir, I don't like lawyers anyway, so that's just fine by me. I'll be back in a few months to collect some of my ten percent."

When they had the money in hand, they left his office and walked slowly back to Stan's Jeep, trying hard not to start laughing. When they got inside the Jeep, they all started talking at once, saying how much fun that was.

Finally Eddie asked, "Is there really a mountain like that with quartz veins like you said?"

"Absolutely," the old man answered. "The directions I gave him were to that mountain and they were accurate. I didn't tell him that folks had filed all the claims possible on that mountain nearly a hundred years ago, and that most any vein there that was worth something had been mined out years ago. I never told him anything that wasn't true; I let him imagine whatever he wanted to as to what he might find. He's been stealing from me for years, so it was nice to get some of it back, thanks to you two. How much do I owe you for the samples Stan? And Eddie, how much for you"

They both told him nothing and Stan volunteered to put him up at his place for the night, after he dropped Eddie off at Margaret's. Eddie was glad to get home; he worried about his mother and Margaret being alone. They weren't really alone though, they had Javier there along with Frio. Still, he didn't like being away when he felt it was his responsibility to watch over them. His feeling of guilt would have been lessened if he knew of Margaret's abilities with a handgun or a rifle. Long ago, TJ had made it a point to teach her everything there was about gun safety, gun handling, and of course how to shoot different firearms. He found out quickly that she was a natural with any kind of firearm, often outshooting him and several other men. TJ had been so proud of his teaching ability that she hadn't the heart to tell him that her father had started her shooting when she was just past nine years old.

When he got in the house, Margaret told him that Jake wanted to talk to him. When he asked what Jake wanted to talk about, she said she didn't know, he had just said, "Have Eddie call me when he gets in."

Jake answered on the third ring, and asked Eddie if he would go with him to the mine, driving the old Dodge. Jake said that he, Alex, and Julie would be driving the Beast and taking some provisions for a couple days. He wanted Eddie to take Javier with him and bring some more supplies, and some building materials. Eddie got a notepad and started writing down all the items as Jake told him what he wanted. After Eddie read back all the items to make sure they hadn't missed any, Jake told him to go by the office and pick up a credit card from Merrian so he could pay for the materials, and get gas for the generator and diesel for the air compressor.

Because it was late in the day, they decided that Jake and Alex would leave early to go to the mine, while Eddie and Javier picked up the materials. Eddie told him that Stan would be taking Prospector back to the mine so he could get his mule and the donkey and go back to prospecting. Jake said that maybe he should go to the grocery store and pick up more provisions.

Eddie said it would be good idea, since the old man had eaten almost all the food in the shack, but he did pay for it, sort of. Jake asked how he'd paid for the groceries and Eddie told him with gold nuggets and some dust. Jake was skeptical and said it was probably 'fool's gold'. Eddie told him no, it was real; he'd compared it to the real thing at the assayer's office. Jake was now very curious as to why they had been to the assayer, so Eddie told him the entire tale of how Prospector had been cheated for years and him and Stan had sold the assayer a "gold mine" worth nothing for the amount of five thousand dollars. Jake laughed and said that the assayer was so greedy that he had probably packed up already and headed for the mine.

That evening the group sat down to a very nice meal at Margaret's. Des had decided to drop by with Michele and the kids, just to visit or so he said. Rosa and Margaret put the dinner on the table and it was fantastic. Together they were great at making meals that made you hungry just looking at them. Michele mentioned for about the tenth time that Rosa should quit the cleaning business and start a restaurant. She again protested that she didn't have the money that it took to start a restaurant, but this time Des cut her off and told her he had the money to invest if she would think seriously about the idea.

He also said that he and Jake had tossed the idea around a little, and if she were to include a bar or cantina in the building, Jake would invest some also. He said he needed to find a job for Alex and if there was one thing Alex knew about, it was bars. They all got a laugh out of that one, especially since Alex had not only joined Gamblers Anonymous, but also Alcoholics Anonymous. The rest of the evening was spent discussing what the interior should look like and so forth.

Eddie and Javier went outside to check the area near the house and barn. Frio was there, it was one small comfort to Eddie knowing that the big dog was his friend. The cars were all locked in the barn, something Jake had told him to do when they first talked, and the barn was locked. Only Michele's mini-van was parked in front of the house. It was locked also, but that didn't stop Javier from looking inside and underneath. He straightened up quickly and called Eddie over to look.

Eddie also looked underneath and then slid on his back as far as he could to see why there were wires hanging down. He could see where two wires had been deliberately cut, but there was nothing attached to them. He crawled back out and dusted himself off, and then the two of them went back into the house. He pulled Des aside and told him what he'd found. Des said to not tell the others, it would just cause a lot of panic for nothing, that he would call the Sheriff's office.

[294]

When he called, Des was lucky enough to get a dispatcher who knew Julie and listened while he explained the situation. She said she knew who to send and they should be there in about twenty minutes. Des was surprised when Deputy Thorpe was at the door to investigate. He had two other people that weren't from the Sheriff's office and when Des asked he was told they were EOD personnel from the Navy. He told Des to relax and stay in the house, they would see if there was a reason to be alarmed. Des handed them the keys to the mini-van and closed the door after they left. He could see Eddie and Javier watching from the living room window, so he joined them. It seemed like forever, but it was merely thirty minutes later that they returned to the house to let them know it was all clear.

Thorpe motioned for them to come and look and then explained the circumstances to Des. Whoever had attempted to place something in the van couldn't get the hood latch to open, based on the pry marks that they'd left there. They then apparently decided to attach something underneath, but were either interrupted and didn't get it attached, or it fell off during the ride to Margaret's house. The van was now alright to drive, but they should probably re-attach the wires. Javier volunteered to take care of the wires.

They were standing there talking about when they heard gunshots and as one they started toward the house, but Thorpe yelled at Eddie and Javier to cover the back of the house in case he tries to escape. As Des followed Thorpe into the house he could smell the gunpowder and heard his grandchildren crying. When they got to the kitchen, Des saw Rosa sitting in a chair, making the sign of the cross over and over and muttering something in Spanish.

Michele had her arms wrapped around Margaret who was sobbing violently; Davis was dead on the floor, or what was left of him. When Rosa and Michele saw Des there they both tried to explain what had happened and it wasn't making sense. He yelled at them to shut up and it got very quiet. Davis's corpse was making a twitching motion, so Thorpe bent over it cautiously and tried to check for a pulse, but there wasn't much of his head and neck left.

Margaret had fired five rounds from the shotgun into him at close range aiming for his head, so there wasn't much there now. Rosa had been splattered with blood and other things, so when Eddie came in the back Des told him to take Rosa out and around the front door to get cleaned up. Thorpe told them to wait, please. He ran and grabbed his camera from the squad car and returned. He took several pictures of the scene from different angles, including a few of Rosa. He then said she could go wash up, but instead of going out the back like Des suggested, Eddie took her past the children toward the bathroom and the oldest child must have figured out what the mess was, because she threw up on the carpet.

Des wanted to be mad at Eddie for not doing what he'd said, but he just let it go. Michele had finally gotten Margaret to calm down enough to answer some questions. Des stopped her, advising her that she didn't have to answer any questions she didn't want to.

Thorpe said he wasn't interested in making an arrest; he just wanted to know what had happened.

After letting Des get his little recorder from his briefcase, Thorpe started asking Margaret questions.

"Why did you have a shotgun in your hands when Davis came in the back door?"

"Frio was acting funny. He was sitting by Rosa and he started growling at the back door, so I thought that if he were here and you all were out front, he could kill all of us before you could get back to the house. I went down the hall to my bedroom where the shotgun was and got it. I was coming toward the kitchen when I heard Rosa say something and she had Frio by the collar so he wouldn't attack.

I saw part of him by the back door but couldn't see enough of him to get a clear shot. I took two more steps and that's when he heard me and turned toward me with a gun in his hand. I began firing and didn't stop until he was down. I was worried that I was too close to hitting Rosa as well as him, has she been hit?"

[296]

"I don't think so," Des said. "She was very shaken up and kept muttering a prayer or something in Spanish, even when Eddie took her to get cleaned up. I'll go check on her now."

Thorpe was still curious, so he asked, "Where did all the guns come from?"

"TJ collected them over the years, he loved guns you know. I thought it would be safer if everyone had one in case something like this ever happened," she answered, and then as if she remembered a very important fact she also said, "I wouldn't let Eddie have one because he's on probation and I wouldn't want him to get in trouble."

Thorpe smiled and then said, "Margaret, you and I go way back, so believe me when I tell you I'm on your side. I know he works for you and Jake and I wouldn't do anything to jeopardize that boy's chances to start over."

They continued talking, waiting for Des to return. A few minutes later, he came in and reported that Rosa had been hit by two pellets in the upper arm but neither had done any damage to speak of, they were both lodged in the fat tissue and not into the muscle. They were apparently those that had penetrated Davis and gone through him to hit Rosa. She had been very shaken up, and was now quite calm; thanks to a shot of tequila that Eddie had brought her. She had said to tell the deputy to wait that she wanted to tell him what a savior Miss Margaret was, and that he better not arrest her.

Des thought for a minute and asked if anyone had told Jake what was going on. Getting no answer, he called the house and Julie answered.

"Is Jake there with you?" he asked.

"Yes. He dropped Alex off at his house a little while ago and just got back. What's going on?"

"Davis is dead. He came to Margaret's house and she shot him in the head. Deputy Thorpe is here now taking statements and photos of the scene. I thought you and Jake should know."

"Thanks Dad, I'll tell him. We'll be there in a few minutes. I'm sure Jake wants to check on Margaret, he treats her like his own mother. Don't leave, we'll be there."

When Jake got there, it seemed as everyone in town was there. Alex and Merrian followed him through the door; Jake had called them before he left the house. Margaret was sitting at the kitchen table, sipping her coffee. Jake went over to her and asked if she was alright, she calmly stated that right now she was doing okay, but she still didn't understand why Davis had kept coming after them. Jake said he didn't know either, there had to be something really serious in TJ's past to have someone hate him that much. Des interrupted and told Jake not to worry about it tonight; tomorrow he and Margaret would explain it all when the other people weren't around.

Thorpe asked everyone to be quiet, and after about a minute when it was finally quiet, he asked that all of them take extra precautions when opening doors or starting their cars. He said that Davis may have left a few bombs at their houses or even at the places they worked. His caution brought everyone back to their senses. Shortly thereafter he left along with the EOD guys from the base.

Michele had removed the pellets from Rosa's arm and she came in all bandaged up, but smiling. Javier had fixed the wires on her van, so she started rounding up her kids to leave. Des wanted to stay, so she said she would be alright by herself at home now that the threat was over. Jake said he would bring Des home later. Javier and Eddie went to check the cars in the barn, just in case Davis had somehow gotten in there.

Alex and Merrian were introduced to Rosa and Margaret because they hadn't met before, little Jacob was in helping Michele get the kids all together and then in the van.

Rosa was very happy when Alex started talking to her in Spanish and even making a joke or two. Soon they were lost in their own conversation, ignoring the others. Julie took Margaret and Merrian in the other room and told them she may have an announcement in a few weeks, she thought she was pregnant. Margaret was very happy; she started crying and then laughing. The events of the evening along with Julie's news had her on an emotional rollercoaster. She calmed down and then said that she wanted to hold a shower for Julie and the baby, and Merrian said she'd be glad to help. She and Alex had already made some friends at the church they were going to, and when the time got closer, then she would invite some of them.

The coroner arrived and soon he and his assistant had the body in a bag and out to their wagon. Rosa asked if it was alright to start cleaning, and the coroner said that he thought so, but he'd check with Thorpe. He came back a minute later and said they could start cleaning any time. Rosa was soon doing what she did best, cleaning up a mess. In the back of his mind there was still something nagging at Des, what had happened to Karen Davis?

Jake and Alex said their goodbyes and told Eddie they wouldn't be starting too early in the morning. They planned on getting enough groceries to stock the shack for a week. That reminded Jake of what Eddie had said about Prospector paying for the food he ate. He asked if Eddie still had the pouch with the gold in it. Eddie handed it to Jake, reluctant to part with it. It was the first 'raw' gold he'd ever seen.

Jake felt the weight of the pouch and looked inside, then handed it to Alex to inspect. Alex also hefted the pouch and peered inside and afterwards raised his eyebrows. He commented on the weight of it and thought that maybe Prospector had overpaid for the food he'd eaten. Both Julie and Merrian laughed and told them to check the price of groceries. Jake took the pouch with the gold and put it in his pocket and started toward the door. Julie grabbed her purse and followed him out. Mr. and Mrs. Chang followed them out. Des told them to wait; he needed a ride home and grabbed his briefcase.

When Jake and the others in the Beast got to the mine, Stan and Prospector were already there loading the pack on the little donkey. Stan told Jake he'd inspected the mine and the cave, but he didn't find anything out of place. When Jake told what the plans were for the day, Stan volunteered to stick around and help. It had been some time since he'd done any real work, he said, and if they were cooking lunch and dinner he would definitely stay. He started helping Julie and Alex unload the Beast and put things in the shack.

Jake was at the location where he'd told Eddie to level off the ground. He had some stakes and a hammer and was starting to layout the foundation of the house. When they finished unloading the Beast, Alex and Stan joined him. Together, they had the entire foundation laid out in short order and started digging. Jake showed them what he wanted done with the top layer of sand and then where to pile the white clay. Alex still couldn't believe that people actually paid what he called 'big money' for dirt, but when he was told that he owned a percentage of that 'dirt', he was suddenly glad that women liked to have their faces covered with it.

Julie asked Jake where she was supposed to keep the perishable items they'd bought, there was no refrigerator. He told her to put them in the cooler chests and top them with the ice they'd bought in Trona, then when she had that done, she could store them inside the mine where it was much cooler than outside. He didn't tell her that last night he'd told Eddie to get a small refrigerator when he picked up the other materials.

Julie finished packing the perishables and called for Jake to help her move the chests to the cave; also she needed to speak to him alone. He was grumbling about being interrupted when they got into the cave, but he became very quiet when she told him that he was going to be a father. She was completely surprised when he started crying. She teased him, saying that martial-arts masters weren't supposed to cry, what kind of example would that be for a child to see his father cry. He asked if she was sure that she was pregnant and she told him that she needed to have a doctor's exam to be sure, but she was pretty sure.

He suddenly got up and said I've got to get back to work, the baby needs a home and we just barely started on this one. He walked back out of the mine babbling about all the things that need to be done. A few minutes later she heard a shout and a couple voices yelling congratulations. When she came out of the mine, they were fixing a comfortable spot for her to sit and supervise the house-building. Rather than argue with them, she graciously thanked them for their concern and sat down. She thought that men can be the most difficult and also the easiest creature to understand.

Eddie and Javier arrived a few hours later, in time for the lunch that Julie had prepared. As they were eating, Eddie asked if Prospector had left. Stan told him that the old man had left early and headed south along the side of the mountain. Eddie sat up and stated that he and Javier had seen several vultures and some ravens circling overhead at an area about two or three miles to the south. Eddie said he was worried about Prospector carrying all that money, that someone might have found out and hurt him or even killed him to get his money.

When Julie asked what money, Stan told her the story of how the old man had sold the crooked assayer a "rich gold mine" to get even with him for being swindled all these years. Stan had to tell everyone how Eddie had helped and what a great actor he was. Julie told Stan about the first time Eddie had helped when Des was going to buy the Beast and had saved them a couple thousand dollars. Jake laughed and said it's because of that innocent baby-face of his; everyone just wants to believe him. Eddie told them not everyone, that Des had set him straight a couple of times when they first met.

As they were finishing their lunch and about ready to go back to work, Stan saw a figure at the top of the far ridge to the south. At that distance, no one could tell who it was, but the person didn't have any animals following, so it couldn't be the old man. Alex told them to wait and he rummaged though his duffel bag and pulled his spotter scope out. He watched for a moment and then told them it was an old man and he was alone, walking toward them.

Prospector finally got within shouting distance and called out, "Hello the camp." Jake yelled back at him, "Come on in." The two of them sounded like a clip out of an old western, Eddie thought. When the old man finally got into camp, Julie had some cold water from the cave waiting for him. Prospector was very polite and took the canteen and drank some of it before talking. When he did talk, it was unlike anything Eddie had ever heard. He could see it was the old man talking, but the words he was using were totally unlike him at all. He sounded like one of Eddie's English teachers from the way he was talking.

"Thank you so much for the water, madam. I don't believe that we've been properly introduced. I am Gerald Ford, however most of the people in this area prefer to call me Prospector. May I have your name, please?"

Julie was shocked to hear such perfect grammar coming from the old man, so shocked she almost didn't answer and then she stammered, "Julie, uh Julie Larson, no wait it's Julie Kozan now. Jake and I were married not long ago. It's certainly nice to make your acquaintance at last, I've heard so much about you."

"Yes, well, you should never take the word of others unless you can trust them completely. Now, if you will excuse me, I need to talk to Jake and the men alone, please."

When she had gone back to near the entrance to the mine Prospector told them of the grisly find that he encountered on his travel to the south. "If I'm not mistaken, it might be that Davis woman you were worried about. If it is, you needn't worry anymore. Jake, if you'll come with me, I'll show you the body, or what's left of it. You might want someone to tag along with you and bring a shovel."

Jake and Eddie went with the old man. Alex had protested that he should be going until Jake reminded him that his leg wasn't completely healed yet, and Jake didn't want to have to face Merrian if something happened to Alex. They both agreed that was something neither of them wanted. And besides, Jake told him, he needed Alex to stay and watch out for Julie in her delicate condition. She had definitely overheard that part and was headed toward him so he hastily said good-bye and they left.

The body was badly mutilated when they got there, but Jake could positively identify it as the Davis woman. He helped Eddie dig a grave and together they were able to slide the body over to the edge and push it in. They covered it with a sufficient amount of dirt and rock to keep the scavengers away from what was left and then stood there for a moment. None of them were very religious, so they just said that it was God's problem now. Eddie stuck the shovel in the ground at the head of the grave so the Sheriff's Office could find it easily when they phoned it in. They hadn't checked the body for identification, not wanting to interfere with any future investigation.

Prospector gathered the reins of the mule and tied his donkey to the ring on the saddle and mounted. As he said his good-byes, he flipped a coin toward Eddie. It was a very old coin made of gold with strange markings on it. Prospector told them there were more like it not far from where their mine was, but he wouldn't go in that hole for all the money in the world. He said there too many buzz-tails in there and they were nasty aggressive, actually coming forward to bite anyone who tried to enter there. He also said that when he was in the mouth of that little cave he felt very light-headed and cold, even on an extremely hot day. He then rode off headed toward the south and whatever he might find out there.

When they got back to the mine, they showed everyone the old coin and told them what the old man had said. Most of them decided that he was just telling another story, that there wasn't any cave full of gold guarded by snakes. Javier told Eddie that he thought the old man was just crazy. Julie didn't agree with them, nor did she disagree, she just said it might be a legend that had been passed on to the old man from someone else.

They had two sides of the foundation excavated when they decided to stop for the day. None of them noticed the man over by the seep filling a water bag. Eddie saw him first and was startled until he recognized the man as el Indio. He waved and told him come down and fill his bag from the water inside the cave, it was cooler and tasted better. Alex was intently watching the man as he approached them and suddenly he said something in Chinese. Indio stopped immediately, not wanting to come closer. They all watched Alex as he spoke again and this time Indio answered in the same language. They went back and forth in Chinese for a couple of minutes, and then Alex said something and motioned for Indio to come closer.

When he was close enough for everyone to see his face, Alex introduced him as Ta Mao Ming, a descendant of the great

[303]

Emperor Ming. Alex told them that Ming wouldn't give a straight answer as to his age, but Alex guessed him to be about eighty years old. Indio bowed slightly toward Alex and the others while Alex was talking, but when he came to Jake, he prostrated himself on the ground. Alex barked something in Chinese at him and he got back to his feet. They went on for a couple minutes, chattering at each other, apparently arguing about something.

When they were finally done, Alex explained that Ming thought Jake was a great warrior to have defeated Alex and that he would give his life for the great warrior if he were allowed to stay until the birth of his son. Alex said that "Indio" had the mystic power to see into the future and that "Indio" knew that Jake had the same power. For a white man to possess such ability was unheard of where he came from, and he wished to stay and learn from Jake. He vowed to guard Julie and Jake's unborn son if allowed to stay. Alex was curious as to how the man knew that Julie was pregnant, unless someone told him and no one in this camp had seen him until just now.

Jake told Alex to tell him he was welcome to stay, but before Alex could say anything "Indio" or Ming said, "Thank you," and walked past them all to get some water from the spring in the cave.

Later that evening, "Indio" told them in very limited English that he'd been sold to a war lord when he was very young. Alex helped him with the words he didn't know. He'd been taught how to fight in many different styles and was very good at fighting. The war lord was afraid that Ming would turn on him some day, so he sold him to some slavers. They in turn sold him to a merchant ship's captain to be his personal bodyguard. He went wherever the merchant ship went and during that time he learned a few more languages, Spanish being the one he knew best.

When he had the chance, he jumped ship in San Pedro harbor where lots of people spoke Spanish. For some reason they kept calling him "Indio" and he accepted that as a name. He had heard that there was a desert not far away and because it was like the country where he'd grown up, he decided to stay here. He earned money here and there by doing odd jobs, like picking up the pistachios. He made do with very little money because he also used what nature gave him like the snakes that tasted so good, and the mesquite beans that he could boil and eat or grind them into flour and make an unleavened bread similar to a tortilla.

He'd found some gold nuggets here and there, but he thought that they cheated him when he went to sell them because they would only give him two or three dollars each for the nuggets. He showed them a couple of nuggets he had in his pouch that hung from his neck. Jake hefted the one and told Alex that for this one nugget he would give the old man at least a hundred dollars, maybe more. Alex translated what Jake had said and "Indio" just shook his head no, these were to be a gift to the child when he was born, so that as long as he had these, he'd never be sold into slavery.

Jake was in a somber mood after dinner, he wasn't talking to anyone and he just sat and stared at the fire. Julie had learned that the best thing she could when he got like that was to just sit next to him and hold his arm. This time when she sat next to him he just turned and asked, "Why did they want to kill TJ?"

"I'm not sure, but it may have something to do with the information you were supposed to get from Margaret and Des this morning. I didn't think of it until late this afternoon when you and Eddie returned. Des seemed to think it was very important that he and Margaret be with you as you read what they'd found in the vault.

Maybe you should take a break from being a house-builder and go into town and go over those papers, I think Alex can pretty much handle the job here until you get back. He's so unlike what you told me about his past, sometimes I think you made those stories up. I know Eddie and Javier look up to the two of you as if you were gods or something." She pointed to where Alex was showing the two young men a basic defensive move, "See. He loves teaching them and it certainly doesn't hurt them to learn how to properly defend themselves. Alex really seems to care about them. He's so very gentle with them."

Jake looked at her as if she were speaking Greek, "Gentle? Are you kidding me? Alex gentle? Do you remember how beat up I was when you saw me in the hospital, that was gentle?"

She laughed at him and said, "Good, you're not brooding anymore. I thought I could get to you, but I wasn't sure. Come on Jake, we'll tell the others that we're going into town tomorrow."

They got into town at mid-morning and called Des. He told them to come by his house and they'd talk. While they were driving to his house, Des made a call to Margaret's, but only Rosa was home. She said Miss Margaret had gone to work this morning and had planned on meeting with Jake and Des on the week-end. He relayed that information to Jake and Julie when they arrived. They both asked how Margaret was dealing with fact of having to shoot Davis and Des told them that she was fine, that she was actually smiling when he last saw her. Then he told them that in his opinion that wouldn't have mattered if Davis was holding a gun or not, he thought she would have killed him on sight no matter what the circumstances. Jake remarked that Des was a very smart man.

They had taken the old Dodge into town with the idea that after talking to Des and Margaret they would pick up supplies and head back to the mine. Jake knew that Margaret got home after three o'clock, so he told Des to stay at home, when they were done shopping for supplies they'd pick him up and all go over to Margaret's. They stopped by the office to check the mail and say hello to Merrian and there was a small oblong box and a letter from Susanville Correctional Center. Jake took it and the box with him to read later. The box was heavy for its size, which made Jake wonder until he saw the return address was from Ernst Buchold.

They stopped and had lunch at the taqueria that Eddie had told them about. Jake was not impressed with either the service or the food. He'd had a few samples of Rosa's cooking and could definitely understand why Des thought she should open a restaurant serving Mexican and American food. Jake told Julie that he wished Angelina lived closer, he really missed her cooking. Julie just frowned and said that he'd have to 'suffer' through her meals until she learned how to cook, but she didn't think she'd ever be as good as those two. Jake immediately knew he was in a no-win situation, so he said that it wasn't cooking that he married her for, and left it at that.

Jake tried to question Des about what kind of information he was supposed to be looking at when they got to Margaret's, but Des just put on the lawyer face and didn't say anything. They pulled into the drive and were greeted by Frio, his usual noisy self.

Margaret stepped out on the porch and waved for them to come on in. She had just made coffee, so Des poured while she went to her bedroom and brought out the diary and the papers. She handed Jake the diary first and as he read, Julie watched his face. She could see the questions building, and then as he read the last two pages, he began to relax and he smiled.

"Now I understand," he said. "He never talked about his past or when he was growing up. I didn't ask because if he wanted me to know, he would have told me. It's hard for me to believe that a family feud like that has been going on for nearly two centuries. He just didn't seem the type to do that, but I guess we all have secrets then, don't we."

Jake then read the will that TJ had written out and that Margaret had witnessed. When he was done, he said, "Margaret, you don't have to abide by this will if you don't want to, I will gladly step aside and let you have all the property. All I ever wanted from him or you was your friendship."

She smiled and said, "This is the way he wanted it and I agreed. As long as I can live in the house and help with the orchard and the harvest, I'll be happy. I'll be even happier if you and Julie bring your children around to play once in a while. And the same goes for Alex and Merrian and their children, she told me that they want to have a couple more kids, if they can."

"We have to get back to the mine tonight, or we'd stay for dinner. Is there anything you need before we go?"

"No, I'm fine now. Rosa is a wonderful companion and keeps me from being lonely. She's teaching me Spanish and I'm trying to teach her English and some of the accounting skills she needs to run her business. Now you run along, you've got to get that house built before the baby gets here."

They dropped Des off at his house and headed back to the mine. They got there just as Javier was starting to clean up after dinner, he quickly got things back out and fixed them each a plate. They were eating when Jake remembered the package and the letter from Ernst. He asked Eddie to go to the Dodge and get the letter and package. Alex asked who Ernst was, he didn't remember the name. When Jake said the 'man-mountain', he then remembered and said, "Your puppy-dog".

Jake opened the letter and read it out loud so all of them could share.

"My friend Rabbi Jake, I finally got your address from Tyler so I could send this present to you. I have been learning more and more each day thanks to you and Tyler. The guard who told me he was an undercover agent is helping me get a hearing in front of the parole board next month. He thinks there may be a chance for me to get paroled or transferred to a low security prison where they have better teaching for inmates like me. It doesn't matter if he doesn't get it for me, I've been behaving and not letting people make me mad any more. I have some bad news. The Reverend hanged himself in his cell when they let him out of the hole. Guard Crenshaw said that may be he did it himself, but he thinks he might have gotten some help. He was trying to get transferred and take the money that belonged to the Aryan Brotherhood. I don't belong to them anymore. I finally understood what you said about there isn't a super race of people. Tyler said you were right too, that we are all better at some things than others and they can be better at other things than we can. Mike Smith said that you were one of the best teachers he had known. He likes teachers because his Mom and his Dad were teachers. He doesn't hang with the Brotherhood either. He said they were basically stupid and that he and I could just hang together. He asks about you, but I didn't have anything to tell him until Guard Crenshaw told me that you married that lawyer lady. He said she was really pretty and very smart. He said you have to be smart to be a lawyer. I hope you will write to me, I miss you a lot. Your friend, Ernst."

Jake opened the package and in it was a piece of board with the following letters painted onto its face, Solitude, Population 1.